IN THE LINE
OF FIRE

ALSO AVAILABLE BY ROSALIND NOONAN

IN THE LINE OF FIRE

A Laura Mori Mystery

R. J. Noonan

CROOKED
LANE

NEW YORK

Published in the United States by Crooked Lane Books, an imprint of The Quick Brown Fox & Company LLC.

Crooked Lane Books and its logo are trademarks of The Quick Brown Fox & Company LLC.

Library of Congress Catalog-in-Publication data available upon request.

ISBN (hardcover): 978-1-64385-015-3
ISBN (ePub): 978-1-64385-016-0
ISBN (ePDF): 978-1-64385-017-7

Cover design by Melanie Sun
Book design by Jennifer Canzone

Printed in the United States.

www.crookedlanebooks.com

Crooked Lane Books
34 West 27th St., 10th Floor
New York, NY 10001

First Edition: August 2019

10 9 8 7 6 5 4 3 2 1

For Helyn Trickey Bradley

With heartfelt thanks for her insightful, steadfast assistance in preparing this manuscript

PROLOGUE

If he was stupid enough to make one, he'd call his YouTube video "How to make one hell of a payday in one easy evening."

He parked his car a block from the main drag of Bonita Street in the shadows of a tree-lined residential street. Getaway was key. Park close to the bank but away from the laser eye of security cameras. Far enough away so that no one from the bank can see you get into the vehicle.

Time of day could be a bonus. Some guys liked the three-o'clock hour when most cops were changing shifts, but he understood the benefits of a winter evening after sundown when the cover of darkness slid over their eyes like a velvet blanket. No one was sure of what they saw in the dark. On a cold winter night, by five o'clock, workers yawned and set their sights on getting home to dinner.

He was a fan of the partial disguise. Nothing like the ski mask or stocking over the face. That would draw immediate attention, set off all the alarms. He pulled on a wig and baseball cap, adjusted them in his visor mirror. Good enough.

He stepped out of the car, plucked the black backpack from the seat, and left the car unlocked. Nothing of value in there. Not yet.

The streetlamps overhead illuminated the bones of the trees and cast odd shadows on the lawns he passed. He slipped on his winter gloves. Under the wig and baseball hat his head itched like crazy, and he rubbed the tops of his ears one last time before crossing the street to the bank sidewalk.

It was so easy.

Someone, probably the manager, had sprinkled rock salt on the icy path, so the frozen slick was breaking up and his boots sank into the ice melt. The glasses steamed up a bit as he walked through the glass doors, but he ignored it.

He couldn't stop now.

He sidled up to a counter, slipped off his gloves, stuffed them in his pockets, and wrote a simple note in block print, the same handwriting he'd practiced over and over again at the kitchen table. Easy to read. No mistakes. Nothing too hard for the tellers to decipher.

He got in line like a regular customer and stood behind a lady with a little kid who wanted to roam the bank like a drone at a concert. The kid bumped into his leg and looked up at him like it was his fault. He leaned down and put out a hand for a high five. The kid just scowled up at him.

"Sorry," the mom said. "He's full of energy. Jeffie, come here." And she picked Jeffie up and took him over to a heavyset teller with glitter eyeshadow.

At last, it was his turn. The ponytail teller with the big Bambi eyes. Poor ponytail girl; sure didn't see these headlights coming right for her.

Her smile drained from her face as she read the note. She was freaking a little. He could see it in her skin, splotches of red creeping up her neck to her cheeks.

Don't panic, Ponytail. Just do as I say and you'll be fine.

He worried that she might freeze for too long, attracting attention. But she snapped out of it, pulled out all the big bills from her till, tucked them neatly in the backpack he gave her, and pushed it toward him.

He didn't move to take it.

For a second they locked eyes, and a lump the size of a fist formed in his stomach.

Come on, Ponytail.

He cocked his head to the side just a little, then glanced down at the small hammer he was holding in the deep pocket of his sweatshirt, the one that looked just like a gun when he held it at a certain angle. Her eyes followed his gaze. She stiffened her spine, inhaled, and slid off her stool to open the safe under the counter.

That's right, Ponytail.

He leaned toward the counter for a better look, knowing she was unlocking a small safe. In a few seconds she straightened and put a pack of hundred-dollar bills with a mustard-colored band on the counter.

Jackpot.

He nodded. That was ten grand right there.

He felt a surge of energy, like he could run three marathons in a row without getting winded.

They didn't tell you that part.

When your bank robbery kicked ass, you felt electric.

He watched that fat bundle slide into the backpack, then took it from her and turned to leave. Do not linger. No whoop of celebration. Get the hell out of there.

The getaway was where most robbers screwed up.

Walk briskly. Don't run. Get in the car. Take off the hat and wig, and drive the car toward the interstate and freedom. Don't speed, just blend your vehicle, your invisibility cloak, in with the other cars. Don't stop for a cheeseburger at McDonald's, no matter how much your stomach grumbles.

And the most important rule of all? Never tell anyone. Not your best friend, not your own family. Most people get caught because they don't go solo; you need to stick to a conspiracy of one.

Don't trust anyone, and you won't get caught.

1

reached out to the terrified bank teller sitting beside me and took her hand. "You're okay now," I told her. "You did the right thing, and no one got hurt."

"I was so scared, Laura! I couldn't breathe. I thought he was going to hurt me." Her voice cracked, and her brown eyes filled with tears.

"It's very traumatic, what you just went through." I gave her hand a squeeze, then moved the box of tissues closer to her. We sat in visitor chairs at a desk in the cubicled section of the First Sunrise Bank where people discussed loans and mortgages with a false suggestion of privacy. Across from us in the main desk chair sat my partner Zion Frazier; eyes wild, dark skin clammy, he looked more like the victim than Ashley Earnhart.

Outside the glass doors of the entrance, the darkness was punctuated by a few streetlights in the parking lot. It wasn't even six yet, but December days were short and night had come. Until we'd gotten the call, it had been a typical Tuesday evening marked by freezing rain, strings of diamond-white lights, and holiday shoppers.

Behind us, a forensic technician in booties moved through the area we'd taped off, combing the counter and tile floor of the center of the bank in search of hair or fabric or even skin cells the robber might have left behind. Although this was the first bank robbery of my six-month career with the Sunrise Lake Police Department, my partner Z had suffered through a deadly bank hit years ago. Hence his near panic attack.

"Nobody tells you how scary it is to be one-on-one with an armed robber," Ashley continued. "I wish I could stop thinking about him, but when I close my eyes, he's there. He's the only thing I see. It's like we were the only two people in the bank." She scraped a few stray hairs back toward her ponytail, but it didn't alter her frazzled appearance. "His image is burned in my brain."

"It will fade, eventually," I reassured her, "but it takes time. Can you tell us what he looked like while he's fresh in your memory?"

"Some old guy with big googly glasses, not the kind of person you'd normally be afraid of. But I could see his eyes shifting back and forth. That made him even more intimidating. I couldn't tell what he was thinking, except once, when he showed me he had a gun. A gun!" Terror added a squeak to her voice. "I was so afraid of being shot."

I nodded sympathetically. "Can you describe the gun?"

Ashley shook her head. "I didn't see it. Just the outline of it underneath his sweatshirt."

Z shifted uncomfortably as he listened to Ashley recount the robbery. Usually cool and stoic, my partner was a ball of nerves. His jaw was tight as he wiped perspiration from his forehead, even though it was cold enough in the First Sunrise Bank for me to wear my fleece-lined winter coat.

"So the robber told you he had a gun?" Z asked.

"No." Ashley's eyes grew glossy with more tears as she thought for a moment, then added, "He just kind of motioned with his head for me to look down, and that's when I saw the outline of it in the pocket of his dark sweatshirt."

"I see. You're doing great, Ashley," I said. "Good recall."

I remembered Ashley from Mr. Goodman's chemistry class at Sunrise Lake High, the school we'd both graduated from six years ago. She'd been a decent student—better than me, that's for sure.

We'd sat several rows apart in chemistry class, but everyone always mistook us for sisters, which was ridiculous considering I'm first-generation Japanese-American and Ashley's mom is a Pacific Islander. "Hey, sis!" Ashley would call to me in the halls between classes. "Wanna coordinate outfits tomorrow?" We'd laugh it off together, but I was stung by our classmates' inability to see me as an individual. Sure, I was shy, but I'd been a student in Sunrise Lake schools for nearly my whole life and still felt like I could've gone missing and no one would have noticed.

We don't all look alike! I remembered wanting to scream at Rodney Blumenthal after he came up to me at my locker and told me he liked my singing in the school play, *Bye Bye Birdie.* I couldn't carry a tune, but Ashley was a really gifted singer and had a great part in the play. After such a nice compliment, I couldn't bring myself to tell him I was not the girl he so clearly had a crush on.

Now Ashley sat in front of me, shaking with fear and recounting a terrifying robbery. And Z was looking worse by the moment, too. He'd eased out of his jacket but was still sweating and shifting nervously from one foot to the next. No stranger to panic attacks myself, I saw Z was about to spiral. And no wonder. Although it had been just a few years since he'd seen an officer gunned down at another bank robbery, trauma had a way of sparking back to life with certain memories.

"Hang on, you two, I'm going to grab us all some water." Passing the reception area of the bank, where customers sat waiting to give their statements, I went through the door behind the tellers' stations to the hidden rooms of the bank. Inside the break room, two other bank employees were being interviewed by my colleagues Cranston and Rivers. Moving silently, I grabbed a few cold bottles from the refrigerator and ducked out. The whole bank was crawling with forensic technicians and cops, and nearly a dozen staff and customers remained. At a computer terminal in the corner cubicle, my boss, Lieutenant Charles Omak, was working with the head teller to capture images from the bank cameras.

It was a fairly comprehensive response for a town the size of Sunrise Lake, but that was no wonder after the string of bank robberies several years ago that had gone unsolved and resulted in the murder of one officer—Franny Landon. The whole town of Sunrise Lake had been stunned by the robberies but nearly undone by Franny's murder. Dark things like that just didn't seem possible in this sweet bedroom community of Portland, Oregon, where one of the biggest debates the city council had every year was what kinds of flowers to plant in the hanging baskets that lined the main streets from April through October. I'd been away at college back then, but I'd gotten updates from my mom, who had insisted that everyone in our family keep away from Sunrise Lake banks until they caught the bandit. Her warning had faded a few months after the robberies mysteriously stopped.

As I squeezed past two uniformed officers taking statements from customers, I noticed the trembling fingers of one thirtyish woman who struggled to tap a message into her phone. Dressed in tie-dyed tights, a raspberry scarf, and a puffy black jacket, her blonde hair pulled back off her face, she looked as if she'd been on her way to the gym when she stopped into the bank. I kneeled beside her and offered a bottle of water. "How's it going?" I said. "Sorry you have to wait a bit."

"It's not the wait." She took the bottle of water but didn't crack it open. "It's the horrible feeling of coming face-to-face with him and wondering what might have happened if I got in his way. I'm shaking to the core."

"Wrong place, wrong time." I patted the sleeve of her puffy jacket. "It's scary, I know. I'll interview you next, okay? Just give me a few minutes."

She thanked me, and I rose, assessing the others in the waiting area. Before we wrapped things up here, everyone in the building would be interviewed. One man paced, and a white-haired man patted the hand of the woman seated next to him as she leaned close and whispered something. They seemed to be watching a woman with an antsy toddler, who was already being interviewed by Jeremy Ramirez, who seemed mildly amused as the mom kept chasing the boy after he broke free and ran across the bank.

Another cop was talking with a woman with dark dense curls and large, moonlike eyes, who seemed to have more questions than answers. How much had been taken? Was the robber going to hit again? "Is my life in danger?" she asked. "I think he got a good look at me. What if he finds out where I live?"

"That's usually not how these things work," the officer answered as I made my way back to Ashley.

"Here you go. Take some deep breaths and drink this." I handed them each a bottle of water, then took a seat. Patience. Kindness. Those were my trademarks, something special that I believed I brought to police work. I removed the small notebook from my bulky uniform jacket and turned to a clean page as Ashley took a sip and let out a sigh. With the tension somewhat eased, I went back to the narrative. "Why don't you walk me through what happened again."

"Okay." She capped the bottle and, squinting to concentrate, provided the same details as before: older man with long white hair, baseball cap with UNCLE KOMBUCHA logo advertising a local brand of the popular new drink. Black-framed glasses and dark sweatshirt. Slight limp.

"Did you get a sense of his attitude?" I asked. "Did he seem mean or rushed? I know it's hard to tell, but did he smile at all, or were his hands shaking or did he seem steady and calm?"

Ashley paused, mulling it over as she smoothed one side of her hair back over her ear.

"His hands. Or at least the one hand I saw." Her forehead wrinkled as she strained to remember. "His hands weren't shaking, but I noticed the one hand without the glove looked so pink and plump. Not wrinkled like you'd expect for an old man. No lines or calluses. It kind of struck me because my boyfriend works in a shipyard, and his hands are so rough. 'Man hands,' he calls them. But the robber's hands looked young and smooth. And he's definitely not doing rough manual labor."

Young hands. Ashley hadn't mentioned this the first time. "This is great information, Ashley." I wrote the details in my notebook, wondering if anyone else had noticed his hands. Was he a younger man wearing a wig and faking a limp to appear older? Possible.

"And he didn't seem too nervous. He didn't run out or push anyone aside when he left the bank. He just walked, as if he were doing a normal errand." One corner of her lips hardened in a frown. "That makes it seem even colder, him waltzing out of here."

"Let's talk about the note," I said. "Were his gloves still off when he slid it over to you?"

"Yeah, his glove was on the counter, and he slid the note over to me and I couldn't believe it. I mean, we're trained for this and all, but I never thought it would happen to me. Not here in Sunrise Lake."

I nodded. I'd already seen the note with its blocky, handwritten print: GIVE ME YOUR FIFTIES AND HUNDREDS. Straightforward, no nonsense. Forensics had collected it for prints, and the fact that he'd handled the note without a glove made me hopeful. But we wouldn't have results for a day or two. "Then what happened?" I gently prodded.

"He didn't say anything, so I started filling his backpack with higher-denomination bills from my drawer, just like the note said. I was still holding my breath when I pushed the bag over to him, but he didn't take it. He just gave me a stern look, like a disappointed teacher. Then he cocked his head sideways. That's when I saw that he had a gun in the pocket of his sweatshirt. Pointed right at me the whole time. I hadn't noticed it until then, but it . . ." Her voice broke. "It freaked me out."

"You did great," Z said to Ashley. "You stayed calm." I could see him trying to get back into police mode after his panic at being called to this crime scene. I hoped he'd find his usual swaggering, sarcastic voice soon.

"I wonder why he showed you the gun," I said.

"I know why," Ashley said. "When he cocked his head and nodded, I knew exactly what he wanted. The money in the safe below the counter. And he waited for me to unlock it with my code." She hesitated. "I added a strap of hundreds to his bag and pushed it back to him. I feel really bad about that part. The strap is ten thousand dollars. So much money!"

Z held up a hand to Ashley. "It's only money, and the bank is insured. Your actions might have saved lives today."

"That's right," I said. "You did the right thing, my friend. But I wonder how he knew about the safe under the counter."

Ashley took a sip of water, glancing over to the tellers' stations. "Maybe he's been watching us. Which is creepy."

"But a real possibility," I said. "Many bank robbers research the banks they rob, visiting a few times to observe the daily routines. Do most banks have teller safes?"

"I don't know about other banks, but for us it's not a big secret. Many of our regular customers know about our teller safes. Business owners like that feature. It saves us trips into the vault, and it's a way to keep a smaller amount of money in our cash drawer. Fewer mistakes that way."

We went over the story again and covered a few more questions, but no new details emerged, and I could see that Ashley was beginning to get shaky now. Sometimes when adrenaline receded, exhaustion and shock set in.

I thanked Ashley and released her. "I see your mom over there by the door." I waved at Mrs. Earnhart, who approached us with Ashley's purse and jacket. "You've been a huge help. Why don't you take my card and head out. We're going to be processing this scene for a few more hours at least, but you should go home and try to relax. We can touch base again tomorrow."

"Okay." Ashley stood and let her mother hold her jacket while she shrugged into it. Childlike, she turned back toward me. "I can't shake this bad feeling, Laura. I don't think I'll ever feel safe here again."

I hugged her. Not exactly protocol, but then again, we'd been high school friends. "Take it one day at a time," I told her. "And if you remember anything else about what happened here today, anything at all, please call me anytime."

Ashley gave me a hug and then walked out of the bank with her mother's arms around her shaking shoulders. Even if she didn't reach out to me, I would call her tomorrow to see how she was doing.

While Z ducked into the restroom, I quickly compiled my notes and ran them by the boss, Lieutenant Omak. Tall and trim with graying hair around his temples and posture that pointed to time in the military, Omak was fair and equally demanding of all his cops.

"I want to get a BOLO out, and here's what we know," I told him. The sooner other law enforcement agencies could "Be On the Lookout" for our robber, the better the chance we had of apprehending him quickly.

Lieutenant Omak looked over my description of the perpetrator. "Keep it short. Limited to physical description," he told me, then went back to the security camera images.

Pacing the perimeters of our crime scene, I got on the phone with Officer Perry Lister back at the precinct and made sure the alert went out.

I spent the next half hour helping the response team interview the customers and staff.

I learned that the blonde woman in the workout clothes, Sidney Maynor, had passed the robber when he'd been heading out of the bank. "The only remarkable thing was that he pushed out the door as I was approaching, and he didn't hold the door for me. I was like, thanks a lot, dude, but when I saw him struggle to skirt around a patch of ice, I let it go. Thank God. If I'd confronted him, I might be dead now."

"Did you see that he had a gun?" I asked.

"I heard he pointed it at one of the tellers." Sidney had not seen his gun—no one had—but rumor of it had traveled quickly among our witnesses.

"Please . . . just tell me what you personally observed about him," I told her. "Did you get a look at his hands? His face?"

She glanced up at the ceiling and gave this some thought. "Hands? No. I think he was wearing gloves, but I did get a peek at his face, and he was smiling. Kind of smug and satisfied and young. Way too young to have long gray hair. He didn't run. Maybe because he was walking with a limp. Oh, and I don't think those were prescription glasses. He stripped them off and held them swinging in one hand as he disappeared down the street. Is any of that helpful?"

I assured her that every detail mattered as I filled in a report with her statement. The image of a man in disguise with a fake gun in his pocket was beginning to take shape as I completed the paperwork and added it to the stack Z was collecting.

After that I joined Omak and the head teller, a fortyish blonde woman with puffy red eyes named Kirsten Mitter. I was curious to see what they were looking for. One thing I did know was that right off the bat a timeline for the robbery would need to be established, and organization was one of my cornerstones. With the narratives from the witnesses and the information caught on camera, we'd get a solid time frame. Kirsten was a master at navigating through footage from different cameras. I tried to join in unobtrusively, taking notes on the video and culling time stamps from Omak's notes. As a rookie detective, I still had lots to learn, and it was fascinating to watch Omak analyze the video. Omak observed the suspect's uneven gait and pointed out his interaction with the little boy. "He's trying for a high five with the kid. At least he's not completely heartless." The high five was left hanging—a high five with his right hand, I noted.

"See that?" Omak had Kirsten freeze on an image of the suspect writing at the table holding deposit and withdrawal slips. "What do you get from that, Mori?"

"He's right-handed," I said.

Omak rubbed his knuckles against the dark shadow on his jaw. "True. I didn't catch that. I'm thinking that he's touching the counter, only one glove on. Let's make sure we focus on lifting prints from that surface as well as the counter by the teller."

"Got it," I said, turning around to make sure the technicians were still here. "I'll talk to them, make sure they pick up everything they can from those areas."

I went to the edge of the cordoned-off area and called to the technician, Tonya Miller, who moved cautiously through an area spattered with white and black dust. She wore coveralls over her clothes, and her thin dreadlocks were tied back with a bright-red scarf. Her paper booties whispered as she made her way to me, navigating around three numbered markers on the floor indicating where samples had been collected.

"How's it going?" I asked.

She shrugged. "Not bad. I haven't worked a bank crime scene in years."

"Omak noticed on the bank video that the suspect made contact with the teller barrier and that counter where he wrote the note. You should prioritize any prints you find there."

"Will do. I lifted a few prints from the table that holds the deposit tickets, but since it's a public space, they could belong to anyone. It does help to have the shiny surfaces. That smooth stone countertop really grabs prints."

I nodded toward the markers. "Find something of interest?"

"Five hairlike fibers."

The tiny hairs at the nape of my neck tingled at the news. A find that might help us build a case. It was one of the things I liked most about police work—puzzling things out. Second only to having a way to connect with people and help them. In my short time on the job, I'd learned that most things a cop did were in the name of service, not enforcement. Sure, it was satisfying to nab the culprit, but the stories that unfolded and minor problems that could be soothed or patched up in the course of an investigation kept me perennially intrigued with my job.

"Two of the fibers were white, more than five inches," Tonya added. "That matches the description of your perp, right?"

"It does." I pointed to one of the markers. "And the robber was standing right there. He bent down to talk with a little boy waiting in line."

"Really?" Tonya glanced back at the spot. "I'll make a note of that. We should know more when we get them to the lab, but it could bode well for your case."

"It could be instrumental in the case." I tried to contain my enthusiasm as I thanked Tonya and turned away, feeling eyes on me. Cranston was watching from behind a post in the bank. Arms crossed, he wore that scowl of disapproval I had come to know when he'd been my field training officer a few months ago.

Cranston could always be counted on for a sour response. What was his issue now?

2

ignored Cranston's scowl—after all, he wasn't my boss—and returned to the corner cubicle to make notes as Omak and Kirsten reviewed the digital images. Half an hour later, with the important moves of the bandit documented, Omak worked with the bank manager to copy the video footage onto a disk to be used for evidence. I rolled my chair away from the computer terminal, tucked it under a desk, and stretched my spine. Close, technical work could be tedious, but it was all part of solving the puzzle.

I found Z watching the operation—the technicians inside the crime tape, and the small conversation groups at the fringes—from a desk chair. "Are you hiding over here?" I asked.

He shook his head. "I'm right in plain view. I was just going over the witness list: bank employees and customers. Omak has released all witnesses, but a lot of them are hanging on. Looks like we're about done here. You can always tell when the crime scene begins to resemble a frat party." This was the old Z, the guy I was accustomed to: blunt and animated, with a hint of tartness.

"Detective Mori, Detective Frazier . . ."

A little thrill rippled through me when I heard my title. I hoped it didn't show, because I'm really not an egomaniac, but my stomach fluttered whenever someone called me detective. Inside, I was still a little giddy about my promotion. After Z and I had worked together to solve the Lost Girls mystery just a month before, Lieutenant Omak had been instrumental in getting us promotions. Not everyone liked the idea of me being the youngest female to make detective in the history of Sunrise Lake, and I knew some on the force resented the promotion of a young black man like Z. Cops like Cranston and Brown grumbled about us under their breath, but I liked to think that was out of jealousy rather than racism. I'd done good work, and I would show them one way or another that I deserved to be a detective.

"Let's pull together what we've got here." Omak said, switching his gaze from me to Z. His eyes lingered on my partner. "Detective Frazier, you look terrible. Coming down with something?"

"Yeah, Detective, you look like you been rode hard," Cranston chimed in, joining our group. "What gives? You got a tummy ache?"

Z ignored Cranston. "Just running rough, Lieutenant. Didn't sleep well last night."

Omak nodded. "I need to update the media in a few minutes," he said, nodding toward the glass doors of the bank. Outside on the street, news vans and satellite trucks with lights and cameras had congregated. "Let's huddle and figure out what details we can release. No mistakes this time."

Omak's last comment had to be a dig at Cranston, who had taken heat for sloppy work on several high-profile cases lately. Maybe he'd been an effective cop when he was younger, but in the few months I'd known him, I'd gotten the impression he was trying to skate by until his retirement.

"Detective Mori, I want you leading the field on this one. You'll report directly to me." Behind Omak, I saw Cranston frown. Not that it was a competition, but many of the senior cops hoped to be assigned investigative cases, with the possibility of overtime pay and promotion to the level of detective. I wondered if Cranston had wanted this case, or maybe he was simply annoyed to see me rewarded with it. A champion of the old guard, Cranston wasn't happy with the way the demographics of the department had changed in the twenty-five years he'd been on the job.

"What do we have so far?" Omak asked.

I squared my shoulders and got down to business. "We have statements from all witnesses. You approved the alert we put out," I told Omak.

"Can you repeat the perpetrator's description, in case anyone here hasn't heard it," Omak instructed. He had his small black notebook out, probably checking details for the press conference.

Going back to my notes on the BOLO, I reeled off the characteristics of our Oregon bank robbery suspect: white male, five feet ten; anywhere between 185 pounds and 220 pounds; Uncle Kombucha dark-blue baseball cap; navy-blue or black sweatshirt; faded jeans; white hair or possible wig; small black backpack; dark winter gloves; black-framed glasses.

"And what's our timeline?" Omak asked.

"We have him coming into the bank lobby at five ten PM. We're still working on the outdoor security images, but since it was dark at that time, the images are shadowed and grainy. He entered at five ten, paused at that table over there, and removed a glove to write a note on a deposit ticket. Forensics is trying to get prints from the paper and pen. He went to the first teller window at five thirteen. Ashley Earnhart was the teller. She's twenty-four, local, graduate of Sunrise Lake High. She gave him the denominations he asked for from her cash drawer. Then, after he nodded to what she thought was a gun, she handed over ten thousand dollars from the safe below the counter. A weapon was never revealed. The security cameras have him leaving the bank at five seventeen. We think we have an image of him heading down Bonita Street, past the paint store on foot."

"Too bad the old coot didn't slip on the ice patch out there," Cranston said. "That would have made for a story."

"Cranston." Omak shut him down. "Keep in mind, we don't know if the old man persona is a disguise."

I ran through the other pertinent information as Omak made notes for his press conference. I recommended we keep the details of the note, the robber's slight limp and his swollen hands out of the press, and Omak agreed. We would search for security footage from other businesses in the area, but most were not as security minded as a bank.

I took a deep breath. What I had to say next was not easy, though it was probably obvious to everyone here.

"Sir, I'm seeing some similarities between this crime and the Twilight Bandit."

In the silence that overtook our group of cops, Omak looked up from his notebook and focused his eyes on mine. I was on thin ice. No one liked to discuss the Twilight Bandit, a robber who had hit nine banks before a robbery had ended with the killing of a police officer three years ago.

I swallowed hard, but pushed on. "Same time of day. The robbery happened after sunset, when visibility was low outside the bank. And the perpetrator appeared to be an old man, in his twilight years. Same MO. I'm just connecting the dots."

A flicker of tension shot across Lieutenant Omak's face. His sister Franny Landon had been the police officer gunned down at the last Twilight Bandit robbery. I knew it might open up old wounds to bring up the unsolved case, but over the years the homicide and robberies had remained unsolved.

"That was three years ago," Cranston piped up. "Weren't you still in middle school when that happened, Mori?"

"It is kind of a stretch." Z gave me a hard, strained look as he shoved his hands into the pockets of his jacket. "Plenty of perps wait for the cover of darkness, and bank robbers favor disguises. It's circumstantial."

Omak flipped his notebook shut. "Thank you, Detective Mori, I've got what I need to address the media. We're still in the early stages of this investigation, and we'll proceed according to protocol." He paused and looked around at all the other officers. "Officially, we are not drawing any similarities between this robbery and the Twilight Bandit. Everybody clear on that?"

Everyone nodded as Omak turned and headed for the bank's front door. You had to admire the way he carried himself, confident yet polite, as he stepped up to the lights and microphones. I could hear the clamor from reporters as they pelted the lieutenant with questions. Somewhere out there my roommate, Natalie, and her camera crew jockeyed for a good position. I hoped Natalie would get a chance to land a question in all that mayhem. Must be a slow news day, because even the Portland news crews were waiting for Omak's remarks.

Inside the bank on Bonita Street, the glass entryway doors and countertops were dusted with powder, some black as soot, some like a coating of flour. Officers and forensic technicians finished up their work and began packing their equipment. The mood had lightened now that the hard work of processing the crime scene had finished, and several groups of cops and bank employees stood around chatting.

The bank manager, whom I had noticed milling around the crime scene, answering questions from detectives and comforting his employees, approached me. "Maybe I wasn't supposed to be listening, but I heard you mention the Twilight Bandit. Do you think today's robbery is connected?"

"It's a possibility we need to consider. I hope you can keep it to yourself. You're the manager, right? I'm Detective Laura Mori."

We shook hands. Polite grip.

"Martin Lopez." Broad-shouldered with dark hair and a goatee that resembled a smudge on his chin, Lopez had a very tight demeanor, though personally I'd have been pretty keyed up if my place of business had just been robbed.

"Not to butt in on your investigation, but I've seen the Twilight Bandit before."

"Really?"

"I was a teller down the street at Lakeside Savings several years ago when old Twilight hit our bank, and tonight I noticed some similarities. Same height and body build, and the hair looked about the same. The robber appeared to be elderly, and he struck after dark, like all the others."

I studied Lopez, clean-cut and affable, a valuable potential witness. "Were you the teller who was robbed at Lakeside?"

Lopez shook his head. "No, but it wasn't busy when the Twilight Bandit came in, and I didn't have any customers. I was finishing up some paperwork, and I looked up at him as he entered. Didn't think anything of him at the time—just some old guy—but as he left, I noticed that the hair on the back of his head seemed pretty far off his neck. A wig, I figured. That made me wonder if the old guy look was just an act."

"Did you tell the police that?"

"I did." He frowned, crossing his arms. "But back then, no one seemed bowled over by my brilliant powers of observation."

"Well, I'm impressed that you remember. And I'd love to take a statement from you sometime this week. I'm sure I'll have some other questions about your staff and typical bank procedures." I handed him a card. "Do you think they're the same guys, the Twilight Bandit and the robber today?"

Lopez paused before answering. "It's possible. This guy tonight seemed puffier than before, but a man can put on some pounds in three years." He tugged on the lapels of his suit jacket. "I know I sure have."

I smiled. "Thank you, Mr. Lopez. You've been very helpful. We'll get this all wrapped up in the next half hour so you can get the bank locked up and go home."

"Let me know if there's anything else you need. I'm going to encourage the rest of my employees to head on home, unless you need them here."

"We're good. We've gotten statements from everyone in the bank. And your staff should definitely go. People need to destress. But here." I handed him a thin stack of business cards. "If you don't mind handing these out. If anyone has any questions or recollections, I'd like to hear from them."

"I'll make sure my people know how to reach you, Detective." Lopez nodded then headed toward the back room.

I went over to Z, who seemed more relaxed now. "Did you hear that?" I asked. "This case looks more and more like the Twilight Bandit is back in business."

Z shook his head, eyes on the sheets of written statements as someone piped up behind me.

"Geez, Mori. If you were any greener, we'd have to water you twice a day." Cranston leaned in between Z and me. "Your lack of experience is embarrassing. Did you not hear what the boss said?"

"I heard him," I said, keeping my annoyance in check. "But that doesn't stop me from investigating connections."

"What connections? A couple of similarities?"

"There may be more." I looked to Z for support, but he just put down the paperwork and started texting on his phone. No help at all. "I would have to get more information on the Twilight Bandit."

"You're talking to the expert. It was my case," Cranston said. "In fact, I should be the one handling this case, since I've got experience. You can talk to the boss about passing it on to me."

I gave Cranston a dry smile. He wasn't doing me a favor. He wanted the possible overtime and promotion of a high-profile case. "You'd do that for me? Aren't you sweet."

"I'm the obvious choice. I took over the Twilight Bandit case. That's how I know the thief dried up. Probably died or left the state. That's what we figured in the end."

"Really?" I had never heard that. "Did you know that theory, Z?" I asked as I felt my pocket buzz.

"Nope." My partner shook his head and went back to the paperwork. Totally checked out, but I couldn't blame him. You couldn't win an argument with Cranston.

"Thanks, Cranston, but I'm going to stay on this one." I reached for my phone. Maybe it was Ashley remembering something important? I looked down. It was a text from Z.

Shut it down, Mori. It's trouble.

I shot Z a confused look, but his face was unreadable.

Unlike Cranston's gloating smile. "Don't say I didn't warn you," Cranston said. This was a man who found joy in getting under your skin.

Giving Cranston a steely look to end the discussion, I grabbed some of the witness statements from the stack and got back to work.

3

It was after ten when Z and I got into our cruiser to head back to the precinct. The brisk December night air energized me a little and cooled down my thoughts on the robbery.

"Damn, what a haul." Z shook his head. "Seventeen grand for seven minutes worth of work." He whistled out loud, a long, descending sound.

"You must be feeling better," I said, starting the vehicle.

Z nodded. "Yeah, sometimes the monster recedes when you face it."

"You sound like my dad." My father was a big fan of proverbs. "You want to tell me why you shut me down in front of Cranston and the others?"

"You know the answer to that. The Twilight Bandit case is not to be discussed."

"Says who?"

"Says the culture of the department. Let it go, Mori. We're both too beat to fight about it, but I can dream about the cash. Seventeen grand."

"More than the usual heist, which is around six thousand."

Z squinted at me. "Don't tell me you looked it up."

I nodded. "I had some time to kill in there. So it turns out that the additional strap of cash from the safe significantly increased the robber's cash."

"What would you do with that kind of money?" Z asked. "If seventeen thousand bucks landed in your lap?"

As I focused on the white line marking the curve of the ridge road around the lake, I considered my easy life. I had a decent place to live, and, yeah, I had to have a roommate to make ends meet, but I liked living with Natalie. She was fun to be around and made independence a little less lonely. I didn't make a ton of money as a police detective, but I also didn't have expensive tastes, not like my mother, who loved to shop and have her hair and nails done at expensive salons. I kept my dark hair blunt cut over my shoulders, pulled back in a ponytail when I was working. All very simple.

"I guess I'd travel," I told Z. "I'd go visit my best friend from college, Neen, in Sweden." A part of me wanted to be brave enough to fly away from Sunrise Lake and explore other parts of the world, but a bigger part of me was comfortable living among the manicured lawns and quiet parks I'd grown up in. Our small town was seeing changes in demographics and technology, but it was still my small-town home. Truth was, I liked living close to my parents and sister Hannah, though that would change soon when she went off to college.

"Sweden, huh?" Z looked over at me. "What, Sunrise Lake isn't white enough for you already?" He laughed. "You know they put one of the few black cops and the only Asian cop together for a reason, right? We're like a rolling brochure for diversity."

I smiled and shook my head. This was one of Z's favorite topics to riff on.

"Hey, what would *you* do with the money?" I asked.

Z smiled. "Oh, I know exactly what I would do. No hesitation."

"What?"

"Her name is Tammy."

I shot him a look of shock. "What?" Damn. Did Natalie know? They'd just started dating a few months ago, but I'd never taken Z for a jerk.

"She lives over on State Street at Sunrise BMW. She's dark blue with tan leather interior. A five series."

"A car?" I feigned a yawn. "Predictable."

"Really, Miss Sweden? Judging?" He shook his head. "Besides, my beater is on its last transmission. That car is a money pit. Used to be a sweet ride, but all good things must come to an end. I swear the car knows when I drive past Tammy on State Street. It starts to sputter. That's what I need for Christmas, Mori, a new set of wheels."

"Speaking of Christmas, I got us tickets to the SLPD's holiday party." I pulled into the parking lot of the precinct and parked under a bright streetlight. Z's rust bucket was parked nearby, and I kind of felt sad for it.

Z shook his head. "No way."

"Oh, come on. Don't make me go alone."

"Don't go, then."

"I'm still a rookie, and I want to get to know my coworkers better. You can understand that, right? Nobody talks to anyone around the precinct. It's all business."

"You don't need a stupid holiday party to talk to people, Mori. Besides, who do you *really* want to know better? Ward Brown? He's just a bitter smokestack with one too many head injuries from his days in the Marines." Z paused for a second to look at me. "Or maybe you're dying to chat up Cranston, the biggest misogynist on the force? That amazing man knows everything. Or so he thinks."

"He really does think he's all that." I cracked a smile.

"Oh, I'm just getting started, Mori. I bet you're dying to get some one-on-one time with Scooter Rivers. He's got the personality of a water snake. The man is a belly-crawler. He only looks up to ask whose boots he can lick next."

I was laughing now. For all of his strong opinions, Z's assessments were right on.

"And Chief Cribben? Why do you think they call him Crappin' Cribben? He logs a lot of time on that throne in his private office, if you know what I mean. Reads all his daily reports with his pants around his knees."

"Ew, no. TMI." I shook my head, swiping at a tear. "There are plenty of decent people in the department . . ."

"Name one. Fast. Don't think."

I opened my mouth, pressing my tired brain to come up with someone.

"*Eeeeeeepppp!* Time's up."

I was glad Z was back to his old self. I'm sure it wasn't easy, handling another bank robbery case after being on-scene three years ago when his partner was gunned down.

"You seem fully recovered," I said.

He nodded. "I'm fine. Superhero fine. Invincible."

"So, you won't mind telling me the inside scoop on the Twilight Bandit. I mean, you were there. Tonight's robbery really is similar, right?"

Z stared straight ahead, the joy drained right out of him.

"Come on, Z," I said, getting irritated. Why was no one on the force willing to tell me the inside details of one of the most important crime sprees in Sunrise Lake history? There'd been nine robberies, but the string of crimes had ended abruptly after Officer Franny Landon was killed.

"It would be a huge favor if you would just tell me what you know about that night."

Z stared straight ahead.

"I'm sorry," I tried again. "I know you don't like to talk about it, but I wasn't on the force when it happened, and some inside knowledge of that serial robber might help us solve this new case. It would really help if you filled me in."

He grunted, and in the dim light of the dashboard I could see his eyebrows were raised, a sure sign he was annoyed. "Just stay out of it, okay? It's bad enough one cop got killed." He ran one hand over his close-cropped hair and then pushed open the door. "I gotta go. Natalie's making pizzas and I'm starved."

"But Z." I pushed open the door of the patrol vehicle to hop out and call after him. "How am I supposed to stay out of a case when I'm investigating a similar crime? It might be the same perp."

He paused and turned to me. In his dark jacket and trousers, he cut a stark silhouette against the lights that bathed the police station behind him. "You know how to work a case, Mori." His breath formed puffs of steam in the December night air. "You comb through witness statements and forensic data and you follow every lead. Stick to today's case and you'll be fine."

He was right. I knew he was. At the moment I had plenty of information and clues to pursue from tonight's robbery without comparing it to past crime patterns. But I still wished he would open up about that night three years ago. That's just me, probing until I have all the answers. "I could use your help inputting witness statements," I called, a last-ditch effort.

"When there's a pepperoni pizza calling my name? Uh-uh. See you later, Mori." He kept on walking toward his beater of a car, boots scuffing the sandy pavement.

Pizza night. My shoulders sank a little as I watched him go. It was tempting, but not enough to lure me away from the investigation. Hoping for some quiet time at my desk to get organized, I went into the quiet precinct. The night shift desk sergeant, Sherry Joel, nodded as I passed, not missing a beat from her phone call. Most of the night shift was on patrol. A lone cop talked with one of the dispatchers as I headed toward the shadowed squad room, which now loomed empty since detectives didn't work the graveyard shift unless they'd been called in on a priority crime scene. But as soon as I reached the back office, Lieutenant Omak snagged me.

"Didn't you work a two-to-ten tonight?" His voice was stern, as if he'd caught me with my hand in a cookie jar. "Your shift is over, Mori."

"I did, but I wanted to start framing up the case for our bank robbery. Have you loaded the bank videos into our database yet?"

He shook his head. "You can dig into the case in the morning."

"But I like getting a head start," I insisted. "Sometimes the details are sharper when they're fresh in my mind."

"I understand that, Mori, and I appreciate the work ethic, but a nonviolent crime like this gets low priority. Tomorrow is soon enough, so for tonight I'm giving you the boot."

"Oh." Even the mildest forms of rejection stung when you tried to be perfect. I looked away to hide my disappointment.

"I appreciate your dedication, but you need to pace yourself, Mori," he said. "No burning out on my watch. Everything will still be here in the morning."

"Okay. I'm just going to make copies of these witness statements before I head out." With a sour taste in my mouth and the pressure of weariness filling my head, I put the stack of crumpled statements into the feeder of the copy machine and let the machine chug through the task as I ducked into the small women's locker room. Suddenly tired, I shoved my street clothes into my duffel bag, leaving my uniform on until I got home. I stopped in the squad room to tuck the copies in my bag (for later reading) and place the originals in the in-basket of the admin assistants, the invaluable clerical staff who inputted police reports.

As I passed the front desk, Sgt. Joel's face reflected the odd light from her computer monitor as she kindly advised a homeowner about local noise regulations. "We've gotten a few complaints about the music in your Christmas display," Joel said, phone pressed to her ear with one shoulder as she tapped the computer keyboard with one hand. "Can you make sure it's off by nine?"

That was the typical police action in Sunrise Lake: noise complaints, missing lawn ornaments, an elderly citizen who'd wandered off.

The robbery at First Sunrise was a big deal, and I felt honored that Lieutenant Omak had made me the lead on the case.

Outside I saw Lieutenant Omak walking in the shadows at the edge of the parking lot, pacing like a restless tiger. He stared down at his cell phone, occasionally swiping up. It was chilly, but he wore no jacket.

Something about the boss mystified me. Not personally. Happily married with a couple of kids, he seemed as squared away as a former military man could be. Of all the supervisors in our department, Omak was the one who seemed best prepared to stand tall and make a decision. But that courage was tempered by a thoughtful side, something enigmatic and distant that always left me wondering what he was really thinking.

"You're going to catch a cold," I said, sounding like my mother.

"Colds are caused by viruses, not weather," he said as he took measured steps through an empty parking space. Finally glancing up, he smiled. "See you tomorrow, Mori."

"Good night, Lieutenant." I sensed that he would remain at the precinct awhile tonight, doing whatever supervisors did to juggle the police operations of a community. And for Omak, there was something more at stake—an investigation of possible police corruption, which he'd told me only because I was about to unearth one of his plants, Officer Esme Garcia. I'd been on the verge of reporting her for suspicious behavior when he'd explained that she was working an inside investigation and I was to back off and keep it confidential. My lips were sealed, though I was curious to know more. I always figure knowledge is power.

As I drove home, I kept running the details of my new case through my head. Older male. Baseball cap. Black-framed glasses. Slight limp. White hair, possibly a wig. Right-handed. Young-looking hands.

I was eager for the microanalysis of the hairs at the scene, as well as any fingerprints. The lab would be one of my first stops in the morning.

The grainy image of the perpetrator lingered in my mind: glasses too big for his face, hat bunching up in places. I'd noticed him on camera wincing a few times as he scratched at the edges of his cap. Either an itchy scalp or an uncomfortable wig. And the glasses were probably part of his disguise, since he seemed to be glancing over them when he was writing the note.

Ashley's mention of his hands intrigued me, and Sidney Maynor had said his youthful face didn't match that white hair. I wondered just how young the robber could be. What if he was a teenager, a high school kid robbing the bank on a dare from friends? Or maybe someone in his early twenties, desperate for money to feed an addiction. I recalled the grainy image of the robber's face that had been captured on the bank cameras. Did the picture show enough of his features to run it by some administrators and teachers at Sunrise High to see if they recognized him? Possibly. But I couldn't reach out to the high schools and local community colleges until I had some confirmation that we were dealing with a younger person.

* * *

I pulled up in front of the little white cottage I shared with my longtime friend Natalie Amichi and noticed Z's car parked in the driveway. The silver door he'd had the body shop replace on the passenger side gleamed in the light of our porch lamp. Z had been seeing Natalie for weeks now, so I got the double whammy of seeing him both at work and often at home. Usually I was fine with that, but tonight it was going to be a little bit awkward for us with a new case and Natalie trying to report on it. The best way to avoid accidentally spilling confidential information was to not discuss the case at all, which was easier for Z than it was for me. Once I dig into an investigation, it's hard for me to extract myself from the weeds.

As I swung the front door open, music, laughter, and the amazing smell of freshly baked bread hit me, a reminder that I hadn't eaten since lunchtime. Z's booming voice filled the kitchen as he did another of his spot-on impressions. For a moment I felt my heart thud in my throat, and I knew I wanted something like what Z and Natalie had: the fun, the flirting, and the thrill of a close kiss. That kind of relationship hadn't happened for me. Not yet.

"Hi, guys," I said, entering the kitchen and putting down my heavy work bag.

"Hey you! We're making personal pizzas and you're just in time. I bet you're starving, working through dinnertime." Natalie poured a healthy glass of red wine and handed it to me. "I believe this has your name on it."

I accepted the glass and dared a glance across the butcher-block island to Z. Somehow the awkwardness was gone, melted away in the glow of our kitchen as Z raised his wine glass. "To working less and drinking more."

I lifted my glass in a toast. "I'll drink to that."

"Hey, pick your favorite toppings, Laura. I've got them lined up over here," Natalie said, then turned to Z. "Hey buddy, aren't you supposed to be grating more cheese?"

"Sorry, boss! No falling down on the job for me." Z continued scraping a block of mozzarella cheese over the metal grater.

I washed my hands and put on a cute little apron decorated with dancing forks and knives. I loved it. Natalie had purchased it for me as a housewarming gift when we'd first moved in together, trying to reassure me that our new living arrangement would work out fine.

It had been hard at first, living away from the home I'd shared with my parents and sister Hannah. As much as I loved my comfortable childhood bedroom, I'd been feeling a little silly for not venturing out on my own. I guess I'd been most afraid of loneliness. And how would I stay current on the family restaurant gossip that was passed around the table more readily than the shoyu? Would Hannah and I grow apart? Already we sparred over stupid stuff, like which one of us ate the last Pop-Tart, but would we want to talk at all if we didn't have to?

Our elder sister, Koko, had already won the family gold star by going to law school, marrying a handsome man of Japanese descent, and promptly having two darling children who immediately cast a spell over my parents. Our older brother, Alex, was in medical school in Michigan, and I missed him dearly. When he'd lived at home, we had talked in a sort of shorthand, understanding each other on a very basic level. As a teen, I had relied on Alex for a male point of view on various subjects. But now that he was off in the Midwest, immersed in med school, our sibling connection was strained over phone or text. I hoped he made it home for Christmas this month.

Things were changing with my younger sister, too. Hannah's star status was about to explode. Any day now, she'd start hearing from colleges, Hannah's early-admissions choices, some of which had wooed her more intently than any of the boys who texted her all the time. Another brilliant and popular Mori child.

Sometimes it felt hard to breathe the same air as my high-achieving siblings.

But nights like tonight helped. It felt good to be assigned another important case, and I quietly relished the easy way Natalie and I had seamlessly fallen into our own domestic routine. As I settled into the cozy evening, all the stress of the day dissolved as the three of us laughed together while outside a cold wind churned up the fir trees that stood sentry around our little cottage.

Within minutes bubbling-hot pizza appeared on the table, and we ate on stools gathered around the island. After a few minutes of greedy silence, we slowed down, and Natalie began to recount her crazy day, which had been tame until news of the First Sunrise Bank robbery broke.

"Next thing I knew, I was taping a live shot in front of the bank on Bonita Drive for the evening news broadcast." She picked up a fallen piece of roasted onion and popped it into her mouth. "I didn't know you guys were there, but I suspected as much, since there were only like ninety police vehicles on the scene."

"Ninety vehicles." Z nodded, wiping his chin with a napkin. "Was that the official count, or fake news?"

"Wise-ass," Natalie teased. "But we got some decent coverage for the eleven o'clock news. I even got a question in at that crazy press conference with Lieutenant Omak."

"I was wondering how that went," I said. "It looked like a madhouse from inside the bank."

"It was crazy. I mean, a bank robbery in Sunrise Lake? It's been years since that happened. Do you remember, Laura, when we were still in college and there was that rash of bank hits?"

"I do remember that," I said, shooting a glance at Z. He took another bite of pizza and ignored me. The two of us always had to be careful not to divulge any information about any active Sunrise Lake investigations around Natalie. She was respectful of our boundaries, but with a little too much wine, details could slip.

"I mean, this looks a little like the Twilight Bandit's MO." Natalie pointed a crust in the air for emphasis. "At least that's what all the reporters were whispering about at the presser."

"Oh yeah?" I said. "What's their rationale?"

She dropped her pizza crust onto her plate and leaned forward. "First, it's the same time of day all the other robberies took place: dusk. Second, he wore another baseball cap. And again, it had a logo from a local brand."

"That could be a coincidence," Z said.

I was nodding. "It's a disguise that doesn't attract attention. The visor of a ball cap covers a lot of the facial features."

"But the local logos are a pattern." Natalie grabbed her phone. "You guys have got to see these pics I downloaded from our news archives. Extracts of surveillance footage from all the different robberies. This Twilight dude loves his hats." She scrolled through dozens of pics with her thumb, the light from her phone illuminating her face. "Oh, here, look at these. They're hilarious."

I took Natalie's phone from her and watched as a series of grainy pictures of an older guy flipped in front of my eyes. In each picture, the robber wore a baseball cap with some sort of logo: FREIGHTLINER TRUCKS, ORTHO FERTILIZER, KELLS IRISH PUB, HENRY WEINHARD'S PRIVATE RESERVE, mostly local brands. I shared the photos with Z, who looked on with mild interest.

"It's like he's got a bad hat fetish or something," Natalie observed as she took her phone back from Z. "Do you remember how our parents kept warning us back then, Laura? Everybody in Sunrise Lake was on edge after that police officer was killed."

"I do remember that," I said. "We were away at school, but our parents were freaking out. When I came home at Christmas break, my mom wouldn't let me go near a bank."

"I remember getting the call in my dorm. My parents were so worried," Natalie said. "And that police officer getting shot was really awful. That's when it crossed the line, terrifying people."

Z stood up from the table, pushing his empty wine glass forward. "I've got to get going."

Natalie turned to him, her forehead creased with concern. "Babe, what's wrong?"

He stretched. "I'm just tired."

I looked at them both. "That cop who was killed? Franny Landon. Z was working with her that night. He was there." I swallowed hard. I didn't know if Z would be angry or relieved that I'd brought up Franny's death, but I thought Natalie needed to know.

I could see her searching Z's face. "I had no idea . . ." Her voice trailed off as she went to hug him.

He embraced Natalie easily, rubbing her back. "I don't like to talk about it. In fact, I've been told by my boss not to talk about that night. I almost lost my job over the whole thing. Nearly lost my mind, too."

"I'm so sorry. That's really tough, hon." Natalie sat down at the table but kept his hands in hers. "Are you okay about it all now?"

He shrugged. "Truth is, I don't really remember much about that night. There are lots of blanks for me. I was really angry about that for a long time, but lately I started talking to the department shrink. Working with her has helped. Kind of. She diagnosed me with PTSD."

"I didn't know . . ." Natalie said as a phone made a *brring* sound in the kitchen. She slid out of her chair. "That's me, but who would be calling me at this hour besides you guys? Z, please don't leave. Not yet, okay?" He nodded, and she hurried into the adjoining room.

"Z . . . post-traumatic stress? I had no idea," I mumbled under my breath. I'd known Z kept mum on the Twilight Bandit case, but I didn't know the level of trauma he'd endured. It made me that much more determined to learn the details of the Twilight crime spree and Franny Landon's death. "I'm really glad you're getting help," I said.

"Thanks." He nodded. "I appreciate that, partner. I wish I could be more help, but a lot of that night is a total blank. There's something really funky about that whole investigation, but the stuff I do remember, and it's not much, is a total nightmare."

"My mom!" Natalie rounded the corner. "She worries about everything. She's calling to make sure I lock my car. She saw me on TV and is afraid the bank robber saw me too. Like he's going to come after me. The things she comes up with in her head . . ."

Z smiled as soon as he heard Natalie's voice behind him.

"Sounds like my mom, too." I said. "Hey Nat, you made dinner, so Z and I will clean up the dishes. Why don't you pick out a movie for us to watch while we scrub up?"

"So you're staying?" Natalie asked Z.

Z nodded. "Yeah, we got this, babe. Find us something good to watch. Extra points if it's got some action in it."

Natalie bounded into the living room and bounced onto the couch. "Hey, sweetie. I just want to tell you I'm sorry you're having to go through all this." She paused, snatching up the remote. "If it's anything like being blackout drunk, I get it. Not remembering. Piecing things together. I've been there—I mean, not since college, but . . . never again." She winced, and her whole neck flushed red. "And, wow. I can't believe I just admitted that. So embarrassing."

Z leaned in over the sofa and kissed her cheek. "Thanks for understanding. It means a lot to me. Not everybody can deal with a wise-ass cop who has PTSD."

In the kitchen, Z scrubbed dishes while I dried and stacked them. We were quiet for a bit as we listened for Natalie to start watching movie previews. Finally, we heard music blaring from the other room.

Rinsing a baking tray, Z kept his gaze on the sink. "Don't go thinking I'm crazy or anything, Mori. I got it all together."

I wrapped the towel around the cheese grater, careful to avoid the sharp edges. "I question a lot of things, Z, but your sanity isn't one of them."

"Good. Don't start now."

I smiled. How could he not understand that it was his offbeat, sometimes unhinged sensibilities that drew people to him? After a short pause, I added, "Is the counseling helping with your memory of the night Franny—"

"Some. The department made it mandatory, my visit with the shrink. It's helped to talk the case over with someone with no skin in the game. The therapist is nice, but honestly, Mori, I don't know if I want to remember."

I dried the last dish and stacked it neatly on our kitchen counter. Z and I worked well together, but I wasn't sure how this new case was going to work out with my partner still reeling from the trauma of a string of previous bank robberies. This was going to be tricky.

4

That night I slipped into bed and lay under the comforter thinking about my new case. Cracking the First Sunrise Bank robbery was a big responsibility, and the possibility of letting down my coworkers, my community, and my family was daunting. I didn't want to doubt my own capabilities, but in the dark crevice of the night, worry needled its way under the door. Why had the lieutenant picked me as lead investigator? Could Cranston be right? Was I too young and inexperienced to head up this investigation?

New challenges encourage growth. I could hear my father's deep voice in my head. All our lives, the Mori kids grew up hearing Koji Mori's words of wisdom. When we were little, Koko, Hannah, Alex, and I would impersonate him, mimicking the quiet cadence of his voice. As kids, the four of us were convinced anything we said, as long as it was delivered in our father's measured tone, sounded wise and important. *Taking out the trash is good for your soul,* our brother Alex intoned as he dutifully carted garbage bags from our home to the can at the end of the driveway. *Letting your sister borrow cherry lip gloss builds bridges of understanding,* Hannah whispered to Koko as she fled the bathroom with our eldest sister's favorite lip color.

These days, though, I yearned to hear my father's calm, clear advice. Life seemed to get more complicated with each passing year, and failure seemed weightier. Once, as a teenager paralyzed by stress over an upcoming SAT exam, my father sat me down and looked into my pinched face with his calm, dark eyes. *Laura, if there is any action you can take at this moment to alleviate the situation, do it! If not, let the stress roll like water off your shoulders.*

Was there any action I could take right now?

I threw off my puffy goose-down comforter, retrieved the batch of witness statements I'd copied at the precinct, and settled back into bed with them. Reading usually relaxed or bored me to sleep, but the statements had just enough surprises to keep me going.

Most of the other tellers hadn't noticed a robbery was happening until Ashley called for Mr. Lopez and hit the alarm button after the robber had departed. The perpetrator had managed to remain calm and blend in. The teller working beside Ashley, Farrah Palmer, had noticed Ashley opening her safe and wondered about it, since the tellers were supposed to get a manager to approve it first. But Ashley had seemed fine, so Farrah had continued on with the transaction she'd been processing.

The woman with the young child had been floored because the robber had seemed so nice, pausing to try to talk with her son. The woman who'd been there with her husband had noticed the robber's white hair, deemed it artificial, and had wondered why any man would wear such a cheap, clownish wig when a bald head was perfectly fine. After the fact, she had regretted not figuring it out on the spot.

I let my eyes close for a second. When I awoke, it was after three and the papers lay on my bed in the light of the side lamp. I gathered them up, turned off the light, and went back to sleep.

* * *

When I arrived at the precinct the next morning, it was hours before my usual shift, but the patrol cops beginning the day tour were lined up for roll call in the meeting room. I noticed that the admin box was empty, a sign that the witness statements were in the process of being inputted to electronic files. I brought my peppermint-mocha latte into the locker room and quickly changed into my uniform.

Back at my desk, I savored the latte of the season as I quickly completed the basic incident report—time, place, basic narrative, and witness list—and put together a timeline of last night's robbery based on the time-stamped film and the observations of witnesses. I was able to draw from the bank video Omak had posted in our electronic file and the written witness statements I'd taken home. So far, none of the witness statements had been entered in the electronic file, though I had noticed Michelle typing away in her cubicle and expected to see them any minute now.

When I finished the timeline, I dug through the file for the statement from the bank manager, Martin Lopez, and dialed his cell number. He agreed to come in after lunch for a more detailed interview. While I'd been intrigued by his former brush with the Twilight Bandit, I was more interested in the bank's current staff and any record of improprieties among personnel at the bank.

As I ended the call, I moved to the front of the squad room and peeked over the rim of Michelle's cubicle. Her work area was strung with a silver garland and featured a bowl of peppermint patty bites that I would find it hard to resist in close proximity. A petite woman with long gray hair always wrapped in a bun or a wispy twist, Michelle turned away from the chart that was open on her monitor.

"Hey, there." I rested one arm on the divider. "How's it going with the statements from the First Sunrise robbery?"

"Was I supposed to do them?" She whirled around in her chair and looked over at the in-box tray outside her cubicle. "I didn't see them land in the in-box. Nope. Not there."

"I put them there last night," I said, wondering what had happened to the statements. "Did Omak take them?" It wasn't unusual for a supervisor to review aspects of a case.

Michelle shrugged. "When you find them, I'll dig in."

I thanked her and headed off to find Omak, who was usually on his feet, watching over the main desk, roll call, or the squad room. But this morning I heard voices coming from his office. An irate voice complained about something as Omak's baritone voice countered with rolling thunder. I paused at the open doorway, not sure if I should interrupt.

"It will be fine, Chief. I'll be supervising," Omak said calmly.

"But I don't like a newbie leading the case. Not her. I've got important people calling, breathing down my neck. The mayor, and the town council. Businesses, banks . . . Nobody wants another crime spree, especially at Christmastime."

"We're well aware of that, sir, and you can count on Detective Mori to conduct a thorough and—" Having turned toward the door, Omak spotted me and motioned me into the office. "Mori, we were just discussing the First Sunrise case. The chief wants us to make it a priority."

Cribben stared down at me, his jowls shifting to a frown. "The heat is on, Detective. People are worried about this thing. I know it's only been one bank hit, but no one wants it to spread. Two of our banks permanently closed branches after the last rash of burglaries."

"Which included a homicide," Omak pointed out. "That's not the case here."

"I understand the urgency, sir," I said, "and we're moving as quickly as possible with the investigation."

"Is that so?" Cribben pursed his lips, unimpressed.

Omak nodded toward me. "Why don't you fill the chief in on where the investigation stands?"

"We've established a timeline and we've time-stamped video from the bank," I said. "I just completed a review of witness statements. I called a few people back for further questioning. And I was about to head over to the lab to meet with forensics."

"I want a copy of the timeline and the bank footage," the chief said.

"Yes, sir."

"And if this is the Twilight Bandit, back for more, I need to know it." Cribben thunked two fingers against his puffy chest. "I'm the one under fire for high-profile crime, so I need to know. Is this the same perp, Mori?"

I shot an unsure look at Omak, who simply raised a brow. "It's too soon to say, Chief," I answered.

"Well, when you know, you come to me. I need you to give me regular updates on the case, up-to-the-minute developments." Cribben's blue eyes were icy with doubt of my abilities, but then I wasn't afraid of hard work and accountability. It would be nerve-racking to report in to the chief, but I respected his need to be on top of the situation.

"Mori and I will keep you updated on all developments," Omak promised.

"Fine. I'll take the timeline and bank video now."

"I'll get those for you, Chief." I hurried down the hall to print a timeline and copy down the link so the chief could access the video. When I delivered them to Cribben, he didn't make eye contact, but Omak thanked me and gestured toward the door, making it clear he had more to discuss with the chief in private.

So Cribben wanted someone else leading the investigation. What if he looked in our database and saw that the witness statements weren't posted yet? I strode straight to the locker room, unzipped my bag, and removed the copies of the witness statements for Michelle to input. I would tell Omak about the missing originals, but not just yet, not while the chief was around to completely lose confidence in my detective skills.

"I'll have these in a jiffy," Michelle said when I handed her the stack. "Where'd you find them?" she asked.

"Stashed away somewhere," I said, trying to be vague as I grabbed my winter jacket and slid it across my shoulders. A visit to my friend over at the forensics lab off Terwilliger Avenue was in order. But first, a coffee run.

* * *

Rex Burns smiled and accepted the double-shot macchiato I brought him from the La Provence Bakery. "You sure know how to grease the pan, girl," he said as I sipped from my own double-shot vanilla latte. "Let me just sip this down before I admit that I don't have a lot of good news for you." Rex led the way over to a standing desk, where he logged in to the computer. His blond hair had recently been shaved in a fade on the side, and the top portion, which had once been waxed into a Mohawk, had grown into a fluffy poof of hair that was tinted green, probably in anticipation of Christmas. "That bank note that your robber passed yesterday?"

"At First Sunrise. Yes. Were you able to get anything from it?"

"Only a partial print. It doesn't match the teller's prints, which we had on file. Earnhart, right? So it might be his partial. Or it could belong to another customer. Sorry." Rex scrolled down the screen. "And the pen was a bust, too, though we thought it would be. Too small a surface to get a good grab. And the countertops gave us seven different prints. Three that match staff. Four unknown. We're still looking for matches to prints in the FBI database."

"I was hoping for a nice, juicy full print that pinged immediately when we ran it," I said.

"But the guy wears gloves most of the time, right? I don't think you're going to ID your bank robber through a print. But I do have something that might be helpful. Those hairlike fibers found at the scene? Turns out three of them are human hair with follicles attached. That means they were shed naturally. But the five-inch white hairs? They're actually artificial fibers from a manufactured hair piece. If these came from your culprit, he's wearing a wig."

"Interesting," I said, hope glimmering in my smile. It didn't prove anything, but it lined up with the suspicions of a few witnesses who'd thought he was wearing a wig. The evidence—fake glasses, young hands, and likely wig—seemed to indicate that the thief was a younger man wearing a disguise.

The chief's question rang in my ears: *Is this the same perp, Mori?*

Had the same white-haired wig been the modus operandi of the Twilight Bandit? I was going to have to research the old case, probably in secret since no one in the precinct wanted to revisit it. There had to be someone in this department who wasn't emotionally caught up in that case.

I looked over at Rex, who perched on a stool to enjoy his coffee drink. "Do you remember the Twilight Bandit case?"

He looked up with crossed squirrel eyes. "You seem to have confused me with a history buff. I'm a science nerd. Different discipline, equally outcast."

"It was that rash of bank robberies that ended three years ago when—"

"Yeah, yeah, I've heard of it, but I was still working at a funeral home and getting my master's when it all went down. My job as a forensic lab tech was just a dream back then."

"You worked in a funeral home?"

"Don't judge me. And it's decent money. The point is, I didn't have the time to pay much attention to local crime stats back then."

"So you wouldn't know if the suspect in those nine Twilight cases wore a wig? Or do you happen to have the fiber samples handy somewhere in a drawer or file?"

"Ha-ha, Mori. You know this is a laboratory. We don't keep case files or evidence here. What you're looking for would be in the back of this building, in the evidence locker."

"I knew that."

Rex grinned. "But you were hoping that I remembered the details of those cases so you wouldn't have to do your job."

"I love doing my job," I said, lifting my latte from the counter. "It's the sloppy paperwork in previous investigations that gets under my skin."

"Not me; it's everyone else. I feel ya."

"If all goes well, I'll be back shortly with some wig fibers for you to compare to our First Sunrise evidence."

"I'll be here." He toasted me with his coffee cup. "Always eager to come up with something macchiato worthy."

It was raining lightly as I left the lab. I stayed under the narrow overhang and circled around the nondescript one-story building that housed the morgue, forensics lab, and evidence locker for every police and sheriff's department in three counties. The door squealed as I pressed into the evidence section, a shadowed warehouse of objects culled from years of crime. Z called it the graveyard of broken laws. Suddenly, I wished he were here to bring some life and humor to this place. Only authorized personnel were permitted in the archives, as a sign on the front desk reminded me, but I could see the rows of floor-to-ceiling shelves through a mesh wall that resembled cyclone fencing.

The silver bell on the counter made me want to laugh. Apparently a high-tech facility. I pinged the bell and waited with an encouraging smile as a lanky cop with a shiny head and a fringe of short white hair emerged from behind the wall.

"All right then, plan it for Thursday. I gotta go. I'll get back to you on that." He hung up the phone and slid it into a pocket. "What can I do for you, Detective?"

I checked his nameplate. "I'm looking for the hairs found at the scenes of the Twilight Bandit bank robberies," I said. "I'd like to check them out and take them over to the lab for a comparison to another crime scene. Yesterday's robbery at First Sunrise Bank."

"Whoa, whoa, whoa, there. This isn't a library, and our filing system doesn't work that way." Hands on his hips, Officer Balducci rolled back on his heels. "You can't just walk in here and check out evidence."

Clearly I had stomped on his territory. "I stand corrected. What's the procedure for pulling evidence to run a crime scene analysis?"

"Here's the requisition form you need to fill out." He tapped a stack of papers on the counter. "Evidence is cataloged by crime scene date and location. It's not like we have a big fat file marked Twilight Bandit."

"Of course you don't," I agreed.

"And you need authorization from a superior officer," he said. "A signature."

I bit my lower lip as I glanced down at the form. I didn't relish the thought of driving back and forth with a permission slip. "Would a phone call do? Chief Cribben has moved this case to top priority; I'd hate to lose time on a formality."

"Have your supervisor call me and I'll see what's what."

"Sounds good," I said, peeling off a few of the forms. "I'll fill these out and get them right back to you."

He shrugged. "I'll be here."

Out in the car I turned on the engine for a little heat as I began to fill in the forms. Was I supposed to know the dates of the Twilight Bandit's hits by heart?

I clicked the pen closed and called Omak. "Here's what I know, and here's what I'm trying to find out." I told him about the hair-like samples from yesterday's crime scene that had been identified as wig fibers and then explained about the evidence I was trying to "requisition" from the Twilight cases for comparison.

"And you met Balducci, gatekeeper of the evidence locker."

"I just had that privilege, and I can tell he doesn't trust me."

"He'll come around." Omak went into the database to find the dates and locations where white wig fibers had been found after Twilight Bandit hits.

"I knew there would be some wig fibers in evidence," I said, jotting down the information.

"There were, but it's kind of a long shot, working with hair samples. They don't have the identifying characteristics of fingerprints."

"I'm just trying to go with the evidence we have," I said.

"That's all you can do," Omak said. "Oh, and when you get back, come see me. I've got a surprise for you."

A surprise? It wasn't my birthday, and Omak wasn't a prankster. "What's that, Lieu?" I asked.

Too late. He'd already ended the call.

5

After Omak called the property clerk and vouched for me, Officer Balducci warmed considerably. The property clerk promised to pull the evidence I needed by the end of the day and deliver it to the lab next door for analysis.

"Wig fibers." Rex seemed concerned when I doubled back to update him. "I've been thinking about that. We might need to send it out to another lab, someone who has experience in fiber analysis. Our lab can decipher whether a fiber is human hair or synthetic, but we don't have the technical expertise to do a complete analysis here."

"Don't you just look at it under the microscope?"

Rex launched into a long explanation on how to identify fake hair, including scaling, recognition of fish eyes, and irregular cross-sections.

"You lost me at scaling," I said. "But what does that mean in terms of time?"

"Two days, maybe three."

"I need it right away," I said, thinking about the chief's mandate. "Anything you can do to expedite things and I'll owe you a thousand macchiatos."

"We'll do our best," Rex promised.

Even after my visit to the satellite facility, I arrived at the precinct before ten. In the squad room, Z was on the phone with the director of an assisted-living facility in Sunrise Lake, where a rash of burglaries had residents on edge. The interaction with the facility director forced my partner to be on his best behavior, polite and earnest. Inside, Z had a heart of gold, but not everyone got to see that. I was glad he had that case to keep him away from my tiptoeing through the old Twilight Bandit case.

*   *   *

Back in the squad room I found Z at his desk scrolling through pages of witness statements. Apparently, a few thefts had blossomed into a mini crime spree over at Sunset Pines, a ritzy assisted-living facility off Carmen Drive.

Z looked over as I put my coat on the back of my chair. "Take a picture, Mori. It lasts longer."

Had I been staring? "Sorry," I lied. "I'm reading witness statements over your shoulder. Who steals a ceramic cat with green glass eyes?"

"There's a whole world of souvenirs and cheap statuettes we know nothing about. And the thief at Sunset Pines seems to be stepping it up. People are getting upset, particularly the women there. They could use someone sympathetic to listen."

"Are you asking me? Is that a compliment?"

"Just a fact. Can you go over with me and do a grip-and-grin while I process a few more missing objects? It should only take a half hour or so."

"Maybe after my interview. I've got a pretty packed day. The chief told me to make this case a priority."

"Ooh. Under the microscope. Can she take the pressure?"

"Shut up," I said quietly, stifling a grin. As I spoke, I logged in to my computer and checked the file for the First Sunrise case. The witness statements had been inputted, which reminded me of the momentary panic that morning. I told Z about how the statements had gone missing, and he paused, rubbing his knuckles against his jaw.

"Did you figure out who took them?"

I shook my head. "I still need to talk with Omak. Maybe he wanted to have a look."

"Maybe," Z said. "But it's not like him to just swipe things."

I knew that, but I couldn't imagine what else might have happened to the papers. For all of our faults, our precinct functioned fairly well with administrative tasks. I wanted to review the bank video from yesterday's robbery on Bonita Street, but first I had to take a peek at the old Twilight case. I found the nine burglaries lumped haphazardly into one file in our database. A second file held information on the homicide investigation. I'd known this was a long shot. Maybe there was no relationship between my case and this string of robberies, but I wasn't going to leave any stone unturned.

Scrolling through to get a sense of the scope, I was amazed at how little information was here. I skimmed, not looking for detail but measuring the content of the paperwork on each bank robbery. The incident reports had been filled out for each robbery, but beyond that the files lacked any sense of order. Pieces of evidence were listed without explanation. There were copies of forensic orders Landon or Cranston had placed, but the results were not in the file. Only a handful of witness statements for each crime. And no sign of analysis, theory, or notes from the lead investigator, Officer Landon. A meticulous officer like Franny would have recorded equally meticulous notes.

I quickly brought up another of Franny Landon's cases, a simple theft charge from a local bike shop. It was supremely organized. The file was small but immaculate, with interviews dated and annotated and filed in order. Evidence photos were included with relevant lists of stolen items. Her work on this case was vastly different from the Twilight files.

Puzzled, I slumped back in my chair, tuning out the chatter and noise of the precinct. What had happened to Franny Landon's work on the cases?

There were no links to video on the case, so I studied the black-and-white photos of the bandit Franny had incorporated in her report. Hard to tell, but in a few of the close-ups he did have the weathered look of an older man. Witness statements were so spotty that I started searching for the details I was looking for in Franny's summary of statements. In the third and fourth robberies I found confirmation: the robber seemed to be an old man, though the long white hair might have been a wig. The perpetrator was courteous, thanking tellers and twice holding the door for other customers. And Franny had surmised from video footage that the Twilight Bandit appeared to be left-handed. Unlike the First Sunrise robber.

I made a mental note: Twilight seemed older, courteous, and left-handed.

Next I clicked on the homicide investigation for Franny Landon. The narrative showed that Z and Franny had been two blocks away when the call came in about the robber, and thus they had responded quickly. They had split up in pursuit of two differ- ent suspects, and after the sound of two gunshots Z had found Franny on the ground with a bullet wound in her head.

Squirming in my chair, I moved away from the narrative and scrolled through the rest of the file. Where was the coroner's report? The timeline? The statements from witnesses canvassed at the scene?

So much information was missing.

* * *

"Hey, Mori," Cranston called from the doorway, jarring me from my thoughts. "There's someone here to see you."

I saw the bank manager lingering beside Cranston, looking a little unsettled. The precinct atmosphere could do that to people. I grabbed a pad of paper and a small portable recorder from my desk drawer and went to join him.

"Mr. Lopez, thanks for coming. We're just going to go down this hallway to find someplace quiet to talk," I said, gesturing with a friendly smile.

As Lopez headed off, Cranston nudged Brown and smiled. "See that! She's solved the case already."

"Ace detective," Brown muttered.

My smile hardened. A little good-natured ribbing was fine, but I didn't want these two upsetting my witness. "I'm doing my job; how about you? If you guys are in here, who's out there defending our streets?" It was lame, but at least it was a stab at defending myself.

"Somebody's cranky today," Cranston said.

I turned away from them and guided Martin Lopez into a small interview room with a table and three chairs, and we both took a seat. He declined my offer of water or coffee—smart move, as the precinct coffee was awful—and agreed to my taping the conversation.

I started the tape and then leaned toward him, trying to make the mood less formal. "How's it going down at the bank the day after?"

"We're open for business as usual, though everyone is a bit tense. Looking over our shoulders. I find myself staring at each customer who comes in, trying to test their character and see if they're going to pull out a gun and harm someone on my watch. On a normal day we stay alert, but today we're all pretty shell-shocked."

"That's to be expected after a frightening encounter like that. Does the bank offer counseling service for a situation like this? Ashley seemed to be in shock yesterday, and I suspect she's not the only one."

"We have a counselor coming in to meet with everyone after closing tonight. After that, she'll schedule private sessions with anyone who needs them."

"That sounds like a solid plan. Sometimes people don't realize they need help until it's offered. "

Lopez gave a tight nod, and I noticed the dark smudges under his eyes. Too little sleep, too much stress. It must have been a long night for him. "I have a list of your employees who were working the day of the robbery, but I'd like to flesh it out to include every employee on staff, including cleaning staff or maintenance."

"I can get you that info, back at the bank."

"Thank you. I know it's one more task at a busy time, and I appreciate that. I also wanted to ask you about former employees. Anyone who resigned or was fired in the last six months or so. Any disgruntled employees?"

"We had one person resign for health reasons, and another that we had to let go, but I don't know that either of them is disgruntled."

"What can you tell me about their circumstances?"

"Mia Anderson is the young woman who resigned to work on her health. She was a reliable employee, though after the fact I heard from some of the staff that she was inebriated during her shifts. I never noticed. She's young—midtwenties. I thought she had an eating disorder, but it seems that alcohol is the problem. I'm glad she's working on it. Nice kid."

I wrote the name MIA ANDERSON on my notepad. "Was she ever under suspicion for stealing money?"

"Never. Her drawer was short more than once, but that happens. As I recall, the amount was always small, less than a hundred."

"And how about the employee you terminated?" I asked.

"You could say he was not a good fit for commercial banking culture," Lopez said, frowning down at the table. When he looked up at me, he seemed apologetic. "I don't know how much I can legally tell you. I mean, this is an investigation, but there are employment laws that protect people's privacy."

"What was the employee's name? I can contact him directly."

"Quincy Blackstone." He stared down at my paper as I wrote. "His father is the owner of the Blackstone Vineyard out in wine country. Nice family."

"But their son was not a good employee."

"No, he was not. But it's not so hard to fire a guy whose survival doesn't depend on his paycheck. Still, we went by the book."

"I'm sure you did. Was there ever a time that Quincy Blackstone was under suspicion of taking from the bank?"

His face strained as he tried to navigate a safe answer.

"Whoa. That expression says a lot," I said with a knowing smile.

"It's complicated. Quincy's drawer was never short. He was impeccable that way. It was . . . his lack of professionalism with customers. Too familiar. I guess you could call him an opportunist."

"Did he part from the bank amicably?"

"Quincy kept saying it was no big deal, but he seemed annoyed with us. But not menacing. He doesn't strike me as the sort of guy who would ever hurt anyone."

I nodded, wondering if this Quincy might have been annoyed enough to plan a vindictive robbery. "Moving on . . . did you notice anyone new visiting the bank repeatedly? Not a regular customer, but someone who might have been observing operations?"

"You mean the burglar, scoping out the place?"

I nodded.

He raked a hand through his hair, mulling it over. "I'll have to think about that, and you might want to talk to my assistant manager, Vance Hausser. When the bank isn't busy, it's his job to work the front of the bank, open doors for customers, meet and greet. We try to make it a friendly ritual, but in truth he's profiling the customers, looking for potential security risks."

This was new to me. Although I'd talked with a greeter at my bank, I hadn't realized he'd been profiling customers. "And if Mr. Hausser sees a potential problem? How is he supposed to respond?"

"It's sort of a social weeding process. Often the 'inappropriate customer,' say, a group of teenaged kids or a displaced person, turns away after they've been engaged in conversation. If they've come on legitimate business, Vance gets them to a teller or handles it himself."

"Interesting." I added his name to the list and asked if Lopez had contact numbers. He had all three numbers in his cell phone. "Is there anything else you think I should know about your bank? Anything unusual that's occurred there in the past few months?"

He leaned back and looked up at the ceiling, thinking it over. "Nothing off the top of my head. We've got a good crew, hard workers, nice people. I hope they stick around and weather the storm."

I thanked Lopez for taking the time to come into the precinct and walked him out. When I reached the lobby, I saw Omak going over the day's schedule with the desk sergeant. "We're a little light tonight, with the Christmas party," Omak said.

"We can deny time off to some of the junior cops," said Tisch, a short, stocky sergeant who had enough seniority to work steady days.

"No, let them go to the party," Omak said, signing off on the schedule. "We'll manage with a skeleton crew."

"Okay, Lieu." Sgt. Tisch grabbed the paperwork and headed toward the offices.

Maybe it was the kid in me, but I was kind of excited about the party tonight, the prospect of getting to know some of my colleagues a bit better. There was a part of me, that conscientious worker who aimed to please, that wanted to skip the party and mine the depths of my new case. But Omak had made a good point last night; pacing was important.

Omak leaned one hip against the desk. "Going to the party, Mori?"

"I'm planning on it. So what's my surprise?"

"You may not like it." He folded his arms. "I got a call from the FBI while you were out. It's protocol for them to get involved in bank robberies, and they're assigning an agent."

"How does that work?" I asked, trying to ignore the tension that rose in my chest, prompting me to argue. In most of the prime-time police shows, there's a running feud between local law enforcement and the FBI, which seems to take over and take credit. "I mean, who, what, when, and does that mean they'll take over the case?"

"They're sending someone out in the next day or so, and no, they won't take the case away from us. Contrary to what you may have heard, I've found the Bureau helpful when I was supervising investigations in Atlanta. For now, keep forging ahead."

What else was there to do? It was still a crime that needed to be solved. I switched topics. "A batch of papers went missing this morning—the original copies of the witness statements from First Sunrise. Did you take them to your office for a look?"

"I don't move paperwork without notifying the owner. Did they turn up?"

"I was hoping you had them, but no. I've asked around, but they just vanished. Thankfully I made copies last night."

"For your take-home assignment. Don't think I don't notice."

I was pleased he had noticed that I took work home. That didn't make me a suck-up, did it?

"We'll need to report to the chief on progress at the end of the day," he said.

"I'll pull my notes together for that. Something else I wanted to ask you about: the case files for the Twilight Bandit case. I've started sifting through them, looking for comparisons, but there's so little there."

Omak nodded. "I've gone through all of them, more than once."

"Really?" It was hard to imagine Omak sitting still long enough to view all that bank video.

"Since Franny was my sister, it's not a case I can get involved in, but the paperwork was a mess. I did have one of the admin assistants clean the files up, add links to the bank videos, basic elements of an investigation. The files were lacking, and I wanted to be well versed in the crime patterns here in Sunrise Lake."

"I heard that Franny was the lead investigator on the case, but I don't see any of her notes in the files."

"Odd, isn't it? Apparently, they disappeared from the files. Deleted. Cranston said he had to start a lot of the reports from scratch when he came along."

"That explains some things," I said. "It's just hard to get the gist of a case when the investigator's analysis is missing."

"Do your best." He tipped his head toward the precinct door. "Was that the bank manager?"

"Martin Lopez. He gave me a few leads to pursue. Have you ever heard of Blackstone Vineyards?"

Omak's dark eyes opened wider. "My wife loves their Cabernet."

"One of their clan is a person of interest."

He nodded. "Keep me posted, Mori."

6

Back at my desk I ran the names Lopez had given me:

Mia Anderson
Quincy Blackstone
Vance Hausser

First I ran a search for arrest records on LEDS, the Law Enforcement Data System. Negative. No surprise, since the bank would have done a background check on each employee before he or she was hired. Next I searched their names with the Department of Motor Vehicles, which gave me their addresses. Quincy Blackstone lived on Cedar Hill in an enclave of million-dollar homes that backed up to wooded state land. I wondered if he lived with his parents. The men had clean driving records, and when I studied their DMV photos, I noticed that Quincy Blackstone wore oversized black glasses, similar to those worn by the First Sunrise robber. Probably just a coincidence, but worth noting. Mia Anderson had a DUI conviction and another one from ten years ago when she'd gotten a citation for an MIP—minor in possession of alcohol.

I called the number Lopez had given me for Mia and left a message. There was no answer when I called Blackstone, and his mailbox was full. The guy needed to get himself organized.

Vance Hausser was easier to reach, as he was working at the bank today. "I could meet with you, sure," he said. "But tomorrow or later in the week would be better. It's pretty tense here, and Martin and I are working to keep things moving smoothly, if you know what I mean."

"Of course." I asked him what he had done on his day off yesterday. Just making conversation as I clicked on a map on my computer, checking out the location of Hausser's residence in West Green.

"I went to visit my girlfriend. She's out in the Hood River."

"That's a hike," I said. "She lives out there?"

"Actually, no. She's . . . I shouldn't say."

Suddenly my perfunctory question had new meaning. "Is your relationship a secret?"

He let out a husky sigh. "Sort of. Ugh. Most people here don't know about it." He lowered his voice. "I'm seeing someone who used to work here . . . Mia Anderson."

"I see." Interesting. "Actually, I've been trying to reach Mia."

"She's not around these days."

"Because she's in Hood River," I said. "The weather's a little spotty for the gorge right now." It was not a good time to vacation in Hood River, where two of the primary draws were hiking and wind surfing on the Columbia. This time of year the river gorge often iced over, causing state police to close the highway that ran out to Hood River. "Is she staying with someone or vacationing?"

"Ah, well." He hesitated. "Actually, you'll find out sooner or later. She's doing alcohol rehab in the Gorge at Clifftop."

Some juicy info. Clifftop is a high-priced treatment facility—a rich man's rehab, people call it. The fact that Mia was there was probably not pertinent to the robbery, though it would place both Mia and Vance far from the scene of yesterday's bank robbery. "I'm glad that Mia's getting help," I said. "I understand she's had a long history with alcohol addiction."

"Since high school. She's only gotten serious about dealing with it recently."

"How long has Mia been at Clifftop?" I asked.

"Three weeks. It's a sixty-day program. And she's doing well. But don't tell Lopez or the others at the bank. Can you not tell them?"

I didn't see why the bank needed to have this information. "They won't hear about it from me." We talked about a possible time to get together later in the week, and Vance promised to get back to me to confirm. I ended the call with a feeling of progress. For now I could cross two names off my list.

My phone call to the Clifftop Addiction Treatment Center put me in a cycle of phone hell that required me to introduce myself every ten minutes and explain that I was seeking information for a crime investigation. "I just want confirmation that Mia Anderson is a patient there, and I'd like to confirm someone's visit to her yesterday," I kept saying. At one point while I waited in phone hell, Z and I looked at each other in a moment of shared ennui, as he was spending the morning trying to reassure residents at Sunset Pines that their claims were being investigated.

As I waited on the line, I clicked through photos of Clifftop, a majestic compound of craftsman-style buildings set on a hilltop overlooking the Columbia River. With sweeping views of the river gorge, sparkling water, towering trees, and blue sky, Clifftop looked more like a resort than a rehab center. At last, a representative came back on the line with a compromise. The facility took patient privacy laws quite seriously and consequently required that I submit my request for information in writing. I quickly sent them an email with my formal request. I knew I could get a court order for the information, but I didn't want to have to take the time for that, along with a visit to the Gorge, which would suck up most of my day.

I called Quincy Blackstone again but got no answer. Most likely I would have to track him down on foot. I logged on to the case and saw that Rex had posted the lab report on the white wig hair found at the scene. It wouldn't hurt to proceed on the theory that yesterday's robber was a younger man. I clicked on the bank video and bookmarked the sections that gave the clearest view of the suspect's face. I downloaded those sections to a thumb drive, found a directory of numbers for staff of Sunrise Lake High School—particularly vice principal Astrid Vitagliano. She didn't answer, but I left a message that I'd be dropping by.

It was after two, and I could feel my energy flagging. Z was still on the phone, but I caught his attention and gestured toward the door with my thumb.

He nodded, and his voice switched to that "ending the call" tone. "Okay then, Mrs. Eckersall, I've got your Statue of Liberty paperweight on my list, and we're working hard to stop the thief there. Yes, ma'am. You're welcome. Thank you. I'll be in touch." He hung up the phone and slumped onto his desk. "Kill me now. Save me from consoling one more grandma about her missing button collection."

"That's the hunger talking," I said as we headed out of the precinct. "I was thinking of hitting that salad place on State Street."

"Nah. We need something rib sticking for a cold day. How about Guber's?"

"Sure." The old sandwich shop had been on Second Street for decades, and it offered something for everyone. Z ordered chicken and dumplings, and I got chicken fajita soup with crusty bread on the side. Not wanting to create a stir in the restaurant dining room, two cops in uniform, we got the food to go and drove to the back corner of a park near the high school.

As I set up my bread in my lap and my soup in the center console, I finished explaining my morning to Z. "I think the next step will be a trip out to Cedar Hill to track down Quincy Blackstone," I said. He wasn't answering my calls, and there was no way to leave a message.

"I wouldn't mind seeing how the Blackstones live. I've been out to their vineyard in the summer, and it's pretty nice. You can tell they sunk a lot of money into it."

"So come with me," I suggested, blowing on a steaming spoonful of soup. A major part of an investigation—phone work and

Internet searches—was best done solo, but when venturing to unknown places, I preferred to have Z come along.

"What about Sunrise Pines?"

"I'll go help you meet with the seniors tomorrow if you help me with this today. I would kick it down the road a bit, but the chief stressed that he wanted this investigation to move."

"All right, Mori. As long as you come out and soothe the old folks tomorrow. You're good at that."

"And after we track down Blackstone, I want to stop in at the high school. I'm still acquainted with one of the vice principals, and I want to see if she recognizes the man in the bank images."

"Why would a school administrator know this perp?"

"Because she's been at the school forever—more than twenty years—and she always took pride in learning the name of every student in the school. If the perp grew up in Sunrise Lake and went to SLHS, Ms. Vit will know him."

"That's a lot of ifs," Z said. "If he went to that school. If she can even make out the grainy image."

"Worth a try," I said as I put the lid on my empty soup container and balled up the trash. Z was almost finished, so I started the car and headed out of the park area toward the high school. School was out—I could tell by the near-empty parking lots that dotted the hillside. The main parking area with marked spots for teachers was still nearly full, and I pulled up close to the front door and parked the unmarked police vehicle in a visitor's spot.

Z checked his cell phone before he opened the car door. "Let's not make this a homecoming visit, Mori. We're both up to our necks in investigations."

"Short and sweet," I promised, holding open one of the double doors for Z.

As luck would have it, Ms. Vit stood in front just inside the main doors, in a group of male students, two of whom towered over her. With glossy silver hair, black glasses, and a flowing black dress accented by a gray scarf, Ms. Vit was elegant yet sparking with energy. "Do you have a ritual for game day?" she asked. "Lucky socks, or peanut butter toast for breakfast?"

The guys smiled down at her, braces showing their youth. "Not me. But I always eat breakfast," said one student with hair buzzed short.

"We try to stay positive," said another kid with blond hair that tumbled over his ears. "And the coach lets us play psych music in the locker room. That helps."

Just then the radio on my collar chirped, and the group looked over at us, the guys a bit wide-eyed. Sometimes people got that way at the sight of a uniformed cop.

"Laura Mori, is that you looking all official?" Ms. Vit opened her arms wide, and I gave her a quick hug. "Or should I say Detective Mori. Promoted in the first six months on the job."

"It's good to see you, Ms. Vit." Throughout the challenges of high school, I could always rely on Ms. Vit to be warm and encouraging.

"Hey, guys. Detective Mori is an alumnus of Sunrise Lake High." She patted my arm. "I always say that you kids have great possibilities in your future. And these guys," she said, turning to the students, "are some of our star JV basketball players."

"You guys got some juice this year?" Z asked.

"Doing our best. We'll see next month," one of the guys said, fist-bumping him.

Ms. Vit sent them on their way, clapping them on their shoulders and reminding them to get enough sleep. On the way to her office I introduced Z, and they chatted about the high school he'd attended on the east side of Portland.

"Your message was intriguing," Ms. Vit said. "How can I help you?"

"I have some video from a bank robbery that took place yesterday, at First Sunrise Bank."

"I heard something about it."

"The perpetrator seems to be wearing a disguise—a wig, hat, and glasses. But we're beginning to think he's a younger man, someone who might have attended Sunrise Lake High."

"What are the chances of that?" she asked.

"That's what I said." Z nodded. "An experienced thief wouldn't plan hits in his own town."

"Still, I'd like you to take a look at the video, see if you recognize him." I fished the thumb drive out of my pocket. "You've known every student in this school for what? Twenty years?"

"Twenty-six," Ms. Vit corrected me. "But who's counting. Of course I'll take a look." It didn't take long to go over the close-up video that I'd copied onto the drive. Ms. Vit squinted behind her glasses as I replayed the segment and paused it, but I could tell it was a no-go.

"Maybe it would ring a bell if the photo was clearer, but truly, I don't think the man in the film is anyone I know. I'm so sorry, Laura."

"No worries," I said, trying to cover my disappointment. "Thanks for giving it a shot."

"Anytime." Ms. Vit patted my shoulder and sent us on our way. As we went down the corridor, the smell of floor wax and the posters for the winter formal and basketball tournaments brought me back to high school in a stressful way. All those hours studying for exams and SATs. All the essays and hopes for As when I ended up getting Bs and Cs. High school had introduced me to the notion of personal failure and panic that came with unmet expectations; it was a struggle that I had learned to deal with, but at times it still nipped at my heels.

You are a worthy person, I told myself as took a deep breath and pushed out the double doors.

7

Back in the car, Z had the good grace not to say, "I told you so."
I exhaled four years of stress, plugged Blackstone's address
into the GPS, and put the car in drive. "If our next stop is as
brief, we'll have time to make it over to the senior living center
before the party."

He groaned. "I was hoping you'd forget about the party."

"Nope. I'm on it. Determined to turn you into a social
creature."

"You are stubborn, Mori."

I smiled as we headed up the tree-lined hill to the exclusive
neighborhood where Quincy Blackstone lived. In our community
the mansions with lakefront property were limited in acreage, so
people with money often purchased meandering ranches that
accommodated houses or hilltop property that afforded views of
Mount Hood, the lights of Portland, or acres of dense state forest.
Once in high school I had been invited to a house on Cedar Hill,
where twenty or so teens had been hosted by the Bergeson family
for a pre-prom dinner. Tables had been set in the dining room and
family room of the large house, where Natalie, Becca, and I had
feasted on steak, chicken cutlets, and gluten-free veggie lasagna.
Many of the other girls had been too nervous to eat, but the guys
had grabbed food before heading off to the game room down-
stairs. For me, prom had seemed like a bonus since I hadn't

expected to go. But my friends had convinced me that it was fine to go in a group without dates, as none of us had boyfriends at the time.

As we drove up Cedar Hill, it became clear that Blackstone had chosen a place with an amazing view. Wow. The grand Tudor-style home sat on a rise like a cake on a pedestal. The snow-topped edges of Mount Hood sat majestically on the northeast horizon, while closer in the Willamette River cut through the valley below.

"Pretty swell," Z said as we climbed the stairs and rang the front doorbell. The woman who answered wore a black uniform smock over her rounded figure and seemed concerned as I introduced us.

"Everything okay?" she asked, her eyes opening wide.

"We're looking for Quincy Blackstone," I said. "Is he at home?"

"Mr. Quincy? I don't know if he's home. He lives in the guest house around back. I thought you were here about the Blackstones. They're on a cruise right now, and I always worry about them traveling. I don't like boats."

"Where is the cruise?"

"The Caribbean. Mrs. Blackstone, she loves the Caribbean."

I assured the woman, Julia, that we were here to speak with Quincy Blackstone, and she gave us directions to the guest house, which was down a short lane, past a fenced-off swimming pool with a curved slide and two buildings that seemed to serve as garage space for five vehicles.

"Check out those garages," Z said. "Can you imagine choosing your ride each day?"

"Sometimes less is more," I said, content with my reliable car.

"Clearly you are missing out on the beauty of a fine driving machine," Z said as the guest house, a two-story Tudor, came into view. We parked in the empty driveway and went to the front door. There were no signs of life as we knocked and pressed the doorbell.

"Nobody home," Z said.

I stepped back from the front entrance, staring up at the well-kept house, its trim painted a rich brown, its beveled glass windows shining despite the gray day. "This Quincy Blackstone is proving to be hard to find. Let's take a look on foot. Maybe he went for a walk."

"On such a beautiful gray day?" Z said sarcastically as we walked a wet gravel path that meandered between the house and a stand of fir trees that afforded the place some privacy. It wasn't raining, but the damp air was bordering on drizzle as stones crunched beneath our boots. The side of the house was landscaped with shrubs masking the foundation, and a wooden deck jutted out from the back of the house.

I caught the burnt-ash smell of marijuana around the same time that I noticed the movement of someone on the deck. He sat in a deck chair under the open umbrella, bundled against the weather in a down jacket and an orange, red, and black print Pendleton blanket. His legs were propped on another chair, and his hand held a joint as he stared off toward the trees.

"Somebody's smoking the ganga," Z said.

I nodded. "Quincy Blackstone." I recognized him from his license photo. Oversized glasses, unkempt pale-brown hair sticking out in various directions, and wide lips that seemed strained in a permanent frown. "Hey, there. You're Quincy Blackstone, right?" I called, introducing Z and myself as we approached the back steps of the deck.

"Did Gloria call you? She just can't accept that weed is legal in Oregon now. Not that I haven't had my card for years. Medical marijuana for gout and glaucoma, and I'm having a bad day. It's painful to walk." Still staring off, he took a hit from the joint.

"We didn't receive any complaints," I said, pausing at the entrance to the deck. "We're interviewing people about the bank robbery at First Sunrise, and we learned that you used to work there."

"And Lopez sent you my way?" He closed his eyes and gave a bitter laugh. "What an asshat."

"We're interviewing everyone who was employed by the bank in the past few months," I said.

"Oh, joy, and that includes me." Blackstone's intelligence and arrogance were amusing but off-putting, the demeanor of a man who kept people at arm's length. From up close I saw a mixture of fear and weariness in his eyes. Was it from his physical pain or his stoicism?

"We're wondering why you left the bank," I said.

"You mean why they fired me? Did Lopez tell you I was sick of making minimum wage while the fat cats that rolled in had hundreds of thousands on the books?"

"It didn't come up in our discussion," I said, shifting away from him. Marijuana wasn't my thing, and as it had been illegal most of my life—and forbidden in my house—it felt awkward to be on duty in such close proximity.

"Well, you're here now, so go ahead. Ask your questions and let's be done with it." He inhaled from the burning joint and motioned us closer.

"Did you notice anything unusual during your time at the bank?" I asked.

"Only me. The millionaire's son working as a freakin' teller. I did the job because my father gave me an ultimatum, but I never liked it, and the day that I started I saw a way to get the hell out of there. I jumped on it, but Lopez and the rest of management didn't like it."

"So what was your way out?" Z asked, moving beside me, into Blackstone's line of vision.

"Venture capital. I have ideas. Big moneymakers. Apps and inventions that just need a little funding to get them going. All it takes is one, you know. One successful product can make a fortune in today's climate."

"And you needed seed money?" I said. "I would think your parents would help you with that."

"Everyone assumes that, but Harry and Gloria have me locked in a gilded cage here. Only a pittance comes my way until they die. They are evil people," he said, bringing the joint to his lips.

Maybe Quincy's parents were manipulative, but at least he had a charming house on the rolling grounds of this estate. But I supposed it was all relative.

"So your parents pushed you to work at the bank," Z said. "Were they pissed when you left the job?"

"Inconvenienced, yes, but I think the old man is a little miffed by the contacts I made there. A retired surgeon and a dot-com king who moved here from California." Quincy's head dropped back as he laughed. "Now I'm the one with the connections. Lopez and the bank management got their panties in a bunch when I courted those guys, but what do they expect? You work as a teller, you help a customer make a deposit, and you see who's got what where. Savings and investments. It's all there on the screen. Boom! And there's nothing illegal about me chatting up the guys who were loaded."

"Sounds very enterprising of you," I said.

"Hell, yeah." He dropped the smoldering paper and ashes into a bowl.

"So what's your relationship with the bank now?" Z asked. "Any bad blood between you?"

"I thought about suing them for termination. I could sue them. I might. But ultimately, I got the best end of the deal. I'm working with my new contacts, putting together deals. I'm better off out of First Sunrise, managing my own firm now."

There was no question that he felt vindictive toward the bank, but was he angry and entitled enough to stage a robbery? I could see Quincy justifying it to himself. He was a possible suspect.

"Can you tell us anything that might help us track down the individual who robbed the bank yesterday?" I asked. "Do you remember any suspicious customers? Any habits of employees that set off red flags?"

"I stayed out of the popularity contest there. Those tellers were all competing for Miss Congeniality." He shook his head. "Waste of my time."

I tried to imagine what it would be like working alongside Blackstone; most likely his arrogance and entitlement would have overshadowed the interesting parts of his personality.

"And there was one problem child," he added. "One girl with the drinking problem. Poor thing. I think she had a hot toddy in her teacup. She was always over or short when she cashed out her drawer at the end of the day. Could never get it right. Maria or Mimi or something."

Mia Anderson. I was glad Lopez had told me about her.

I had one more question for Quincy Blackstone, but before I risked offending him, I wanted to get a peek inside his house. I lifted the collar of my patrol jacket and feigned a shiver. "It's getting cold out here. Do you mind if we step inside to finish our conversation?"

He squinted at me. "Of course I mind. I've watched enough crime shows to know that no one comes in without an invite or a warrant. Since you have neither, we're ending this now." He gingerly lowered his leg from the chair and got to his feet.

"Thanks for your help." I tried to keep things cordial as I edged toward the French doors for a look inside. A small marble table and two chairs sat in the nook beyond the door, but the rest of the area was blocked off by a painted gold Japanese screen. "I just have one more question for you."

His limp was pronounced as he moved to the door. Hand on the door latch, he paused and gave me a sullen look.

"Can you tell me where you were yesterday around five PM?" I asked.

"Really? Do you think ten or twenty grand means anything to me? I swim with much bigger fish."

"Tell us what you were doing and we're out of your hair," Z said. "Can you do that much?"

"I can, but I won't, and I'm insulted by the suggestion. Here I thought we were getting on so well, Detectives."

"A regular friendship fest," Z said.

"It's not meant to be insulting," I called after Quincy as the door slid closed with a jolting sound and he disappeared inside.

* * *

While we were on our way back to the precinct, Omak called to let me know that the chief wanted to see us for a progress report on the First Sunrise case. "Don't worry if you don't have much to report. For some reason he's jittery about this one."

"I was just discussing a possible suspect with Z. We're about ten minutes away." No time to visit the adult community, but I promised to help Z with that tomorrow.

Back at my desk, I quickly checked my emails and confirmed that Mia Anderson had been a patient at Clifftop and that her visitor, Van Hausser, had indeed taken her to dinner last night. An alibi for Mia and Van. Quincy was still an unknown.

I wanted to do more digging on Quincy Blackstone, but it wouldn't do to keep the chief waiting. I tucked my jacket on the back of my chair and found Omak pacing in the back corridor as he spoke on the phone. We took the stairs up and were immediately shown into the chief's office.

"Tell me you've got good news," Chief Cribben said, leaning back in the wide leather chair at his desk, "because I've been looking at the images from the bank, and it seems to me like that damned Twilight Bandit is back. And if he was easy to catch, we would have snagged him three years ago."

"We don't know if it's the same perpetrator," Omak said. "Detective Mori is having the lab compare wig fibers found at the First Sunrise location to the fibers we have on hand from the Twilight hits. We should know more tomorrow or the next day."

"Not soon enough. God knows I hate the waiting game of crime analysis, especially when panic is rising in the community. People are already saying the Twilight Bandit is back. I've gotten more than half a dozen calls this afternoon. Bank CEOs and the chamber of commerce and the head of the garden society. Not to mention the mayor breathing down my neck. We need results. Fast." Cribben folded his arms across his chest. "Any other leads?"

"We're looking at a former employee, fired from First Sunrise recently, disgruntled with management."

"A malcontent who was fired from the bank?" The glum expression lifted from the chief's broad face. "Tell me more."

"His name is Quincy Blackstone, future heir to the Blackstone Vineyards."

"Is that so?" The chief nodded. "I've met Harry Blackstone. Nice people. They turned their hazelnut orchard into a winery and hit gold. What do you have on their son?"

"Nothing that we can make an arrest on, but there's motive. He admits to resenting the bank for firing him, and he's also looking for venture capital to fund some new enterprises. Apparently the parents limit his access to family money."

"So we've got possible motive," the chief said. "What else?"

"As a former bank employee, he would know that each teller has an individual safe under the counter," I said. "Not that it's a huge secret, but it's something an employee would know. His eyeglasses are a style similar to the First Sunrise robber. He also suffers from gout and has a pronounced limp, like yesterday's suspect."

"This sounds like our perp." Cribben wagged his finger in the air. "Maybe we should bring him in for questioning. Get a warrant to search his place. Get his fingerprints at least. He could be our perp, and how good would that look, getting him off the street before some people even heard about the robbery?"

"Chief, we don't have the evidence to charge Blackstone right now," Omak objected.

But Cribben didn't seem to hear Omak as he turned away. "We could bring him in now, before the party," he said, spinning a scenario. "We can send out a press release, saying we have a suspect in custody with details to follow. Then I could make an announcement at the party, saying that we're looking at a possible copycat crime." Cribben grinned. "I do like the sound of that! We'll be closing two cases in one fell swoop."

"As I said before, we don't know that the cases are related." Omak pivoted, blading his body so that the chief could not avoid looking at him. "And we're not ready to make a case against Quincy Blackstone."

"So we catch and release if necessary. Sometimes an arrest is all it takes to calm people down—give them the feeling that we're taking action, things are being taken care of." Cribben clapped his hands and rubbed them together. "That's what we should do. Go on and dispatch some uniforms to pick him up. You can be the arresting officer, Mori. You can write the press release, Lieutenant. Can we put together a media conference by tomorrow afternoon?" He banged a fist on the desk as if it were an empty mug, the act of a man who'd just won a major drinking contest. "Let's lock up our guy."

8

"Let's take a minute and think this through." Omak kept his voice low, but from the resolve in his dark eyes I could tell that he was dug in, standing his ground. "Blackstone just popped up as a suspect, and Detective Mori hasn't had a chance to follow up on his background yet." He turned to me. "Do you know his whereabouts at the time of the crime?"

"He refused to say."

"Quincy Blackstone may have an alibi. Beyond that, we might be able to get a warrant to search his place without arresting him. Follow procedure and build our case." Omak put both hands on the desk and stared down at the chief. "It's too soon to make an arrest, Chief, and we don't want to make a mistake on this and risk losing the public trust."

"But we're close, Lieutenant. There would be a benefit to making an arrest now to calm nerves, and backtrack later."

"And risk the Blackstones suing the police department?" Omak pointed out. "Liability is definitely an issue here. The family has the resources to make a strong case against us."

The threat of a lawsuit was too much for Cribben to gloss over. With a growl of frustration, the chief sat back in his chair. "Damn it. There's definitely a downside to policing in a wealthy community. Having to tiptoe through proverbial rose gardens."

"We all know this investigation is important," Omak said. "All the more reason to maintain its integrity."

As the chief nodded, I realized I'd been biting my lower lip throughout their exchange, surprised by the police chief's desire to move without just cause. Omak, however, seemed to take the chief's zeal in stride and cajoled him to be patient with the calm of a Zen master. The conversation chiseled away at my confidence in the department leader, who perhaps had earned his reputation for cronyism and laziness.

With the command to keep him up-to-date on any developments in the case, Cribben dismissed us. I followed Omak to the stairs.

"Lieu?" I called, but he was moving fast. I finally caught up to him on the first floor. "That was weird. Should I have played down my interview with Quincy Blackstone?"

"No. You did everything right, Mori."

"I just didn't expect him to jump ahead like that. I guess he must be under a lot of pressure to solve the case."

"Community leaders are always under pressure. There's something more to Cribben, but I've given up trying to figure out his politics and motivations." Omak stopped walking and turned toward me. "You'll be okay, Mori. Just stick to your investigation and let me deal with the chief."

"That'll be a relief." We discussed the case and decided to try for a warrant to search Quincy Blackstone's residence. I spent the balance of the afternoon writing a warrant request, citing that Blackstone had been fired from the bank, had intimate knowledge of the workings of the bank and teller safes, had expressed resentment of the organization, and had no known alibi at the time of the crime. As items to be recovered in the search, I listed the wig that had shed fibers at the crime scene, the Uncle Kombucha hat, the black hoodie, and the stolen money. It was my first warrant request, and I hoped that Omak would clean it up before it went to a judge in the morning.

The report was so consuming that I hadn't noticed the exodus from the office as gray light outside the windows give way to inky darkness. When I looked across my desk, the squad room was empty except for Z and me, and the hallway was quiet but for the sergeant chatting with the custodian. Most of the precinct staff had left work early to head over to DeMarco's.

"The party!" I said aloud, leaning back in my chair and stretching my hands wide as wings. "We'd better get going."

"No rush," Z said. "I've got a few more complaint reports on missing items over at Sunset Pines."

"Which can wait until tomorrow," I said, rising from my chair. "Come on, Z. You must be hungry."

"Not hungry enough to torture myself with polite conversation. Nothing I hate more than idle chitchat. Wah-wah-wah-wah."

"Hey, you two workaholics, get outta here." Sgt. Sherry Joel called through the squad room. "Anybody who's anybody is already over at DeMarco's Restaurant."

"I'm not anybody!" Z boomed back at her. He pretended to hide behind a stack of *Law Officer* magazines he kept piled on his desk.

"If you two aren't going, I can find a place for you out on patrol duty," the sergeant countered. "We're running on a skeleton crew tonight."

"God, no, not that!" Z held up his hands as if to ward off the sergeant.

"Looks like it's party time," I said.

He let his head roll back, utterly fed up. "Fine. I'll give you an hour, Mori. Time enough to grab a plate of lasagna and work the room for a bit."

I grabbed my winter coat from the back of my chair. "Let's schmooze!"

* * *

When Z and I arrived at the Italian eatery and bar, the incredible smells of roasting garlic and fresh oregano met us at the door. A full buffet snaked through the main dining hall, and crowds of people extended from the intimate cocktail tables all the way to an outside bar and seating area strung with white lights. Although it was chilly and overcast outside, some people gravitated to the patio overlooking the lake.

I was surprised to see colleagues from the medical examiner's office and the crime lab. I waved at Rex Burns sitting at the bar next to his adorable boyfriend and made a mental note to hang with them later.

"I'm headed for the food line. Coming with?" Z asked.

I shook my head. After the day I'd had, I was looking forward to a strong gin martini with extra olives. Plus, I saw Ellie Colgate, a friend from dispatch, drinking a frosty beer at the bar. I told Z I'd catch up with him in a few minutes and beelined it to Ellie, who was always good for an entertaining dating story or some office gossip.

In her early thirties, Ellie had already been through three husbands and had a four-year-old son. I might've given up on love after three soured marriages, but not Ellie. She dated furiously, and she always told hilarious stories about the dates that didn't go so well. I loved how easily Ellie fit in with the rough-and-tumble cops she worked with every day, taking no guff from anyone.

"Hey, you!" Ellie said as I sidled up next to her at the bar. "I was hoping you'd show. Great people-watching tonight!"

I ordered a martini and asked Ellie how work was going and how her son was doing in preschool. Martinis had become my signature drink in college when I couldn't stand the sugar in the rum-and-Cokes and margaritas my friends favored. Now I leaned against the bar and sipped my gin martini, pure and cool, while Ellie chatted. We laughed about our crazy work schedules.

A few minutes later, the crowd at the bar thinned enough for us to see Ward Brown sitting a few barstools away drinking a bourbon and water. He was smoking a cigarette slowly, blowing the smoke up toward the ceiling like a cowboy in a saloon. This was unnerving the bartender, a young woman with black-and-white tattoos covering her forearms, who kept asking Brown to put the cigarette out or move to the patio area.

"You wanna make me, darlin'?" he said to the bartender.

Brows raised, she tried to reason with him. "Come on, be cool. You *know* there's no smoking allowed inside."

"Brown! You idiot. Put the cigarette out," Ellie bellowed at him.

He smiled, put the cigarette behind his back, and slid his drink down the bar toward us as he moved closer. A handsome, well-toned guy, Brown reminded me of the Marlboro Man. He had that same rugged sex appeal, that same aloof sense of power.

"Ellie Colgate, when are you going to ditch your dead-end job and sail away with me?" Brown slurred his words, and I picked up on the sickly-sweet smell of bourbon emanating from him. How many hours had he been here drinking?

"I'll think about that, Brown. I really will. When do you think you'll be able to afford a boat big enough for my family?"

His dark eyes twinkled. "You never know, Ellie. There may come a day when you regret not taking me up on my offer." He looked down at his wristwatch, a distinctive Rolex plated with turquoise and gold. It sparkled, even in the dimly lit restaurant, and I wondered how he could afford a luxury like that on a cop's salary. "I'm not as down-and-out as you might think. I've got a place on the river, and once I pack this job in, I'm sailing off to see the world."

"We're so impressed," Ellie said flatly. "But right now, you just need to sail away."

He took a drag off his cigarette and blew smoke through the side of his pursed lips. "You two gals make misbehaving so much fun."

"Do the right thing, Brown," I said.

His eyes focused on me, and he laughed out loud. "So arrest me. I think I might like that. We both might." Brown picked up his glass, swirled the liquid, clinking the ice as his gaze lingered on me.

I wanted to squirm, but I wouldn't give him the satisfaction. Instead I gave him my most scalding stare.

"You're killing me, tasty boy," Ellie said, her face in a deadpan expression. "But we're saving this spot for a man who's smoking hot, not just smoking."

I laughed. Why couldn't I think of comebacks like that on the spot?

Finally relenting, Brown tipped his ashes off on the bar and walked across the restaurant to join a loud group of cops who straddled the doorway to the patio.

Ellie watched him go. "You know he's dating the office shrink, right? Can you even imagine the conversations they might have? He's cute, but that attitude wouldn't cut it for a minute with me."

"The office shrink?" I wasn't sure who Ellie meant. Could this be the same therapist Z was seeing?

"Daphne MacKenzie. Blonde. Legs up to here." Ellie motioned to her chin with her left hand. "Have you met the wives' club over there yet?"

I looked over where Ellie motioned and saw a tall table with a group of women, each one more stylish than the next, sipping cocktails and laughing together. I knew Deborah, Cranston's wife, who looked too nice to be with such a grizzled cop. No accounting for taste, I guess. Deborah was talking animatedly to Scooter River's wife, Joanna, but the woman who most caught my attention was a dark-haired beauty who sat quietly listening at the table. Her hair was styled and shellacked and looked as if you could bounce a tennis ball off it without disturbing one hair. Her well-manicured nails lay neatly on display as her hand rested on a spangled clutch bag.

"Who's that?" I asked Ellie.

"Oh, you mean Dolly Redmond?"

"As in, Ron Redmond, the mayor?" I answered.

"Yup."

I'd heard of the mayor's wife, Dolly, but I hadn't seen her in person before. My mother volunteered with Dolly at the Sunrise Lake Women's Club. And occasionally I'd hear from my father how the mayor and his wife came in to dinner at our family restaurant, Sakura's, but that they always ordered the same food, vexing my dad, who regularly tries to get customers to try one of the nightly specials he labors over. No dice. Still, my father loves that our restaurant is an icon in Portland, where important people like to mingle. Sakura's is enough of a landmark that the Sunrise Lake mayor and police chief would have visited just to be part of the Portland social scene. Everybody knows and loves Koji Mori, and our restaurant flourishes in part because of my father's easy personality and his ability to welcome anyone.

I wished I'd inherited my father's ease in crowds. I felt like a fish out of water at the party, but this wasn't a new sensation for me. My parents had always hoped I'd become something they could brag about. A professional with a job that would guarantee a lifetime of financial security. They'd latched on to my childhood desire to be a psychologist, and although I'd moved away from that, I worried that my parents still held on to it as a dream for me. I'd hoped that my early success in solving the Lost Girls case and making detective would win my mom and dad over, but instead they both seemed more worried than ever about my safety.

Z approached and nudged me with his shoulder. "Are you going to get in on this, Mori?" He brandished his plate, piled with gooey lasagna and green salad. It smelled delicious. "Seconds. It's awesome."

"Yeah, I guess I should before it's all gone."

"I'm all about it," Ellie said, heading toward the buffet.

Just then something bright and shiny caught my eye: the blonde hair of a beautiful woman walking through the bar. She looked confident, as if she floated through crowds every day and knew just what to say and do in every social situation. She wore a beautiful crepe teal suit with a skirt that stopped just above her knees. I wondered how she could possibly walk in those nude-colored stilettos that made her legs look taller than Portland's Big Pink Tower, but she moved flawlessly. I would've already tumbled half a dozen times. The blonde woman stopped at the bar and smiled. Whatever secret code she was sending, the bartender knew it, nodded, and poured her a glass of white wine.

"Who's that?" I asked Z. He turned from his plate of lasagna and stopped midchew.

I waited.

"You know how I told you I was seeing a police shrink about this memory problem?"

"Uh-huh."

"Well, that's her. Dr. Daphne MacKenzie, the psychologist. I guess she decided to make the holiday rounds."

"Really?" I couldn't believe *this* was the staff psychologist. So sophisticated. So confident. MacKenzie carried her wine over to a big group of male cops and joined in their loud conversation. How did she do that so seamlessly? I worked side by side with these guys, but still I had trouble striking up a normal conversation with them. "You're way too serious," Cranston used to tell me when he was my training officer. "Lighten up, Mori." Good advice, though at work I had two speeds: serious and intense.

"How is it that I've never seen her before?" I asked Z.

He shrugged. "She splits her time between a few agencies. We share her with the Vining and West Green police departments, so she hardly ever comes into the precinct. I always see her in her offices over on Channing Avenue."

As Z and I watched, Ward Brown reached over and played with MacKenzie's long hair. She smiled back at him and laughed at something he whispered in her ear.

"I guess it's true. Ellie said Brown was dating the psychologist."

Z raised an eyebrow. "No accounting for taste, I guess."

As we stood talking, MacKenzie looked at us, recognized Z, and walked over, balancing her wine as she picked her way across the restaurant in those impossible heels.

"Hello, Zion," she said, extending a hand to him. Z accepted it and smiled.

"Dr. Mack, good seeing you here." Z's stiff nod tipped me off that he was a little uncomfortable. The easy smile that usually spread across his face like a sunrise was missing. "I recommend the lasagna."

She laughed. "Good to know." Although she said it like a woman who found the world fascinating, Dr. Mack didn't strike me as a person who ate something as pedestrian as lasagna. Judging by her flawless figure, she didn't look like she ate much of anything. But she did smell divine. I caught a whiff of her perfume—sandalwood and sea salt—and took it deep into my lungs. One bottle of that incredible scent probably cost as much as my rent for a month.

"And who is this?" she asked, looking at me.

Z made quick introductions.

Dr. Mack tilted her head as she smiled at me. "You solved the Lost Girls case, right?"

I breathed in quickly. How did she know about that? Had Z told her? At any rate, I wasn't used to people openly crediting me with the case, even though it had been the reason for my promotion to detective.

"Yes, I was part of that team," I said.

"You're being modest." Raising one brow, she leaned in close so that her blonde hair brushed my cheek. I inhaled the sandalwood and sea salt as her hand rested lightly on my arm. "We need to own our accomplishments," she whispered. "If you're smart, grab the credit."

Before I could say anything, Dr. Mack graciously made an excuse to join the women at Dolly Redmond's table and left the two of us standing at the bar.

"It's weird seeing people out of context," Z said.

"Yes," I agreed, elbowing Z in the ribs. "I think something is happening over there."

Mayor Redmond and Chief Cribben were standing at the corner of the room, readying themselves to take a small stage with a podium. Dolly Redmond stood tall next to her husband, absentmindedly playing with a strand of pearls that hung from her slender neck. The two men couldn't be more physically different. Redmond was a petite, wiry man with sharp features. Everyone in town knew he ran marathons, training daily with morning runs around the lake. I saw him all the time when I was driving in to work.

Redmond and Cribben had each grown up in Sunrise Lake, even played football together in high school, but after college Redmond had moved to northern California, where he had made his fortune in a tech start-up. A renowned millionaire, Redmond then moved back to Sunrise Lake, married his high school sweetheart, ran for mayor, and won. A real hometown hero story.

Chief Cribben was Redmond's opposite: tall and expansive, with wavy graying hair and sparkling blue eyes. His face was doughy, and though you might blame that on age and stress, pictures hanging in city hall showed a vital, early-career Cribben with an equally fleshy face. Every cop on the force knew Cribben had worked his way up through the ranks, rising from a beat officer to a detective and finally top of the heap: chief. His story was part of Sunrise Lake lore. Anybody can make it here! That's what the Cribben Myth was all about. I wanted to embrace the world of possibilities. I liked to think that Z and I were evidence of changes in that culture, but still, the path was riddled with obstacles.

"Happy holidays, everyone!" crowed Redmond. "I'd like to welcome to the stage our chief of police, the big guy himself, the skipper of the Sunrise Lake Police Department: Chief Cribben."

Everyone clapped, but the table where Cranston, Brown, and Scooter Rivers sat erupted in a loud cheer as the men beat the table with the palms of their hands and whooped loudly.

Cribben took the microphone from the mayor. "Skipper, huh?" He paused. "Well thanks, Gilligan."

Cranston's table roared. And as the mayor and chief bantered back and forth, I looked around the room. The two men seemed to relish cutting each other down to size, and most of the people here enjoyed it as well. I noticed Lieutenant Omak standing near the back door, watching his bosses entertain the room. He didn't crack a smile. I wondered if this "friendly" rivalry between Cribben and Redmond was rooted in something darker.

"And now I'll turn the microphone back over to my little buddy here," said Cribben, stooping his body down to Redmond's height as the two men passed on the stage.

"We all appreciate your service, Skipper," chirped Redmond, "but let's remember it wasn't Gilligan who grounded the Minnow."

After the speeches, most of the crowd followed the two leaders out to the lit patio overlooking the lake to light up cigars and make toasts. Not part of the "in" crowd, Z and I stayed behind at the bar, nursing a couple of weak drinks.

Maybe Z had been right about this holiday party. Trying to break into the "boys' club" that was the SLPD seemed more daunting than ever.

9

A dart whizzed past me and landed squarely in the center of the dartboard. Another ace shot by Officer Kurt Van Der Linde, who smiled broadly at me. I was losing the dart game, but I didn't care. For the first time this evening I was having fun. Z took a turn next and landed his dart in a respectable outer ring. Kurt took off his glasses and handed them to Z.

"Maybe these will help next time?" Kurt suggested with a laugh.

"No, thanks." Z pushed his hand away. "You need those more than I do, old man."

"That's rich coming from a punk who's seventy-five points in the hole."

Amused by the trash talk flying back and forth between Z and Kurt, I leaned against the bar and waited for my turn. The crowd had thinned enough to make the space more comfortable, and Cribben's group had settled in with cigars and rounds of whiskey shots outside on the deck. As much as I wanted to get to know my coworkers better, there was no way I could approach that tight knot of men whooping it up outside. That particular group had common ground that I would never invade. Hunting trips, fishing excursions out of Tillamook, climbing excursions on Mount Hood. I had overheard them joking about how they'd actually forgo the hunting or fishing to spend days in the cabin or cottage drinking and swapping stories. Which sounded even less appealing than holding a fishing pole for hours on a bobbing boat.

Besides, I knew some of the guys didn't think I belonged on the job. Whether it was my gender, ethnicity, or lack of experience, Cranston and Brown had made it clear they didn't see me as a peer. I suspected the witness statements from the First Sunset robbery had been pulled by someone wanting to sabotage my success.

As I watched through the large, gleaming windows, a slightly stooped man with white hair broke away from Cribben's followers and lumbered through the dining area to the bar, where we were hanging out. He carried a blue Danish cookie tin with both hands, holding on to it tightly like a little boy. I watched as he limped past the bar and caught my eye.

"Wanna cookie?" he asked me, offering up an open tin filled with homemade cookies iced to look like tiny SLPD badges.

I nodded and chose one off the top. "Thanks."

Z skidded over, abandoning the dart game in favor of a cookie. If he'd been a Labrador retriever instead of a man, Z would've been a pushover to train: *Sit down. Treat. Roll over. Treat. Chase the bad guy. Treat.*

"Can I have one, please?" Z asked the man.

The guy smiled and handed over the tin. "You two make a cute couple."

Z's head snapped to attention. "Oh no, uh, you got that wrong. Mori's my partner."

The older guy lifted both palms up in a dramatic mea culpa. "Whatever you young people are calling it these days . . ."

"No, no, no," Z said. "We work together. You know, uh, like Batman and Robin, Starsky and Hutch, Scully and Mulder."

I cocked my head. "Some days it's more like SpongeBob SquarePants and Patrick."

Z smirked.

"Too bad," the man said. "Nothing like having a spouse you can count on. I had the best. Mary Louise. Married for nearly thirty years before cancer got her."

"That's a good, long run, my man. Wanna join our game?" Z asked. I wondered if Z was angling for more cookies, but the man nodded and walked over to join Kurt.

"Who is that?" I asked Z.

"His name is Donny Gallagher, and he's a retired cop. It's sad. He's kind of losing it. He had to retire six or seven years ago due to early-onset dementia. Then he lost his wife a few years after that. Nice guy. Probably only in his fifties when it came on."

I was floored. "That's terrible."

"Yeah, the old boys' club keeps in touch with him pretty well. Cribben trots him out like some sort of mascot on the holidays, but I think they try to keep him busy and involved."

Z and I joined Kurt and Donny in the dart game. Donny had true aim and took a bull's-eye his first round.

Donny raised his left hand and pumped his fist like a prize-winning boxer. "See that? And left-handed, which they used to say was a curse of the devil."

"Not bad for a lefty," I teased.

"Yep, still got it. Even the nuns couldn't change me. Broke more than a couple of rulers over these knuckles trying, though!"

"That must have been tough. No way to treat a child."

"Yep, more than a couple of nuns would roll over in their graves tonight if they knew old Donny Gallagher went on to become a cop." He looked at me closely. "It's too rough a job for someone nice like you. Go be a lawyer or a veterinarian or something."

"Now you sound just like my mother," I said, still trying to keep the conversation light.

"Well, she's right," Donny went on with an odd fervency. "You'll never get rich off a cop's salary, and it's hard, dirty work."

I shrugged. When would people get it through their skulls that I *did* want to be a police officer? More than anything. Ever since I was a kid watching reruns of crime shows, I had loved the way layers of deception were peeled back to reveal the truth, which detectives pieced together like a puzzle. If I had a gift, it was for getting people to open up and talk to me, which helped me get to the nut of the matter.

Z gathered his darts and put them on the table. "I gotta dash."

I looked at my watch and smiled. Natalie would be home from her shift in just a few minutes. "Tell Nat I said hi."

Z rolled his eyes. "You don't *know* me!"

"I think I do," I said, laughing.

"Don't stay out too late with these hustlers and thieves," Z said loud enough for the other guys to hear as he made a straight line for the door.

I threw my last dart and struck an outer ring. Not great, but I was secretly relieved that it was on the dartboard at all. I plucked my three darts out and stood off to the side.

"Your turn again." Kurt nudged Donny gently. But the older man was staring at the multicolored string of holiday lights draped around the bar.

"I just love this time of year," he said. "Reminds me of my mother and how she would take us kids ice skating on Parcher's Pond and warm us all up later with homemade hot cocoa. I miss my mother. They're all gone. All gone." Donny's face sagged.

"Hey, you can't give up now, Donny. You're winning," I cajoled.

"It's all about the stance and throw." Donny went to the side table and picked up three green darts. "My mother always said I could come home no matter what. No matter what I did that was bad, I could come home. I tell Christopher that, you know. I make sure he knows that, too."

Donny stood in throwing position, lost in reverie as he aimed at the board, but couldn't bring himself to release the dart. "No matter what, I tell him, you can always come home. You can come home, but you got to learn to live with yourself. That's the hardest part."

The game had come to a stop, and Kurt and I looked at each other.

"Hey, man, how about a drink?" Kurt offered.

I elbowed him. "Or maybe some coffee?" I suggested.

Donny shook his head and mumbled something about forgiveness and fate. When he finally went to take a shot, his arm flinched and the dart flew to the side. I stepped back as it came toward me, arching low and hitting my boot before bouncing off. "Whoa! You got me, palsy."

"Now look what I did!" His face turned red as his eyes filled with tears. "I hit you!"

"I'm okay," I insisted.

His eyes looked tired and despondent as a tear streaked down one cheek. "I didn't mean to hurt anyone, Mom. I really didn't. It was an accident."

I rushed forward and placed a hand on his arm. "Really, I barely felt a thing."

Donny clung to my arm, and I patted his back. What could he be talking about? Was he back on Parcher's Pond, ice skating? Had something happened to one of the kids Donny had been playing with?

He let out a sorrowful moan. "I swear I didn't mean for her to die."

"Nobody died, Donny," Kurt said.

"I'm fine. Really," I insisted.

Behind me, I heard someone clear his voice. "Gallagher, get yourself together, man."

I bristled. Chief Cribben came around me and got in Donny's face. "Hey, buddy. You're making a scene here. Whaddaya say we take this back outside?"

"We were just talking and having a dart game," I explained. "He's okay."

Cribben looked at me, his cold gaze held mine. "It's best for Donny to stick close to his friends. Isn't that right, Donny?"

Donny nodded. "Sorry, Chief. I didn't mean for her to get . . ."

"It's fine," Cribben said, cutting him off. "And I'm surprised to see you here, Mori. Don't you have a warrant to write?"

"It's done," I said, feeling like a kid called out on a late homework assignment.

"Good. I'll make sure it goes through tomorrow." He looked away from me, as if I no longer existed. "Come on, Donny."

"Let's go, buddy," Cranston said, coming around behind Donny and threading his arms around the man's chest, physically pulling the big guy away from me. "You're missing the party out here on the patio."

I watched them usher Donny back to the patio, all the while cajoling him about wandering off as if he were a child.

I turned to Kurt, who shrugged and said, "That was a buzzkill. Can I get you another drink?"

I declined and told him I was heading out. If anything, this night was turning out to be more disappointing than I'd thought possible. Not only had I not cracked the odd social matrix that was the SLPD, I'd managed to irritate Chief Cribben and upset a retired cop with dementia. Maybe I had picked the wrong career path for myself. Sure, I loved the investigative police work and the idea of helping my community, but working with colleagues who on a good day ignore you and on a bad day ridicule you was taking a toll.

I had grabbed my coat and was walking toward the exit when a stocky man wearing sweat pants and a black fleece jacket appeared in the doorway. He saw me standing by the entrance and asked if I'd seen his dad, Donny Gallagher. I nodded and explained I'd been playing darts with him earlier.

"So you're family?" I asked.

He nodded. "I'm his son, Christopher." He hesitated. "Has Dad stayed out of trouble tonight? I was worried because he seemed a little agitated before he left this evening, but he was really looking forward to the party, so I wasn't going to hold him back."

"Yeah, he's been pretty chill. Handing out cookies to everyone and anyone," I explained, trying to reassure him a little. "He got a little weepy a few minutes ago, but Chief Cribben and friends took care of that."

Christopher looked relieved. "My old man's lucky to have friends who still look after him, especially since my mom died a few years ago. He's just getting a little hard to predict, so I worry when he stays out too long."

I found Donny's coat for Christopher as the younger man fetched his father. I was glad that Donny had a son who could take care of him. Their relationship sparked a memory of my own mother walking my late grandmother to bed each night, making sure she didn't slip and hurt herself. That's what family does, I thought.

Outside, the cold air slapped me awake, and I trotted quickly toward my car, which was parked on a side street. Above me, the moon and stars spangled the night sky. When I reached my car, the windows were covered with condensation and the vehicle seemed crooked, as if I'd parked it in a gutter. As I rounded the front fender, I could see that the car was definitely listing toward the curb. The reason? The tires on the passenger side were now completely flattened. I shone the flashlight of my cell phone on the front tire, bending down to take in the multiple slash marks.

Creepy.

I glanced up and down the street, a quiet residential block with tall trees between the ranch houses that had been updated with cedar facades and driveways of custom stone. I'd come to this street when the restaurant parking lot was full, thinking it was a nice neighborhood, not a place where someone would slash your tires. A few of the porch lights were on and many of the houses had lights on inside, but the street was empty.

Pushing the toe of my boot into the front tire, I suspected this was personal. Someone was trying to send me a message.

A snap in the bushes behind me, and I jumped out of my skin. Swiveling around, I didn't see anything, but it was nearly impossible given the dark, inky night.

Is someone watching me? I wondered. Whoever it was, they'd get a kick out of seeing me freak out. I could feel my heart hammering in my chest and sweat beading at my hairline. I hated to admit it, but the irrational prickle of panic stabbed my chest.

A slight wind shifted, and I caught the scent of cigarette smoke, but there was no telltale glow that I could make out. Ward Brown's defiant face came to mind. Was he the creep responsible for this?

Another snap of a twig, this time closer to me. Wheeling around, I caught a whiff of sandalwood and sea salt. Doctor MacKenzie? But as much as I craned into the darkness, there was nothing. Then I remembered that Dr. MacKenzie had squeezed my arm, and I brought my sleeve to my nose and smelled her expensive perfume still lingering in the cloth. Yup, that was it.

As I took out my phone to call the precinct, I noticed something odd on the back of the car. Letters were scrawled in the condensation on my back window:

Back OFF Twilight!

Twilight? But I wasn't even investigating that case, not really. The angry letters had been quickly scribbled, with little attention to detail. The O wasn't closed all the way; the exclamation point looked haphazard, as if the writer had already been stepping away from the message before finishing.

I felt like screaming, but cops don't lose it like that, I told myself. If someone was watching, I definitely didn't want them to know they'd gotten to me. Who didn't want me asking questions? I wondered if the missing witness statements were related to this. Was the culprit's goal to avoid investigation of the serial bank robberies, or to harass me? I snapped a picture of the message scrawled on my window, then jumped in my car and locked it.

No reason to stand out alone like a target.

And that's what I was now: the object of someone's wrath.

10

've never felt an excess of support from Sgt. Joel, but when she answered the phone at the supervisor's desk, relief flooded through me. "Sunrise Lake Police, this is Sergeant Joel."

"Sarge, this is Laura Mori, and it's not an emergency, but I need to report a crime. My car has been vandalized, tires slashed." I hoped that my voice was steadier than my heartbeat, which now thundered in my ears.

"Are you in a safe location? Off the highway?"

"Yes, Sarge. I'm on a residential block a few blocks from DeMarco's."

"And you're sure you didn't just get some flats?"

"This was deliberate. Both tires on the curb side. I found the slash marks."

"I'll send a unit over for a report. Do you need a tow?"

"I'll call my auto club."

"All right, Mori. Stay safe."

Within three minutes a patrol car pulled up, and relief washed over me as I got out and met Jeremy Ramirez. "They've got you on night shift?" I asked, trying to appear casual and calm.

"Overtime, covering for the party. What happened here, Mori?"

I showed him the damage and the message, which was starting to frost over on the rear window.

"'Back off Twilight,'" he read aloud. "Is Twilight a nickname of yours?"

"No. I think they're referring to an old case." As I spoke, I realized Ramirez had been in the department for only a year. A transplant from Colorado, he wouldn't necessarily have heard of the serial bank robberies and homicide that had occurred three years ago.

"I see. Well, it's late, and I don't want to alarm people. But I'd like to know if any of the neighbors saw anything," he said, looking toward the houses on that side of the street. "And it's possible the homeowner has a vendetta against anyone parking in front of his house. I've seen that before."

"Parking wars." I nodded. Suburban homeowners could be very territorial.

As we spoke, the door to one of the nearby houses opened and a man stepped out in a jacket and slippers. He nodded toward us and came down the walkway.

"Well, there's one curious neighbor to talk with." Ramirez went off to meet the man as I stayed near my car, thinking it would be best to let him handle it. Keep personal separated from professional.

In the time it took the flatbed tow truck to arrive, Ramirez spoke to three of the neighbors, who reported no unusual noises or events on the street that night. The neighbor across the street came over to check on me and offer me a hot drink. Although touched by her concern, I declined the drink, eager to see my car off and get home.

* * *

I was relieved to see Z's car in the driveway when the Uber dropped me off at the house. I needed to talk about the slashed tires and message scrawled on my car window, and he was the best prospect. My parents would freak out, and Natalie would have a million questions that I could not answer without revealing confidential information.

Inside, Z and Natalie were curled up together on the couch watching reruns of *The Office* on television. They looked so sweet together that I hated to break up their snuggle fest. I wondered what it would be like to have someone you felt close enough to sink into at the end of a hard day. Just the thought made a hard lump form at the back of my throat.

"Hey Laura," Natalie said, noticing me as I tiptoed into the living room and put down the leather messenger bag I used as a purse and computer case. "How was the party? Z said it was boring."

"I nearly fell into a coma," Z corrected her.

"You missed all the weirdness," I told them.

Z sat up. "Well, Mori, I thought it was pretty weird to begin with, so I can't imagine how it could've gotten much worse."

Z and Natalie sat up and watched me with bright eyes as I recounted the odd behavior of the police chief and his buddies when Donny accidentally hit me with the dart and started crying.

"It's like they were pissed that I was talking to him," I said.

"That's the old boys' club. They don't let anybody into their inner circle," Z replied. "Four years on the job and I still don't have the magic password. Some days I'm not sure I want it."

"And what's up with the weird bromance between Redmond and Cribben?" I asked. "Those two rib each other so hard that I'm convinced they actually hate each other."

Natalie sat up a little straighter. "Oh, I have the scoop on those two." She turned toward me. "A couple of years ago, I researched a fluff package on the mayor, and it was really interesting."

Z smirked at me. "Is she still speaking English?"

I shrugged. "You get used to the weird TV news lingo after a while."

"Like you two aren't always speaking your super-secret cop language all the time!"

"Who, us?" Z laughed.

"Anyway, I produced a biography on Mayor Redmond, and it turns out he and Cribben went to high school together, even played on the same football team together. They even dated the same girl. Guess who."

"Tyra Banks?" Z said.

"No. Dolly."

"Wow," I said. "Rivals in every way."

"The thing is," Natalie went on, "everyone I spoke to who knew them in high school said they hated each other. Major rivals. Cribben was a star player on the football team, and he made quarterback his senior year. Unfortunately, he blew out an ACL and never played again."

"Ouch." Z grimaced.

"Yeah, but here's the interesting part: Redmond replaced Cribben as quarterback and played like a maniac. He's smaller, but he's fast. Got a scholarship to Stanford, while Cribben, on the other hand, stayed local and never left Oregon. Worst part, though . . ."

Z and I both leaned in.

"Cribben's girlfriend Dolly left him and went to California to be with Redmond. When Redmond came back to Sunrise Lake ten years later, he and Dolly were married and he'd made his fortune in the high-tech sector."

"Ooh. That had to hurt the chief," I said.

Natalie shrugged. "Maybe Cribben and Dolly had cooled on each other way before she left him? Who knows? Cribben never married, so he's probably not the type to settle down. Besides, Dolly and Cribben serve on a lot of the same town committees, and they've always been really cordial to one another, as far as I've seen."

"I can see the made-for-television movie now: *Love Triangles on the Lake*," I said. "But seriously, it's kind of sad for Cribben, ending up all alone."

"Don't feel sorry for Cribben." Z swiped my concerns aside. "The guy's driven. He rose through the ranks from beat cop to chief, and he never lets anyone forget it."

"Hey, who wants popcorn?" Natalie asked, getting up from the sofa. "I need a snack."

Z and I both nodded. I wasn't hungry at all, but I needed a second alone with Z to show him the photo I'd snapped of the message on my car window. I hit Z's shoulder to get his attention and then sank down beside him.

"Look what I found scrawled on my window tonight as I left the party," I whispered.

"Damn, Mori." Z used his fingers to zoom in on the message: BACK OFF TWILIGHT.

There it was again. I could almost smell the cold and the pine trees and the cigarette smoke and Dr. Daphne MacKenzie's expensive perfume. It all swirled in my nose. My head began to feel light-headed, but I fought the sensation.

"Could this be because I was asking questions about the Twilight Bandit?"

Z shrugged but kept looking at the picture, his finger tracing over the words etched on my window.

"I don't know, but I don't like this, Mori. You gotta be careful."

"You sound like my mother." I pulled my phone back. "I'm always careful."

"Yeah, sure, but that bank hit yesterday got me thinking. You know it's the last thing I want to think about, and I know it was three years ago, but Franny's killer was never found. There's a cop killer out there somewhere."

"Well, since I can't ask anyone else about the night Franny was murdered without getting stonewalled or ruffling feathers, why don't you tell me something?"

Z exhaled slowly. "I'll try."

"The night Franny was killed, who was the supervisor on the scene?"

"Sergeant Stanford. Gil Stanford. But I don't remember when he got there."

I knew Stanford, but not well, since he now worked the midnight shift.

"It's all a big jumble of panic," Z said. "I mean, I'm not even sure if the memories I *think* are true are reliable."

"Okay," I said. "Where was your backup?"

"No units available. I called in a code eleven ninety-nine."

I nodded. That code made the hair on the back of my neck stand up. An officer uses an 11–99 only if they're under fire from an active shooter.

"I remember hearing Franny yelling. Franny chased a man running toward the street, and I was on foot pursuit in the drive-through after a guy on a bike. Turned out my guy was unarmed, a dishwasher for Victor's on his way to work. As soon as I cleared the guy, I doubled back and saw Franny from across the parking lot. She was down, like she'd fallen onto the sidewalk near the corner of Fir. Not moving. I couldn't believe it. She'd been shot, and the blood . . . I knew it was bad."

"Who was on scene?"

"You need to look at the reports because my memory is wrecked. Garcia and Brown. Sergeant Stanford, I think. And Cranston came, even though he was off duty. Pain in the ass."

"Is there anything that sticks out in your memory as weird?"

"Besides the blocks of amnesia?"

I nodded.

"Just a feeling of desperation and a weird bell ringing in my ear. Nothing I can make sense of.

"And then, days after, there was Cranston, blaming me, ranting that Franny and I had messed up. He was so pissed. He used to be my training officer, and he kept badgering me, like he was teaching me a lesson."

"He has a temper. We've seen that."

"Thing is, Mori, we *were* following procedure. Franny and I waited for backup outside the bank and only pursued when we thought two individuals were fleeing the scene. I'll regret that decision until the day I die, but at the time, Franny and I thought it was the right thing to do. Eight other robberies, and the Twilight

Bandit had never shown a gun. We didn't even know for sure he had one, at least not until that night."

"Cranston is big on blaming everyone else when things go wrong," I said. I'd spent some time training under Cranston, a cop steeped in old-school methods of policing. He was a carrot-and-stick kind of guy, sometimes a bit of a bully, especially when things weren't going his way. The whole time Cranston had been my training officer, he'd tried to talk me out of becoming a police officer because it was "no job for girls." His obstinacy had toughened my resolve to complete my training and prove him wrong.

The smell of fresh-popped corn wafted in with Natalie. "One bowl has butter, and the other is just salted," she said, setting them on the coffee table.

And so my conversation with Z ended on cranky old Cranston. I scooped up a handful of popcorn and fell back onto the comfy chair with a sigh. Time to unwind and put the stress away until tomorrow.

Which was easier said than done.

The chime of my cell phone pulled me away from the TV. I was grateful for my mother's end-of-the-day phone call. Sometimes the call was an annoyance, but after the vandalism on my car and Z's account of Franny Landon's death, I was glad to hear my mother's voice on the other end of the phone.

The note stayed on my mind as I showered and put my pj's on. A threat. Someone didn't want me poking around in the Twilight Bandit case. A little ironic, their message, since it wasn't really my case, and besides, digging into a case was the stuff of detective work. Much as I wanted to dismiss the note, it was still a threat.

And it left me with a bad feeling.

I would need to be more alert than usual. Eyes wide open, always on guard.

11

The next morning I heard the rain pounding on the roof of the precinct as I buttoned my uniform shirt in the women's locker room. After a restless morning I'd left home early in an Uber, since my car was in the shop.

My early morning nightmare reflected my stress. My mind kept serving up this recurring dream that I was trying to get help, but the keypad on my phone wasn't responding. I kept pressing the numbers, and the screen would go dark. My first response was frustration; then panic set in as the feeling of danger mounted.

Danger from what?

"It was just a dream," I muttered as I sat on the locker room bench to pull on my black boots. I'd woken up in anxiety, but not the acute fear of the panic attacks that I sometimes suffered from. My parents thought it was kind of ridiculous that someone who experienced panic attacks had become a cop, but most of my attacks hit during the night at a time when they didn't interfere with my work. And the panic attacks were my Achilles' heel, a problem that had existed before I'd even imagined becoming a police officer.

Somewhere in the next row a locker slammed, and I jumped out of my skin. I'd thought I was alone in the small women's locker room, which wasn't unusual, as there weren't that many female police officers in the SLPD. I listened for footsteps or the telltale sound of a shower starting, but nothing followed. My breath caught in my throat. *Stop being so paranoid*, I told myself, but after last night my body and mind were on high alert.

I pulled on my second boot and edged closer to the end of the bank of lockers. Just then, Officer Esme Garcia rounded the corner. I jumped back.

"Nervous much?" Garcia laughed as she finger-combed her short, brown hair.

I shrugged. "Someone's been dogging me. My tires were slashed last night, along with a message to stay out of the Twilight case."

"A threat." Garcia's face grew somber. "Any idea who it came from?"

Not wanting to place credence in the smell of cigarette smoke and perfume, I shook my head.

"I don't like the sound of that at all." She folded her arms. "Could it be related to your new case? I heard you caught the First Sunrise robbery, right?"

I nodded. "I'm not sure, but it's got me on edge. Any advice?"

I'd always admired Garcia's ability to blend in on the force, to play well with others. She'd somehow become an accepted part of the old guard without losing herself.

"Yeah I do," she said, looking around and lowering her voice to a whisper.

I leaned in.

"Don't trust *anyone* except Omak," Garcia said with a solemn nod.

Wow, I thought, sure that she was exaggerating. *Nobody* else? First off, I knew Z was a clean cop, a straight shooter of the first order, and I was sure there were other decent cops on the force. "That's a tall order. What should I be looking for?"

Garcia straightened her shoulders. "I can't say. But watch yourself." She leveled her gaze at me. "And talk to the lieutenant about the threats Franny got when she worked on the Twilight Bandit case."

I shook my head. "I went over the case notes. Nothing was mentioned."

"Talk to Omak."

"I will, but I'd love to pick your brain on—"

A door creaked, and Garcia swiveled away from me. "Man, this rain is the worst," she said loudly. "I hope it stops before I have to go out on patrol."

"I hear ya," I answered, our exchange turning perfunctory. I tucked my blouse into the waistband of my navy trousers, closed up my locker, then left the locker room without a second glance at Garcia. But her warning rang in my brain like a fire alarm.

*　*　*

In the break room I made a fresh pot of coffee, which would be better than the coffee machine in the hall but worse than the java artistry from any local coffee shop. The office coffee would quickly burn and grow sour, but still, the dark brew smelled magnificent. After tossing a dollar into the coffee club bucket, I grabbed two creamers and returned to my desk, where the fat Twilight Bandit file sat beside my ream of notes on Sunrise Bank employees. I had printed the file to mull over it, but so far, seeing it on paper hadn't brought on any epiphanies.

"You are trouble," I muttered, recalling my damaged tires.

I tucked the file under a floor plan of the First Sunrise Bank and breathed in the peace of the quiet squad room. There was one detective on call during the night shift, and the others took turns alternating days and evenings, so early mornings were serene in this room. Checking my email, I read an admin notice about scheduling time off over the holidays and an email from Omak that had come in just after midnight. The lieutenant had made a few changes to the Blackstone warrant before he passed it on to Judge Elliot Howard for signing. Of course, he'd copied Cribben on the email. I hoped it would pacify the chief, who had been nothing short of imperious last night at the party.

"Mori."

I looked up to see Lieutenant Omak standing at my desk, a folder under one arm. "I was looking over last night's activity, and I saw the vandalism report on your car. How are you doing?"

"I'm fine. My car will be in the shop until after noon."

"And they left you this." He opened the folder on my desk and pointed to the photo of my car's rear window. The menacing message was clear in the black-and-white image.

"That's right. I thought the slashed tires were random until I saw that." I shook my head. "Weird, isn't it? I'm not working on the Twilight case. Not really."

"Perception can be everything. Ask one question about a case, and people assume you're in up to your neck."

"I guess."

"Ramirez's report says you didn't see anyone around your car. Neither did the neighbors. And there were no other incidents of slashed tires in the precinct last night."

"I wish I knew who did it."

"I need to advise you to be careful, Mori. This is not the first time we've had threats related to the Twilight case."

"What do you mean?"

He looked over his shoulder, but the squad room remained empty. "It's not public knowledge; I don't even think the cops around here know about it. But Franny Landon started getting threats when she was working on the Twilight case."

"What kind of threats?"

He pointed to the file. "Messages like this. Phone calls, too. Franny was unable to determine the source, but the message was clear, and I don't think the few people she told in this department took the threats seriously. The culprit did not want Franny investigating the Twilight Bandit."

But Franny had kept her investigation going, and someone had killed her. Was there are correlation? I closed the file and looked up into Omak's dark, troubled eyes. I didn't want to, but I had to ask. "Do you think Franny was killed because she persisted in investigating the Twilight Bandit?"

"I'd say that's highly likely." He held my gaze, studying my face. "Do you want off the bank robbery case?"

"What? No! Of course not. For all we know, the tires were slashed by some wild kids and Cranston stumbled across my car and wrote the message so I would stop complaining about how sloppy his casework is."

"And the cow jumped over the moon," Omak said. "But really, be careful, Mori. Watch your back. Remember, we're here if you ever need backup."

"I'll remember that, Lieu."

He tucked the file under one arm and left the squad room, a quiet vacuum sucking up the space around me.

A glimmer of panic stabbed at my chest. If I let it, a full-fledged attack could bowl me over and leave me quivering.

But I wasn't going to let it.

I'd learned a few techniques to stave off an attack, and they usually worked in the light of day. Taking some deliberate, deep breaths, I imagined pushing the weight of fear from my mind and settled into another search of Quincy Blackstone's background. A search of news articles covering the Blackstone family brought up various stories about the development and success of the Black-stone vineyard and winery out in Newberg, where the Blackstones had joined some neighbors in turning their hazelnut orchard into a vineyard for Pinot Noir grapes.

If these news photos were any indication, Quincy had not been a happy kid. One photo showed him as a toddler, his face pinched in a storm of tears. There was the boy Quincy sneering at the camera as Harry Blackstone kneeled in the dirt beside a slen-der grapevine. A teenaged Quincy frowning at his father, who jovially toasted people from a dais. An adult Quincy with fists plunged into his pockets in a stoic stance as he posed for a family photo. He was the only one who was not smiling. The adult Quincy had not struck me as a gleeful person, and I sensed that whatever weighed him down had been pressing on him since childhood.

The database for arrest records came up blank, but a different search showed that Quincy had been the subject of a medical-assist action by police a few months ago. The case notes indicated that he had been found wandering the Max train tracks late one night near the Moda Center, the huge arena on the east side of Portland where our pro basketball and hockey teams hold their games. Incoherent and dazed, Quincy had been taken into custody under suspicion of being intoxicated or under the influence of drugs, but testing had proven that he'd been sober. During a three-day hospital stay he'd been diagnosed with kidney disease, and doctors had determined that the episode had been delirium caused by kidney failure.

Delirium? I hadn't known that was a thing, but a Google search told me it happened when toxins that could not be expelled by the kidneys affected the brain. I wondered if he was now on dialysis, but I didn't have access to all his medical records. I felt a new empathy for Quincy. With his many medical conditions, Quincy would have had to work harder than most to hold down even the most basic job.

Quincy had no military service record, but I managed to pull up his transcript from high school—Bs and Cs at the exclusive Cascade Academy—as well as a partial transcript from Meriwether College, a private institution where Quincy had earned more than twenty credits with lackluster grades and a number of withdrawals.

An hour had passed since I started my research, and many of the desks at the squad room were now occupied. I picked up my empty mug and was considering another mediocre cup when my phone rang.

"Detective Mori."

"Chief Cribben," the voice said. "I want to see you in my office ASAP. What time does your shift start?"

"I'm in the building now," I said. "I'll be right up."

When I arrived on the second floor, which houses the police chief's office along with an expansive hall used for community meetings and ceremonies, Cribben was standing beside his assistant's desk. He held up a hand to silence me as he listened in to her attempts to reassure the caller, saying "No, sir" and "Yes, sir" and promising that the investigation was ongoing.

"They just won't quit," he muttered, motioning me away from the desk to stand beside a portrait of a younger, leaner Buzz Cribben. "The phone's been ringing off the hook since this new bank robbery, and my patience is shot. We need to end this, Mori. Make it stop."

"I'm doing my best, sir."

"Well, I've stepped in to expedite things. I called Judge Howard to let him know that the request for the search warrant was a major priority. His office tells me he's going to sign it this afternoon when he's finished with court. It should be ready by one o'clock. You're to pick it up in Portland and search Blackstone's premises immediately. I want to be able to announce the arrest by the end of the day."

I couldn't promise an arrest, but the chief had to know that. "I'll take care of the warrant, sir," I said. "I'll be at Judge Howard's office by one and will let you know how the search goes."

"Of course you will." He nodded. "That's all for now."

I went down the stairs, wishing that I could find something to like about the head of our department.

Back in the squad room I found Z at his desk talking on the phone as he squinted at the computer screen, trying to find a pattern in the small-time thefts that were alarming residents at Sunset Pines. *He's a good cop*, I thought to myself. Z liked to mock everything, but he always threw himself into whatever case was before him, no matter how small.

He tried not to let his trauma affect his job, but the strain was there, an undercurrent tugging at his feet, pulling him off balance. I knew he'd been through hell, but I hadn't realized how much it still tortured him. I hadn't known about the memory gap and the PTSD from the night Franny was killed. All along I'd thought he refused to talk about it because he was guarding a secret, when in fact he'd been haunted by his inability to make sense of it.

I was about to dig deep into the files again when I noticed they were missing from my desk. In their place was a yellow sticky note from Omak asking that Z and I come to his office ASAP.

Z snapped his fingers at me to get my attention as he asked the caller to hold on. "You got a new partner on the bank robbery case," he said, covering the phone, even though the hold button was blinking. "An FBI agent showed up this morning."

"Catch her name?" I asked.

"Yeah, she's a dude. Starts with a *D*." He paused and looked up to the ceiling, feigning contemplation. "Agent Dickhead, I think. Real charmer."

I took a deep breath and walked slowly to Omak's office. Behind me, Z quickly ended his call and got up to follow. I pushed back the dread at meeting the FBI agent assigned to this case. I worried about coming up short and getting sidelined in my own investigation, but I also knew that the case would benefit from more resources.

Omak smiled as I entered his office. Beside him stood a tall young man in a dark, tailored suit. "Detective Mori, meet Nick Derringer, FBI."

Derringer was all business. Brisk handshake. No smile.

"And I think you've met Detective Frazier?" Omak added. The two men shook hands, but Z didn't make his usual offer that he be called by his first initial. I wondered if Z didn't like him or if he was slightly intimidated by the three little letters that came after Derringer's name.

"Detective Mori is our lead detective on the case," said Omak.

"Please, call me Laura."

Derringer nodded. "Your lieutenant has been kind enough to let me set up my operations on a table here in his office." He motioned to a desk in the corner, where there were two coffee cups, a banana, and a laptop. Splayed open on the desktop were the Twilight Bandit case files that I'd left on my desk earlier this morning.

"It's no problem." Omak waved away the attention. "I'm rarely in here. I usually pace around the precinct. Keeps me connected to what's going on." Z and I exchanged a knowing look. We remembered how Omak walked in circles around the desks and hallways of the precinct, especially during tense discussions like in our first case together, the Lost Girls. Omak seemed to think best on his feet.

"You guys can sit," Omak said.

Z and I took the visitors' chairs while Derringer wheeled over the chair from the corner desk. Omak remained standing, resting one hip against his desk.

Derringer asked me questions about the First Sunrise robbery on Bonita Drive but quickly drew comparisons to the Twilight Bandit. I turned to Omak, who had directed our investigation to the First Sunrise robbery.

"Right now we're viewing the First Sunrise robbery as a stand-alone case," Omak said.

"But there's a definite pattern." Derringer's brows rose, as if he was shocked that we weren't all over the connection. "I didn't handle the Twilight case," he said, turning to me. "And that was before your time, right?"

Behind him, Z rolled his eyes.

"I remember reading about it in the news, and I've familiarized myself with the facts of the Twilight case," I said. "I know that the Twilight Bandit—"

"Hold on," Omak said, interrupting. "Let's be clear on this: Laura's assignment is the robbery that took place Monday night. The Twilight case was three years ago, and so far we don't have compelling evidence that these cases are connected."

Derringer looked from Omak to me, as if this were a joke. "Of course they're connected. The old man wig, the limp, the hits after dark."

"On the surface they may be similar," Omak said. "But right now we're focusing on the active case."

"And this week's robbery varied from the Twilight case," I said. "I see a few details that lead me to believe that Monday's robbery was not the same culprit but a copycat crime."

"Really?" Derringer reached back and grabbed a pad from the desk. "What are the discrepancies?"

I took a deep breath and dove in. "The thing that sticks out the most is that the robber at First Sunrise seemed to be right-handed. He used his right hand to write the note, hand over the bag, push open the door. But according to the case files the Twilight Bandit was left-handed."

"Interesting." Derringer had been looking down at some notes he'd scribbled on a yellow legal pad, but now he stared up at me with sudden interest. His gaze was intense, and I could feel electricity start to climb my spine. "But maybe he's ambidextrous."

"It seems odd to make a change like that three years later," I said. "And when it comes to jotting down the note that quickly, you can't just switch hands on the spot and print legibly."

"True. What else?"

"The teller thought his hands looked young, not the hands of an older man. On the other hand, everyone thought the Twilight Bandit was at least in his sixties. More weathered skin. And another witness thought he had a young face and attitude. He didn't hold the door for her, which is sort of a millennial thing, while the Twilight Bandit was known to be courteous, holding doors and thanking the tellers."

"Excellent observations," Derringer said slowly. I could see the spark of recognition light up his face. "I need to take a look at the video from Monday, compare it to the Twilight videos we have on file."

"Of course. I posted it on an internal link. Let me give you the info." I leaned in toward him to jot the information on his notepad and realized too late that I was pushing into his personal space. He smelled clean, like Ivory soap and citrus.

"Where are you on the case now?" Derringer asked.

Glad to be back on track, I told him about our prime suspect, Quincy Blackstone. "We'll know more this afternoon, after we search his place," I said, explaining that the chief had told me that a search warrant would be signed by the judge.

"That was fast. I guess the chief pulled some strings to move it along," Omak said.

"What about evidence from the crime scene?" asked Derringer.

"The fingerprint evidence isn't going to help us much. The thief was wearing gloves most of the time. But the technicians found some hairs and fibers that appear to have come from a wig. Right now the synthetic fibers are at an outside lab for comparison to the wig fibers found at the scene of some of the Twilight robberies."

"Nice work." Derringer nodded. "We might be able to connect the cases based on the wig fiber comparisons. And this fired teller sounds like a good lead."

"Laura has been asking all the right questions," Omak agreed, and Z shot me a quick smile. It felt good to float an original theory to a roomful of seasoned cops and be taken seriously.

I wondered if my parents would be at all impressed. As a younger girl, I'd always wanted to make them proud, but it was hard. My parents expected me to be quiet, studious, and a good listener, but outside my Japanese-American home, the world rewarded assertive, confident people. It was confusing, and in the rush to please my parents and the world around me, self-fulfillment had taken a back seat.

My parents had stressed academics for me and my siblings, but I had struggled in school, more interested in watching *Law & Order* reruns on television than studying algebra. I found real refuge in police work, where my attention to detail and good listening skills really paid off. Sometimes I just wished my mother and father could be flies on the walls of our precinct on days like today, when our lieutenant, my partner, and the FBI agent were listening intently to my theories on a case.

Derringer looked down at his phone. "I've got to return my supervisor's call." He shot me a vague look, and I couldn't tell if he was pleased with the detective work I'd presented or thought I had gotten a lucky break. "Do you have witness statements and a timeline from Monday?"

"Yes, I'll get you copies. And I have a question. I know the FBI had an open case on the Twilight Bandit, and I'm wondering if I could have a look at your data?" I tried to find the right words, not wanting to throw anyone under the bus. "The case files I inherited are difficult to organize."

"Since you're working this case, we can certainly share any information we have. I'll send you the files," Derringer said.

"In the meantime, I'll get you a copy of the fingerprint analysis from the lab and a simple timeline."

"Detective Mori?" Omak said as he neared the door. "Remember what I said about watching your back."

"I got her back." Derringer looked up, his dark eyes determined. "We'll be working together on this, and I take care of my partners."

Although it seemed presumptuous, Derringer's response was also reassuring. I smiled at him, but he only nodded and wheeled himself back to the corner desk as Z and I got up to leave.

The lieutenant was the first one out the door, striding down the hall. Confinement was Omak's Achilles' heel; he couldn't stand it for long. I wasn't offended. Everyone had their thing.

"Let me get Derringer set up, and then we can head over to Sunset Pines," I told Z as we headed back to the squad room. "I've got a few hours to meet with your peeps before I have to head into Portland."

"Trust me, the residents of Sunset Pines are not my crew," he said. "But they'll be glad to see your sunny smile."

Back at my desk, I was transferring files when Z smiled at me. "Aren't you glad you get to work with Agent Dickhead? Be careful he doesn't swoop in and take all the credit for your good ideas."

I swatted off the comment, but privately I was worried about working with Derringer. Truthfully, I couldn't read him well. He listened intently, but he also seemed very serious. And attractive, yes, but lacking in joy. I wondered if anyone ever got the man to crack a smile.

12

Z hated the smell of lavender. It always made him want to sneeze. And right now, as he waited in the lobby for Mori to finish up her interview with another resident of the Sunset Pines assisted-living facility on Carmen Drive, all he smelled was lavender potpourri. The management probably pumped it through the building's vents.

This case took the grand prize for weird calls. Nearly thirty different residents in the last month had complained of missing junk. Not valuable items. No expensive jewelry or prescription medication. Nutty stuff like cat figurines, door stoppers, knitted afghans, napkin holders, a silver bell of great sentimental value.

The older residents were shaken up, so Z was glad Laura was with him this afternoon. She was good at calming people down and reminding the residents to lock their doors when they went to meals. It was her superpower. Laura didn't know it yet, but she was great at reading people and telling them just what they needed to hear. He'd noticed that during the Lost Girls case when she'd talked a pair of homeless kids into trusting her enough to give up valuable information. Nothing short of genius.

"Odd case you caught here, Z." He could tell from the slight grin on her face she was amused they were investigating missing cat figurines.

"Don't you know, *no call is too small in Sunrise Lake*," Z said, recalling the unofficial SLPD mantra.

"You know, at least half of the residents I interviewed today report seeing a cop on the premises lately, but the management call log and visitor sign-in sheet don't show any police officers being here at Sunrise Pines," Laura said.

"I noticed that, too. Most of the victims kept asking me when the 'polite police officer' would be responding to their complaints." Z shrugged. "So what am I, the rude cop?"

"Nooooooo," Laura joked. "You're not grumpy or rude or short-tempered or ill-mannered . . ."

"Damn, you make me sound like one of the seven irritating dwarves."

"You, irritating?"

"Seriously, we need to figure out the identity of this mystery cop." He finished typing notes into his laptop.

"Do you think there's a correlation between the cop and the missing items?" Laura asked. "Maybe someone is impersonating an officer to gain access to the elderly residents."

He closed up his laptop and rose. "Could be. But why go to so much trouble just to steal trinkets? The thief left behind checkbooks and cash at a few of the apartments."

"Another possibility is that this is a real cop, just visiting his family. Maybe he's even one of ours, visiting but not signing in. You know how cops feel like they're above all the rules."

Z nodded as he tucked his laptop under his arm and nodded toward the door. "That's possible, too. Let's get out of lavender land."

Laura and Z had turned toward the main entrance when they encountered Dolly Redmond, the mayor's wife, coming in the sliding-glass doors to the atrium. She was carrying three blue tins of Royal Dansk Danish butter cookies, stacked high, with her chin holding on to the top. Mori jabbed him in the ribs and they veered over to say hello.

Dolly blinked nervously and offered a weak smile as they introduced themselves.

"I don't believe we've ever met," Z said, "but we saw you with the mayor at the holiday party last night. Good times," he said, trying to sound enthusiastic.

"Yes, it was a hoot, wasn't it?"

"A hoot for sure," Z answered, worried that he was a terrible liar.

Laura shot him a look that said *just stop!* and took over. "You've sure got your hands full there. Need some help?"

Dolly shifted the tins in her arms, half surprised. "Oh, no. I'm fine, thanks."

"You must be a big fan of butter cookies," Laura said in that sweet, genuine way she had of winning people over.

"These aren't for me. My great-aunt Peg just loves these cookies. She's a little . . . a little off," Dolly said. "She's in the memory care section, you see."

"Sorry to hear that, ma'am." Laura said diplomatically.

"Lots of cookies for one aunt," Z said.

"Well, she was so good to me when I was a child. Practically raised me after my mother died. The least I can do is keep her in cookies."

"That's so sweet of you. We'll let you get on with your visit," Laura said. "Please tell the mayor we said hello."

"Will do."

Z and Laura politely waited as Dolly walked through the atrium with her load of cookies. They kept quiet as they got into the car, but once the door was shut, Z said, "What the hey? Three blue tins of cookies?"

"The Girl Scouts have got nothing on Dolly Redmond."

"But that was the same kind of tin Donny was carrying last night. Donny comes into the party with a blue tin of cookies, and the next day the mayor's wife is walking around with the same kind of tin."

"Maybe Danish butter cookies are a thing for older people. Maybe Dolly gave him the cookies to hand out."

Z shook his head. "Maybe, but my grandma's in her eighties and I never saw any blue tins in her house. Let alone five."

"You're just sad she didn't offer any to you," Laura teased.

"I *am* hungry."

"Well, good. We need to pick up my car from the shop, and then I need to be in Portland to pick up that warrant by one, so we have almost two hours to finally get you a tour of my family's restaurant."

"Seriously? A tour with food?"

"Of course." Laura laughed. "My parents wouldn't let you go without sampling a few dishes."

Z felt a new enthusiasm for the afternoon as he got into the car. "You know, Mori, I have always liked your parents."

* * *

As they drove past Pacific Lake Bank, Z flashed back to the night of the last Twilight robbery. He and Franny had been at loose ends. Two rookies who didn't like the partners they'd been paired with. Franny had complained that Cranston was sexist and critical of every move she made. And Z had been closed out by Brown, an ex-military guy with acres of bravado. Brown had acted like Z had a contagious disease and rarely spoke about anything that didn't have to do with his time at war. Brown had stones for balls and liked to share battle stories that proved it. These partnerships had made both Franny and Z feel uneasy, and the two rookies bonded over the situation. Z had thought Franny was a good cop, though they didn't know each other well because they rarely got to work together.

Z remembered something else about the night Franny was killed, something about the way Cranston had called in at the last minute. What had been his excuse? A family issue? It had left Z without a partner, and he'd thought he'd end up typing reports or answering phones in the station house, except that Brown had been doing some special construction detail over on the highway, leaving Franny without a partner. So the two rookies had ridden together.

At the time, nothing about that arrangement had seemed odd. But maybe something else had gone on that night. Z had always felt responsible for Franny's death, but recently, something about the way that night had evolved felt wrong. Some truth lingered below the surface of his subconscious, just beyond his reach. He had to find a way to access it, even if the probing was painful. You had to keep trying, picking at the wound. The day you stopped trying was the day you lost.

13

We arrived at Sakura's in the thick of lunch hour, and since the small parking lot was jam-packed, I wove down the next block and turned sharply down a narrow alley.

"Where the hell are you going?" Z asked.

"My secret parking spot." The brick walls pressing in on both sides made me want to inhale and shrink my car as I edged deeper into the tight alley. The corridor was wider than it seemed, as delivery trucks backed down here all the time, but they didn't come in the middle of the day, so I figured my car would be fine here.

"Follow me," I told Z, guiding him through the back door and into a steamy, bright kitchen filled with a savory, smoky smell. Servers breezed in and out. Sauces bubbled on ranges as men and women dressed in black-and-white-checkered pants, white shirts, and white aprons chopped vegetables or tended fryers.

"Mori? I don't think we're supposed to be back here," Z said, backing against the white tiled wall as a server swept past him balancing an armful of plates.

"Relax," I said as we threaded through the workers in the narrow space. "Excuse us," I said. "Sorry!" Z followed me to a corner of the kitchen, where my father stood worrying over a pot of bubbling soup.

"Hi, Dad."

He turned and his creased face lit up.

"Laura!" He hugged me with his eyes squeezed shut.

"Z, you remember my father, Koji Mori." They had met briefly at our promotion ceremony.

Z held out his hand and Koji took it firmly. "Laura's partner! Laura always says so many good things about you."

"Dad, please," I said. "He'll get a fat ego."

"Thank you, sir," Z said. "It smells delicious. What are you making there?" Z nodded toward the bubbling pot Koji had been tending.

Koji spun around looking for a spoon. "You must try it. It's *suimono*. Made from matsutake mushrooms. Delicious."

Z leaned over the soup as my dad swept the steam with his hands toward Z's face.

"The very best part of this soup is the fragrance. You can smell the herbs, the *mitsuba*, the citrus rind," my father said.

I watched in satisfaction as Z closed his eyes, taking in the savory aroma. "He's hooked you already," I said.

In the dining room, Dad sat us at a cozy table in the back where family members or close friends sat to eat. It was good to be out of the way, as sometimes guests noticed our uniforms in restaurants and worried that something was wrong. I told my father we had an appointment at one, and he assured me there was plenty of time to relax and eat. I waved to my mother, who was seating a large party in the front room.

"Did you see your sister?" My father looked back toward the kitchen. "Hannah is working today. She finished her winter finals early for Christmas break." All the Mori siblings had worked in Sakura's during winter break and summers.

"Lucky duck," I said. "We'll find her."

Z picked up a menu, but Koji waved him off. "No ordering. I'll plan a special meal."

"Dad, we just want something simple. Maybe some soup and tea."

My father chided me playfully. "You're kidding, right? Only convicts and monks ask for soup and tea."

Z grinned at Koji. "Well, I'm neither, so fire away!"

A few minutes later dishes started appearing from the kitchen. Shrimp tempura. Flavored Thai noodles. Crispy deep-fried cutlets that we called *tonkatsu*. Nothing made me happier than seeing someone enjoy my father's food, and I couldn't help but smile as Z busied himself trying every dish. I ate my fair share and wondered if Quincy Blackstone would pan out as a suspect.

"I can't wait until we get a look inside Quincy's house," I said, fantasizing about finding a stash of cash from the bank or the white-haired wig worn by the perpetrator.

"What's this 'we' business? I thought that FBI dreamboat was your partner on this one? Where's he?"

I wiped my mouth with a napkin. "He's meeting us there." I sank deep into the oversized red booth and finished my bowl of soup. "This tastes just like my childhood."

"Heaven is a Japanese restaurant." Z waved his hand, indicating the entire table.

"Some of those dishes are not Japanese. You've got Thai noodles and the sesame chicken is Chinese. Dad is testing an Asian fusion menu."

"It's all delicious." He wiped his mouth with a cloth napkin and went back to the sesame chicken. "Growing up in a restaurant must've been awesome."

I tilted my head, giving the statement some thought. "In some ways it was. My sisters and brother and I ended up working in the kitchen a lot. And we did dishes, too, so . . ."

"Yeah, I can see the downside."

"What downsides?" The question came from above the two of us. I had been chin-deep in my soup bowl and hadn't noticed my mother, Keiko, approaching the table. She looked perfect, as always: her soft makeup expertly applied to accentuate her heart-shaped face and dark eyes.

Z jumped. "Hello, Mrs. Mori. I'm Z, Laura's partner."

"I remember you." Keiko smiled, revealing a row of evenly shaped teeth. Such an elegant smile my mother had. She slid into the booth next to Z and across from me.

"This the man I want to talk to," she told Z. "You can tell me what my daughter really does all day."

"Mom, I work!"

"Laura, you should eat some noodles. Fatten you up a little. Too skinny," she complained, reaching across to pat my arm with a hand heavy with shiny cocktail rings.

Turning her attention to Z, she said, "I think this job is far too dangerous for Laura. She's out there on the streets dealing with miscreants."

If only she knew about last night's vandalism. I didn't look up from my soup.

"Not a lot of miscreants wandering the streets of Sunrise Lake," laughed Z.

"Maybe so, but these bank robberies bother me." Keiko shook her head. "And that female police officer murdered a couple of years ago. That was terrible."

Z pushed a plate of half-eaten tofu away and nodded. "Awful," he agreed. "But you should've seen your daughter work the Lost Girls case. She really held her own."

"Hello?" I said. "I'm here, while you're discussing my career as if you two are in control."

Mom cast an agitated glance at me, and I sat up a little straighter under her scrutiny. Mom's voice was heavy as she said, "I recall sitting beside my daughter in the hospital at the end of that investigation."

"Yes, but she cracked a hard case and brought justice to a lot of people," Z said, squinting at me. "She's tougher than she looks."

My mother drummed her well-manicured nails on the table. "I hope so."

"Where is Hannah?" I asked, trying to change the subject. "Maybe she can have some tea with us."

"Hannah's busy in the kitchen. Probably helping your dad on the dessert station." Keiko looked over to Z. "Are you ready for something sweet?"

Z puffed out his cheeks. "No way. I'm stuffed, but it was delicious, Mrs. Mori. All compliments to the chef."

My mother got up and patted my shoulder. "I'll send over more tea, then." She left the table and immediately greeted a crowd of regulars who came bursting through the front door with a gust of wind.

"Hard to please?" Z jerked his head toward my mother.

"A smidge." I paused. "The whole family wants me to be a doctor, lawyer, or some well-paid professional in a trade that people will always need. A profession that will provide long-term security. Even making detective didn't win them over. Sometimes I wonder if I should've been a psychologist like Dr. MacKenzie."

Z raised his eyebrows. "Really? You'd make a good shrink."

I felt like that was true, though my math phobia had prohibited me from grad school—particularly a degree that required statistics.

"But I'm not sure that would be a good fit for you," Z went on. "You love police work. You like figuring out puzzles. I know, because I do, too."

A swift movement on the other side of the restaurant caught my eye. Someone was running out of the kitchen. Was there a fire?

Z swung around to see what had caught my attention as Edgar, one of the prep chefs, zigzagged through the tables. Clearly in distress, he waved us over.

"Me?" I stood up and moved toward him, staying close to the wall in an attempt not to disturb the patrons. Z was behind me as we closed the distance and came face-to-face with Edgar. "What's going on?"

"Out back, in the alley," he said breathlessly. "Please, come . . . Miss Hannah is hurt."

14

The door to the alleyway stood open. Outside, a few feet from my car, my sister Hannah sat awkwardly on the pavement in a sea of broken plastic and shattered glass. My dad squatted beside her, leaning over her, trying to comfort her.

"Oh my God, Hannah!" I flew to her and touched her hair, her cheeks, her shoulders. "Are you okay?"

She nodded, looking at me through the tears that filled her brown eyes. "I scraped my hands on the ground when he pushed me."

"Who? Who pushed you?"

"There was a guy out here. I heard a noise, and I came out and saw him beating up your car. When I told him to stop, he shoved me to the ground."

"You protected my car? Oh, Hannah." I hugged her close, thinking of the horrible things that could have been so much worse. "I'm so sorry you got hurt. Did you hit anything else when you went down? How about your head?"

"No, just my hands, and I think I tore a hole in the knee of my pants."

"Let's get you on your feet," our father said. "Can you stand up now?"

Dad and I each took one arm and helped Hannah to her feet.

"There you go," Dad said. "You gave us a scare, but you'll be fine." His confident words belied his worried expression, the wrinkles in his forehead as he eyed Hannah as if she were a precious doll.

"That loser messed up my hair," she said. She was quivering and pale, but seeing her pull out her ponytail and toss her head reassured me that she really was fine.

Able to breathe again, I had a chance for a wider view of the situation: the smashed headlight on my car, the shiny broken glass on the ground, Z pacing the periphery, Edgar worrying the strings of his apron as he waited by the door.

"Thanks, Edgar," I said. "You can go back inside. Everything's fine."

"Are you okay, sir?" he asked our father.

"Fine, fine." Koji stepped away from Hannah and clapped Edgar on the back. "Your quick response was a blessing. Thank you." He nodded as the prep chef went inside.

Z came over to us. "I've already called it in. The Portland police are on their way."

"But you guys are the police, right?" Hannah asked.

"We need to file a report with the local jurisdiction," Z explained. "Cops don't investigate their own families." He shot me a look. "Well, not usually. I let Omak know. He'll send someone else for the warrant if we get held up here for a while."

"Who was this man, Laura?" Dad asked. "This attacker?"

"I don't know, Dad, but I'm going to find out."

"Your sister—"

"I know," I said. "It's scary that someone would hurt her—"

"I'm right here," Hannah said, delicately picking at her palm.

"But don't you see, they were trying to hurt you?" My father's voice grew soft in that way that made me melt inside. "I'm worried for Hannah, but also for you, Laura. This man must have followed your car right here."

I had realized this was true, but I hadn't wanted to upset my dad more than necessary. "We're going to find out who did this and stop him from hurting anyone else."

"I trust you to do that." My father looked me squarely in the eyes, as if extracting a promise. "This is your job now."

This was new; a dawning recognition of my vocation. "Yes."

The pact was sealed.

"I need to get back to the kitchen," he said, turning away.

"Dad?" I called after him. "Can we not tell Mom?"

He turned and gave a dismissive wave. "As you would say, good luck with that. Sooner or later, your mother knows everything that happens here."

"And how about your security cameras?" I said, nodding toward the black mechanism mounted over the door. My father had installed security cameras years ago. "Are they working?"

"Everything is in working order here," Dad insisted. "You need some video? We can get it from the computer in the office."

"I'll go see about the footage," Z said.

Hannah pressed her head onto my shoulder, and as I slipped one arm around her, I could feel that she was trembling. "Are you cold?" It had started to rain, that fine sputtering drizzle.

"Just shaken. I need to go inside and wash up. Back to the dessert station."

"In a minute. Tell me about the guy."

"He was cute. Rugged cute," she said. "Dark hair, I think. It was hard to tell because he wore sunglasses and a black hoodie over his head. Enough facial hair to look chill without going full-on mountain man."

I nodded. Strangely enough, I knew exactly what she meant.

"And he had a tattoo on his neck. The hood didn't completely cover it. I could make out a blue star tattoo with a yellow lightning bolt."

"On his neck?"

"I know. He's gonna totally regret that ink in five years. But I didn't see the tattoo until later. At first glance, he seemed okay. When he asked about you, I thought you had a secret admirer, and I was excited." She looked down at her hands. "I didn't realize."

"You talked to him? What did he say?"

"Just 'Laura Mori?' As if he thought I was you. When I said that you were my sister, he said, 'Close enough,' and took a swing at your car with a tire iron. Then I realized that had been the noise I heard. I'm sorry. I was slow on connecting all the dots."

"It's not your fault. Did he say anything else?"

"He said, 'Tell your sister to stop Twilight,' or something like that. Does that make any sense to you?"

"It does. About how old would you say he was?"

She shrugged. "Hard to say. He was covered up. But when he took off down the alley, I noticed he was in decent shape. He moved like a young person, twenties max."

"Your description will be helpful, and we probably have video of him," I said. "But I wish I knew who he was."

I tried to tamp down the eeriness as I looked up and down the alley. Two threatening messages in two days. Someone did not want me poking around the closed Twilight case. Why? Because I might find something had been missed in the first investigation? It scared me to think that someone had followed me here, to my parents' restaurant. Whoever it was wanted to spook me, and I hated to admit it was working.

While the Portland cops talked with Hannah, Z and I inspected the back entrance to the restaurant. It was raining, just enough to wash down the pavement, and there was no sign of anyone matching my sister's description. Nothing seemed out of the ordinary.

Resolve was fueled by a burning sense of anger as I crouched on the wet pavement looking for clues that weren't there. For the first time in my life, I felt vulnerable in what amounted to my second home: my family's restaurant. It was time to turn things around, take control.

Time to become the hunter instead of the hunted.

* * *

Although I had thought that it would feel victorious to pick up the search warrant, our spirits were dampened as Z and I drove back to Sunrise Lake with the document. We drove straight to the hill and wove our way to the rear of the Blackstone estate, where Derringer waited in a dark Ford Escape.

"I heard your car was vandalized in Portland," he said by way of greeting. "Are you okay?"

"I'm fine," I said as the three of us began to walk toward Quincy Blackstone's front porch. "But he gave my sister a hard shove and smashed one headlight of my car." I turned to Z. "News sure travels fast."

"Omak told me," Derringer said. Fine bits of mist were accumulating on the broad shoulders of his dark suit jacket, and I was struck by the way he filled out a suit. He looked strikingly dark and handsome against the gray sky and landscape. "Do you think it's connected to this case?" he asked.

"It's related to Twilight. He left a message telling me to stop the case. And this guy was young, taller than the bank robber, and no limp at all. No disguise, not even a hat. He's not the bank robber."

"Which indicates that our Twilight bandit had an accomplice," Derringer said.

"Someone trying to cover for him," I agreed. "I'm just glad that Hannah wasn't seriously hurt."

"No doubt," Derringer said. "We'll check in with the Portland police as soon as we're done here."

I felt a new camaraderie with Derringer as Z knocked on the door and rang the bell. After a minute's wait, the door opened, revealing Quincy Blackstone. Wearing jeans and a hunter-green cashmere sweater, he raked through his wild hair and glared at me.

"I thought I was done with you guys trespassing and harassing me. I mean, do you know who my parents are?"

"It's not trespassing today," I said, handing him the paperwork. "We're here with Agent Nick Derringer from the FBI, and we have a warrant to search these premises."

"What?" Quincy leaned out to get a better look, his eyes growing round as he spotted Derringer. "You brought the FBI? Whoa. Do you think I'm a terrorist?"

"This is in connection to the robbery at First Sunrise Bank," Derringer said. "We'd like for you to step aside so we can get started."

"Yeah, okay." Quincy released the door and stepped back so that we could enter a small living room with a leather sofa and love seat. With a white shag rug, warm yellow lamps, and fleece throws on the couches, it was much neater and warmer than I had expected from Quincy's arrogant, cool demeanor. "Did you train at Quantico?" Quincy asked Derringer.

"I did. Is there anyone else in the house right now? Any firearms?"

Quincy answered no to both questions, and he agreed to stay put as we began our search. While Z and Derringer searched the bedroom and living area, I went to the kitchen, where I came across eight prescription pill bottles and cartons stacked into the corner of the granite shelf. Medications prescribed to Quincy Blackstone. From what I could tell, the pills were treatment for gout, high blood pressure, and kidney disease. I took a picture of the bottles and quickly jotted the names into my notebook.

In the pantry I found a decent supply of canned beans and soups, boxes of pasta, and an expensive juicer. Nothing out of the ordinary.

When we finished the initial search, we switched areas and double-checked each other. I was halfway through the living room when Quincy let me know he had called his lawyer. "He's emailing a document over to your precinct. To your boss." He smiled, one brow arched. "You're going to be in big trouble now."

I wasn't scared. "Thanks for letting me know," I said, leaning down to shine my flashlight under the sofa.

We worked together to check the small attic room and dank crawl space. In two hours of searching we found nothing that would tie Quincy to Monday's robbery. Just to be sure, Derringer confiscated Quincy's laptop and a few files from a banker's box he kept in the closet. Quincy was angry about the laptop, especially after his lawyer had sent Omak a document that seemed to remove Quincy Blackstone from our suspect list.

"It's an unsigned affidavit, but basically it gives Quincy Blackstone an alibi for the time of the robbery Monday evening," Omak explained over the phone. "The lawyer is saying that Quincy was in treatment Monday beginning at four PM. Dialysis takes around four hours, so that wouldn't put Blackstone back on the street until eight o'clock. We'll make sure we get a signed statement and corroboration from the medical facility, but I'd say Quincy Blackstone is clean."

"That's what we're seeing on this end," I told Omak. Already my mind had shifted away from Quincy to focus on other possible suspects . . . another bank employee, a career criminal from the FBI's most-wanted list, a copycat robber, a person with some connection to the Twilight Bandit. That last possibility stuck in my mind, as it would help explain the threats I'd been getting.

For all his objections, Quincy seemed disappointed when we left his home; I think he had enjoyed the attention.

On the way back to the precinct I saw that I had a missed call from Rex at the lab. I called him and left a message. "I bet he has lab results on those wig fibers," I told Z, who didn't share my enthusiasm.

Back at the precinct, we unloaded the confiscated items, tracked down Omak, and filed into his office. "I'm a little worried about the chief's reaction to clearing Blackstone," I said.

Omak shrugged. "You had reasonable cause to search. I wouldn't worry about it."

"It's not about Blackstone's rights. It's that Cribben was counting on making an arrest tonight," I said. "He told me he had his contacts in the media standing by."

"He'll need to rein it in for now," Derringer said. "This sort of thing happens all the time."

I put the Blackstone files on the corner desk and looked at Omak. "Do you want to tell him?"

"We'll go together," Omak said. As Z went back to the squad room, Omak called upstairs to the chief. "Let me call him. I learned a while back that he doesn't like to be surprised," he said, taking his phone out to the hall.

"Sounds like your chief is under a lot of pressure to produce," Derringer said as he restacked file folders on his desk.

Leaning against Omak's desk, I nodded as I stared at the door. "He wants an arrest," I said.

"And he's not picky." Derringer swung round to face me. "Any warm body will do."

"Round up the usual suspects," I said, turning to face him, glad that he got it. I was quickly losing faith in Buzz Cribben as the chief of our department, but my sense of loyalty and mission didn't allow me to say much more.

I called Rex again, and he picked up. "Where the hell have you been?"

"Executing a search warrant," I said, as if it was the sort of procedure I conducted every day. "Did you hear from that outside lab?" I asked.

"I've got the results in front of me, but they need some explanation."

"Hold on, I'm putting you on speaker phone," I said. "FBI Agent Nick Derringer is here with me, and he's part of the team working on the case."

"Okay, then. Let's start by saying that synthetic fibers are not like human hairs. We're able to analyze the wig fibers by color, shape, which means curly or straight, and exterior and interior structure under the microscope. But it's not like evaluating the definitive DNA in human hair. A wig fiber isn't one of a kind. In fact, one wig could have fibers from various different sources, fibers that don't necessarily match."

"I get it. So are you telling me that the results are inconclusive?"

"Not exactly. The lab got positive matches on some of the fibers, but not all. So there's a good chance that the fibers came from the same wig. It's possible but can't be proven at this point."

"We'll go with that for now, but send on the analysis when you can." I gave Derringer a questioning look and he nodded at me. "Thanks, Rex."

As I ended the call, Cribben plodded in with Omak behind him. I straightened up, nodding deferentially, but the chief's sour expression didn't soften.

"You let me down, Mori," Cribben said. "I thought we were going to bring Blackstone in, ask questions later."

I held up my hands as if to a say *oh, well* but stopped short of apologizing. My father had taught me that it's unwise to apologize for things beyond your control.

"We decided to do it by the book," Omak said from the doorway.

"I'm kidding. Well, only half kidding." With squinty eyes, Cribben turned toward Derringer. "Are you the FBI agent?"

"Yes, sir." Derringer rose to his full six feet plus, smoothed down his tie, and introduced himself. He had polished the introduction, a cool, professional presentation and look that seemed to engage the police chief.

"I guess it's good that you're here, Agent Derringer. None of our people have had much luck solving bank robberies around here for a few years now."

"Detective Mori seems to be on point," Derringer said.

"She hasn't brought me anything that I can take to the press yet," the chief complained. "Unless you have a suspect on standby."

"We don't, though we have some news from the lab," I said. "Their analysis shows that the wig fibers found at the scene of some of the Twilight robberies are a possible match with those found Monday at First Sunrise Bank."

Cribben scratched the back of his neck. "What does that mean?"

"It means there's a good chance that the same wig worn in the Twilight robberies was used Monday," Derringer said. "It's possible that the Twilight Bandit has struck again."

The chief winced. "Not what I want to hear."

15

After the chief left in a glum mood, the three of us brushed aside his disappointment and dove back into the matter of the bank robberies. With the related wig fibers and the dismissal of Blackstone as a suspect, we were back to square one in a sense. Agent Derringer and I decided to split up the work of piecing together any patterns of the Twilight Bandit spree and matching them with details from Monday's robbery at the First Sunrise Bank. Omak let me log on to his computer so that Derringer and I could compare notes as we combed through reports. We worked in companionable silence as the gray light from the window gave way to the overhead fluorescents.

For starters, I read through the FBI case on the Twilight Bandit—a far more logical account of the robberies. There had been nine bank robberies in the span of fourteen months—November through December of the following year. All robberies took place late in the day in the darker months—November through March. All robberies had been in Sunrise Lake at dusk or after dark, and each time the robber scored more than ten thousand dollars. No gun was ever pulled inside a bank. No need. The robber passed a note and the tellers dutifully filled a backpack. No funny business. There'd been no arrest in the case, despite one fatality: Officer Franny Landon. The main FBI investigator who'd handled the case had passed away while the case was still open, and Chief

Cribben had unceremoniously called the case cold, handing Detective Cranston the unsavory duty of buttoning up the case files. From my look at the SLPD files, it appeared Cranston had taken that assignment about as seriously as parking meter duty.

What made the ninth Twilight Bandit robbery different from the others, aside from Franny's murder, was that the bank's exterior cameras were not working. None of them had caught an image. Turned out, we discovered later, that the outdoor cameras had been covered with duct tape. But the videos from inside the bank still worked and showed the same thing—an older man with a baseball cap pulled low over his eyes.

I pulled video recovered from Monday and watched it closely, clicking on replay again and again to study details. The recent robbery was strikingly similar to the Twilight, though this time the cameras were working, inside and out. The thief was elderly or had disguised himself to look that way with a white wig and glasses. Wearing a tan baseball cap and dark jeans and jacket, he could've been a trucker, a farmer, even a lawyer. No way of knowing. The robber stopped at the bank counter, took off his right glove, and, using his right hand, wrote instructions on a deposit slip in block print. GIVE ME YOUR FIFTIES AND HUNDREDS. No threats. No visible gun. The note had been enough to scare Ashley, the teller, into handing over money, which he'd loaded into a black backpack before turning and striding out into the darkness. The robbery was fast and seamless.

Next, I clicked on the link to one of the Twilight Bandit robberies. The grainy footage revealed what seemed like an elderly man approaching the counter. He removed a glove and wrote his note in the same blocky, oversized lettering.

What the copycat had gotten wrong, though, was using his right hand to write the note and hand it to the teller.

There was also the text of the bank robbery note to consider. The same blocky lettering. The same message, word for word. It was as if the First Sunrise culprit had studied the Twilight's handiwork. I pointed this out to Derringer.

"Wasn't the Twilight Bandit note released to the public?" asked Derringer. "I thought *The Oregonian* ran it."

I shook my head. I'd scoured newspaper clippings and local television reports, and nowhere had the contents or a description of the Twilight Bandit note appeared.

"Our First Sunrise robber had access to inside information about the Twilight Bandit," I told Derringer. "Someone who would have had access to the text of the other notes. That points to a bank employee, though I've screened everyone at First Sunrise Bank. No leads there."

I didn't want to push into a murky area, but there was an obvious possibility. "Maybe our new burglar is a bank employee or a cop. Someone who would have had access to the text of the other notes. I've screened the employees at First Sunrise."

"Which leaves the law enforcement community." Derringer looked up from the computer, where an image of the First Sunrise robber was frozen on the screen. "Cops and investigators also have access to inside information like the text of the note."

"But a cop wouldn't rob a bank," I said, quickly recognizing my own bias. "Or, at least, that's unlikely."

"Because you don't want to think that way of someone in law enforcement."

"Exactly. I love my job, and I want to believe everyone I serve with is also serving with integrity, giving it their best."

"That's a noble view. I'd like to agree, but in a logical investigation you can't rule out a cop."

I thought of Cranston, who'd mucked up the files on the Twilight Bandit. If the investigation turned in that direction, he'd be first on my list. Again, my bias.

"There's also the chance that First Sunrise was robbed by the Twilight Bandit. I know you've found differences, but maybe he changed part of his MO to throw us off."

I nodded, liking the way Derringer rolled out the possibilities. It would be good for me to work with someone who wasn't so closely woven into the community. "Anything jumping out at you?" I asked him.

Derringer looked up quickly and pointed at his screen. "I was just going over the Sunrise Lake case files from the Twilight Bandit case. What a mess, huh?"

"Yeah, it's kind of a dumpster fire, right?" I agreed, surprised that in the course of a day we had learned a new shorthand, talking like old friends.

He grinned. The man had a sense of humor, after all. "There's so much missing, it's hard to draw any conclusions."

Even though the door to Omak's office was closed, I lowered my voice to a whisper. I wasn't sure if I was at liberty to reveal to Derringer that the SLPD was already under investigation for corruption and that Lieutenant Omak was spearheading that shadowed effort. Derringer and Omak shared an office, but did they also share information? I didn't know.

"I have a proposal . . ."

"Go on," he said.

"Reading the narrative from the FBI report on the Twilight robberies helped things gel in my head, but the case is weak on corroborating evidence. I checked at the evidence locker, and a lot of specimens were inventoried and never analyzed. Teller notes, fingerprints, bags of duct tape found on the outdoor bank cameras. Do you think we could take a new look at things, build the Twilight case from the ground up?"

"Rerun the evidence?" Derringer asked.

"In an outside lab. And for now we'll keep any notes or evidence involving the Twilight case out of the SLPD database. I'll run it by Omak, but we can change security settings so that files can only be accessed by the three of us. We know that someone doesn't want me on this case. Better not to give them any indication of progress we might be making."

"That's a great idea. I didn't know there was unprocessed evidence." Derringer nodded. "We'll use the FBI lab in Seattle. I can run the evidence there myself."

"That might help us move the case," I said. "For now, I'm going to go talk with the coroner about something in the FBI version of the homicide investigation." I handed him the pages I had printed out from the medical examiner's report on Franny Landon's autopsy and checked my watch. "Almost five. Shoot. I'd better call over and see if Dr. Viloria is still there." I grabbed my phone and shot a text to Rex, asking him how late Dr. V would be working.

"What am I looking for here?"

"It's the coroner's report. Did you notice her report on the angle of the bullet? I'm having trouble making sense of it."

He studied the report, frowning. "It didn't jump out at me before, but now I see what you mean. It looks like the bullet couldn't have come from a fleeing suspect on the street."

"I need to go ask Dr. Viloria about it."

"Mind if I come with you? I'd like to hear the explanation first-hand, and, to be honest, my supervisor keeps telling me I need more field investigation. I guess I'm an office nerd at heart." As he spoke, he rubbed above his ear, and I caught sight of a scar on his skull that was visible underneath his closely cropped hair. He caught me staring at his head, grinned, and rubbed the scar with his fingertips.

"Kicked in the head by a horse."

"What?"

"When I was a kid," Derringer explained. "My parents told me not to run out into the pasture to feed the horses. I was supposed to keep a fence between our neighbor's horses and me at all times. But I didn't listen, and I ran out with sugar cubes in my hand to feed the neighbor's palomino. She was a beauty. I walked behind the horse. It kicked. I ended up in the ER with eighteen stitches and a good story."

"So, you've literally been kicked in the head by a horse?"

Derringer tipped his head and gave me a mischievous look. "Yes, ma'am." He smiled, at last. "So, I have an excuse if I do anything stupid."

"Good to know," I said. "Full disclosure?"

"Yes?"

"You don't seem the stupid type. Or an office nerd."

"I don't know about that, Laura Mori, but I can tell you I still enjoy bending the rules now and then."

I secretly wondered if Derringer's disdain for rules applied to his personal life, too. God, I hoped so.

16

A car pulls up in front of Donny Gallagher's door, and he stands up from his favorite brown recliner that he sometimes positions in front of the bay window so he can keep an eye on the comings and goings of the neighbors and their kids. It's been a gray, boring afternoon, but the evening is starting to look up now that he has visitors.

He limps toward the front door, his left ankle—an old injury from his crime beat days on the force—stiff from disuse.

A yellow school bus trundles down the street. Gotta be the late bus, the one for the kids who stay after school, since it's nearly dark now. After five. Donny knows all about the comings and goings of cars, trucks, and buses in the neighborhood. Life in the fish bowl, he likes to joke. If he had nothing going on, he'd go out to the street and post himself as a crossing guard, help the kids get across the street. Especially now, dark so early these days. But right now Donny is all about the visitors, and in the yellow light of his porch he sees a man in uniform step out of the passenger side.

It's the guys!

Donny loves getting visits from his old buddies on the force, though they visit less and less since the girl was killed.

Donny opens the door and folds his arms, huddling against the damp wind. It's cold this afternoon, and the bare tree limbs are soaked and dripping. Not supposed to happen. The weather-man said it wouldn't rain this late. Wrong again.

He can't see who has come to visit as the two figures get out of the vehicle. Whoever it is, Donny's hopeful they will drink a beer with him and stay awhile. He's been lonely since his wife died. His son, Chris, drops by to check on him, sure, but Donny loves it when his buddies, the ones who remember him when he was healthy, stop by.

Donny smiles at the two cops at his door, except he's confused. They're wearing masks, and Donny is pretty sure it's not Halloween.

"Hey, guys!" Donny doesn't see the left hook coming from the shorter of the two officers. The blow slams into Donny's jaw, cracking a couple of teeth.

"You broke the deal, Donny."

Donny is howling as the cops push him back into his house and shut the door behind them. The pain—it's raw! Donny tries to bat their hands away, but he's quickly pulled to his feet and pushed against a wall.

"What the hell?" Donny yells. "Show your faces, you lousy pieces of shit."

The tall one pushes a flashlight against his throat, making Donny squirm and choke.

"No more bank hits, remember? You said it first." The shorter one kicks him in the groin, and Donny's stomach lurches.

"I know who you two cowards are, anyway. Your masks don't fool me." But Donny is bluffing. He's not too sure who these guys are. His memory lets him down all the time these days.

"Shut up, old man, and show us where you've stashed the money," the taller one spits at him. "Since you're doing bank hits on your own now, we'll take a cut for protection."

Donny coughs. "I haven't done any banks. I swear it."

The cop with the flashlight to Donny's neck punches him hard in the gut. "Like we're going to believe that," he says.

"I saw that hit at First Sunrise on the news, but I didn't do it. I swear." It's a struggle to get words out with that steel rod crushing his throat.

The flashlight eases away from his neck, allowing him to breathe as the punk cop talks up close. "Think hard, now. I know your memory is fuzzy, old man."

It's true; lately he's been having trouble separating dreams from memories, his own actions from characters he's seen on TV. "I didn't hit that bank. I don't remember it."

"As long as you remember where the money is stashed, you'll be fine."

"I've got no money. I'm broke." Chris tells him that all the time. *You're broke, Dad. Where did all your money go?* "I got nothing."

"Bullshit," snaps the shorter guy. "Sure you didn't just forget where you put the cash? Mind if we look around a little?" The flashlight is removed, and Donny gasps, dropping to the floor, where he struggles to breathe. He lies crumpled as the two of them riffle through his kitchen cabinets.

Donny knows he's been slipping. He forgets things. He finds himself standing in front of his own refrigerator wondering if he's already eaten lunch. He forgets his passwords to most websites he visits, and he texts his grocery list to Chris three or four times a day. Donny loses track of time easily, and he sometimes forgets appointments he's made. But he isn't a zombie quite yet, and he'll be damned if he's going to let a couple of thugs knock him around.

From his sitting position on the floor, Donny lunges at the tall guy's knees, easily taking the man and Donny's favorite lamp down to the floor. The lamp smashes, light popping, then out. The room is dim, but Donny can see enough to throw a strong punch at the tall cop's windpipe. Donny turns to attack the second guy, but he finds a revolver two inches away from his face and cocked.

"You're gonna kill me over this shit?" Donny asks. "What's your story gonna be? Self-defense in my house? Good luck. Talk about a career ender." The thug holding the gun hesitates a second and then lowers his gun.

Donny is just about to lunge for the cop and disarm him when something rock hard smashes into the left side of his skull. Red-hot pain ricochets through his brain. Donny reaches up instinctively to cover his head with his arms as the world around him goes black.

And at last, he feels no pain at all.

Just the sweet, Irish stout foam of nothing.

17

Most people felt uncomfortable or even ill when they entered the tiled, astringent morgue, but Derringer seemed sharp and polished as I introduced him to Dr. Viloria, the medical examiner. Dr. V and I had worked together during the Lost Girls case, and I hoped she'd have the time and inclination to talk to me about another closed case that was inching open bit by bit.

"Franny Landon?" Dr. V was short, under five feet tall, with slick, shiny dark hair that she usually wore pulled back. Creases marked her forehead as she looked at the ballistics report I'd taken from the cold-case file. "Of course I remember that case. You don't forget a gunned-down cop, at least not in Sunrise Lake."

She flipped through the report and nodded several times. "The bullet came from a .38 automatic handgun. No surprise, as it's a common weapon. But the angle of the bullet was surprising. I remember that we were a bit confounded by this at the time. A weird angle, and the shot came from a distance," she said.

"How much of a distance?"

Dr. V. scrunched her nose as she studied the report. "Anywhere from twenty to twenty-five yards, we estimate."

Derringer rubbed his jaw, considering the possibility. "That's a long trajectory for an automatic handgun, isn't it?"

"It is," Dr. V conceded. "But I've definitely seen it before. The shooter would have to be experienced with a firearm or darn lucky." She peered over her glasses to look directly into my face. "I already told all this to the investigating officer at the time, you know."

"Yeah?"

"I mentioned it a few times, for emphasis. I remember because he seemed a little distracted."

I snorted a little. "Bald guy? Bit of a goofus?"

She nodded.

Cranston. Why wasn't I surprised? I asked the coroner what she made of the odd angle of the bullet.

Dr. V took another look at the ballistics report, flipping through the pages until she reached a section with a drawing of the victim and the bullet's point of entry.

"We know that the bullet came from some distance away. Around twenty yards. And see this?" Her finger traced a dotted line. "The bullet entered at the top of the skull on a downward trajectory, so it probably didn't come from street level. We see something like this when someone has been shot from an elevated location—the rooftop of a building, or sometimes a hilltop in a combat situation."

"So the shooter had to be far away and above Landon?" I asked.

She looked at the pages again. "I'd say so." Dr. V looked at me, her brown eyes stern like my mother's. "This case is more than three years old. I thought the chief had closed it."

I shrugged. "A case isn't really closed until it's solved." I paused. "Can we keep this conversation off the record?"

Dr. V's mouth wriggled to one side as her dark eyes studied me. "What conversation?"

* * *

Back at the precinct, Derringer and I decided to take a dinner break and then dig in again. He had the idea of creating a map of the Pacific Lake Bank crime scene, which gave me the idea to have Z walk us through it. I didn't know that bank well, and after the revelation from the coroner it would be great to get a sense of the bandit's escape route and the homicide scene.

"I'll be back in an hour," I said, leaving Omak's office. I felt a little bad leaving him on his own. Derringer had proven himself to be a diligent, fair worker today, but there was still an awkwardness of newness between us.

I found Z in the squad room, hard at work on his report. "I'm trying to get the administration at Sunrise to update their security system, at least replace the broken cameras," he said.

"How's that going?" I asked.

"It's not."

"Wanna grab some dinner?" I asked.

"Hell to the yeah."

We signed out a department Jeep, since my car had a damaged light. Deciding on a cozy barbecue joint that had a roaring fire in the back, Z pulled onto Ridge Road.

Leaning back against the headrest, I shut my eyes.

"Tired?" Z asked.

"It's been a long day, and it's still not over."

"Well, Fancy's Barbecue will fix you right up. And we're definitely splitting a mac and cheese. It's the cure for just about everything."

I smiled and took a deep breath. Maybe a catnap on the way.

Just then the police radio crackled to life.

My eyes opened and the skin on the back of my neck prickled at the code as Ellie's voice came on the radio: "All available units to respond to a home invasion, possible homicide on Oakwood Road."

It was an unusual call for Sunrise Lake.

"We're close," I said.

"We got this. Hang on." Z flicked on the lights and sirens and sped the rest of the way to the scene.

We zeroed in on the address from the lights of a patrol unit already on scene. The flashing blue and red beams from the turret lights swept the yard of a one-story house as the two of us walked up the cracked cement walkway.

Time: 7:32 PM.

I recognized the young man sitting on the stoop, crying. Ward Brown stood over him, smoking a cigarette and talking quietly to the distraught man.

Officer Scooter Rivers stood in the doorway, his shoulders slumped in despair.

"I know this kid," I told Rivers. "What's the deal?"

"The kid is Chris, Donny Gallagher's son."

I nodded, remembering them from the party.

"Donny's inside. It's a bad scene. I can't believe he's gone," Rivers murmured to me as I pushed past him into the house. Z followed behind me.

Donny's body lay on the floor, his face in a pool of blood. His body was bent in an odd angle, half on an area rug. Had he struck his head while falling? Once I knelt down, a closer look at Donny Gallagher's face revealed cuts and fresh bruising. He had been beaten.

"How long since the paramedics pronounced him dead?" I asked Brown, who'd left Chris and wandered back into the house.

"No need for paramedics," Brown answered. "I know dead when I see dead."

"You guys didn't call the paramedics?" Z asked, incredulous.

I pulled on latex gloves, knelt down next to Donny, and gently touched my fingers to the carotid artery in his neck.

"Jesus, guys. You're not docs," Z hissed. "The least you can do is call a bus just in case."

Donny was still warm to the touch, and I thought I felt a faint pulse. "He's still alive!"

Z called for an ambulance as I loosened the top button of Donny's shirt and heard a slight groan. He was breathing. I looked up and waved off the men who crowded around us.

"Give him some space." I felt the air clear a bit as I stayed there, holding Donny's hand, whispering to him, trying to reassure the elderly man that help was on its way.

Just then Cranston burst into the house, a napkin tucked into his collar. "I was on meal when I heard the call on the radio and recognized the address. What the hell?" He stumbled forward, ripped the napkin from his shirt, and knelt beside me. "Aw, no . . . Hang in there, big guy."

"Paramedics are on their way," I said quietly. I wasn't exactly thrilled to see him, after my speculation about his involvement with the Twilight Bandit, but in this moment he showed some humanity.

Cranston cupped Donny's cheek, as if tending to a child. "Hold on, buddy."

Omak arrived just as the paramedics wheeled in a stretcher and took over Donny's care. I could see the darkness in the lieutenant's eyes as I left the paramedics to their work and walked out to my car to grab a notebook. As I rounded the corner of the house, I saw Brown and Cranston arguing in the alleyway, but I couldn't hear what they were saying. From the looks of things, both men were pent up about something.

After Donny was loaded in the ambulance, I helped string crime scene tape around the front of the one-story house with fading blue paint. As we worked to secure the scene, all of us heard Omak scream at Brown and Rivers in the driveway on the side of the house.

"When you go to medical school and become doctors, you can pronounce. Until then, do your damn jobs!"

I'd never seen Lieutenant Omak lose his composure like that before, but I thought if anyone deserved the dressing down, it was Brown and Rivers. It was strange that these two seasoned cops would make the presumption that a victim was deceased. Especially a victim who had been their friend.

I went around the side of the house, staying out of the way but close enough to hear their conversation as I started stringing tape along the garage door.

"It was an honest mistake," Brown said, his thumbs looped into his black equipment belt. "We're sorry, sir. Donny was our friend, and we're pretty broken up here."

"Was? Again, you've got him in the grave," Omak said quietly. "What the hell is wrong with you, Brown?"

"I didn't mean that, Lieu." Brown winced, looking down at the ground. "Rivers and I would like to stick around to work the crime scene. We want to help. Whatever it takes, for Donny."

What? Now they wanted to help Donny, after leaving him for dead? Brown's logic stunk like week-old sushi.

"We've got enough personnel here to process the crime scene. Your skills are needed on patrol right now," Omak said firmly. "You'd best head on out. And I want you to think hard and long about your duty to provide first aid to victims in the future."

"Yes, sir." Rivers respectfully turned away and walked toward their squad car, his eyes downcast. Brown followed, but without the humility. He moved with ease and entitlement, a man without conscience who was always right. God help our small police department.

As Z and I waited for crime scene technicians, I found Chris and offered to get him a ride to the hospital. "But first I need you to answer a couple of questions for me. Think you can do that?" I asked gently, taking my notebook out of my jacket pocket.

Chris nodded. His face was red with emotion, and tears streamed down his swollen cheeks. He told me he'd come to check on his father around six PM after he closed up at the cleaners. "Dad usually springs out of his chair and comes to the door. He sits at the window waiting. But today there was no answer, even after I tried a few times, and it was dark inside. I noticed his truck parked in the garage, so I started getting worried and used my key. When I got inside, I noticed things out of place. The lamp plugged into a timer was knocked over and smashed. The coffee table was turned over, and part of the wall had a chunk out of it, like someone had whacked it with a hammer. And then I saw him on the floor, bleeding, and so still." He pressed a hand to his mouth, sobbed. "I thought he was dead. I can't blame Brown for thinking that. I thought the same thing. I mean, he's old beyond his years now. Failing. What kind of a person attacks a man who is losing his mind? I mean, what kind of a bastard does that?"

I shook my head. "Any ideas, Chris? Who would want to hurt your dad?"

He looked away, his face twisted with pain. "I don't know. I should go. I don't want him to wake up alone."

I nodded. "Let's get you to the hospital." I stowed my notebook away in the pocket of my jacket and asked one of our cops to transport Chris to the hospital, where he was instructed to stay with his father.

"We'll talk again when things settle down."

Chris nodded, his gaze on the ground.

Once Donny and his son were removed from the premises, the forensic team began to spread out, starting to photograph and sweep the area. Since a handful of cops had traipsed through the house, the crime scene was far from pristine, but we did our best to preserve what we had. I looked out into the growing dusk and saw that Derringer stood in the middle of the lawn with two technicians. Tamping down my relief to see him here, I approached him. He seemed engrossed in a conversation with Tonya Miller, the dark-haired young woman who was an expert on lifting fingerprints. Why did it bother me to see them involved in close conversation?

I cleared my throat and asked him how he'd landed here.

"Omak suggested I come over. He said he had to pull two uniforms off the scene. We figured another set of eyes and hands is always good."

Nodding, I filled him in on what we knew so far. Now that Cranston, Rivers, and Brown had been sent away by Omak, I could tell Derringer about their involvement with Donny, though Z and I went over the details in a back bedroom, not wanting anyone else in the department to overhear.

Trust no one.

"They seem to have a sort of friend's club, a network that Donny was involved in even after he retired," I said.

Derringer nodded, soaking it up immediately. "That's often how corruption looks from the outside," he said. "Let's keep this to ourselves for now. Don't mention it to anyone but Lieutenant Omak."

"Absolutely," Z said.

The door of the small bedroom opened with a creaking sound, and we fanned out to search the house, avoiding the living room until the crime scene techs finished up.

Almost immediately, Z called from the kitchen, "I've seen this a few times before." A blue Royal Dansk Danish butter cookie tin sat open on the kitchen counter, junk spilling over from the tin. There were pens, coins, old lighters, and broken reading glasses.

"Reusable cookie tins," Derringer said, lifting the lid. "When I was a kid, my grandma would fake me out with them. Every time I'd see one of these, I'd get excited for cookies. But then I'd open the lid and find Grandma's sewing kit or button collection in there." He shook his head. "Major disappointment."

"That's heartbreaking, Agent Derringer. Do you need to take a moment?" Z teased.

Derringer's eyes were lit with amusement. "I think I'll survive."

Smiling, I turned away from both men, relieved that a rapport was developing between them. My eye caught sight of something familiar on top of Donny Gallagher's refrigerator. A pile of blue cookie tins.

"Hold on. I think we've hit the mother lode." I grabbed a step stool and positioned it so that I could reach the top of the fridge.

"More cookie tins?" Z looked over at me.

"Looks like it, and I'm afraid you're going to be disappointed again. Not a cookie in sight," I said, opening the first tin, which was jammed with used plastic shopping bags. The second and third were filled with odd trinkets. I opened a fourth tin and saw that it was filled with actual cookies. "Jackpot."

"Cookies?" Z looked up from the evidence he was bagging with gloved hands. "Please tell me there are cookies."

"No snacking on evidence," Derringer called gruffly across the room.

"You know, it's really odd that Donny has all these containers and we saw Dolly Redmond with this same kind of cookie tin walking into Sunset Pines," I said. "I mean, how popular are these cookies, anyway?"

"Apparently Danish butter cookies are the treat of choice among the elderly of Sunrise Lake." Z walked over to look at the tins I'd pulled down from the top of the refrigerator. "If I played the stock market, I'd put some money into their company."

Z put a gloved hand in one of the canisters and started rummaging through the figurines, wristwatches, and old keys. He got serious as he held each new object and inspected it. "Most of this stuff fits descriptions of items taken from residents at the assisted-living facility. I mean, exactly. A bronze Statue of Liberty and a pickle Christmas ornament? This can't be a coincidence. I think this is some of the stolen stuff."

"Really?"

"Yeah. I mean, I'd have to match it up with my reports," said Z, "but these pewter saltshakers were reported missing just a week ago. How did Donny get all this shit?"

"From putting on his old police uniform and going down to the assisted-living home to impersonate a cop," Derringer said. "It's that simple."

"It seems that way." I suspected there was more to the situation than Donny playing cop, but I needed to mull it over some more.

Later, as I was pulling out boxes from Donny's bedroom closet, I came across a taped-up box large enough to fit a pair of boots. With one gloved hand I broke the seal. Immediately I saw the white wig, along with black glasses and a collection of baseball caps matching those I'd seen in the Twilight Bandit surveillance footage.

For a second I just stared, openmouthed.

"Guys? Check this out," I called, holding up the wig and a cap as Derringer and Z looked into the bedroom. "I think we just found the Twilight Bandit."

18

By the time Derringer and I arrived at Evergreen County Hospital, Donny Gallagher was in postop, having undergone surgery for severe head trauma. His doctors predicted Donny would survive his injuries, but it was too early to determine what permanent neurological damage he might've sustained. We peeked in on Donny, saw Chris napping in the bedside chair, and backed out.

It was after ten PM, shift change for many of the nurses on the third-floor surgical unit of the hospital. Derringer and I stood between the elevators and the nurses' station, watching as fresh-faced men and women arrived, laughing with their coworkers, reviewing charts, and receiving important updates on particular patients. The clang of activity and low hum of fluorescent lights thrummed in my ears.

Lowering myself to a seat in the waiting room, I felt my energy drain as the temporary adrenaline surge dissipated. Finding Donny Gallagher beaten to a pulp had taken a toll, and once I got back to the precinct, I would need to add to Z's report about the scene of Donny's assault and the collection of evidence that seemed to dovetail into two active cases. I needed a hot cup of coffee and some sugar to power through what was shaping up to be a long night.

"I'm grabbing a snack," I told Derringer. "Want something?"

"Coffee?" He scanned the hallway with a sharklike intensity that I admired. "I'll go with you."

The cafeteria had closed for the night, but a nurse directed us down one hall to a row of vending machines that sold coffee, sandwiches, and snacks. We took our stash back to the intensive care waiting room and devoured our small feast. The coffee was decent, and it went well with the Kind nut bar I'd gotten from the machine. Derringer quickly polished off two sandwiches, but we both savored the coffee.

"I wouldn't mind pressing Chris Gallagher for more details," Derringer said thoughtfully. "I think he knows more than he told you."

I could tell he was gnawing at the bit to grill Chris himself, but I thought a softer approach was sure to give us a bigger payoff, and I told him so. "Besides, his father is in serious condition. We need to take that into consideration."

He shook his head. "A cop is lying in intensive care and Chris Gallagher knows more than he's letting on. If anything, that guy needs to be leaned on hard."

"Before we do a push, let's do some research." I straightened in the stiff chair and nodded toward Derringer's black satchel. "Does that computer have access to crime databases?" I wanted to run some searches on the Gallaghers, but that would mean returning to the precinct to use the computer system there.

"This computer has magical capabilities," he said, "as long as the hospital Wi-Fi is reliable."

He put his coffee aside and opened up the small laptop that he'd seemed glued to in Omak's office. At this time of night, there were no other visitors in the intensive care unit waiting room, so it seemed okay to huddle close and take care of some business.

"Let's run a search on Donald Gallagher first," I said. "I'm wondering if we can get some financial information on him too. Whether he was in debt. Gambling debts that he owed people."

"We'll see what we can find." In a matter of minutes Derringer had compiled an extensive pedigree on Donny, which had quickly unfolded once he'd accessed Gallagher's social security number from employment records.

"Wow," I said. "It's scary what you can do."

"It would be scary in the wrong hands."

Donny Gallagher came up clean. His mortgage was paid off, he received social security and a police pension, and he had sixty thousand dollars in the bank. Not a rich man, but he seemed financially secure.

Christopher Gallagher had graduated from the county vocational high school four years ago. He had been employed by Regal Cleaners for at least two years.

"But he's not a saint like his father," Derringer said. Chris had a criminal record with two DUIs.

"A drinking problem," I said. "I sort of wondered about that."

"And there's something else here. He was never charged, but he was arrested more than once for shoplifting in Portland department stores. The charges were dropped in all three cases, which often happens. You pay the store a fee and promise never to shop there, and they decline prosecution."

"Interesting," I said.

"What did I tell you?" Derringer said. "This computer tells all."

"And now I'm more eager than ever to talk to Chris Gallagher." Derringer turned toward me and loosened his tie just a smidge. His eyes looked serious. "How about if I take a crack?"

I could feel heat flaming my cheeks. Derringer was asking politely enough, and really, he had as much say in the investigation as I did. I was nervous about making a mistake in the case, and maybe I was being too soft on Chris. Besides, I'd never seen Derringer's interrogation style, and I was a little curious to see his technique. As much as I wanted to question Chris again, I had to do what was best for the investigation.

"The ball's in your court, Agent Derringer," I said, turning to look out the large cathedral-style windows adorning the west side of the building. "I can always mop up afterwards."

He raised an eyebrow. "Challenge accepted. I'm going to pull Chris out of his father's room. I'll shoot you a text when I'm ready to question him."

Not sure how I felt about this approach, I grabbed a cup of coffee from a vending machine. As I sipped the warm liquid, I looked out the tall glass windows over the trees of Sunrise Lake, taking in the glowing lights of houses and streetlamps in my hometown. The sky was a deep purple. From up here, everything looked calm and quaint. The streets appeared silver from the freezing drizzle that hung in the air. It sure didn't look like a place where cops were shot dead or beaten up, but I was quickly discovering that looks can be deceiving.

* * *

Twenty minutes later, a text from Derringer instructed me to meet him in the fifth-floor waiting room. It was secluded up there, outside the pediatric ward, but still not the private place I'd hoped for when we talked about interviewing Chris Gallagher.

"You see, Chris, we found some incriminating evidence in your father's home that doesn't look good for Donny," Derringer was saying, already in the thick of it as I approached the brightly colored waiting room. Chris, visibly shaken, sank deeper in the plastic waiting room seat as Derringer stood hulking over him.

"How long has your father been robbing banks?" Derringer asked.

The younger man scowled. "What? That's crazy. Before he got sick my dad was a cop, and a good one."

"Really. Then how is it we found all the elements of the Twilight Bandit's disguise in his bedroom closet?"

"Planted." Chris shook his head. "Someone must have planted that stuff."

Derringer leaned in, training his penetrating eyes on Donny's son. "I want to believe you, Chris. But your story sounds pretty farfetched. I think you've been watching too many crime dramas on TV."

"My father has dementia, for God's sake," Chris said. "He's being used."

"Who's using him?"

Chris turned his head away. "I don't know, and I don't want to talk about it."

"The more you help us . . ."

"Bullshit." Chris spat the word across the room. "You want a fall guy for the robberies and that lady cop's death, and it's easy to pin it on the old guy who can't think straight. But even though he's losing his mind, he's still a good person. He's the go-to guy in the neighborhood, a neighborhood watchman. He keeps a chair near the front window so he can sit and watch over the street. He looks after neighbors, signs for their packages and keeps them safe until they get home from work. He knows the kids' bus schedule and sometimes goes out to the bus stop in front of his house and plays crossing guard so the kids get home safely. My dad is one of the good guys."

"He sounds like a kind man." Derringer grabbed a chair, turned it around, and sat down across from Chris, who folded his arms across his chest. "Look, we found some pretty damning stuff in your father's house, and I think you know more than you're saying."

Chris clenched his jaw and gritted his teeth. "I don't know anything, man."

"Why don't I believe you?"

"That sounds like your problem, not mine." Chris jerked his head to indicate the hospital room where his father lay clinging to life. "My problem is down in ICU, barely breathing."

"What's with all the cookie tins in your old man's house?"

Chris furrowed his brow. "He has a sweet tooth?"

"Some sweet tooth."

Chris pulled his winter jacket closer around him. He was in his twenties, but he was acting like a petulant teenager. I could only assume the stress of his father's beating was taking a toll.

Derringer looked over at me and shrugged.

I shot him a look that said, *Ready for me to take over?*

The FBI agent shook his head and circled Chris again. "I think you can tell me what we found in your old man's house. I think you already know."

"My dad is a pack rat, okay? There's no telling what trash you found stuffed in his closets."

Derringer turned his head sharply. "Closets?" He swiveled to look at me. "Did I mention that we searched Donny's closets?"

"I don't recall you mentioning Donny's closets," I said.

Chris looked up at Derringer, panic crowding his eyes. "I just assumed . . ."

"What did we find in your old man's closets?"

Chris scowled. "Hell if I know."

"But you do know. You were over there every day. You knew what your old man was involved in."

Chris leaned forward and looked over at me. "Would you get Hulk Hogan here off me? He's full of shit, and all I want to know is if my dad's going to make it." He looked Derringer in the eyes. "Not like you give a rat's ass either way. In fact, you'd like my old man to die so you can pin everything on him, write up a lot of paperwork and put a check in your win column, you lazy sonofabitch. Instead of doing real police work like my dad would've done, you're over here harassing me."

Derringer got quiet. "What do we want to pin on your dad, Chris?"

Chris looked up at both of us, his eyes hollow from exhaustion. "How the hell should I know?"

Derringer turned to me and raised an eyebrow. I took the signal, walked over to Chris, and sat down beside him. He smelled like beer, and I wondered if he'd been drinking earlier in the day.

"Hey, it's been a long, stressful day for you. Would you like a Coke? Maybe a sandwich?"

Chris looked up at me with bloodshot eyes. "A Coke would be great. And a cheeseburger?"

I nodded. "There's a fast-food place down on the next block that's open until midnight. I think we should move this conversation to a private room, and then we'll get you something to eat."

I think it was a concession of defeat that Derringer removed himself, offering to go down the block to grab some food. While he was gone, I managed to track down the charge nurse and arranged for the use of a private conference room for an hour or two.

Once we were all settled with burgers, chips, and drinks on the conference table, Chris seemed less agitated. As my father always said, a little food could make a huge difference in temperament. As Chris slowly ate his food, I began lobbing softball questions his way. Derringer sat apart from us, taking notes and staying out of the interrogation. We both saw that Chris responded better to my gentler approach.

Chris relayed how his dad had started to decline around five or six years ago while he was still on the force. At first it had been hard for the family to confront Donny about his declining mental state, but Chris's mom had made it easier on everyone, smoothing things over with that grace she possessed. Once Donny had accepted the dementia diagnosis, he was pretty easy to handle. He willingly stopped driving, and he was pretty good about taking his medication, but the one thing Donny hadn't wanted to do was retire. He cried to his family about how much he was going to miss his "brothers in blue." Chris's mom had intervened, stirring up some support from the cops, and the department bigwigs had been pretty kind to Donny, at first. Cribben had asked if Donny could come in a couple of times a week to help him with department odds and ends, and many of the older cops would invite Donny out to lunch with them or take him golfing on their days off.

"Sounds like it worked out relatively well for your dad," I said.

"It did . . . at first."

"What went wrong?"

Chris hesitated, looking toward the hallway. "The doctors know I'm in here, right? They'll come get me if he wakes up."

"Your father is sedated," I assured him. "The nurses expect him to sleep through the night at least, and they do know we're in here."

"I can't lose him now," Chris said. "I need to make him proud. I want him to see me graduate from college and follow in his footsteps and join the force."

"You mean, the police department?" Derringer asked.

Chris nodded. "That's the plan."

He was lying.

I wrapped up my half-eaten burger, my appetite waning. There was no way Chris would be hired onto a police force with two DUI convictions and a history of shoplifting. Worse, from the looks of his bloated belly, I figured Chris for an alcoholic. Any one of these facts would've kept Chris from joining the force, and as the son of a cop, Chris would know this. Bottom line: Donny's son was lying to us.

I changed tactics. "You seem a little uncomfortable around some of your dad's cop buddies." I was going out on a limb, but back at Donny's house I had noticed the way Chris had shied away from Brown and Rivers.

"Do I?"

"You know, like Cranston, Brown, and Rivers . . . those guys. And Chief Cribben. Did he come around to see your dad, too?" I asked, recalling the way Cribben had toted Donny around at the holiday party.

Chris nodded. "The chief used to take Dad golfing."

"But not anymore?"

"Last time was probably six months ago. I think Cribben just lost interest. At first, all his cop buddies thought they were being really kind to Dad." He snorted. "I should've known better. They manipulated him even when he was healthy. They bullied him, mocked him."

"How did they manipulate him?" I asked.

"They pushed him, convincing him that it was all right to do their dirty work."

"What kind of dirty work?"

Chris looked up at me. "You know."

"They set him up to rob the banks," I said, watching Chris for a reaction.

"They created the Twilight Bandit, the old guy who strikes after dark, takes the money, and disappears. No gun. No one gets hurt. The cops protect the bandit. And everyone shares the money."

There is was—the scheme laid out for us.

Derringer looked over at me, but I didn't want to look away and break the connection I had with Donny.

"Did Donny enjoy being the Twilight Bandit?" I asked.

"In the beginning. It was like a game to him, and it made his friends so happy."

"But that didn't last, did it? Did they argue about money?"

"They didn't let Dad keep his fair share." Chris crumpled up his napkin, his eyes flared with anger. "They cheated my father. Somebody was getting rich off those robberies, but it wasn't Dad. They set him up to take all of the risk and cheated him. Bastards."

"Tell me how they did it, Chris."

He scoffed. "Rat on the rats?"

I nodded. "They used your dad. They don't deserve your protection."

He let out a disgusted puff of air. "Dad carried out the burglaries with the glasses and the wig and those stupid hats. And the SLPD cops found different ways to slow response times so Dad could get away." Chris popped the last chip in his mouth and crumpled up the bag. "You know those cookie tins you found in Dad's kitchen?"

I nodded.

"That's how the money got passed around."

"Really?" I remembered Donny at the holiday party carrying a blue cookie tin. And then there was Mayor Redmond's wife carrying a load of those tins in to her aunt Peg. Were they all involved? "So they moved cash in the cookie tins?"

"Yup. But somehow, most of the cash seemed to be moving out of Dad's house. I think they rooked him."

"Who was cheating him? Who on the SLPD was getting your dad to rob banks?" I leaned in close, trying to get Chris to trust me enough to hand me the masterminds.

He slid further down in his chair. For a second, he looked like a miserable teen I'd just had to ground for a month.

"I don't know who's really in charge. I mean, Brown and Cranston are questionable. They both hung out all the time with my dad, taking him to lunch. Both make fun of him a fair amount. Especially Brown. And Rivers used to be in on the weekend golfing with the chief."

Chris laid his head down on the table. When he lifted it again, he looked twenty years older. He explained how he'd always thought Cranston was a true friend to his father, but now he wasn't sure about anything. "The whole scheme might go all the way up the chain to Cribben," he said. "Maybe even up to the mayor."

It was a big tale to swallow. Dolly's husband, mayor of our town. Blue cookie tins. A failing officer turned robber to impress his buddies, and a few rotten cops pulling the strings. Inside my boots, my toes wriggled as my mind flitted over the possibilities.

"You may not know this, Detective Mori," Chris continued, "but my dad was a good cop. There's no way he could've pulled this stuff off by himself. After my mom died four years ago, Dad's memory went downhill fast. It was like she held him together somehow, but he became unraveled after she passed. I'm not sure which cops are pulling the strings behind this operation, but they're trying to pin it on an old man with dementia."

"We get that, Chris," I said sympathetically. "And I like your dad. He's got a big heart. But three years ago, the crime spree went beyond bank hits. Franny Landon was murdered during the last robbery."

"No!" Chris straightened up and leaned forward. "You've got that part wrong." His mouth was a grim line as he looked from Derringer to me. "Dad had nothing to do with that lady cop's death. My dad would never kill anybody."

"Not even if he got spooked during the robbery? Maybe he got cornered and panicked?"

"No. Dad told me he was already running from the bank when it happened. Dad heard a shot behind him, but he didn't stop running. He just kept going. The whole thing freaked him out."

"Homicide tends to do that to people," Derringer chimed in, driving the point home.

"And he ran from a victim, Chris," I pointed out. "He wasn't concerned enough to stop and help."

"He wasn't in his right mind." Chris didn't shrink from our criticism. "I know it looks bad for Dad, but he was completely undone by the news of Franny's death. It threw him into a new depression for weeks. Made him afraid of the dark. Made it hard to get him out of the house, even out of bed. He was angry and confused, and I couldn't get him out of it that winter. Proven by the fact he stopped robbing banks. Finally in the spring, he packed up his bandit stuff. Sealed his fake glasses and hat and wig in a box and promised never to rob another bank as long as he lived. And that was the end of that."

"But someone quite similar to the Twilight Bandit hit a bank this week." I looked Chris dead in the eyes. "Maybe your dad decided to come out of retirement one last time and not tell you. Maybe he missed the thrill of the chase after all."

I realized this was something of a stretch—that the bandit on camera seemed younger, and that Donny would have had to learn how to write well with his right hand to pull off the subterfuge. Still, I threw it out there.

This time, Chris didn't take the bait. "You saw my father. He doesn't have an ounce of aggression left. Do you really think he has enough grit left to do a bank heist?" He shrugged and looked away. "Can I get another Coke?"

As I went down the hall to the soda vending machine, I realized Chris was right about his father's level of skills. I didn't think Donny had the clarity, stamina, or will to pull off the bank robbery at First Sunrise. Plus, the new bandit appeared to be right-handed, opening up the field of candidates wide enough to drive a truck through. I wondered if Donny's cop friends had been grooming a replacement for Donny. Someone new to carry on the work. If so, were they planning another hit sometime soon?

Derringer tapped me on the shoulder and motioned with his head that we should talk privately.

"One second." I popped back into the conference room and handed Chris his can of soda. "You're free to go, Chris. If you want to wait here, we'll go see about your dad's condition."

He looked drained, but he nodded.

Outside the conference room, Derringer raked his dark hair back with one hand, his eyes skeptical.

"Nice work in there," he said, looking down, suddenly fascinated by his shoes.

"Thanks . . . I think."

He looked up quickly. "No, no, you did a great job at getting Chris to spill his guts. Seriously, you just cracked Chris Gallagher open like a sunny-side-up egg. Good job."

"You got him started," I said, trying to share the credit. It had been a team effort, and the ramifications of Chris's statement were still settling in my mind. Donny had robbed the banks, but his accomplices were among my colleagues. That part was pretty awful.

"Where do you want to go from here?" Derringer asked.

"We have confirmation that Donny is the Twilight Bandit. I suspect that when we compare hair samples from that wig from our crime scenes and check the logos on those baseball caps, we're going to find a match to the Twilight Bandit."

Derringer ran his fingertips over the scar on his head. "You're right. I hope the county lab can get to that evidence quickly. And with integrity. Maybe I should run it up to our lab in Seattle. I'm leery of trusting the local facility, all things considered."

All the evidence collected at tonight's crime scene was being processed at our county lab. "Rex will handle it. He's thorough, and you and I will make sure to follow up on everything. But the bank thefts are only part of the case. We have strong evidence that Donny is the Twilight Bandit, but Chris's statement about the homicide rings true for me. I think someone else is behind the shooting of Franny Landon."

"I agree," Derringer said. "From his profile, Donny Gallagher didn't seem to have the guts for a crime of violence. The Landon murder is almost another case altogether."

"And then there's the case of Donny's assault," I said. "Who did that do him, and was their intention to keep him from spilling the truth about the Twilight case? If some of our cops were accessories in the robberies, maybe they were afraid that as Donny became more debilitated, he might spill the incriminating truth."

"Right." He frowned. "And there's where things get complicated. You've been threatened twice regarding the Twilight case, Laura. Twice in two days. And then tonight, someone busts into Donny's house and assaults him, an attack that's probably related to the Twilight robberies."

"I understand the seriousness." I squinted at him. "What are you saying?"

"Maybe you should step off this case for a while. Until the heat dies down."

I blinked up at him. Step away? But I was part of the investigation.

My cheeks flamed with indignation. Would he have suggested this to a male detective? Probably not. Though I suspected his intentions came from a place of protection.

I stood tall, arms folded across my chest. "Really, I'm surprised you would even think that way." I couldn't help myself; I had to ask. "Are you advising me to back off the case because I'm a woman?"

"What? No, that's not it. It's the fact that you've been targeted, twice. I would recommend it for anyone who's been targeted, male or female." He didn't seem flustered, which made me suspect he was being honest.

"I appreciate your concern," I said, "but detective work is what I do. If someone doesn't like that, well, I think I have the tools to defend myself if push comes to shove."

"I'm sure you studied self-defense," he said.

"In the academy, not too long ago." I fixed my gaze on his dark eyes. "So, Agent Derringer, you're not going to get rid of me that easily."

"That wasn't my intent."

"Of course it wasn't." I smiled at him, working hard to hide any trace of insecurity over his suggestion that I surrender.

"I just wanted to give you an out. For your safety. But anyway, I guess we should go check on Donny," he said. "If he's conscious, we might be able to get a statement from him, especially now that his son is talking."

"Of course," I said for the second time, feeling a new strain between us.

"And I think it would be wise to have a cop sitting on Donny. If Chris is right, there are some cops in your department who see Donny as a liability."

"He needs protection," I said, annoyed that I hadn't thought of that myself. "I'll call Omak and see if he can assign someone here."

* * *

In Donny's hospital room, nothing had changed. A nurse checked his vitals and fussed with the machines that beeped and squawked beside him. The doctor appeared and repeated the information from earlier. For now Donny was heavily sedated, his prognosis guarded. It was a game of wait-and-see.

Derringer excused himself to make a call to his supervisor in Seattle, and I lingered beside the former cop's bed. He seemed fragile and gray under the bandages and tubing. Taking his hand, I squeezed his cold fingers and listened to the intermittent beeps from machines that constantly measured his vital signs.

"Who did this to you, Donny?" I asked the battered man.

We might not know for a week or two or ever. In the meantime, a good detective would follow the trail to wherever it led. And I was a good detective, despite whatever weird vibe Derringer was giving me.

It was time to look more deeply into Donny Gallagher. Who would have profited from Donny's robberies? And who would have something to lose if he was caught? I didn't know these answers . . . yet.

For tonight, I would wait here until a night shift officer arrived to take his or her post as Donny's guard. After all, he was a suspect now. A suspect someone had assaulted, and I wasn't about to let that happen again.

I gently rubbed a spot on Donny's arm that wasn't attached to medical paraphernalia. "You, my friend, are going to be in protective custody. Sleep well."

19

That night, when I called the lieutenant to check in from the hospital, he told me to go home and get some rest. "You've just worked a traumatic crime scene," Omak said. "Sometimes the shock and violence don't hit until later. Go home. Tomorrow is soon enough to start with report writing. Start your shift later in the morning so you can sleep. By then you'll have some forensic reports on the crime scene at Gallagher's house. The lab might even have some analysis on the Twilight Bandit evidence found at Donny's place."

"I'd love to have some answers tomorrow," I said.

"We'll try for that. For now, get some rest."

Exhaustion was so heavy on my brain that I didn't argue with him as I pulled out of the hospital parking lot. Zombielike, I headed home, letting out giant, tearful yawns at each traffic light. Maybe sleep would help remove the image of Donny sprawled awkwardly in a pool of blood. Maybe rest would alleviate some of my misgivings over discovering the connection between this seemingly sweet, failing man and a string of bank robberies that had ended with a homicide. Yes, it would be awesome to close the case, but I didn't want to ruin an already diminished life in the process.

And then there was Derringer, the guy who made my heart race, the guy who'd shown me how brown eyes could warm you like a sip of sherry. Something had flipped with him tonight, and I couldn't put my finger on it. Was he really trying to get me off the case, or just pointing out the danger of being targeted? I couldn't get a good bead on Derringer, but that shouldn't have bothered me. And somehow it did bother me. I felt we were on the edge of cracking these intertwined cases wide open, and after they were solved, Derringer would go back to Seattle and we wouldn't work together anymore.

That really bothered me.

I was glad to see Natalie's small car parked in front of the house, but when I got inside, her door was closed, the house quiet with one lone light on. She'd gone to bed, which was where I needed to go, too. But before I could relax, I needed to scrub off the negative images of my checkered day.

The steamy water of the shower was refreshing, and I lathered up in sweet-smelling soap and then stood with my face in the stream of water. My friend Becca, who was always dabbling in mystical things like tarots and crystal balls and Reiki, had told me that sometimes needy souls attached themselves to you, and the only way to cleanse them was to rinse in cold water. No cold water for me, but I liked the image of washing away clingy spirits.

As I shampooed my hair, I thought of Donny Gallagher, pale and bruised in the hospital bed. I tried to imagine him moving through banks, writing the notes, slipping them to the teller, then moving briskly out of the building, but courteously holding the door. Could he have pulled off the robberies three years ago?

Feasible, if he'd possessed sharper cognitive skills and a pur-pose. He still had a dead-on aim in darts, and he seemed fiercely loyal to his friends, his cop buddies. I could see him pulling the bank hits for the game of it. A way to please his buddies without really hurting anyone.

Until Franny Landon was killed.

Hard to imagine Donny gunning down a woman in cold blood. What had Dr. Viloria said about the projectile of the bullet? The shooter was above Franny, and far away. If Donny had been running from his crime, he wasn't the shooter. But who was? There was no way to visualize that crime scene without going there. I needed to go to the scene, explore the property around the bank.

I rinsed the conditioner out, shut off the water, and stepped out into the steam, which swirled around the open slit of the window. It was up above eye level, but it made me feel vulnerable, exposed to the world. With a towel pressed against my chest, I slammed it shut and locked it. Done.

I wrapped a towel around my head, pulled on my fluffy robe, and texted Z to see if he was still up.

He called back right away. "It's late, Mori. You okay?"

I fell back against the pillows of my bed. "Just tired. Today was a *seriously* long day."

"But a great day, right?" The pride was evident in Z's voice. "I mean, you caught him! You caught the Twilight Bandit! Case closed, right?"

"If the evidence checks out, one case will be closed, Donny's assault is a new one, and there's another still unsolved. It appears that Donny wasn't the shooter. But then you always suspected that, didn't you?"

"Yeah, there's something shady about that whole night."

"Which brings me to my issue. A favor."

"Mori, I've granted enough wishes today. We'll talk tomorrow."

"We need to visit the bank in the morning. Late morning. We both need sleep."

"We getting a joint bank account?"

"Not at Pacific Lake Bank. You're going to give me a tour of the premises."

"Crap."

"Tomorrow morning."

"Do we have to do this? You've solved the damn case."

"Not the homicide. Besides, I need some visuals to get the shooting straight in my head before I can write up this report."

"Mori . . ." He let out a gritty sigh. "The things I do for you."

"It won't take that long. Thanks, Z. Sleep well."

*　*　*

By the time I arrived at work on Thursday morning, there were two trucks from Portland TV news networks in the parking lot, which was crowded with cars and pedestrian traffic. On closer observation, people seemed to be packing up and leaving. While searching for a spot, I saw Natalie standing off to the side of the precinct door, speaking in front of the camera.

Something had happened.

"There was a short press conference called by Chief Cribben," Natalie explained after I'd parked the car and run over to catch her. "It ended a while ago . . . almost thirty minutes. He announced that the Twilight Bandit has been caught."

It was like a punch in the face. The police chief had announced the progress on my case, and no one had mentioned it to me. "Oh, really?" I played dumb.

"I know, it's a shocker, after all these years," Natalie agreed. "It's big news, but the chief was somber, given the circumstances. The bandit was a retired cop, suffering from dementia. Donny Gallagher. Possible motive is that the poor guy needed the money for medical bills."

Medical bills? Thanks to the city of Sunrise Lake, police officers retired with excellent medical insurance coverage. I suspected that this detail was one of the mayor's fabrications to alter the background of the story and hide any hints of what had actually happened to the money stolen from the bank.

"I'm sorry I missed that," I said. "Since I worked so much overtime last night, I decided to come in later today."

"You didn't miss much," Natalie said. "Considering the way Chief Cribben likes to boast, there was a minimum of fanfare. Here's a copy of the press release with the salient details. You can keep that. I have plenty."

I glanced down at it. "Did the chief happen to mention who was responsible for the apprehension of the suspected bandit?"

"He didn't mention any names. Just said 'our detectives.'" Natalie's eyes opened wide. "Was this your case?"

"It is, but that's off the record," I said.

As Natalie gushed about how unfair it was to take credit for other people's work, I scanned the press release. There was no mention that Donny had been assaulted. Only that he was being hospitalized for "injuries sustained during his arrest."

"What the hell?" I muttered.

"You okay?" Natalie asked.

I nodded. "But I need to go. A meeting with the boss." Fuming, I ducked inside, hoping the fury wasn't burning in my complexion.

* * *

"I relayed the details of the assault on Donny and the potential evidence found at Donny's house. For obvious reasons, I didn't give the chief information about Chris Gallagher's testimony regarding the Sunrise Lake cops allegedly involved with the bank robberies." With a look of disgust, Omak tossed the press release onto his desk. "This is what the chief had our communications officer write up. It's embarrassing, yes. Downright false. I tried to make some corrections, but Cribben shut me down. When all is said and done, the man outranks me."

"Can you take it up with the mayor?" I asked. "Cribben is lying to the media."

"Mori, the press is the least of our worries right now. You're working on a case that involved possible police corruption, a network that might even involve the chief of police. From here on, it's going to be difficult reporting any developments on this case to Chief Cribben. Until we're ready to press charges, I'll try to handle communications with the chief. In the meantime, be careful."

"I will, Lieu."

"Not just the usual precautions. Stick with a partner. Donny's attack was brutal, and you've been threatened twice over this Twilight case. Someone wants to stop the truth from getting out, and

I'm skeptical that it's really about the Twilight Bandit anymore. I think we'll find that evidence proves Donny pulled those robberies."

"But not the homicide," I said.

"Exactly. But until Donny can tell us more about the robberies and Franny's murder, we'll have to let the chief's false narrative ride."

I nodded, agreeing with Omak's line of logic.

Today's walk-through at the bank might help me visualize things and see the path of Franny's killer. Time for a walk in his shoes.

20

Z hated this place.

The hedges. That fence. The friendly sign for the pre-school with a gingerbread man on it. The perfectly spaced boxwood shrubs that lined the garden at the end of the parking lot. He even hated the tinsel decorations that the city strung on lampposts for holiday season. These were the landmarks of his nightmares.

The small garden and fence that separated the parking lot of Lou's Barber Shop from the Pacific Lake Bank shouldn't have raised the hair on the back of Z's neck, but it did. This was where he'd chased a robbery suspect the night of Franny's death.

Three years, and he still hated these Christmas bells. He didn't understand why the lady in the sleek blue BMW would want to beeline into the parking lot and saunter to the ATM of the bank that haunted him on this Friday morning. He didn't know why anyone would put their kids into that preschool with the weird winking gingerbread boy on the sign. Actually, he didn't know why anyone would want to have kids, anyway.

Z sunk down into the passenger seat and slammed the car door shut. "How long do we have to stay here?"

"Long enough for me to get the lay of the land." Laura handed him a paper cup from the patrol car. They had to ride around in a marked car today because Laura's headlight was getting repaired and Z's rust bucket with its growling muffler was deemed too unprofessional. "You didn't even touch your mocha. With whipped cream."

"You're killing me, Mori." She knew he had a weakness for the sweet drink, but he didn't want a mocha right now, and no amount of whipped cream would ease his mind as he wandered the street where Franny had been shot dead. Many of the details from that horrific night were a blank space in his memory, but sometimes images came back to him in a rush of nightmares that woke him in a cold sweat. He didn't want to go there.

But Laura looked determined, and yeah, he wanted to help her find Franny's killer. Maybe if he walked the scene with Laura, well, maybe he'd come up with something to help move the investigation.

Z took a deep breath and nodded. He listened intently as Laura laid out the details of the case that most cops on the force didn't know: the ballistics report indicated Franny had been shot from a distance of at least twenty yards and from an elevated spot, which made it highly unlikely that she was shot by Donny as he fled from the robbery.

"Seriously?" Z picked at the bottom edge of the paper cup. "Where'd you hear that?"

"It's not hearsay," Laura told him. "It's from the coroner's report in the FBI file."

"Really. And no one followed up on it?"

"Apparently. I went over the report with Dr. Viloria. The information is solid."

Z rubbed the back of his neck, trying to process the fact that someone had been sitting on this. "Cranston is a scumbag. This was his case, and he dropped the ball."

"Right. But now I'm picking it up and trying to run with it. My question is, who did the shooting and from where?"

Z took a breath. "So, what do you need from me?"

"Give me the lay of the land," Laura said. "Where did Franny go down? Where was the gun found? And show me where you were when it all happened."

"All right. I'll try." Z could feel his blood begin to pound in his temples. Just being back here made his skin crawl with perspiration and guilt. The bank was a wedge-shaped building on a parcel of property with a front door that opened up to Bloom Street. At the wide end of the bank, the rear doors and the ATM all faced the parking lot and Fir Street. Lou's Barber Shop sat beside the bank in the plumb corner spot, though their parking lots were separated by a tall fence.

As they stepped out of the car to walk the property, Z's heartbeat began to accelerate, thrumming in his ears. Images of that night flashed in his mind: the adrenaline, the gunshot, the shock of watching a life slip away.

He tried to swallow back some of the tension as Laura scanned the perimeter. "Was that preschool across the street there three years ago?"

"With that winking gingerbread man that creeps me out?" Z nodded, swiping the moisture from his forehead with the back of one hand.

"You okay?" Laura touched his shoulder. "You're sweating in December."

"Let's just get through this, okay?" Imagining a steady straight line, Z steeled himself to keep his emotions as flat as that line as he walked Laura through what he remembered of that night.

Three years ago, he had been riding with Franny when they got the call for a bank robbery in progress. They'd arrived on the scene just in time to see two men leaving the bank parking lot in separate directions. Franny had followed one suspect on foot around a fenced enclosure at the bank parking lot on Fir. Z had followed the second suspect, fleeing on a bike through the drive-through on the opposite side of the bank. It turned out that Z's mark had been a restaurant worker on a fifteen-minute break from his job. Z had been taking down his information when he heard Franny shout. "I ran across the parking lot to find Franny and saw her lying on the ground behind the fence over there." He pointed to the corner of Fir and Bloom streets.

When he'd reached her, Franny had been unconscious. And there had been blood. So much blood. She'd been shot in the head, though Z hadn't known that then. He'd begun CPR prior to the paramedics' arrival—at least that's what Brown and Rivers had written in their reports. That part was a blank in his mind.

He led Laura around the fenced-in area to the thin strip of grass in front of the barbershop where he had found Franny.

"She went down right there. I don't remember much at that point except starting CPR." He glanced back toward the barbershop, because even three years later he still had trouble looking at that patch of ground. The shop wasn't open yet, which explained the lone car sitting in the lot.

"You can't see this intersection from the bank, and even if the exterior cameras had been working, none of them pointed around the fence," Z said.

"But the barbershop has a prime view," Laura pointed out, "And they were open at the time."

"Right, but those frosted windows kept anyone inside from seeing what was going on out here." Z had to force himself to keep breathing. Even working with the shrink for more than a year hadn't helped all that much with the nightmares or the night sweats or the feeling of doom hanging over his head when he woke up.

In the months after Franny's murder, Cranston and Brown had taunted him.

"You need help, man," Cranston had told him. "You got it bad."

"The department has a shrink, you know. I mean, you walk around here all the time like you want to put a fist through the wall," Brown had needled him.

Back then Z hadn't wanted to punch walls as much as he'd wanted to punch his fellow SLPD officers, who seemed to want to get over her murder without catching the dirtbag who had killed her. Whatever had happened to backing up a fellow officer?

"I'm just saying, you want someone to talk to, you could do worse than Dr. Mack," Brown had told him.

"Thanks for the helpful advice, guys," Z kept telling them. "You're really the best." He'd walked away as if he hadn't heard them, though he'd found himself calling the confidential phone number and making an appointment with the police shrink. He'd wanted to meet with someone who knew the stresses of police work, and he knew Dr. MacKenzie floated between several police departments in the region. He'd figured he couldn't get worse talking to her, right?

Meeting with the shrink in her office was about the only time he'd let himself go, let himself express doubt that this case was far from settled. It was the first time he'd been able to say out loud that a cop had been killed and the department had missed the truth, though Z wasn't even sure what that was. Dr. Mack had suggested that he needed to return to the scene to help lay things to rest in his mind, and this morning, walking the parking lot with Laura by his side, Z was beginning to see the merit in her advice.

They moved beyond the bank fence and past the barbershop to the intersection of Bloom and Fir, where a garland was now strung across Bloom Street and ornaments like large tinsel bells and stars dangled high over the road.

That garland had been up when Franny was killed. The image of a fake bell dangling silently overhead filled his mind.

"That damn bell . . ." Z pointed to the decoration on the lamppost. "I remember hearing it while I was doing CPR. But it doesn't ring. No clapper."

Laura touched his shoulder. "You were probably in shock."

"Probably. According to the reports, the gun was tossed in those bushes over there." This time, Z pointed to a well-manicured hedge that lined the fence on the bank side of the property. "I think Cranston found it."

Laura folded her arms over her chest and looked from the patch where Franny had fallen to the row of bushes where the shooter had tossed the gun.

"Something doesn't make sense here," Laura said. "If the bandit was fleeing past the barbershop and Franny followed him, why would the shooter come back this way to throw the gun away?"

"Exactly." Z folded his arms across his chest. "Why would the shooter kill a cop and then run toward the victim to dispose of the firearm? This murder investigation has never made sense."

Laura turned and walked back down the street, just far enough so that she could look into the parking lot of the bank. "I've always had a hard time picturing this crime scene. Now I get it. The fan shape of the bank lot is unusual, and I've been looking at the satellite images on Google Earth. But those photos don't show sight lines from the ground, and some of them were taken during the summer months, when all the trees around here have leaves on them."

Z spread his arms wide. "In the winter, with all the branches bare, you can easily see the preschool across the street, and the office building beyond that." He pointed in the direction of the school.

Laura swiveled to take in the 360-degree view of the bank, its parking lot, the preschool across the street, and the barbershop on the corner. "Yeah, I see it now," she said.

Bells jingled over at the barbershop as the door opened and a guy rolled out an industrial vacuum. The cleaning crew. He nodded at Z and Laura on his way to his car.

Z pointed to the door of the barbershop. "That's where the bell sound came from." There'd been a brisk wind that night, and Z had never forgotten the sound of the bells hanging on the shop door. He'd hooked his mind on to the soft tinkling sound, letting it pull him away from the chaos. The wreaths had swayed in the breeze, and he'd heard the cheerful chimes that had seemed so out of place in the nightmare that had occupied him. The part he couldn't remember past dropping to the ground beside Franny, trying to keep her alive with CPR.

Had he done everything possible to save her life? Damn, he wanted to know he'd done the right thing and not curled up like a coward. But he had his doubts. Why?

Had someone pushed him away from Franny?

I'll take over.

Someone had come along and taken over CPR. Standing here now, Z was pretty sure that was a memory and not a fantasy.

Had it just been the paramedics?

No. Before the paramedics came, someone had been there to take over the grueling task. But who?

Someone from the barbershop? Someone from the bank?

Z was on the verge of remembering. One more session with Dr. Mack and maybe he'd get the whole picture.

He wished Dr. Mack were here now . . . leading him to the truth.

So damned close.

"Hello, Officers. Is there something I can do for you?" The bank manager had noticed Laura and Z walking around the parking lot and come out to inquire. Z was too shaken to answer, but luckily Laura knew the manager, a friend of her brother, and struck up a friendly conversation. She was good at that, and Z was grateful he could skate out on talking to anyone. He was shaking inside.

He went to the patrol car and ducked inside. As soon as he slid into the seat and heard the thud of the door closing, he crumbled. Memories from that night were crowding his mind, and Z shut his eyes and tried to erase the scene of Franny's death. It was too much.

"Something's not right with you," Z's mother had told him at Sunday dinner. And she'd been right. Z had been haunted for years by a murder he couldn't remember, and it was draining him. "It's like a tiger's got you by the tail, and you can't shake it loose," she'd told him.

But something was coming loose. As Z waited at the intersection of Bloom and Fir, glancing from the barbershop on his right to the preschool on his left, scraps of memory came to him. A flash of light in the dark. Cranston and Brown arguing. Or maybe they were shouting, but about what? And that tinkling bell, the cold blast of wind on Z's cheek, and an eerily calm voice next to him, in his ear. Warning him? Threatening him? Z couldn't remember, and he trembled, knowing that the key was locked somewhere in his memory, somewhere dark and distant and unreachable.

But it was there.

And as Dr. Mack had told him, if it was there, someday it would float to the surface.

21

After our survey of the bank property, Z claimed he wasn't hungry, but I drove to the Covered Wagon Diner anyway, knowing he'd bounce back once he got a whiff of bacon and griddle cakes.

"As promised, breakfast is on me," I said. "Since I dragged you out under protest." He hadn't wanted to revisit the bank property, but now that it was over, I was grateful he'd made the sacrifice.

"Thanks, Mori." He looked up at the waitress and handed her his menu. "In that case, I'll take the Wild West Breakfast Special."

"Sausage or bacon?" asked the waitress.

"Both."

"Whipped on the pancakes?"

"Sure."

"Seriously?" I lowered my menu. "Why don't you get sprinkles and chocolate chips, too?"

Z flashed the waitress a hopeful look. "Can I?"

"Of course. That's called the Slappy Pappy."

"The Slappy Pappy," I said, reading from the menu. "'For hungry little whippersnappers.'"

"Whoa, wait now. Sounds like I'm ten," Z said. "Just give me chocolate chips and whipped."

"Fruit or hash browns?"

"Hash browns, always."

The waitress, a thick teen with a nice smile and blonde hair that lobbed over one eye, scribbled away and then turned to me.

"I'd like two poached eggs with whole wheat toast and fruit," I said.

"You're always on a diet, Mori," Z said.

"That's right. A normal one," I retorted, though I was glad to see Z's appetite and soul had returned. Once the waitress headed off, I had to ask him one question. "Was it as bad as you expected, returning to the scene of the trauma?"

He slid the pepper shaker to his right hand, then back to his left. "Actually, not so bad. No picnic, but I think it jogged my memory some."

"Care to share?"

"I'll let you know, once I've gone over it with Dr. Mack. She's helping me separate my raw memories from nightmare visions. And she thinks I'm getting better at it with time. Feels like I'm getting closer. I need to see if she can fit me in tonight or tomorrow."

"Is she a good psychologist?" I asked. My impression from the Christmas party had been a woman of sophistication and poise—two qualities I didn't possess.

"I think so. But can we talk about something that's not going to ruin a good meal?"

"Sure. But thanks for showing me around. It helps having a picture in my head."

Z seemed lost in the matching salt and pepper shakers, and I felt a twinge of guilt for dragging him to the bank today. It wasn't good to be personally involved in a case; I knew that. But I couldn't help but think that Z's post-traumatic stress would ease if Franny's killer was arrested. It made me want to solve this case that much more. "So . . ." I floundered, trying to change the subject. "Got any plans for this weekend?"

He took a swig of orange juice. "Natalie wants to go to the Grotto, see the lights, hear some Christmas music."

"Aw. That's so romantic."

He shook his head. "You are going to destroy my reputation, Mori. And I hope we're done scoping out locations for your case, because now that we found all those souvenirs at Gallagher's house, I've got a truckload of inventory to match up, and I need to get over to the adult community and start getting people to ID Donny as the cop impersonator."

"You can get back on it," I said. "Thanks for helping me out."

"You're welcome. And I will let you pay for this meal."

After that we didn't chat much—hard to talk over a mouthful of pancakes, eggs, bacon, sausage, and whatever else was on Z's platter—but it was an easy silence, as my thoughts went to the case that Z couldn't really be involved with anyway.

* * *

I let Z drive back to the precinct as I texted Omak and asked him to pull some personnel files for me. It was an unusual request, and I felt a little squeamish asking for personal information on my colleagues, but if the line of suspicion pointed in their direction, they needed to be scrutinized.

We arrived at the office with two cups of black coffee from the Wagon Wheel and headed straight to Omak's office, where I found Omak pacing as he ended a phone call. Derringer's desk was empty, and I remembered he'd gone to Seattle to run evidence up to the FBI lab this morning. I didn't want to admit that I missed him.

"I come bearing coffee and some new information." I handed Omak a cup, barely able to contain my latest discovery. "Can we try to get Derringer on speaker phone, so he stays in the loop?"

"Absolutely."

It took a few minutes, but Derringer was able to find an empty office and call us back.

"How's it going up there?" I asked cheerfully. "I was just going over the grounds of Pacific Lake Bank with Z, trying to get the coordinates clear in my head."

Omak nodded, removing the black lid from the cup. "I just got off the phone with the branch manager. He was concerned."

"Well, I'm glad he's on his toes," I said. "The layout of that branch is crucial in figuring out the homicide from the Twilight hits. If Donny is the Twilight Bandit, the glaring question stemming from those robberies becomes, who shot Franny?"

As I sat down in a chair, I was aware of Derringer's silence. Was he curious, intrigued, loving my initiative or resentful of it? I wish I could read him better.

"Any theories, Laura?" Omak asked, leaning against the window frame.

"I don't have particular suspects in mind, but I think I know where the shooter was positioned. The coroner's report shows the angle of two bullets that entered Franny's body came from above her. A significant height, and a significant distance away. So the fleeing bandit could not have shot her from the street."

"I don't think I've seen this report," Omak said.

"It was in the FBI file," I said. "Somehow it dropped out of our case."

Omak crossed his arms. "Okay. We know the bullet came from a .38 automatic. What was the range?"

I swallowed hard. "The coroner estimates anywhere from twenty to twenty-five yards."

Omak whistled, a piercing sound that slid down the scale quickly. "Wow, that would be an impressive couple of shots."

"I know. It's a challenge to hit a target that far away with a handgun," Derringer said, "but it can be done."

"Yes," I said, pitching forward in my chair just a little. "It indicates that our expert shooter is former military or trained in law enforcement."

"But the height . . ." Omak began. "How could that happen from street level?"

"I just found a higher vantage point as I was walking the crime scene with Z. Across the street from the bank parking lot, there's a preschool with a tall play structure. Half the year it's completely obscured from sight by a small grove of oak trees. But in the winter, you can clearly see it from the bank parking lot."

While Z had waited for me in the car, I'd quickly run over to check out the lay of the land at the preschool, where toddlers had been wandering over the soft rubbery surface and moving plastic trucks in the sandbox. I had shown my ID to one of the teachers, who had let me explore the schoolyard for a few minutes. Near the edge of the fence closest to the bank parking lot was a colorful play structure with a metal slide attached. I'd climbed to the top and peered over. Voilà! A perfect view of the section of the parking lot where Franny had been gunned down. I think the teacher was a little surprised when I went down the slide, but one of the kids got a chuckle out of it.

"What kind of psycho hides in a child's play structure to gun down a police officer?" Omak whispered across his desk. I saw, for the first time, the deep shadows that lived under Omak's eyes, the strain of his sister's death written all over his face.

"A killer," Derringer said simply.

Omak took off his glasses and wiped at his eyes. "I'm sorry."

"She was your sister. You never have to apologize for your grief," I said.

Omak exhaled. "Thank you. Both of you. I can't tell you how good it is to know that you two are on the trail of a murder that should've been solved years ago." He nodded toward the door. "I'm going to grab some fresh air."

"Sure." I stood so that Omak could easily exit the cramped office.

Derringer waited a few seconds, then spoke. "I think you're onto something, Laura. And the time of day . . . it was after five when the shooting happened, right? There wouldn't have been kids on the playground in the cold, after dark."

"Right," I said. "The preschool's latest pickup time is six, but at that time of year, the children are always playing indoors at the end of the day."

"So the killer struck from the play structure?"

"There's nowhere else in the vicinity with the kind of height and trajectory needed to fit the ballistics report on Franny." I exhaled. It felt like forever since I'd breathed out. "It's the only place that makes sense."

"Play structures are pretty small, and our killer was more than likely a guy. I know *you* fit up there, but could a man comfortably fit and get a good shot?"

"I'm not *that* small, Agent Derringer." Was he flirting with me? I was probably reading too much into his attempt at humor.

"I'm six three. Would I fit up there?"

I thought of his broad shoulders and long legs, and my cheeks burned. I was glad this wasn't a video conference.

"You'd fit," I said. "Not comfortably, but I'm sure you could get up and down."

"But it was nearly total darkness when Franny was shot," Derringer countered.

"I thought about that," I countered. "The parking lot and street by the bank are fairly well lit, not a real problem for a good marksman."

Derringer tugged at his necktie, considering these new facts. "If the shooter was at the school, it would point to premeditated murder. Not a spontaneous shooting. The killer planned it. He was in position to shoot when the robbery went down."

"True." I nodded, having considered the same line of logic. It meant that the shooter was in deep, not just someone acting recklessly or in self-defense. Franny's death had been planned.

Omak returned to his office, looking composed and serious. The storm had passed. "Thank you, Officers. I'm ready to hear more."

I nodded. "So, after shooting from the play structure, the killer would've had to descend and toss his weapon into the bushes on the opposite side of the street and beyond the fence. Ordinarily the spot where the gun was found would have been in range of the bank cameras, but they had been disabled. Still, someone would've seen the shooter milling around that area in the minutes following the shooting. But the people holed up in the bank and barbershop awaiting the all-clear signal from police saw nothing unusual, just cops on the scene in the aftermath of the shooting." I took a deep breath before saying the next statement. "So, while I don't have any specific suspects, I believe it was a cop who shot Franny."

Omak sat in the room, grim-faced. Neither man argued against my theory.

Finally Omak spoke. "Motive?"

I sipped my warm coffee, hoping to have the courage to say this to the victim's brother.

"I believe Chris when he says that one or more cops were putting Donny up to these robberies. Maybe Franny was getting close to busting the case wide open?"

"It fits," Derringer said. "Laura's theory explains why Donny was nearly beaten to death last night, too. What if Donny went out again on his own and the cops got pissed that he was going rogue? They'd be afraid the old man knew too much about them and their involvement in Franny's death. They had to silence him."

"Or maybe the cop buddies were upset that Donny wouldn't continue the robberies," I suggested. "It might have been a cop who robbed First Sunrise on Monday. One of Donny's right-handed buddies, who knew the MO, knew where Donny kept the disguise stashed. And he could have planted the wig and glasses at Donny's place to end the trail of evidence with Donny."

Omak rubbed his face with his hands. "So, who's the dirty cop?" Omak asked quietly. "One or more?"

I told them I wasn't sure yet. Plenty of suspects, though. Brown and Rivers had nearly let Donny die instead of calling in the paramedics. Was that just lazy police work, or something more sinister? Had the two cops beaten Donny up in the first place? And then there was Cranston, who'd interrupted his dinner to rush over when he heard Donny's address come over the radio. A creaky explanation, as I'd never known Cranston to be vigilant about listening to radio calls while on meal.

"To narrow it down, Rivers is no marksman. He sometimes has trouble qualifying at the range," Omak said. "He wouldn't even try to make that difficult shot from the preschool play structure."

"You would need a trained shooter," Derringer said.

"Whoever shot Franny did have the advantage of a lit street, but still, it couldn't have been easy," I said.

"Both Cranston and Brown are excellent marksmen," Omak volunteered handing over files. "I've checked their qualifying scores from the shooting range, and they both are in the top tenth percentile every year."

Better than my score, I thought. But then, I hadn't held a gun in my hand until two years ago in the academy. I'd never had reason to.

I leafed through Brown's records. "I remember Brown mentioning that he served in the military," I said, scanning the file. "And here it is. I thought he bragged about being a sharpshooter. Here's a commendation from a special sniper unit. That's the sort of marksman it would take to hit a target across the street in semidarkness."

"So it seems that Donny's closest friends were Cranston, Brown, and Rivers, right?" Omak asked.

"And the chief," I said. "Cribben took him golfing."

"This is where worlds collide." Omak rubbed his jaw. "There's a possibility that this investigation ties into the internal investigation we've been conducting since I joined this precinct," Omak said, his voice low so that I had to strain to hear. "Some things shouldn't be discussed in this building. I'm going to arrange an off-site meeting for you two to talk with my undercover on the corruption case."

"Garcia?" I whispered.

"I don't want you two stepping on each other's toes. She's been secretly investigating Cribben, and she used to partner with Brown, so there's that."

"Just let me know when and where," I said.

One more question for you, Lieutenant," said Derringer.

"Yes?" Omak asked.

"How was your sister's murder case dropped without further investigation?" Derringer asked him. "There were obviously leads that could have been pursued."

Omak frowned and looked down.

"Whenever I ask questions around the precinct, I get the idea that many of her fellow cops were so traumatized by her killing that it sort of shut down," I offered.

Omak fidgeted in his seat before making eye contact with each of us. "I wish it were that innocent, but I'm afraid there's something really rotten in the SLPD, and I'm not the only one to suspect it. Laura already knows this, but Mayor Redmond hired me to pinpoint suspected corruption in the department."

"Lieutenant, you can't be part of your own sister's investigation . . ."

Omak cut him off. "I'm not." The lieutenant pressed his fingertips to his desk and looked directly at each of us. "I'm working the fringes of a larger corruption case. We all know it's a small department, and you'll probably know the people you're investigating pretty well. That said, I've stayed away from Franny's murder case, hoping another sharp detective would rediscover the Twilight Bandit case, uncover evidence, and bring Franny's case back to life." Omak looked at me. "I could assign it to you, Laura. You've got no personal connection to her murder."

I swallowed hard. "So you believe your sister's murder was premeditated?"

"I do. I've spent a career trying to counsel and help cops who got jammed up or landed in stupid trouble, but this is different. Someone was threatening Franny. I believe it was someone in this department. A cop has crossed the line, and they don't belong among the good men and women who serve here. And you know I'd feel that way whether or not the victim was my sister."

"It's clear that Franny's murder should be investigated separately from the Twilight Bandit case," Derringer said. "Given the evidence that you've uncovered, Laura, I know my supervisor will want the FBI on this one."

"What happened to the FBI agent who was working Franny's homicide?" I asked.

Derringer explained that the agent assigned to the case, a man named Paul Melnick, had died of cancer during the investigation. After his death, Chief Cribben had declared the case closed—too many dead ends for it to go anywhere.

Hearing that, something burned inside me. The truth of Franny's murder was out there, within reach, and for various reasons investigators had kicked around it but never tackled it head on.

"I want this case, Lieutenant."

Omak paused. "Okay, but you'll work it together. Under the radar. No one outside this office knows. I don't think I need to remind you that one good cop is dead. It can't happen again." Maybe it was the light, but I thought I saw Omak's eyes tear up again.

"Yes, sir," I said.

"We're all on the same page here," Derringer said earnestly.

"Good." Omak turned away and absently shuffled files on his desktop. "And good job figuring out the Twilight Bandit, Laura. Unexpected, but nice work."

"Really good work, Laura," Derringer added.

His tone was genuine, and it might have been the first time he'd called me Laura. I felt the tension between us shifting like a changing weather front. Maybe he realized he was stuck with me for a while longer and had decided to be nice. Or maybe there was more to it.

Ha. That would be a first.

"I'm glad you're staying on these investigations," Derringer said. "Glad but concerned. You need to be careful."

I smiled, feeling a glimmer of hope. "We'll make a good team on this case."

"Yes, I believe we will."

"So . . . hurry back so we can wrap this up." Was that too personal? Well, maybe I meant it that way.

22

My afternoon was spent connecting all the dots on the Twilight Bandit case. Reports from the lab revealed that hair and fibers from the wig and collection of baseball caps found in Donny Gallagher's home proved to be a match for the serial bank robber. For me, the hat collection was the most surprising. Freightliner, Nike, Kells Irish Pub, Deschutes . . . exact matches to the robberies of three years ago. You would think he would've destroyed the evidence, but the collection of hats worn by the Twilight Bandit was completely intact, not a single one missing. Donny was nothing if not sentimental.

I went through the canvassing reports from Officers Garcia and Milewski, who had gone door-to-door in Donny's neighborhood last night to see if residents had heard or seen anything out of the ordinary. Nothing unusual there.

But something Chris had mentioned stuck in my head. He'd said that his father had watched over the neighborhood, that he helped out neighbors and knew the school bus schedule. There was a good chance the school bus drivers knew Donny, too.

The bus company put me in touch with Clive Spaulding, a school bus driver who knew Donny. "I was sick about it when I heard he got attacked and beat up like that," Clive said. "Donny is the nicest guy. Really good to the kids."

"He's a sweet man," I agreed. "How long have you known him?"

"Two or three years now. My route goes past Donny's house. There's a stop right in front, and Donny usually comes out and helps the kids get across the street. Stops traffic. Sort of plays cop. I think it's the highlight of his days, and the kids like him."

"I see. Did he come out yesterday when your bus went by?"

"Yeah, in the afternoon. But not with the late bus."

"What time was that?"

"After dark. We get to that stop around five oh five. It's the activity bus for the kids who stay late for orchestra or clubs."

"And Donny didn't come out at that time?" Not surprising. He might have been dying by then.

"No, because he had visitors. They cut into his driveway right in front of the bus. A car with two guys in it. One of them was a Sunrise Lake cop. I saw his uniform."

The first responders. "I guess they were responding to the attack."

"No. I don't think so. The cop and the other guy . . . they had these ski masks on, kind of like . . . like I don't know. Teenage Mutant Turtles. It caught my eye, because I have to sit and wait at the stop. I saw Donny open the door to them. I figured it was some kind of inside joke or something."

"I see," I said as the sickening image of uniformed attackers seeped in.

"It was only later, this morning, when I heard about the attack on the radio and knew it was Donny—I don't know. It seems weird now. So I mentioned it to my boss. I thought about calling the police . . . calling you."

"Your observation could prove helpful, Mr. Spaulding," I said. "Thank you. We'll be in touch for a formal statement."

Shaking inside, I found the patrol activity logs online from the previous day and took note of everyone who was working, focusing on each officer's whereabouts from five PM, when the bus driver had spotted Donny's cop visitor pulling in. I made notes, then went to Omak's office.

"And now we have an eyewitness," Omak said when I told him about what Spaulding had seen. "Normally I'd question his timing and recollection, but the bus route timing is pretty specific, which makes it likely he saw Donny's attackers."

I nodded, feeling sick about the possibility that some of my colleagues were thugs.

"Let's check the roll call and see exactly who was working yesterday," Omak said. "See if any of Donny's guys were near the house in the evening."

"I already checked. Cranston and Garcia were driving solo, patrolling the banks." It was a special evening patrol Omak had set up this week to reassure the community; two patrol cars would be dispatched to check on banks around sundown. "They ended the bank patrol at eighteen forty and turned out in a patrol car together. They were on meal when the call came in from Chris Gallagher. But here's the thing about Cranston. He saw what looked like an abandoned car at Golden Pacific Bank and went inside to talk with the manager at seventeen oh five. Patrol log and the manager have him there for a full forty minutes."

"So he couldn't have been the cop who pulled up at Donny's house," Omak said.

I nodded. "It's a tight alibi. Rivers and Brown took meal at sixteen forty-five to seventeen forty-five. They returned to the precinct soon after dinner for an equipment failure. Radio batteries. They were out of service twenty minutes, then back on patrol. They handled one theft report—a stolen bike—before the call came from Chris Gallagher at nineteen thirty-two."

"Our suspects," Omak said. "And throw in the chief to spice things up. We've got some rotten apples in the barrel." Omak frowned as he rubbed his knuckles against his jaw. "I'll call Garcia in, see if she can find out what Rivers and Brown did for meal yesterday. As for our next step—"

"Can we check lockers?" I said. "Maybe do a check of every cop in the precinct, so that we don't tip our hand that we're looking at specific cops?"

"What would you be looking for?"

"The weapon used to murder Donny? Bloodstains? Donny's hair or skin?"

"A long shot, and I would need Cribben's approval, but I can't risk running any of this information by him."

"I'll keep working other angles," I said. On my way back to the squad room, I was searching my coat pocket for mints when I came across the thumb drive I'd used yesterday at my family's restaurant. My mother, who had learned of the alley incident within minutes of its occurrence, had given the Portland police and me copies of the video of the tattooed vandal who'd smashed my headlight. Mom had been more pragmatic than I'd expected, less fearful than Dad. "Laura, you've got to get this guy," she'd told me, and I'd agreed on that.

Hard to believe that had happened yesterday; it seemed like years ago.

I plugged it into the computer at my desk and ran the images. The young man was tall and graceful, with the appeal of a dark, mysterious pirate. But Hannah had been right about that neck tattoo. A bad choice. And quite distinctive.

I called Ms. Vit and asked her if she would take a look at some video for me. "I can email them to you. And this time, the images are sharper."

"Of course! Anything I can do to help. I'm flattered that you think I know every young person in town, but Portland is a growing metropolitan area."

But Sunrise Lake was still a small town. "If you can identify this young man, it would be a huge help."

"I'll do my best."

I had just finished emailing the alley video as an attachment when Z called.

"There's something off here," he said. "You need to come on over to Sunset Pines. I know, you're on a case, tons of work, blah, blah, blah. But it's easier if I just show you."

"Right now, I could use some fresh air."

"Lavender air," he said. "Come on over."

An odd bonus from our evidence cache at Donny's house was a surprising connection to Z's case. The trinkets we'd found in the cookie tins there turned out to match the inventory of items stolen from the Sunset Pines assisted-living facility. Z was thrilled to close the book on that oddball case, though he had not been able to get any of the residents to identify Donny yet.

The sky had faded from taupe to cold pewter Thursday afternoon when I pulled up in front of Sunset Pines. Z was waiting for me in the lobby. "Glad you could make some time for me, Mori."

"You call. I show up."

"Thanks," he said. "This case just got a lot weirder."

"Weirder than missing porcelain cats?"

Z held up a photo of a smiling Donny Gallagher. "Here's the thing. I've been showing Donny's ugly mug around the whole place, and no one recognizes him. That's strange, isn't it? A personable guy like Donny hangs out at the home in his old uniform, you'd think people would remember his face."

I nodded, thinking of how much Donny's face had been marred in the beating he'd sustained. We were still waiting for him to regain consciousness. Still hoping he would recover enough to name the men who'd attacked him. I had a feeling he would lead us to Franny's murderer if he could regain consciousness.

"Hey, remember Dolly Redmond's mentally fragile aunt Peg?"

"Yeah?"

"I want you to meet her."

"Z, really? We've both got our cases . . ."

"Trust me. It will be worth your time."

Aunt Peg's apartment smelled of lilac and Bengay cream. Within minutes of our arrival, it was clear that Dolly's aunt Peg really did suffer from dementia. But what Z and I found most intriguing were the blue Danish butter cookie tins she'd lined up along her living room shelves. There had to be twenty or thirty tins, and who knew how many more this little old lady had stashed in other rooms.

"Boy, you know who loves butter cookies, Aunt Peg?" Z asked.

The elderly lady looked at Z and smiled but made no move to answer his question.

"My girlfriend Natalie loves them."

"Oh, you do?" Aunt Peg turned to me.

I stepped back. "Oh, no. I'm his partner, not his girlfriend."

The elderly lady just shook her head. "I was in denial when I met my Henry. You shouldn't fight love, young lady."

Z put his arm around my shoulders. "Did you hear that, Mori? Don't fight love. And you ought to know, right Aunt Peg? How long were you married to, uh, Mr. Aunt Peg?"

I elbowed Z in the ribs and he dropped his arm, but that didn't stop him from trying to make friends with the elderly aunt of the mayor's wife.

"Can I buy a tin off you, Aunt Peg? Like I said, my girlfriend would be so happy if I came home with butter cookies."

She laughed at Z. "Don't be silly. I only give these tins to my niece, and sometimes to the sweet police officer who comes to see me." Aunt Peg stage-whispered to me, "I think he's kind of cute."

Z looked confused. "Wait, you think I'm cute?"

Aunt Peg guffawed. "No! Not you. That strapping policeman who stops by and talks to me every week." She looked at Z sideways. "But you can have a cookie to eat right now, if you'd like."

"Sure." Z smiled, crossing to the tins lined up against the wall. But Aunt Peg was already motoring slowly toward her kitchen counter.

"Oh, no. The cookies are over here in my kitchen cupboard. Don't be silly, those tins don't have any cookies in them."

Z looked at me sharply. "Oh yeah? What's inside those containers?"

Peg smiled wistfully. "Oh, you know, odds and ends."

"Odds and ends for your favorite policeman?"

Peg scrunched her face up in a little smile but didn't answer.

"Will you show Detective Mori what's in the tins?" Z asked her. "She's great at keeping secrets."

"She seems very nice." Aunt Peg looked from Z's face to mine as she returned to the sofa and plopped a tin onto the coffee table. "But it doesn't belong to me. The tins are mine, of course. But once I eat the cookies, I let my niece use them for storage."

"Your niece Dolly?" I said. "Z and I know her."

"You do?"

"We've met a few times. I don't think she would mind us having a look, right Z?"

"I don't think she'd mind at all," Z said. "In fact, she'd probably want us to take a look."

"Well . . ." Aunt Peg's stoic expression didn't soften. "You're police officers like that nice young man. I suppose it wouldn't hurt to take a peek."

Z and I held our breath and leaned forward as her frail fingers gripped the canister lid and pulled it off.

Inside the tin, fat stacks of money glowed green in the lamplight.

Fifties and hundreds, all neatly bound in rubber bands.

23

Z and I kept quiet about the tins as he walked me to the patrol car. He seemed to be holding his breath as we headed through the corridor, passing one room hosting a cocktail hour and another where a dozen or so residents were lined up waiting for the dining hall to open. Z nodded at a woman pushing a walker as we escaped the lavender air and made it to the cold December air.

"Okay, Mori, stop right there." The air had grown cold and Z's words came out in white puffs of air. "I say we turn around, go back, confiscate those cookie tins, and arrest Aunt Peg for being an accessory to multiple bank robberies."

I stopped walking and turned to face him under a tall streetlamp in the parking lot. "Z, we can't do that."

"Hell to the yeah, we can! Chris Gallagher told us those cookie tins are used for the disbursement of stolen money, and Aunt Peg has a connection to the crime web through Dolly Redmond."

"Do you think the mayor is involved too?" I wondered aloud.

"Chances are, the money grab is part of the nasty thang Dolly does with Cribben on the side."

"That is so not the way I want to think of the chief," I said, pressing my fingertips to one temple. "But bottom line, we can't go in there and confiscate an old woman's money without more evidence."

"That money screamed bank heist. We can't look the other way when corrupt cookie tins are passing under our noses."

I caught a movement in the parking lot beyond him. Someone was talking on a cell phone, despite the cold, but when I looked that way, he appeared to duck behind a van. Probably nothing, but still . . .

"We shouldn't be talking here out in the open," I said. "Easy targets."

"Hell to the yeah," he said, heading toward the patrol vehicle.

Inside the car, we agreed that this was a question above our rank. I called Lieutenant Omak and explained our visit with Peg.

"How much cash?" he asked.

"At least ten packs of fifties and twenties," I said. "I took some photos of it, but we weren't able to see inside all the tins."

"Aunt Peg was getting cranky," Z said. "She kept telling us it belonged to Dolly, and she didn't want us messing with her niece's stuff. But I say we confiscate it now. Maybe we can trace the cash back to one of the Twilight Banks, or to First Sunrise."

We discussed various strategies and possibilities. "Keep it under wraps, but I need to tell you that Dolly Redmond is on Garcia's watch list, as she had been frequently spotted visiting the police chief's home. The two seem to be involved, which had strained my ability to report everything on the corruption case to the mayor. Who seems to be clean. But the love triangle complicates things."

So the rumors about Cribben and the mayor's wife were true.

"Sounds like a scandal brewing," Z said.

"Adultery isn't illegal," I said. "But concealing stolen property is another story."

"For now, we need to sit tight on this," Omak decided. While we could have tried to get a search warrant of Aunt Peg's place, Omak knew that would alert anyone involved in the stolen property ring to start covering their tracks. He asked Z to keep an eye on Dolly's aunt while he was at Sunset Pines.

"Will do, Lieu. I've got a doctor's appointment in two hours," Z said, checking his watch. I knew that meant Dr. Mack had agreed to see him. "But I'll be back here tomorrow to keep an eye on Peg and interview some more residents. So far, I haven't found anyone who recognizes Donny. But as I'm visiting these folks in their apartments, you can bet I'll be on the lookout for blue cookie tins."

"And I'm going to reach out to the state's attorney's office and the FBI to open a sealed investigation. This department needs to be accountable to someone, and right now, it can't be the police chief or the mayor."

*　*　*

Back at my desk, I logged on to Google Earth and studied aerial photos of the bank and surrounding grounds where Franny had been killed. I'd found that switching up perspectives could sometimes loosen my ideas on cases, especially the ones that had me tied up in knots like this one.

I was drinking my decaf latte and rereading the coroner's report on Franny when I heard the shuffle of footsteps behind me in the squad room. Suddenly a handful of uniformed cops were gathered at the desk off to the side, within hearing range.

"So she really threw another cop under the bus?" It was the voice of Scooter Rivers, biggest suck-up in the crowd of blue uniforms.

"That's right. She's got him under lock and key at Evergreen County Hospital." That was Brown's voice. "It's sad, since he's there all alone, with a police guard. Not even his family can see him."

"Oh, give it a rest," I said, swiveling around in my chair to face them. "Donny's son can see him. And did you ever consider that the guard is there for Donny's protection? Someone assaulted him."

"But you're preparing a case against him, even as he's there unconscious." Cranston sneered at me as he spoke. "And that's wrong. Going after one of our own."

"No cop is above the law," I said. It was hard for me to look at them, wondering who might have been the pair of masked cops who attacked Donny. Besides, I didn't like being ganged up on, especially by my peers, but I wouldn't give them the satisfaction of seeing my discomfort. "If evidence shows that Donny is the Twilight Bandit, that's how he'll be charged."

"That's bullshit, Mori. He's an ex-cop with dementia," Cranston protested. "He's part of our family."

I could feel my breath start to tighten in my chest, not from fear but from fury, as I stared at the group pressing closer in the way that mobs move like one mindless organism.

One of you attacked him, and you stand there in judgment of me?

"Hey! What's goin' on here?" There was a rustling at the back of the squad room as Ellie Colgate pushed her way through to me. My favorite dispatcher. Ellie was a petite blonde woman, but she seemed about seven feet tall when she opened her mouth. "Scatter, you morons," she railed at the crowd of men who blocked me in my desk seat.

"Someone over here crossed the thin blue line," Cranston said, nodding at me.

"Aren't you retired yet, old man?" Ellie shot back at him.

Brown stepped back and caught my eye. While Ellie spun around to face the others, he grinned, put a finger to his temple. As I watched, he mimicked shooting himself in the head.

"Decent cops don't stand for corruption," Ellie barked. "You remember that, right? Some of you might have to dig deep. Search those shriveled hearts for some decency and integrity. Jesus H. Christ! I got calls backing up. Night shift better get their ass in gear."

Slowly the cops drifted away from my desk, grumbling to themselves.

"She's not the real problem," Brown grumbled. "It's Donny's son. He was the rat who gave him up. He's the one we should be leaning on."

"Do you hear what you're saying?" I asked. "Are you threatening a witness, Brown? Are you actually advocating tampering with a witness to a crime?" I felt the tension in the room tighten around me, though everyone stood still.

"Geez, Mori. We were just talking." Brown shrugged. "Don't freak out or anything." He began to slink away, and the other guys followed. I walked up to Brown and got right in his grill, so close that I saw gray beginning to edge the hair around his face.

"If any harm comes to Chris, I'll hold you accountable," I said.

Brown laughed. "I was out on the streets working when you were still in your princess diapers. Keep that in mind." He motioned for the others to follow, and the men headed out for their night shift.

I could feel blood pumping in my chest—the precursor of a panic attack—as I walked to the ladies' room to collect myself. What the hell was going on here? My colleagues, my fellow cops, were pressuring me to drop an investigation because the perpetrator was a retired cop. Even worse, Brown had threatened to go after Chris Gallagher, "the rat" who had made a statement against Donny.

The injustice of it spurred me to track down Omak at the front desk. "We need to talk. In your office. Now."

He seemed surprised, but handed off the book to Sgt. Joel, told her he'd sign off on the roll call later, and led the way to his office.

Once inside, I closed the door and leaned against it. "Some of the cops are upset that Donny is being charged. Rivers, Cranston, Purser, and Brown. They took the liberty of looking at the crime scene report and witness statements, and Brown is threatening to take revenge on Chris Gallagher for 'ratting' on his father."

"Great. Nothing like a group of thugs in uniform to ruin the reputation of an entire department." Omak shook his head, an expression of disgust on his face as he sat at his desk. An unusual move for Omak. "Have a seat, Mori. You're going to need to document this for me. Part of our internal investigation."

"Of course," I said, "but I'm worried about Chris Gallagher."

"I understand. I'll have a stern talk with the motley crew. They should know better, especially Cranston and Brown. Those guys are near retirement, and with behavior like that, they could blow it all." He paused, as if catching himself. "That sounds ridiculous in the context of what we're really dealing with here. One or more of those guys is in deep. We know that. They can forget collecting a pension. They're going to land in jail."

"We just don't know who," I said. "If we could just do a locker search . . ."

"I don't have the authority to do it, but I'm working on it. If it comes from the FBI, it will strengthen the integrity of the investigation."

I nodded, tamping down my impatience.

He rubbed his jaw as he pulled the keyboard of his computer closer. "All right, Mori. Let's bang out this complaint."

* * *

When I got back to my desk, Z had returned. Even though I tried to hide it, Z could see I was upset. When I told him about the earlier confrontation and the threat toward Chris Gallagher, Z became indignant.

"Man," he said, shaking his head. "That's messed up."

"Some of them are trying to be loyal to Donny, but to turn on his son?" I shook my head. "The whole pack mentality has taken over. Next there'll be pitchforks and torches. I talked to Omak, and it seems to be contained for now. But I'm worried for Chris."

"And you. You should be worried for yourself. You've had threats. Be careful, Mori."

"I'll be fine," I insisted, unconvinced.

In truth, I'd been able to avoid a panic attack, but I was shaken. It wasn't that I felt in danger from my fellow cops; it was the fact that I lacked the power to protect Chris. I tried to concentrate on my notes and case files, but I was trembling inside. I could feel my throat tighten. I pulled out my phone and texted Hannah, who usually served as my improvised therapist when I felt a panic attack coming on, but she didn't respond. She was probably at work and couldn't check her messages.

Z looked over at me, concerned. "You need to get out of here, Mori. I can drive you. Natalie's making pot roast tonight."

I shook my head. I knew this would pass soon enough, and I really wanted to get some work done. I had a meeting with Derringer in the morning, and I wanted to have something new to show him on Franny's case. "Thanks, but I need to get through this stuff."

Z lowered his head and his voice. "Have you ever thought about seeing a shrink? The last couple of sessions I've had with Doc MacKenzie have been really great. Just now, she helped unlock some things that I'd thought I'd lost."

"You're remembering more from the night Franny died?"

Z nodded. "The void in my memory is filling in. It's scary, I got to admit that, but there's also a sense of relief not to carry that burden anymore."

He looked around the squad room, where another detective was talking on the phone. He wheeled his chair over to my desk and leaned in closer. "I remember giving Franny CPR. And I remember someone pushing me away, telling me he'd take over. Only thing is, I don't think he did CPR. I think he let her die."

"Z, she had a head wound," I said softly.

"He let her die," he repeated.

"Who? Who was it?" I asked.

"That part is still kind of hazy, but the doc says that should slow down and my memories may grow clearer the more I try to access them. You should check her out. It's free, and you're into that psychology stuff, right?"

"I am." At least I had been a lifetime ago, when being a therapist was my dream occupation. As I stared at a weather report from the day of the shooting, I decided to advocate for myself and take Z's advice.

With a deep breath, I dialed the number for Dr. Daphne MacKenzie. I was surprised when she answered the phone and was able to fit me in tomorrow, Friday. I was looking forward to sizing up the woman who was rumored to be in a relationship with Ward Brown, an officer who seemed a little unhinged to me.

Maybe, if I played my cards right, I could find out a little more information about him. And maybe Z was right. It couldn't hurt to see the doc about my anxiety, right?

A call to the hospital indicated that Donny was still unconscious, but I went over to check and make sure his guard was in place. Van Der Linde chatted with me and actually followed me into Donny's bay in the ICU. I was glad he took his assignment seriously.

He told me that Chris had been there most of the afternoon. "He went to the cafeteria to get some dinner," Van Der Linde said. "Poor kid. Donny is all he has."

As I was on my way out, Chief Cribben appeared, looking appropriately somber and sad.

"How's he doing?" he asked me outside the ICU.

I relayed the hopeful prognosis from the doctor, but he shook his head. "A traumatic brain injury . . . he'll never be the same. Poor guy. He was already failing. I understand he could have sustained these injuries from a fall."

"Actually, that's not true, sir." I spoke softly, trying to keep disapproval from my voice. "Who told you that?"

"We all know he was clumsy. Losing control of his motor skills." He shrugged. "I probably shouldn't be so sympathetic since the guy terrorized our community, robbing all those banks, but I chalk it up to his dementia."

Yes, I read the press release, I thought, but I didn't want to go toe-to-toe with the chief. I stopped into the cafeteria to check on Chris, who had nearly finished a platter of hot turkey in gravy, mashed potatoes, and corn.

"It's really good," he said. "You should get some."

But I couldn't eat. My stomach was in knots over the guy sitting across from me and the cops threatening to go rogue.

* * *

An hour later I was crashing on the couch as Natalie worked in our kitchen cooking a pot roast with mashed potatoes and asparagus for dinner. Natalie loved to cook, said it was how she relaxed after busy days at work. I guess today was a whopper for her because Z and I were on the receiving end of a real meal. Z sniffed the air and declared ours the best-smelling house on the block.

I'd changed out of my work clothes and into the blue Columbia sweatshirt Hannah had given me for Christmas and my black yoga pants. I tied my hair back and lounged on the couch with a mystery novel.

"Need any help in the kitchen, honey?" Z called to Natalie. He was seated across from me on the couch, surfing his phone.

"No, I'm good," she yelled from the kitchen. "I'm going to check on the pot roast and then take a quick shower before dinner."

A few minutes later I heard the shower running in the bathroom, so I turned to Z to tell him how strange I thought Chief Cribben had acted today at the hospital.

"I got the idea that he wasn't so hot on the idea of posting a guard at the door," I told him. "He said something like, 'It's not like the old guy is going anywhere.'"

Z was incredulous. "Donny was nearly beaten to death just a few days ago, and he's still in a coma. We still have no idea who did it. Or wait. Do you know more? What's happened in that case?"

I thought back to the day's progress. "Well, there's been an indication that it was two masked people from a patrol unit."

"What?"

I told him what the bus driver had witnessed. "It looks like Donny was beaten up by cops on the job."

"That makes me sick. Shit. So who?" Z asked. "I heard through the grapevine that tomorrow Omak is calling in Brown and Scooter Rivers to read them the riot act for not helping Donny as much as they should have," Z said.

I pressed a fist to my forehead. "I wonder if they could have attacked him, then covered their tracks. Maybe left and changed clothes? And then Chris found Donny and called the police?"

"It's possible. This is going from bad to worse." Z frowned. "I hate being out of the loop on Franny's case. I feel like it's the least I owe her . . ."

"Trust me, you're doing your part by trying to remember more about the night she died," I told him. "Plus, I think you're a little jealous of Special Agent Derringer. One alpha dog challenged by another mighty canine."

Z gave me a look. "For starters, just sayin', *I* would be the mighty canine. And maybe *you* have a little crush on a certain pretty-boy federal agent, and you want time alone with him to make your move."

"Yeah, right. Like I would even know *how* to make a move on a guy," I said, more defensively than I meant to sound.

Z cocked his head like a Labrador retriever. "So, what I'm hearing is that if you knew how to make a move on the nancy fancy boy, you would. Is that right?"

"First of all, he's not a nancy fancy boy."

"Oh! She defends him!" Z threw a pillow up into the air and caught it. "First sign of a crush."

"Please," I said dismissively, hoping to end the conversation right there. The truth was, I did have a big crush on Derringer. When I least expected it, he could make me laugh. And it didn't hurt that he was very handsome but didn't seem to know it. But I knew I was invisible to Derringer. The FBI agent probably had his pick of women to date, and the nerdy detective from small-town Oregon did not even rate.

"You should ask him out, Mori."

I threw a pillow at Z and leapt to answer my ringing phone.

It was a nurse from Sunrise Memorial Hospital calling to inform me that Donny Gallagher had died a half hour earlier.

24

thanked the nurse and immediately dialed Chris Gallagher's number. No answer, but I left a sympathy message on his answering machine.

"Damn," Z said. "I was really hoping he'd recover. I thought we'd be able to talk with him. At the very least, I wanted to know the names of those bastards that beat the crap out of him."

I hung my head. Another killing. Another dead end.

"Should I be alarmed that I can't reach Chris Gallagher?" I asked, thinking of threats made against him.

"Nah. Not after Omak read the patrol cops the riot act. One twisted hair on Chris Gallagher's head and he's holding his cops responsible. Not a lot of leeway there."

"But you'll check on Chris? I would go, but I've got a meeting with Derringer and then that appointment with Dr. Mack and—"

"I'll check on Chris. And good luck with Dr. Mack. Therapy can be intense."

Z told me that in his last session he'd recalled a few more details of that night. "I remembered that there was a flurry of movement from across the street, something bright, a flash, at the preschool," Z told me. "I think someone was up in that play structure."

I could picture this now after spending time at the crime scene. "Maybe you saw a muzzle flash in the dark." If that was the case, then Franny's death was premeditated. Some killer was up there, ready to shoot Franny and Z when they'd responded to the 911 call from the bank. "Wow, that's a milestone."

Z nodded. "It was a pretty intense session. She pushed me to remember the person who pulled me away from Franny. I feel like it was a man, someone I knew." He looked toward the kitchen, then added, "A cop."

"Why is it important to remember this person?" I asked.

"In my mind, this is the guy who killed Franny. I know that part's not rational, but it's embedded there. I need to remember. I want to remember for Franny." Z turned his head away from me, and I could hear the hoarseness in his voice. "It's the least she deserves from me."

I patted his arm. "Anything I can do for you, partner?"

He nodded. "Yes, as a matter of fact, there is." Z paused.

"What?"

"Dr. Mack wants me to go back to the bank parking lot again, to walk the scene where Franny died, but she doesn't think it's wise for me to go alone. She thinks it will help jar the missing pieces of my memory loose." He paused. "Will you go with me this weekend? Maybe sometime Saturday?"

"Of course," I said.

Z nodded. "Good. Dr. Mack wants me to text her when we head over there so she can be around to talk in case I have a real breakthrough." He looked over at me. "She's been really support-ive. I hope she can help you, too."

I exhaled. "Me too, Z. I've had anxiety attacks since my early teenage years. It's hard to handle, especially in our line of work."

"We see some bad shit. It doesn't help," Z agreed.

Natalie, fresh out of the shower and dressed in sweat pants and a T-shirt, plopped down on the couch next to Z and snuggled up to him. She stuffed her fingers in her ears.

"Lalalalalala!" She laughed. "I'm not listening, but I bet you guys are talking about work!"

Z smiled at her. "Hey, I'm hungry and that pot roast smells too good to be true."

"It's almost ready. You guys set the table while I get it out of the oven. Deal?"

"Deal," I replied, more than happy to grab silverware in exchange for a homemade meal.

I was folding napkins and Z filling water glasses when Natalie asked if we wanted to head out to the holiday farmer's market on Saturday. She'd heard there were more booths scheduled to open this weekend, and she wanted to check them out. "Besides, Saturday is a day off this week, right?"

"It's supposed to be," I said, wondering how the investigations would line up over the next few days. "I'll go if I don't have to work. Sounds fun."

"Or excruciating," Z chimed in.

Natalie walked into the dining room with a steaming pot roast and set it in the middle of the table. "Or romantic." She turned to Z and smiled. "It's definitely good people watching. A couple of weekends ago I saw Mayor Redmond's wife buying lavender soap from a booth. So you never know who you're going to see out and about."

"Dolly Redmond, huh?" Z asked.

"Yeah, I saw your boss there, too. Chief Cribben. He was hanging around Dolly at the booth. I guess the rumors are true."

"Rumors? What rumors?" I asked.

Z put down his fork and listened intently.

"Well, I've always heard that those two are crazy about each other. You know, they dated in high school. The rumor goes that Dolly and Cribben had a falling out and took a break from each other, but she turned around and married Redmond. People say it was to make Cribben jealous, but who knows . . ."

Interesting. "Cribben has never married, has he?" I asked.

Natalie shook her head. Always a sucker for a good love story, I could tell this story tugged at her heart.

"Married?" Z hooted. "Who would marry Cribben? He looks like a walking pastrami sandwich. He's sloppy and always flushed . . ."

"Oh, stop it. You're being mean," Natalie teased him.

"I should know. I worked in a deli during college," Z countered. "If anyone here knows pastrami, it's me."

* * *

Friday morning I was on my way to work, waiting in the drive-through at Java Joy, when Ms. Vit called.

"I hope it's not too early, Laura, but I have just a small bit of information about your young tattooed man."

"Never too early for news," I said, faking energy. I wasn't a morning person at all, but I was one minute away from one of the best triple-shot lattes in Sunrise Lake. "Did the images ring any bells?"

"First of all, I don't know your young man. It's not just the tattoo, but his distinctive body type, tall and lithe. I would remember that. But I took the liberty of sharing the image with some of my friends who are administrators. This young man's neck tattoo reminded me of a conversation we once had about tattoos and piercings that might prevent our students from getting hired. I had a little girl who tattooed teardrops under her eyes. Such a mistake! The skin on our faces is so sensitive and hard to repair. A group of us were talking about helping our kids avoid long-lasting mistakes like that. Nose piercings were common at that time, but we've all seen some painful piercings of the cheek and ears. It breaks my heart to see any student disfigured for life. Anyway, Eva Garrison—she's a vice principal over at West Green—and I recalled her telling me about a student with a large and obvious neck tattoo. I talked with her and sent her the photo, and believe it or not, she recognizes your young man."

While Ms. Vit had been talking, I'd moved up in the line, received my latte, and enjoyed my first heavenly sip of the day. "That's great," I said, easing the car forward to the road. "Did Ms. Garrison remember his name?"

"Unfortunately, no. Eva isn't big on memorizing the names of her students the way I am. But she remembers his student record.

He was an average student, but in his senior year he blew a gasket. Major behavior issues. And then the neck tattoo as soon as he turned eighteen, but that was just a small part of the bad behavior. She thinks there were some entanglements with the police. Vandalism or some such thing. Such a shame. He made it out of high school a few years ago, but barely."

"I see." A name would have helped my search, but at least I had a place to start now. When I had the time, I could contact the West Green School District and search their database, possibly identify the tattooed vandal from his school ID photo. For now, I would tell Omak about the development and put the matter on my list while I focused on the robberies and homicides. And I would offer up the tip on the vandal's background to the Portland police in case they wanted to follow up in West Green.

* * *

"Good morning," Derringer boomed as he came into Omak's office that morning and quietly shut the door behind him. "I come bearing news."

I felt my pulse quicken as I looked up into his dark eyes. It was good to have him back.

"Good news, I hope," I said.

Derringer frowned, looking from me to Omak. "Something bad happened here. What did I miss?"

I wrapped my hands around my coffee cup, seeking warmth. "Donny Gallagher died last night."

"Oh, man." Derringer rubbed the back of his neck. "I was hoping he'd make it."

"And we have a witness who saw Donny open the door to two men the evening that he died, around five PM. Two masked men, and at least one of them was a Sunrise Lake cop."

"Really." Derringer nodded. "So Donny's death might be part of the corruption ring."

"Sounds like it," I said.

"What's *your* news?" Omak asked, sipping a steaming cup of coffee behind his desk.

"Well, as we suspected, the partial prints from the copycat robbery are no good."

"Damn," said Omak.

"But I took Laura's good advice and reran much of the evidence from the Twilight robberies. Besides the wig fibers, I found a pattern that is telling. The duct tape that was found on the outside bank cameras in the ninth Twilight robbery was covered with fingerprints. I ran the prints against the fingerprints of the bank employees and the SLPD." He paused. "There was a hit."

"Really?" I hated the suspense. "Who?"

Derringer folded his arms. "Ward Brown's prints were all over that tape."

Omak exhaled, and I was reminded that, for the lieutenant, this case was intensely personal.

"So you found Brown's fingerprints more than once?" I said. "How many of his prints?"

"More than a dozen."

"Really? So Ward Brown might have been the culprit who covered those exterior camera lenses with duct tape." I stood up and began pacing, "And why would he do that? Because he knew what he had planned. Let's say the theory is correct. He didn't want to take the chance that a camera would photograph him shooting Franny or ditching the gun in the bushes or refusing to give her CPR or whatever he did. He covered up those cameras because the murder was planned. Premeditated." I looked down at Omak's desk. "He planned to kill the investigator who was onto Donny Gallagher. Maybe she even knew that some of her colleagues were involved. Maybe she knew Brown was culpable. She was getting threats. In order to save himself and the robbery ring, he had to kill her." I turned to my colleagues. "How would that story play in court?"

"Any decent defense lawyer is going to have a field day with that evidence," Omak said. "They'll say he handled the tape while collecting evidence."

"Yes." I saw Omak's point. "He would have handled the tape at the crime scene, but every cop carries latex gloves for that purpose. Even if Brown slipped procedure once or twice, the number of prints on the tape is overwhelming."

"It's not enough to indict him," Derringer said, "but it tells me Brown had a major role in the Twilight Bandit robberies, and potentially Franny's murder."

Omak nodded. "Good work, you two. Let's keep moving forward, building on what we know."

"The fingerprints are a clue, but we need more evidence," Derringer said, "stronger evidence. Ward Brown is a good suspect, but we should delve deeper into the profiles of the cops on the scene. Brown, Cranston, Rivers . . . even Esme Garcia and Zion Frazier. Sometimes the answers are there, right in front of us. Hidden in an HR file or sitting right on the shelf of an employee's locker."

"Zen crime solving," I said.

Derringer nodded. "The answer exists. It simply needs to be found."

* * *

While Omak went upstairs to update the chief—"I'd rather have a root canal," Omak lamented—Derringer and I discussed ways to proceed. While in Seattle, Derringer had learned that the FBI was expanding its investigation here in Sunrise Lake, looking into police department corruption, based on Lieutenant Omak's request.

"It shouldn't slow us down on the bank robberies or homicides," Derringer said. "From what I've seen, it looks like the corruption case is intertwined with Twilight."

"There's a web connecting some of our officers to these bank robberies and murders," I said. "I'm afraid that uncovering Donny Gallagher's role as a bank robber was just the tip of the iceberg."

I promised him an update on other tangential details when I returned from my appointment. "I feel like we've made a lot of progress. Lots of clues, but we're still lacking the main narrative to draw them all together."

"Classic crime solving," he said.

In the meantime, we agreed that it was best for Derringer to call in officers who'd been at the scene of Franny's shooting and interview them on his own. "With the weight of the FBI behind you, I think you'll command more respect than anyone in this department," I said.

"Respect is fine, but it's the truth that we're really after."

25

W alking into Dr. Daphne MacKenzie's office, I noticed the color palette first. The waiting room and office were tastefully appointed with neutral colors that reminded me of the coast: sofas and chairs in coordinated sand-colored fabric and accented by light-blue and brown pillows. The office was soothing, but it also felt remote. High-end magazines were spread perfectly on a polished coffee table, and soothing black-and-white photographs of sailboats hung on the walls. The office was buffed and shiny beyond reproach.

"Welcome. I'm glad you made an appointment." Dr. MacKenzie emerged from behind a door and extended a hand. She wore diamond stud earrings that caught the light, and I noted her light sandalwood and sea salt perfume. The smell transported me back to the anxiety I'd felt when I discovered the ominous note scrawled on my car window the night of the SLPD holiday party. I tried to keep my breathing steady. I was here to learn as much about MacKenzie and her rumored relationship with Brown as I could, and I wasn't terribly interested in giving her much personal information about myself.

"You must really like to sail," I said, making small talk as we settled in.

She glanced around at the photographs of sails billowing in the wind. "I do. It's what I hope to do full-time one day. It's so relaxing."

"I imagine."

"So, what brings you in today?"

I nodded. "I've been having a few anxiety episodes lately, but I think that might be pretty normal, given my line of work."

"Certainly, police officers can be prone to increased stress and anxiety . . ."

"Like my partner Zion Frasier?"

MacKenzie hesitated. "This is your session, Laura. We're here to talk about you."

"Yes, of course," I agreed. "But we can discuss how my actions affect other people, right? And I'm wondering how I can best support my partner as he tries to work through his PTSD."

The therapist's smile revealed a perfect set of white teeth. "You're a good partner, Laura. Z's told me what a good investigator you are."

"Thank you," I said, looking around her office. "What got you interested in working with police officers? Certainly there are easier kinds of people to work with."

MacKenzie sat back in her seat and curled her shoulders in just a little bit. I'd seen this same body language on suspects I talked with, and it usually meant they were uncomfortable with the line of questioning. Still, she answered the question.

"I like complicated, I guess."

That was certainly true if she was in a relationship with Ward Brown. There was nothing simple about a dirty cop.

"In some ways, I like to live vicariously through the police officers I work with," MacKenzie answered. "What about you? Why did you go into law enforcement?"

"I like solving puzzles," I told her. Maybe I should have told her that being a police officer was considered a stain on my family. That they would have been so much prouder of me if I'd become a therapist like her, counseling cops instead of becoming one of them. She would probably have eaten it up, but I wasn't in the mood to share.

"So, being a detective is your first career choice? I ask because it can be hard being female and on the force."

I nodded. "It has its challenges." I thought specifically of Cranston and his little digs. He was relentless. "But I like helping people, and this is one of the best ways. I'm there for people in some of their worst life moments."

"Yes, you are. But that can take a personal toll, right?"

It could. I'd begun having nightmares during last year's Lost Girls case. My anxiety had certainly surfaced again during this case, but I wasn't going to let it get the best of me. It definitely wasn't going to stop me from solving this case.

"Sure. You have to know how to blow off steam," I said, keeping my answers vague. "Those are beautiful earrings," I noted, leaning forward to get a better look.

MacKenzie lifted one hand to her right ear, as if to cover the jewelry I'd noticed. I noted her immediate reaction, one I associated with a feeling of embarrassment or guilt. Certainly she had enough money to buy herself jewelry, but I couldn't help but wonder if she'd received that jewelry from Ward Brown. Did she know she was potentially involved with a dirty cop? I couldn't tell.

The doc exhaled. "How can I help you today, Laura?" She was resetting. Taking control of our conversation.

"I'd like to know how best to support Z as he deals with his PTSD."

"Of course." She smiled. "Well, Z has told me I can share some things with you, and you know he recently had a breakthrough. I've asked him to return once again to the scene of Franny's death to see if that will continue to release memories. We're at a critical juncture in his memory recovery, and I'm hoping you'll go with him to support him."

"Yes, Z and I talked about it. I think we're going tomorrow."

"Good. Talk him through the events of the night Franny was shot," she advised. "And please text me when you all are headed there, so I can be a phone call away if Z has a rush of memories. I think he's ready."

"Will do," I said. On a small side table under a window, I noted a few framed photographs. I stood up and walked over to the photo of MacKenzie hugging a young, dark-haired man. He was handsome. Maybe I'd been wrong about the doc and Brown.

"My son, Jason."

I looked again. "Really? You don't look old enough to be his mother."

"I had him when I was very young. Another lifetime ago. He's home from college for the holiday break. He's been going to Oregon State in Bend, but he's threatening to stay home now. School isn't his thing, and he thinks he's got a future in video-gaming, but I don't see that as a viable career. There's a little pressure for him to go into police work, but I'm not sure it's right for him."

"Pressure from you?" I pivoted to see the doctor's reaction to my question.

She reached a perfectly manicured hand to her throat. "Not really. Just . . . friends."

I smiled and wondered if it was Brown who was putting the squeeze on the kid. I took one last look at the photo. Mackenzie looked wistful as she hugged a young man brimming with confidence. A young man with a tattoo on his neck.

I gripped the photo, trying not to reveal my reaction as I stared at his image. MacKenzie's son had a blue star tattoo with a yellow lightning bolt on his neck. I took a closer look to be sure.

Yup.

Jason MacKenzie was the tattooed young man who had shoved my sister and damaged my car.

"Handsome, right?" MacKenzie said, walking closer.

I was still staring at Jason's tattoo, but managed to make some sound in the affirmative.

"Girls are not his problem." She sighed and gave a little laugh. "Gainful employment, on the other hand . . ."

A chill ran up my spine. What was MacKenzie's son doing following me around? I suspected Jason was getting some extra work on the side, but it wasn't aboveboard. Had he been recruited by some bad cops to help put the chill on the investigation into Franny's death? If so, Brown was the obvious influence on the kid. I put the photo back on the side table. "I'm afraid I've got to cut this meeting a bit short. I've got to meet a colleague. Thank you for your time," I said.

MacKenzie hesitated. "Are you sure you don't want to talk more about your anxiety? I can offer some tools you might find helpful."

I looked at her. "I don't think I'm ready. Thank you, though."

MacKenzie stood. "Sure. Don't forget to text me when you and Z visit the crime scene."

"No problem," I said. I didn't trust the doc, but I didn't think she was operating out of malice. Still, I couldn't figure out how exactly her son fit into the picture. Had someone recruited MacKenzie's son Jason to scare me away from the investigation? Was it Brown or Cranston? If so, did MacKenzie know her son was mixed up in dirty business? Either way, I had to warn Z that MacKenzie might not be quite as helpful as she seemed.

26

Z followed the manager through the dining hall and back toward the main office. It wasn't even noon yet and nearly every table at the assisted-living facility was filled with residents, all of whom waved at him and wanted to follow up with him about their missing Christmas bells or pottery candy dishes. Z was annoyed this afternoon because, even though he'd recovered many of the stolen items at Donny Gallagher's house, there were new reports of more stolen watches and mini sewing kits and glass bells from Amsterdam. With every visit, Z was astounded by the sheer number of trinkets one thief could carry off. And now that his main suspect, Donny Gallagher, was clearly not involved in this most recent rash of stealing, Z was back to square one.

Z stopped to speak to one elderly woman who had waved him over, and when he looked up, the Sunset Pines manager was nowhere in sight. Oh well. By now he knew the way to the main offices. Z strode through the dining hall and turned down a second hallway, where he saw a police officer ahead of him.

Who the hell was that? Who from the precinct had sent a uniform out here?

"Hey, Officer!" Z called.

The cop turned with a broad smile pasted across his young face, but it faded fast when he saw who had called to him.

"I'll be damned," Z said under his breath. Chris Gallagher dressed in a police uniform, and it was nowhere near Halloween.

Chris took off running down the hallway. Z followed, but the hallways were winding and Z didn't know the layout of the facility nearly as well as Chris did, given that he was able to slip out of Z's sight pretty fast. It didn't help that Z had to stop and search every recycling closet and public restroom he came to, just in case Chris had ducked in to hide.

Z emerged from one hallway near an alcove where two ladies sat leafing through a newspaper.

"Excuse me, have you seen a police officer run by here?"

They both nodded. "That sweet officer ran right by us. He is such a doll," said one lady in a crocheted pink sweater.

"Is he?"

They both nodded vigorously.

"He helps carry my groceries up to my apartment every week."

"What a helper." Z smiled. "I could use his help right now."

"Maybe you can catch him," said the lady in the pink sweater. "I saw him take a left at the end of this hallway, and that leads to the kitchen. Maybe he went to get a snack."

"Maybe," said Z. "Thank you, ladies."

As Z jogged forward, he wondered about Aunt Peg and her cookie tins. Somehow, all these dots were about to connect. He just had to find that punk impersonating an officer.

He came to a set of swinging doors that led to the back of the kitchen and strode through. Z saw a couple of prep cooks and a dishwasher loading a huge tray with china plates from lunch.

Without saying a word, Z put a finger to his lips, flipped open his police badge and held it up high. Slowly the workers stopped their cleaning and looked at Z. He smiled. Using two of his fingers, he mimed someone running through the kitchen, and one of the prep workers smiled knowingly and motioned with his head to the walk-in freezer at the far end of the kitchen.

Z gave him a thumbs-up.

When he opened the walk-in freezer door, he heard the telltale sound of suction and felt a blast of frosty air kick him in the face. Z felt for the light switch on the wall and flipped it on. Chris Gallagher was huddled in the corner of the freezer, hunched down on his knees and shivering. Z grabbed Chris by his arms and yanked him to his feet, marching him out of the walk-in freezer.

"What are you doing impersonating an officer, Gallagher?" Z grilled Chris as he walked him out of the kitchen. "Have you been stealing from the residents of Sunset Pines?"

"No!" Chris shouted.

But Z didn't believe him. "You need to figure out how to know when you've been caught, Chris. I guess the apple doesn't fall too far from the tree, does it?"

* * *

Omak and Derringer came to Sunset Pines to assist Z in making the arrest. Z tried to cajole some information out of Chris Gallagher, but after thirty minutes spent prodding Chris Gallagher about those freakin' cookie tins, the young man remained glum. Z was fed up. He scowled across the table at Chris, who sat handcuffed in a conference room, his face red and stoic.

"I try not to take my job personally, Chris, but your attitude is starting to piss me off."

Chris shrugged, staring down at the table. "Can I get another Coke? Or something warm. It's cold in here. I'm freezing."

"We'll get you a nice hot meal if you explain what you've been doing here, impersonating an officer," Omak said.

"Nothing," Chris said.

"You're wearing one of your father's old uniforms," Derringer pointed out.

"I know." Chris looked down at the SLPD emblem on his right shoulder. "It's comforting to me. Especially now that Dad's gone."

Gone, but not even in the ground yet, Z thought, recalling the controversy that morning at the precinct over the question of allowing Donny to have a burial with police escort—a courtesy for retired members of the department. Cribben deemed it acceptable, but Omak had issues, considering Donny's alleged involvement with Twilight. Z had steered clear of it.

But now, to see Donny's son out peddling the fake uniform when the old man wasn't even put to rest . . . it pissed Z off even more. "Chris, according to the residents here, you've been showing up in that uniform for weeks," said Z. "Impersonating an officer."

"Yeah, so? What're you going to do about it? Arrest me? Oh, right. You already did."

Z clamped a hand over his jaw, a meager attempt to mask his annoyance as he turned to Omak and Derringer. The three men had each taken cracks at getting Chris to spill his guts, but so far nothing had worked. Z was frustrated, wanting to know the connection between those cookie tins, Chris Gallagher's police costume, and Chris's old man.

Omak, leaning against a wall, motioned the other investigators toward the door for a meeting outside. Z followed him, glad to get away from the entitled brat-boy who required extra TLC in light of his father's recent death.

Derringer closed the door behind them, and the three men leaned in to talk.

"We're getting nowhere," Omak said. "I want to take the opportunity to question him, especially since he hasn't requested legal counsel, but maybe some time in a cell will make him want to talk."

Z winced. "True, but I hate to lose the chance we have now. Once he sees the realities of jail, Chris might lawyer up."

"We need to bring Laura in," Derringer said. "She has a way with suspects. People like to talk to her. And she already has a rapport with Chris."

Z maintained strong eye contact with Derringer, getting a new read on the guy. It was good to see the FBI agent appreciate his partner for the capable cop she was, but maybe Derringer harbored a little crush on her, too? "What do you think, boss?" he asked the lieutenant.

"Nothing we're doing is working. Let's bring her over." Omak was already tapping on his cell phone.

27

I had been on a roll, finding two sealed juvenile arrest records on Jason MacKenzie, when Omak called me over to Sunset Pines. Z quickly described chasing Chris down but then getting stonewalled during questioning.

"Your buddy Derringer told us we needed to call in an expert interrogator," Z told me quietly in the hall. "You."

Stifling a smile, I asked a few questions, hit the vending machines, and headed in.

Inside the conference room, I handed Chris a warm cup of cocoa and sat down across the table from him. "That's hot chocolate. I heard you were getting cold, and it is a little nippy in here." I wrapped my hands around my own coffee cup. The vending machine in the building was mediocre, but I had to go with the resources at hand.

"I'm not going to talk to you just because you give me cocoa." Chris blew on the surface of the steaming cup as if it occupied the full scope of his attention span.

"Fair enough. I'm not here to make you talk. I'm supposed to babysit you while the 'big guys' figure out what to do with you." I tucked a strand of hair back behind one ear. "They don't let me handle anything important around here."

Chris looked up at me, curious but neutral.

"It's just a stupid boys' club around here." I slumped in the chair, feigning boredom. "Sometimes I literally feel like I'm back in middle school."

"I didn't realize it was so bad around the precinct. My dad never said anything . . ."

"Well, your dad was one of the good ones, you know." I shook my head. "I'm really sorry for your loss, Chris."

Chris's face tightened. "Thanks."

"I mean it."

The door opened, and Z walked in carrying a tin of cookies. Chris stiffened. Z put the tin on the table and walked out.

"What a serious turd bucket," I said.

Chris's eyes warmed, and a smile tugged at the corners of his mouth.

"They all think they can give the kiddies some cookies and that'll keep us from getting restless?" I complained. "What are we, three years old? Next, they'll come in here with glasses of milk." I reached over and opened the tin, revealing golden cookies in various shapes. "Still, they look pretty tasty. Want one?"

Chris nodded, and I pushed the tin over to him and took a cookie myself. "They're good dunked," I said, lowering a cookie into my steaming cup of coffee.

He rocked a little in his seat as he dropped crumbs all over the table. "My dad really loved these cookies," Chris offered after a long silence. "But he's gone now. I think it might be my fault he's dead."

"Is it, Chris?" I asked quietly. "Why do you think that?"

A tear slipped down his cheek. "You wouldn't understand. No one will."

I leaned in toward him. "I can promise you I'll try."

Chris stopped chewing, his face twisted in pain. "I was only doing it to take care of my dad."

"What were you doing? I'll understand."

Chris took a last gulp of cocoa and then confessed that he had been coming every week to the assisted-living facility. He'd been doing it for three years now, ever since his dad had instructed him to visit Dolly's aunt Peg and bring home cookie tins.

"And the tins had more than just these babies in them," I said, waving a butter cookie in the air.

He nodded. "I told you, that's how they moved the money."

"So for three years you were part of the distribution system for cash from the bank robberies?"

Chris looked sheepish. "Under the top layer of cookies, they hid the cash Dad was owed for the Twilight Bandit robberies. Dad turned all the cash he got in the heists over to his cop friends, and they protected him from interference from the police. As part of the deal, Donny got back his fair share of the dough, bit by bit, in small payments."

"So you knew about the money in the tins," I said. "You knew it came from robbing banks."

"Not at the beginning, but even before Dad spilled the truth, I knew he was involved in some fishy business. Dad was always surrounded by cops, and suddenly, after Mom died, he had cookie tins full of cash. In the beginning, it seemed like a lot. He finished paying off his mortgage and he paid my rent for a year."

"But it didn't last," I said.

Chris shook his head. "It all changed after that lady cop got shot."

"How did that change things?" I tried to act nonchalant, but my pulse was thrumming in my ears.

"It freaked Dad out. He cried about Franny Landon every day, every night. Sometimes he swore to me that he had nothing to do with her death. Other times, he said it was all his fault. But that was his dementia. I know he didn't kill her."

"Who did?"

Chris shrugged. "I don't know. Neither did Dad. But he knew he didn't want to be involved in anything that got people killed. After that, he refused to do any more robberies."

"So he stopped robbing banks."

Chris nodded. "He put the wig and glasses into a box, and that was that. But it wasn't a popular decision. His cop buddies wanted him to hit a few more places while the daylight hours were short. They got rough with him more than once, trying to make a point. I saw proof. A black eye. A swollen cheek. But Dad swore he was done with bank hits."

"That's a terrible way to treat your father," I said. "He was a good man, a loyal friend. In the short time I knew him, he was kind to me."

"And they treated him like crap. When money got tight, there was no sympathy. They told him if he wanted money for a new roof, he'd better pop another bank."

"I'm sorry he was short on funds," I said. "Did he consider robbing another bank?"

He shook his head. "Even if he'd wanted to, Dad was struggling with his motor skills and short-term memory. So I got the bright idea of popping a bank myself. Making it look like a copycat robber."

"So you pulled the First Sunrise hit?" Even as I said the words, I knew it was true. We would probably find the Uncle Kombucha hat in Chris's apartment. And that was why the words of the note had been identical to the Twilight's teller notes. Chris had learned from the master, his father. "You robbed the First Sunrise bank, but your dad didn't know about it."

Chris nodded. "I made sure he didn't find out. After I was done, I packed up the wig and glasses and put it back where I found it in his house. I did it for him. For us, because the money was dwindling. His pension wasn't enough to live on and I make shit at the cleaners. Dad's not old enough for social security yet. I figured one hit, and we could keep it all to ourselves. It would have been enough to pay for the roof with some left over."

"But the cops didn't like being cut out of the profits," I said.

Chris nodded. "I didn't think they'd pin it on Dad. I thought they'd figure it for a copycat. But I was wrong. As soon as I robbed First Sunrise, Cribben was all over Dad. Cribben is the leader, I think. The big chief. 'Tell us where the money is, Donny.' It was awful. And Dad kept insisting he didn't know what they were talking about. They strung Dad along, taking him to the Christmas party and all. I guess they figured he'd tell them eventually, but he had nothing to tell." Chris shook his head. "So Dad paid with his life, just because I did one bank hit." His voice caught in his throat, and Chris began to sob. "I feel so guilty. My dad didn't deserve to die that way. I should be in prison."

"Chris, my friend, I suspect prison will be in your future."

"But I never thought they'd come after him." Tears filled his eyes. "He was their friend! He stuck out his neck so they could line their pockets with cash. I never thought they'd kill him!"

"I believe you."

Behind Chris the door opened, signaling that our interview was over. Derringer, Omak, and Z entered the room, having heard the whole confession on my open phone line. Omak helped Chris stand and read him his rights once again.

"I never meant it to happen this way," Chris sobbed. "My dad is dead because of me."

"Donny Gallagher is dead because dirty cops killed him," Omak said in a calm, almost reassuring voice. "Can you tell us who beat your dad, son? Who killed him?"

Chris brought his shackled hands up to his cheeks and tried to wipe away the tears. "I honestly don't know. Lots of cops hung around my dad. Cribben seemed to be the boss, but he's got a soft heart. I can't see him hurting Dad."

Omak began walking Chris around the table, but Z stopped him.

"Wait a second," Z said. "You've been impersonating a cop here. How long has that been going on?"

"Just a few weeks. Dad didn't know about it, but his uniform fit just fine, and I wore it here one day almost as a joke. But people around here liked me more when I was a cop. They told me I made them feel safe. It was a good feeling for everyone, so I figured it was no big deal."

"Impersonating a law enforcement officer is a class C felony in Oregon," Omak said. "That alone can get you five years in prison."

"But people liked it," Chris argued petulantly, "and I didn't hurt anyone."

"You stole from them," Z pointed out. "All the trinkets and figurines in the cookie tins? What's up with that?"

Chris's chin dropped as he gave me a sad look. "When I was picking up cookies from Aunt Peg, I would occasionally lift a pair of earrings or figurines. I've been a klepto since I was a kid, but it's no big deal," Chris confessed. "It's how I deal with stress."

"It is illegal," I said. "It would be good to find a way to alleviate stress that won't get you locked up."

"I always figured Dad could get me out of trouble if I ever got caught. But that's the fun of it—not getting caught."

"Those days are over, Chris," Omak said, clapping a hand on his shoulder. "Let's go." We watched as Omak finished walking Chris down the hall to the squad car.

"I should've caught on to the kleptomaniac thing earlier," I said. "He had a record of shoplifting, but the charges had always been dropped."

"Hey, we caught another bad guy." Derringer smiled at me, and I felt like I might catch fire from the intensity. "Chris just confessed to pulling the copycat heist at First Sunrise. All because you pulled it out of him. You're really a natural, Laura." His eyes warmed to a golden shade of plum wine when he smiled. "You understand what makes people tick. And in this case, you used it to disarm that kid and get him to confess."

For a second, I wished my parents had been in the room right then to hear an FBI agent compliment my work. "Thank you," I replied, wishing I could bask in Derringer's compliment without feeling weak in the knees. "Unfortunately, Chris couldn't tell us who killed Franny Landon. I was sure Chris would have some inside information through his father, but now I believe Donny kept him out of the loop, trying to protect him."

"Hey, it's progress," Derringer said, "and you've been work-ing on the case, narrowing down the cops who were on the scene the night of the homicide. We'll go back to the evidence and the records. Due diligence. Sometimes that's how cases get solved."

"I know that. So . . . I guess we have some digging in our future."

"We do." Derringer's hands were behind him, pressed against the wall, as if he needed the support. "So . . . I guess I'll see you back at the precinct."

"I guess so," I said, wishing I could come up with some multi-syllabic words, which was challenging when I was looking up into Derringer's eyes. It was going to be a challenge to stay focused on the case now that the door had opened to all this . . . this possibil-ity. "Mori! Let's go," Z called, saving me from saying something gooey-romantic and embarrassing myself forever.

*　*　*

Back at the precinct, things were a little chaotic as we set up tan-dem cases charging Chris Gallagher. Z was working with Clau-dia Deming, the county prosecutor, to write up the petty theft and impersonation charges against Chris, while Derringer and I worked again with the federal prosecutor Mitch Lampert to charge Chris with the robbery of the First Sunrise Bank. Although we were noses to the grindstone, celebration was in the air. Omak brought in sacks of burgers and fries so we could power through the evening hours. Ellie was playing Christmas carols on her iPhone dock, and the lights that had been strung around the win-dows of the squad room blinked merrily as we compiled state-ments and evidence for our cases.

It was hard to resist the festive mood. Some major cases had been solved. But as I worked, the two unsolved homicides niggled at me. The time frame and Chris's statement cast suspicion on Brown in Donny's murder, and I wanted these bank robberies to be done so I could dive deep into that homicide investigation.

Omak and Z knew I'd identified the alley vandal as Jason MacKenzie, but we didn't have time to act on that information tonight.

First, we had to wrap up Twilight.

Mitch called a judge for a warrant to search Chris's apartment, and while that was being processed, we pulled together Chris's confession, the video and evidence from the recent First Sunrise robbery, and Chris Gallagher's criminal history.

Time seemed like small blips of interludes when the judge called in our search warrant, and Derringer and I took Milewski to help us search Chris Gallagher's ground-floor apartment. There were items that made me think Chris was frozen in time. A hot dog cooker. A framed poster from the film *Rudy*. A radio shaped like SpongeBob SquarePants. Chris Gallagher struck me as one of those guys who had gotten stuck somewhere in junior high and never moved ahead. In the bedroom closet was a stack of baseball caps. Derringer found the Uncle Kombucha cap toward the bottom of the pile. And in Chris's sock drawer, stuffed into half a dozen white athletic socks, we found sixteen thousand dollars. "Most of the haul from the First Sunrise bank robbery," I said. "I guess he didn't subscribe to the cookie tin method."

"I've never seen that much cash," Milewski said. "It makes me nervous. Someone could rob us on the way back to the precinct."

"Between the three of us, I think we've got this covered," I told him.

There was still a festive mood in the air a few hours later as the night shift began to file in, most people pleased that we'd snagged a bank robber and the Sunset Pines thief.

"All in one night!" Ellie exclaimed. "It reminds me of that *Christmas Carol* story, where everything changes on Christmas Eve."

"I love that story. Especially the ghost of Christmas future. Straight out of a horror film. But anyway, good job on the case." Esme Garcia gave me a fist bump as she passed my desk. "You rock."

"You've really hit the jackpot, Mori, sewing up two cases in a row," Lister said. "And the Twilight Bandit was a big one."

"Yeah, I didn't think that one would ever be solved," Van Der Linde said as he removed his black leather gloves and rubbed his hands together. "All of this is kind of a big deal, Mori. I hope you know how lucky you got, everything falling together for you."

I nodded, glad for their support.

Mitch Lampert looked up from our shared screen, held up a pen, and pointed to Van Der Linde.

"Hold on, there, Officer. Did you say luck?" Lampert's eyes flashed, silvery and mysterious behind the glare of his spectacles. "Good detective work is organized, meticulous work, strategizing, research, and countless interviews. This suspect didn't fall into Detective Mori's lap. She followed the clues, gained his trust, and extracted a confession. And *that* is how an investigation is done."

"Credit where credit is due," Van Der Linde said.

"Ten-four," Milewski said, nodding. "Good job, Mori. And Z, too. Wherever he is." He was in the conference room, working with Claudia. "He solved the mystery of the missing tchotchkes, right? It's all good, man."

"Thanks, Milewski," I said with a rush of warm feeling. Maybe the entire squad wasn't pitted against me. Maybe the other cops were starting to come around. Well . . . some of them.

The evening shift coming off patrol wasn't quite as thrilled with the way the case had been resolved.

"I'm upset that Donny's boy, Chris, got caught up in this." Cranston crossed his arms, folding himself into a grim frown. "His old man just passed away, and now he's facing jail time? He'll probably miss his dad's memorial service. That doesn't seem right."

"If you do the crime, you've got to pay the time," Brown said, tossing off the comment as if he were talking about something innocuous as the weather, not the likely conviction of his friend's son. It was a stark contrast to his remarks the previous day, when he'd thought Donny should be immune from prosecution because he'd been a cop. Ward Brown definitely had a loose screw. I figured it would take Dr. Mack years to straighten out that twisted mind.

"Come off it, Brown. When'd you get so heartless?" Cranston muttered.

"When the kid walked into that bank and passed the note," Brown said. "He's a crook now. Let him serve his time. You never know. When all is said and done, it might turn out that Chris was the one who offed his old man. Sick of taking care of him. One of those elder abuse situations."

"That's bullshit," Cranston protested.

"Chris wouldn't do that," Scooter piped up.

"You never know," Brown insisted. "Everyone's a suspect. Right, Mori?"

Brown didn't need to know that Chris had an alibi for that evening—his job at the Regal Cleaners. He hadn't closed up the shop until eighteen forty-five, long after the car with two masked men had been seen pulling up at Donny's house.

"Do you have Chris on your list of possible suspects in Donny's killing?" Brown pressed. "You should."

Brown never stopped pushing his agenda. "That's right," I said. "Everyone's a suspect."

Including you.

*   *   *

"That's it," Lampert said. "The arrest reports are done. I'm sending copies of the case file to everyone on the email list. We may have a few loose ends to tie up later, but for now it's good enough for government work." He squinted at me. "That's a joke."

"And I would laugh if I weren't so tired." I rose to walk him out of the precinct. "Thanks for all your help." As a lawyer for the FBI, Mitch Lampert had become an expert on prosecuting bank robberies.

"Agent Derringer, how's the evidence coming on accomplices in the Twilight case?"

"It's moving along," Derringer said. "So far we don't have a lot to show that Donald Gallagher had accomplices, but Mori and I are working on that."

"Great. Keep me posted."

I started to walk Mitch out, but he held up a hand. "I know the way by now. Good night, now."

When I turned around, Derringer was staring at the floor.

"So, Laura. I guess I need to apologize." He looked up, his eyes all smoky and brown. Probably from lack of sleep, but something about those eyes tugged at me. "You know, I really underestimated you."

"Did you?" I could hardly breathe.

"My mistake. You've moved swiftly on what might prove to be three separate cases. You've shown remarkable investigative skills."

I liked a man who could admit to making a mistake. "Thanks, I guess. You seem a little surprised that I might have some talent."

"I'm really stepping on it here. What I want to say is, you're pretty amazing, and I enjoy working with you."

I wanted to tell him that I felt the same way, but I struggled to form intelligent words. "Same," I said. So lame.

Looking nervous, Derringer folded his arms across his chest. "I know we're working a case together, and I don't want to over-step bounds. But I was wondering if you'd like to have dinner with me sometime, you know, after all this is wrapped up."

My heart flip-flopped in my chest. "I'd love that."

Derringer extended a hand to me and we shook, but he held my hand a little longer, and the warmth from his palm floated through my whole body, making me feel a little light-headed. Was this really happening? I couldn't believe I'd caught the eye of a tall, good-looking, dedicated investigator.

"But really, I wonder . . ." I looked around at the near-empty squad room, where a janitor was emptying trash and two detectives on the night squad were going over plans for a DUI checkpoint. "Why do we have to wait?"

He dropped my hand. "Well . . . protocol. It seems more professional."

"Sure. But you could come over to my place and have a glass of wine. Or Gatorade or tea, if that's your thing."

"Wine is good."

"My housemate will be there, and maybe her boyfriend. Z. My partner."

"Sounds incestuous."

"One big happy family," I said, barely able to believe I was putting myself out there. "And with the protocol thing, there aren't really any hard-and-fast rules, so it's not like we'd be doing anything wrong."

"Nothing illegal," he said.

"And you're staying in a hotel, which must be kind of lame after a while."

"It gets stale fast."

"So get your coat and come over," I said, channeling a vixen from a noir film.

"Now?"

"We're done for the night. And I've got a craving for a gin martini."

He smiled, his eyes curious, as if he wasn't sure if I was kidding. "Sounds dangerous."

"Only if you drive home afterwards," I said, getting my flirt on. "Seriously, get your coat, and you can follow me there."

My heart did a rap-beat thing as I rolled out of the precinct parking lot, the lights of Derringer's car in my rearview mirror. I called my mother on the way home, wanting to have the check-in thing out of the way so the night would be free to socialize. While I was talking with Mom, a text from Natalie buzzed in, telling me she would be staying at Z's tonight. Really. Really? Now I would have to live up to the vixen in my invitation.

But Derringer didn't seem to care that it was just the two of us. He seemed to enjoy seeing the house. The arched doorways and old-fashioned picture window. The butcher-block countertop with mismatched barstools. The colored-glass collection in the kitchen window. The mountain of pillows that seemed to be an addiction for Natalie.

"It's a rental, but my first place," I said.

"It's nice," he said. "Feels like home."

"So, have a seat," I said, pushing a bunch of pillows aside to clear a space. "What can I get you to drink?"

"That martini you mentioned sounds pretty good."

"I'm on it." My signature drink, and one I had mastered in college. "Some people like straight vodka in their martinis, but I like the tang of gin." I put two sexy martini classes on the counter so I could give Derringer my total attention. Gin, shaker, ice, vermouth. Large, plump olives, my gourmet indulgence. "And there's always the matter of dry vermouth. Vermouth, or not vermouth, that is the question. How would you like yours?"

"Surprise me," he said from the corner of the couch, where he'd cleared a spot, neatly stacking pillows to his right.

"All right. Then we'll do shaken, not stirred, with a splash of olive juice for that umami flavor." I poured gin into the shaker, trying not to overpour but failing as my gaze kept going to him.

"So when did you become an expert—"

The bang of an explosion at the front window kept Derringer from finishing his question as smashed glass went flying like dandelion seeds in the wind.

A violent wind.

The shock of it roared in my ears as pieces of glass glimmered in the light, sickeningly sharp.

Destructive.

Deadly.

For a split second I stole a look at Derringer, thinking that it couldn't end this way.

Not in a rain of glass.

28

My pulse raced as the front window came crashing into my home. Glass shards shattered and flew into the living room, tearing through the air in a savage fury that sent me collapsing to the floor. Without conscious thought, I ducked behind the kitchen counter as splintered diamonds exploded in the air.

"Derringer?" I called, my voice strangled with fear. I remained hunkered down while the last bits of tinkling shards settled to the ground. "Are you okay?"

For a second, all I heard was the rumble of an engine in front of the house, made louder by the hole in the window. A car tore out of our driveway, its roar ripping the dark silence. I rose above the counter to see Derringer pushing his way out from under the pile of pillows, where he had taken cover when the window had been blasted.

"I'm okay. You all right?" Suddenly he was on his feet and by my side, touching the top of my head, pressing his hand to my cheek.

My racing pulse thrummed in my ears, my senses on alert as I nodded and pointed to the window.

"Someone tossed a rock through your window," he said, forming the conclusion I was too shocked to make. He crossed to the door in four steps, a gun in his hand. The door flew open and he disappeared outside.

"Nick?" I stumbled around the kitchen peninsula, then stopped, afraid to tread on broken glass in just my socks.

Suddenly, Nick was back, holstering his gun as he rushed over to me. "Are you okay?" He put his arms around me, supporting me.

I leaned into him, grateful that he was here. "I'm fine, but shaken. What about you? You were close to the window."

"Saved by the pillows. I tried to get a look at the vehicle, but it was already turning onto the road. Looked like a car, but the plate wasn't illuminated." He held me close for a minute, rubbing my back as I melted against him. "Do you want to sit down?"

"Just for a second," I said, reluctantly breaking contact and hobbling over to one of the stools. "I'll need my shoes to start cleaning up."

"I'll get them. But before we do anything, we need to call this in." He was already on his phone, tapping in the precinct number.

"Are you sure?"

"Laura, this needs to be on record. Someone just attacked you in your home." He handed me my shoes, then began talking to the dispatcher. Probably someone I knew. This was all so weird, so up close and personally menacing.

While Derringer talked to the dispatcher, I went to the rock on the floor and noticed that it was actually a brick. A heavy one that I could use for arm exercises. A piece of yellow lined paper was wrapped around it, attached with a rubber band. I got a pair of latex gloves from my closet, then picked up the brick and opened the note.

DONNY G DESERVED WHAT HE GOT. LET IT GO.

"Donny G?" I said aloud.

The note could have been written by a mobster in the 1920s. Now he wanted me to back away from investigating Donny's murder? Fat chance.

*   *   *

The house felt different Saturday morning when I awoke to the chiming alarm on my cell phone and walked, zombielike, into the kitchen to plunk a coffee pod into the machine and start my morning brew.

Cold seeped in through the boarded-up living room window. Reminded of the night before, I shivered. It was darker in here, and there was a visitor still asleep on my couch. Thick dark hair was visible beneath the fluffy white blanket. Stretched out, he seemed to cover the couch from end to end.

Oh, yeah. My boyfriend.

Hard for me to believe, as I hadn't been involved with anyone since my childhood crush, but there was a definite chemistry between Nick and me.

He had stayed over, but not in my bed.

Things had taken a turn after the night shift cops had taken a report, the glass had been swept up, the window boarded. He and I had found our way to each other, tentative at first, and then bold but tantalizingly slow. I would have happily stayed up all night exploring the landscape of Derringer with my lips, memorizing him with my fingertips. But chivalry was alive in Nick Derringer, who didn't want to take advantage of my vulnerability but also refused to leave me alone after the brick attack.

I was so crazy about him I wanted to laugh and cry at the same time.

I forced myself not to stare at the lump in the sofa that was my handsome new boyfriend and turned to get the milk out of the fridge.

Thank God Derringer had stayed. *Nick.* I had to get used to calling him that. Nick was the only reason I'd been able to fall asleep last night. Just knowing he was in the house, posted near the scene of the crime, had made me feel safe and incredibly cared for.

Cradling the warm mug, I stared above the sofa at the semi-darkness of the living room with one window covered with a piece of particle board Derringer had found in the garage. Turned out he was pretty handy with a drill and hammer, and the steady calm of his demeanor had helped prevent me from spinning into a panic.

I winced at that boarded-up window. Someone had tried to hurt me, but I couldn't let myself imagine the horrible possibilities if things had played out differently. I showered and dressed in my uniform. We had that important meeting with Omak and Garcia, and I had that commitment to Z later in the day. I was going to get out there and show that I wasn't afraid. Even if I was quivering inside, I'd try to put a defiant message out there. Laura Mori would not back down.

* * *

Derringer and I drove together to the off-site meeting in Clover Park, a city green space that backed up into the woods on the north side of town. If you drove in for half a mile, there was an expanse of cleared land that had been turned into soccer fields—eight of them—that hosted matches through much of the year. In the drizzling rain we passed one game that seemed to be a pickup match for men in their twenties.

At the end of the drive was a pavilion used for parties and barbecues in nice weather. A man in a watch cap and an oversized jacket sat atop one picnic table. I wondered if he was homeless, until he turned and I recognized Esme Garcia.

"Nice cover," I said, sliding onto the bench across from her.

"Just in case someone saw me talking with you guys," she said. "I've put too much time into this investigation to be exposed at this point."

The door of an SUV opened, and Omak strode over to us.

"It doesn't look like any of us were followed here," he said, "but I saw your name in last night's crime reports, Mori. What's that about?"

"Someone sent a brick through my window." I still felt shaky as I explained the incident. I left Nick's name out, although I knew he was listed as a witness in the crime report. Omak would have picked up on that.

"And the note told you to stop investigating Donny's murder?" Garcia nodded. "Somehow that doesn't surprise me."

"It's the third threat she's received this week," Derringer said, explaining about the other two incidents. "Though last night was more like an attack."

Omak pressed a fist to his forehead. "We've got to wind up this case before someone else gets hurt. Donny Gallagher's death is a reminder that the person or people involved in the Twilight case are absolutely ruthless. That one will haunt me for a while."

"None of us saw that coming." Garcia removed her cap and ran her fingers through her short, dark hair. "Especially not an attack on Donny. He might have pulled off those robberies years ago, but he was really struggling in the last year or so. It's really a heartbreak."

"But you weren't investigating Donny until this happened?" Derringer asked her.

Garcia shook her head. "He wasn't on my radar. My main focus has been our police chief, Buzz Cribben."

"The investigation actually started when the city council received anonymous tips on the mayor," Omak explained. "Since then, some of Cribben's neighbors have come forward to work with us. It started with some conspicuous consumption four years ago. A Corvette and a Lamborghini. A boat. Sudden riches that were beyond his salary, and he hadn't inherited money. Over the past few years a bit of a feud has developed, since the chief leaves the boat and fancy cars on the street, defying parking regulations."

"And I bet he never got a ticket," Derringer said.

"Exactly," Omak said. "It seems like a small thing, but Cribben's neighbors were angry enough to complain. The mayor asked us to investigate."

"Which got a little sticky when we sat on Cribben's house and began to see a pattern in Dolly Redmond's visits," Esme said. "We don't know if the mayor is aware of the affair. Which isn't illegal, of course. It just complicates things."

"Especially since Dolly is a part of the money distribution scheme," I said. "Did you read the report about Chris Gallagher's statement regarding the disbursement of funds from the Twilight robberies?"

"The cookie tins?" Garcia nodded. "At first I thought it was a joke."

"From what Chris says, Donny turned all the cash over and was doled out a stipend in cookie tins."

Garcia squinted. "During a stakeout I have seen Dolly Redmond bringing blue cookie tins to Cribben's house. Sometimes she has a few, and he helps her unload them from her car. But I wasn't sure what was inside."

"Cash," I said. "One of the tins in the apartment owned by Dolly's aunt Peg was loaded with cash. Stacks of fifties and hundreds in bank straps."

"This is one weird case," Garcia said, shaking her head. "It took us a while to build a case, but by staking out Cribben's place and listening in on his communications, we've collected evidence of police corruption, possibly racketeering, and aiding and abetting multiple bank robberies."

I thought of the chief's attitude toward the case this week: his insistence on updates, his push to get the bank robbery solved, get the public off his back, even if it meant arresting the wrong person as a diversion. At the time his leadership skills had seemed to be lacking; in truth, I think he had been trying to tuck this incident away before anyone started making connections. "If you don't mind my asking, what kind of evidence do you have on him?" I asked.

"We started by taking a close look at Cribben's emails and correspondence," Garcia said. "At first that didn't show us much, but then our tech guy was able to link Cribben's department-issued cell phone into the computer so we could read his text messages. That produced a gold mine. We have records of long calls to Donny Gallagher's residence. Donny didn't own a cell phone. And we have numerous text messages to Dolly Redmond and to an anonymous number. A burner phone. We'll call that person A. Cribben was alarmed by Monday's robbery, which wasn't planned. He texted A that any connection to Twilight would have to be shut down. Stop the investigation."

"So he ordered A to come after me," I said. "'A' slashed my tires, smashed my car. And then threw a brick at my house last night."

Garcia nodded. "I'm sorry we didn't figure out the pattern before now, but we still don't know the identity of A. We have some ideas, but I know you've been working the other end of the Twilight investigation. What's your thinking, Laura?"

"I think it has to be Brown," I admitted. "When I found my tires slashed, I smelled cigarette smoke nearby. And the second threat was delivered by a young man connected to Brown. It's Jason, Dr. MacKenzie's son."

"And Dr. Mack and Brown are dating," Garcia said.

I nodded.

"Hold on, now." Omak rubbed the back of his neck. "This is starting to sound more like *Soap Opera Digest* than an investigation."

"Jason MacKenzie is in his twenties and has a juvenile record. A violent record. It's likely he was the second man in the car that pulled into Donny's house the night he was killed."

"What about Cranston and Rivers?" Derringer asked.

"We know their whereabouts during the time of the attack on Donny," I said. "If they're involved, it seems that they're more on the periphery."

"And there was something suspicious about Brown the night of Donny's attack." Garcia glanced at Omak, who nodded. "For this investigation I've been floating around in the department, working with whoever needs a partner on a shift. It's been my way of gathering information. Yesterday I was partnered with Rivers, and he was freaking out about Brown. They'd worked together the night Donny was attacked, and Rivers sniffed something suspicious about it. Apparently Brown went off to have dinner with his son."

"And since Brown has no kids, that was probably Jason," I said.

"And afterwards, when they returned to patrol, Brown had a stain on his pants. Rivers thought it was blood. Brown said no, it was mud, and they returned to the precinct so Brown could change. Then an hour later, they respond to the bloodiest crime scene Rivers has ever seen. Gallagher's house."

It seemed so obvious. "Oh my God, is he saying Brown attacked Donny?" I asked.

Garcia tugged the sleeves of her jacket over her hands. "Rivers isn't saying that, but he's thinking it."

"Which would explain why Brown seemed so callous that day, saying Donny was dead, leaving him bleeding there. Maybe he thought he'd killed him." The low hum of a warning filled my ears as I looked over at Omak. "This is incriminating for Brown. Will Rivers come forward with what he knows?"

Garcia shrugged. "We might be able to coax it out of him. Rivers is scared, afraid of Brown's wrath, afraid of getting jammed up for not speaking out."

"I'll talk with Rivers," Derringer said. "If he's on the fence, I might be able to convince him to go on the record with what he knows. I've learned a few things about cajoling the truth from a subject," he said, giving me a quick glance.

"I'm not sure about all the connections," Omak said. "I don't see Dr. MacKenzie as a person who would compromise her professional oath."

"Maybe not deliberately," I agreed. "But still, Brown could gain some access through her. Maybe when she shares anecdotes of her day. Maybe he has access to case files that aren't locked up."

"And Brown is no angel," Garcia said. "He used to be a good cop, but the last few years I feel like he's kind of phoning it in. I worked a few shifts with him where he tried to gloss over 911 calls. Didn't want to do the work counseling people and getting to the bottom of issues."

"We have some evidence that points to Brown as the shooter in the Franny Landon homicide," I said, "and now it looks like he's responsible for Donny Gallagher's death."

"We need to bring Brown in," Derringer said. "If nothing else, he's a person of interest."

"If we arrest him, that will put him off the street," I said, "and we can search his locker and his car for traces of Donny's blood. Anyone involved in an attack like that would come away with trace evidence. Maybe we'll find that burner phone on him. And if we search his apartment, we might find the cookie tins with money. We can do a forensic search of his accounts, see if he's got income he hasn't declared or accounted for. We can search for weapons. Or we can get the others to turn on him—the chief or Dolly Redmond." I turned to Esme. "Do you have enough evidence to arrest them?"

"We were hoping to go after everyone at the same time to avoid tipping anyone off," she said. "And we don't want to move on Cribben until we have a warrant to search his home, his personal records and bank accounts." She turned to Derringer. "How's that going?"

"My boss is working on it," Derringer said. "I'll see if he can put a rush on it."

"For now, I'll reach out to Brown, see if I can get him in to talk," said Omak. "I noticed on the roll call schedule that he's put in for today off, so it might take a while to track him down. But as soon as we decide to move on this ring, we need to bring the kid in—Dr. MacKenzie's son. He's young; he might break down and talk to us when he realizes how much he has to lose. I'll work with Agent Derringer on searching lockers and processing evidence. If they think it's a wider sweep, they might not panic as fast."

"I just hate to show our hand by raiding lockers," Garcia said. "Once we let them know we're closing in, they might destroy evidence or skip town. Maybe Brown is already on a flight to Tahiti."

"At this point, it's a chance we have to take," Omak said. "Enough is enough."

29

There were a lot of moving parts to this complex case, but somehow I knew they fit together, and I was determined to figure out how.

Two bank bandits had been caught, but it seemed like we were miles away from a conviction for our cop killers. "Have you ever had a case like this?" I asked Derringer as he drove back to the precinct. "What seems to be a simple bank robbery splits into three or four different cases? A bank robbery. A copycat heist. Intertwined with two murdered police officers, and a ring of police corruption that somehow involves cookie tins?"

Derringer looked over at me curiously. "To be honest, I haven't worked that many cases. But I think you'd be safe to say this one's unique."

"We need to solve the homicides," I said.

"We will."

"I'm worried about Brown being out there. Armed and dangerous. As a law enforcement officer, he has even more power to hurt people."

That bloodstain Rivers had noticed was bothering me, too.

"If Brown and some other guy in the car killed Donny, how do you see it playing out?" Derringer asked.

"I think Brown got angry when he thought his old friend pulled a bank heist without sharing the proceeds. Maybe Brown went over to the house to let Donny know he did the wrong thing, and the beating got out of control. Or maybe Brown just wanted to shut Donny up for good. End any liability of Donny talking too much to the wrong person. Like me."

He nodded. "Makes sense. Where'd you learn about this Jason kid? The son of Brown's girlfriend?"

I explained that a school administrator had remembered him as a troubled student, and then I'd recognized him in family photos at the police psychologist's office. "Which leads me to believe that Dr. Mack has no idea her son is involved in anything illegal right now. But knowing what we know about Brown and not being able to arrest him yet, it makes me incredibly nervous."

"I'll push Omak to bring him in for questioning, and maybe the locker search will give us insight into who killed Donny. I've just got to take care of a conference call as soon as we get to the precinct. My boss and Mitch Lampert need information so we can get the warrant to look at the chief's bank accounts and follow the trail of money in the Twilight burglaries. I haven't yet told the boss that we're going to have to raid the cookie tins of a woman in her nineties at a nursing home."

"A possible PR disaster for the FBI," I said.

"God, I hope not."

* * *

We arrived at the precinct armed with large, rich lattes. I changed into my uniform and, on my way out of the locker room, fielded a call from Dolores Elsinore, an owner of Regal Cleaners, who was responding to my further inquiries about Chris Gallagher.

"He's a good employee," she said. "Always on time and friendly with customers. We're so sad to hear about his father. It's so frightening. I can't believe Chris was involved in that."

"The attack is still being investigated," I said. "While Donny worked with you, did you ever experience cash shortages?"

"No."

"Did you ever suspect that he was stealing from the business?"

"Absolutely not," Elsinore insisted. "We would never have tolerated that. And Donny knows that we have cameras in the shop, one pointed at the cash register."

I thanked Mrs. Elsinore and opened up an email from a former classmate who now worked as a tattoo artist. She was getting back to me on the shape and colors of Jason MacKenzie's tattoo, which I'd been researching to see if it had any gang affiliations.

A text message from Z told me he was waiting in the parking lot. I closed my files, specially coded now so that every cop in the precinct didn't have access, and shrugged into my jacket. Z thought I was doing him a favor, coming along today, but I had my own selfish motives. If he had a breakthrough, we might gain key information about Franny's murder. I was hopeful that Z's memories from that night might break this case wide open.

Footsteps sounded behind me. Someone was following me down the hall.

I turned to find Nick. We were standing in a quiet hallway around a corner from the soon-to-be bustling squad room.

"Hi there," I said.

"Hey." Looking nervous, he moved a step closer to me. "I was just thinking about last night. That, well, we probably shouldn't say anything to anyone about me being at your place. Considering that we work together."

"I know." Somehow, his concern made me want to giggle. This was so junior high, but it was sweet that he was looking out for our reputations. "Professionalism is important for both of us."

"Agreed."

"And you need to be extra careful. A brick through the window is more than a message delivery system. You're in danger, Laura. You could ask Omak to take you off duty until this is all resolved."

"That's not necessary. I can handle myself," I insisted.

We were standing close to each other, savoring the moment, our faces inches apart, when Z rounded the corner.

"Uh. You ready to head out, Mori?" My partner looked slightly amused, but also uncomfortable. "I'll be out by your car."

"I'll be right there." I touched Derringer's arm and slipped away quickly. "We'll talk later," I said, barely able to tear my gaze away from those smoky eyes.

Z and I walked silently through the precinct, passing a grumbling Cranston as he moved toward Omak's office. I suspected that he'd been called in for an interview. I hoped that Derringer would share everything about the interviews and locker searches when I saw him later.

"Word is, Omak's tried to reach Brown a couple of times but he's not responding," Z whispered to me as we hopped in my car.

"Really? Maybe he's sailing off into the sunset. You know that boat he's always bragging about?" I asked, pulling out of the parking lot. Under a gray and ominous sky we cruised down the street toward Pacific Lake Bank.

"It's pretty cold to be on a freakin' sailboat," Z said. "He really is an odd duck. I don't know what Dr. Mack sees in him."

"Besides those cowboy good looks?" I asked.

"Hold on. I need to text Dr. MacKenzie that we're on our way to the bank. And as soon as I'm done with this, we're going to talk about whatever was going on back there between you and Romeo."

"Nothing."

"Yeah, that looked like nothing. It looked *exactly* like nothing. You and Derringer are like two puppies falling all over each other."

"Not true! We're very professional." I shook my head, trying to bite back a smile. "Off the record, I'm crazy about him."

"Off the record? Like I'm writing your life story, Mori. And if I was, I wouldn't be including who stayed over at your house and whatnot." That morning I had texted Z and Natalie a few details about the attack, the broken window, and the fact that Derringer had stayed the night.

"No, there was no *whatnot* last night, but I was really glad he stayed. Truth is, I wasn't sure he was interested in me at all until last night."

Z looked at me sideways. "Really? Do we need to get you a Seeing Eye dog? Are you that blind?"

I grinned. In the months Z and I had ridden together, we had developed a comfortable pattern of teasing and ribbing each other. I finally felt like a real cop with a real partner, someone who would always have my back.

"You can pull into the parking lot," Z said, pointing at the empty area beside the fence and shrubs.

"No way." I turned onto the street in front of the bank, searching for a place to parallel park. "The bank is open for Saturday hours. The last thing we need to do is incite a panic in their customers."

"You're right. Sorry. Got my head up my ass."

"You're preoccupied."

As I shut off the car and removed the keys, I got an eerie feeling there was something I was missing. Z's phone dinged with a text message.

"Okay," he said. "That's Dr. Mack telling me to take it slow and call if I need to talk things through."

"That's nice, but you could talk to me," I said, remembering the psychologist's office—the warm colors, the waterscape paintings, the family photos. "Don't you think it's weird that she has a son who's out of control?" I asked. "Who might end up being a suspect in Donny's murder?"

"That's definitely creepy. But I bet Dr. Mack knows nothing about what her son is up to. We can't control our family, Mori. Ask my mother. Ask your parents."

I frowned, searching for a spot on the street.

"What do you know about Dr. Mack's son?"

"Jason is his name. I researched his ink, and it's not a gang tattoo. I searched online and called a tattoo artist I went to school with. No association that we know of." I pulled into a spot in front of a small office building and turned off the engine. "I need to talk with Jason. See how long he's been following me and who put him up to it."

"I'll bet it's Brown, that nut job. Probably taking advantage of Dr. Mack's kid, using him as a goon to scare you off your investigation. Look, I'll help you find Jason this afternoon." Z's eyes looked heavy from fatigue. In anticipation of today's walk around the crime scene, he probably hadn't slept much last night. His sorry state fueled my motivation to solve Franny's murder. Z needed release, a chance to move on emotionally from that terrible night.

I exhaled sharply. My next question was tough. "Do you trust MacKenzie?"

Z twisted his mouth. "I don't trust many people, Mori. I trust you. I trust Natalie. I trust my mother. Outside of those three people, I'm guarded." He looked out the car window before turning back to me. "But I do know I'm getting closer to remembering what happened that night, and a lot of that is due to Dr. Mack. I'm not stopping until I've got it all back."

*   *   *

Z and I walked the perimeter of the bank and watched a few customers come and go through big glass doors with the words PACIFIC LAKE etched on them. I was quiet, letting Z gather his thoughts about that fateful night. Z turned, and I followed him over to the area at the far end of the parking lot and behind the fence where Franny was shot.

"When I found her on the ground, I didn't want to move her. They say you can make a medical situation worse by moving someone, but I had no choice," Z said, kneeling down on the ground near where Franny had fallen. "She was on the ground here, but I pulled her away. Over there." He pointed to the lamppost on the corner. "Under that damned Christmas bell."

*   *   *

Z hadn't mentioned moving her before. "Why? Why did you move her?"

He shook his head. "I don't know. Or maybe . . . Something whizzed by my ear. A bullet? It narrowly missed me. Not sure what direction it came from, but . . ."

He and I both looked over at the preschool and the top of the play structure, barely visible behind a plot of bare-limbed trees.

"I dragged Franny away from the line of fire, over behind that streetlamp base. Not much cover, but the best I could find. That was where I dropped to the ground to give her CPR. Under that tinsel bell that hung off the lamp."

"These are new memories, right?" I asked.

He nodded as we went over to the streetlamp. "Not the bell, but I didn't remember dragging her until now."

This explained the crime scene photos I'd seen in the FBI file—the long smear of blood that had been measured at more than four feet, a bloodstain that had gone unexplained in the sparsely detailed report.

Z kneeled and touched the ground, then looked up. "That damned tinsel bell was up there, and the bells on the door of the barbershop were jingling in the wind. I remember it now. As I dropped down to do chest compressions, I worried that the shooter might hit me, too, but I couldn't back off. I had to save her."

I nodded, taking it all in. The shooter had shot at Franny. Only Franny.

Not Z or any other cop who had come later.

This had been a specific hit, a way to stop the Twilight Bandit investigation. Stop Franny Landon, the cop who was getting close to the ring of corruption.

"And then he came and pushed me away." Z looked up at me, squinting against the soft drizzling rain that had begun to fall. "I remember it clearly now. It was Brown. He said something about taking over, and he moved me off Franny and bent down over her."

"Ward Brown," I said. "You're sure."

Z took a deep breath. I could see he was fighting to stay composed. "It was Brown. He took Franny's pulse at her neck and insisted that she was dead. Called it in on the radio and said, 'Confirm kill,' like a military sniper on a mission."

30

Z was remembering.

Finally, he knew.

He remembered that Brown was the one who'd let Franny die. That Cranston arrived next on the scene, and he argued with Brown about a gun. The shooter's gun. It had been found in the bushes between Franny and the bank.

Cranston questioned why the shooter would run back to toss the gun and then run away from the bank. Brown kept telling Cranston to shut up and stop asking stupid questions.

And all the time Z was fighting Brown, trying to get to Franny, until Brown finally gave up manhandling him and let Z drop to the ground beside her, restarting CPR.

And then everyone was there—half a dozen cops, Sgt. Stanford, Chief Cribben, the owners of the nearby shops that were still open. Z was treated for shock, relieved of his gun and shield, and questioned over the next few days. A hundred questions with answers he couldn't reach.

Suddenly a phone chimed and buzzed, pulling him back to the here and now as Mori looked at her phone, said it was Omak, that she would call him back in a minute.

"What else?" she asked him, her voice seeming to vibrate through water. "What else do you remember, Z?"

And he slipped back to that night, the darkness coming back to him, swift and fierce now. The iron smell of blood. The rush of paramedics around Franny and him. The panicked feeling stirred by the sirens.

The sound of a shot ringing in his ears.

But the gunshot—it wasn't a memory.

Pain bloomed through his chest and he roared in agony as his body was flung backward, blown off his feet by a bullet to the chest.

No!

He was hit. Z knew the burning sensation meant he'd been shot.

He was on the ground, eyes closed, in a dark place. His vision dimmed. Drops of sweat ran down his face, and he felt clammy and nauseated all at once. His heart beat like a frantic bat in his ears.

As if in slow motion he opened his eyes, saw Mori wheel around and drop down beside him, her eyes wild and panicked. She was yelling at him, asking him something, but he couldn't move his lips. He could only watch her as the pain in his chest swelled and his breath . . . he couldn't catch his breath.

Mori was yelling into her radio, but he heard only bits and pieces.

Finally, her voice filtered through. "Officer down! Officer down!"

Suddenly, the world grew smaller and smaller until it was nothing but a pinhole too small to see anything.

It was his cue to escape. Go. Go before the tiny circle of light closed forever.

And he closed his eyes, faded to the darkness.

31

The gunshot brought me a burst of adrenaline that dulled the edges of my vision and sharpened the sights, sounds, and smells in front of me.

The boom of gunfire, and then eerie silence.

The smell of wet pavement and soil in the drizzling rain, and then the tang of salty sweat and panic.

The sight of Z flying back, as if an enormous bear had shoved him across the sidewalk with a fat, hefty paw. It took me a second to register that my partner's flight from his feet and onto the ground was related to the sharp bang we'd just heard.

The world seemed to freeze over then; time suspended as I dropped to the pavement and tried to help him. Talking constantly, probably nonsensically, I found the pulse in his neck, noticed his ashen, clammy skin, his moans, his panting, his pain.

He was conscious, no blood that I could see, breathing with a pulse.

But he'd been hit, and we had to get the hell out of there before the shooter fired again.

Babbling on about how he was going to be okay, I grabbed Z by the armpits, lifted his head and shoulders, and started dragging.

It was a bumpy ride over the pavement. Probably tearing the hell out of the bottom of his pants and scuffing the backs of the boots that he polished to a dull shine. The thirty feet from the corner of the street to the front door of the bank seemed like a mile, but some man on his way out of the bank rushed to help me drag Z the rest of the way into the vestibule.

Z was out, and I checked for a pulse again as soon as we got him inside the door. Still there. "Stay with me, buddy," I said, then looked up at the concerned man.

"Don't go out there again," I told him, a sixty-something man with a graying beard. "Stay in the bank and take cover." I stepped away from the vestibule and raised my voice, trying to gain the attention of people in the bank as a woman, maybe the manager, rushed over from her cubicle. "There's an active shooter outside," I announced. "Lock the doors and take cover. Stay away from windows and doors."

The bearded man told me he was a retired Denver cop and he'd do anything he could to help. He helped me slide Z inside, to a safer spot behind a wall, while the bank manager—Pam was her name—went to the door with two big keys and locked up. Pam and the Denver cop started corralling people away from the windows while I got on my knees beside Z and started peeling off layers.

As I unzipped his jacket, I saw the bullet hole, clean through the fabric just off-center of his chest. Inches from his badge. A perfect hit, if Z hadn't been wearing his vest. Leaning close in industrial light, I unbuttoned his shirt and saw a tiny hole in his vest. Beneath it, I could feel the small round disk of the bullet, which had compacted into a large bead when it hit the Kevlar. When I touched that area, Z came back with a moan of pain.

"Hey, buddy," I said, tearing at the Velcro ties of the vest.

He moaned.

Which I took as a good sign. A great sign. He was alert enough to process the pain.

"You took a bullet to the chest, but your vest stopped it. The pain you feel is blunt-force trauma." Lifting the vest, I saw a dark, swollen area of impact. It looked raw, and I wondered if some ribs had been shattered. Maybe, but he was alive.

I let the fabric of the vest go and then fastened his jacket closed, knowing shock would make him shivery cold.

I pressed my palm to his cheek. "Hang on, partner. Help is on the way."

Z's eyes opened to a sliver, and he seemed to be focusing, but then he groaned, his head lolled to the side. He needed rest.

As he faded out again, I took out my cell phone and called dispatch. Ellie Colgate answered. I could tell it was her from the sound of her voice.

"Ellie, please. Laura Mori. I need your help . . ."

"What is it, Laura?"

"I'm at Pacific Lake Bank, with an active shooter outside. I think the shooter might be on our radio ban, listening in. Can you get word to the paramedics that the injured officer is inside the bank? He's breathing with a pulse. Looks like blunt-force trauma wound from the bullet. I don't want them going to the intersection and being in the line of fire."

"Got it," she said. "I'll advise the same to the two responding patrol cars. Call me back on this line if you need me."

I ended the call, feeling a rush of relief to know that an ambulance and backup were on their way. A moment of ease. And then it was time to go.

Once again, I crouched beside Z and leaned in close. He seemed peaceful now, as if sleeping. "You are okay," I said, lips close to his ear so that he could hear me. "Z, tell me that you're okay."

He flickered awake at the sound of my voice and stared at me as if I were an alien.

"I'm going after him," I said. "Tell me you're okay, because I've got to go catch that bastard."

He grunted.

"Z. I'm not leaving if you need me. Tell me you're okay. You gonna hold out until the paramedics get here?"

He winced in pain, and then gave a nod. "Hell to the yeah."

It was all I needed to hear.

32

Rage roiled my blood as I left Z in the care of the bank manager and headed for the Bloom Street exit. Knowing that the back door of the bank might still be visible to the shooter, I slipped out the front and hurried to the patrol car on the street.

The cold, damp air snapped me back to the moment. The reality. The need to hurry, but remain calm.

This one couldn't get away.

This one had to be stopped.

For the last few minutes, I'd been on autopilot, dragging Z out of range of another bullet, calling for backup, securing the bank. Tending to my partner. The last three or four minutes seemed like a lifetime. My subconscious mind had formulated a plan, and now I was laser focused on apprehending the shooter.

I would go beyond the shooter, to the far end of the preschool grounds, and come at him from the other side.

Him . . . Ward Brown.

I knew it was him. Had to be, the bastard.

I drove past the daycare center and peered into the parking lot beyond the building, where a lone car sat in the watery light from the gray sky. Was that the shooter's getaway car? Spotting the I'D RATHER BE SAILING bumper sticker, I knew it belonged to Brown, who always bragged about the big boat he was going to buy.

I passed the lot and parked on the street. Gun drawn, I ran to the building and took cover there. A car passed on the street, then another. Typical Saturday afternoon traffic. Then, holding my breath, I moved into the entryway to the preschool parking lot.

Would I come face-to-face with Brown, his gun drawn, his eyes lifeless and craven?

No. As I eased along the side wall, the parking lot was empty but for Brown's car. I covered my eyes against the drizzle and tried to see ahead. Was the shooter still there in the play structure, lingering? Was he waiting for another victim to walk into his sites? Waiting for me? Or maybe he was packing up, getting ready to flee before backup came blazing in.

As far as I could see, there was no motion. No sign of life.

But I sensed him.

Adrenaline surged in my veins, making my head feel light and heavy at the same time as I eased along the school. The back of my jacket swept the bricks as I kept close to the one-story building as a means of cover. Across the pavement, the fat bushes remained still, and if I focused I could see light through them.

No movement. No sound. No one was crouching there.

Kneeling in the wood chips beside the school, I took out my phone and called the dispatch number again. This time I gave Ellie my coordinates and told her I was going to secure the perimeter to keep the shooter from escaping.

"Ten-four, Laura."

Ellie assured me she would keep this call quiet, and I gave her my location. She was going to contact Omak on his private line for backup and promised to keep me on speaker phone no matter what.

"I think the shooter is Ward Brown," I said. "I repeat, Officer Ward Brown. At any rate, we know the shooter is armed and dangerous."

"Don't move in until backup arrives," Ellie said.

"Not planning to. I'm sitting a few yards from Brown's car, and I'm going to intercept him if he makes a dash for it."

"Okay. Hold tight."

As I waited, wedged against the building, I ran the case against Brown in my head. First, he was a trained military sniper, so he definitely had the skill to pull off Franny's murder and the attempt on Z's life. And Brown's military training aligned with Z's memory of him saying "Confirm kill" over Franny's body. Also, he was one of Donny Gallagher's so-called friends. And his fingerprints had been found on the tape used to cover the outside bank cameras. It demonstrated that he had a plan to take action outside the bank the day that he killed Franny—action that he didn't want to be recorded on camera. He had planned and executed Franny's death—a premeditated murder.

Not to mention Donny's murder. I suspected that the locker search and investigation of the burner phone Cribben was known to call would incriminate Brown in Donny Gallagher's murder and the Twilight robberies.

Plus he was dating Daphne MacKenzie, the police psychologist, and the woman who was helping Z regain his memories of Franny's murder. I now realized that today had been a trap. A setup. MacKenzie had advised Z to return to the bank for "therapy" and then tipped Brown off that Z was on his way to the bank. Brown must have realized Z was on the brink of remembering what really happened the night Franny was killed. On the cusp of the vision of Brown as Franny Landon's murderer.

If I hadn't been so scared and angry, squatting in the flower bed of the preschool, I would have blamed and chastised myself for not seeing that one coming. Dr. Mack had manipulated Z and me, and I'd sensed the subterfuge when I visited her office. Stupid me. But there'd be time to kick myself later.

I hoped.

A cold fear soaked through my sizzling fury as I realized I was out here by myself, and Brown was definitely armed. Every instinct shrieked for me to retreat . . . go back to the bank.

But I couldn't back away.

The shooter in this schoolyard had tried to kill my partner. I couldn't let him get away.

I scurried to the end of the building, as close to the parking lot as I could get. Peering around the building's edge, I looked toward the play structure and saw something move.

He was there!

Any minute now he'd get into his car and drive away. I had to stop him before he did.

I ducked back behind the building to steady my thudding pulse and think for a minute. No way could I cross the parking lot, in plain sight. But if I kept to the left, following the fence line that bordered the dumpsters, it would lead to the trees near the playground, where there was some cover.

I could get closer. Take him by surprise.

I could do this. I had to do this.

Inching along the fence, I forced myself to breathe through the fear clenching my body and listen carefully for the sound of him scurrying away, trying to escape. At the end of the fence I dared a glance at the playground and noticed a figure at the top of the play structure.

He was still there!

I hurried away from the fence and took cover behind a small green box, an electrical transformer. My pulse hammered as I took a breath and sneaked another look. Squinting against the cold drizzle, I saw the shooter straighten and lift his gun, pointing toward Fir Street and the bank.

Had someone wandered into the intersection? Was he going to shoot again? No!

Gripping my service pistol, I ran toward him to get within range. Closer, closer . . . thank God he didn't look my way, didn't seem to see me. As I ran, the whoop of a siren was joined by the wail of a police car. An ambulance and a patrol car were on their way to the bank.

Breathless, I positioned myself behind a tree with a trunk wide enough to hide me. I took aim, but he had lowered his gun. Not a threat at the moment.

I was within thirty feet of him, close enough to see the sheen of rain atop his head. What the hell? Holding my fire, I stared at the man standing at the top of the play structure.

Officer Ward Brown wore a camouflage jacket with the collar turned up. His hair was combed and neat but his shoulders were hunched, as if weighed down with the burden of the rifle in his arms. The rifle he had used to bring Z down.

33

The threat of first responders seemed to change Brown's strategy, as he put the rifle down, grabbed the overhead bar of the play structure, and swung himself down to the ground.

He knew he had to get out before the police began to search the area.

I watched as he reached back for the gun and walked casually into the parking lot, fishing in his pocket with one hand as he held the rifle under his left arm. He squeezed the pad on his key ring and his old car chirped, the trunk popping open.

The tree bark was rough against the skin of my cheek as I pressed close and waited. I couldn't let him get into the car and drive away, but I was hoping he would stash that rifle away and close the trunk, putting some separation between him and the deadly weapon.

Brown loaded the rifle into the trunk, then looked around.

The hair stood up on the nape of my neck as I sensed that he could feel my presence despite the fact that I didn't move a muscle, didn't dare breathe.

He scanned the horizon, frowned, then slammed the trunk shut and flipped his keys up. He was walking toward the driver's seat when I stepped out from behind the tree, raised my gun, and pointed it at him.

"Stop right there, Brown! Hands in the air."

"Whoa." He raised his hands but remained cool, eyeing me with a snide smile. "I always knew you didn't like me, Mori, but this is a little extreme."

"You're under arrest," I said. "Stay where you are, and you won't get hurt."

"Under arrest for killing your partner?"

So he assumed that Z was dead. I decided not to correct him. In any negotiation it was always better to have more information than your adversary.

He kept his hands up but fanned them out dismissively. "You should be thanking me for dropping everything on my day off and rushing over here to help you chase off an active shooter. I was doing errands when I heard the radio call, and I hightailed it over here. I thought I might find the shooter, but he was already gone. You can put your gun down now."

I held steady, maintaining my shooting stance. "You stopped by with a loaded rifle in your trunk? How convenient."

"It's a licensed weapon. I use it for hunting, and since I'm off today, I'm not carrying my service gun." He shifted his head to the side, uncomfortable being a target. "Take it easy, Mori. I'm on your side."

I couldn't believe anything he said. There was a good chance he had a small pistol in an ankle holster or the console of his car. I was also fairly sure that his hands, clothes, and rifle would test positive for gunshot residue, the small particles produced when gunpowder explodes. But his attitude was more pleasant than ever, so I decided to play the game. At least until my backup arrived. I kept my gun pointed at him.

"Listen to me, Mori. You're in shock, seeing your partner go down. It's a lot to process, I know."

"How did you hear about the shooter?" I asked.

"I have a police-band radio in my car," he said. "You know I'm kind of a buff. I heard the call on the radio, saw something over here, and came to check it out. But by the time I brought my car around the building, the shooter was gone."

Although I didn't believe any of it, I decided to go along with his story, pretend that I understood the things that had motivated Brown to take a wrong turn. I kept my gun pointed at him but moved closer, giving up the cover of my large fir tree for a thinner one. "I wish you'd snagged the shooter," I said. "I'm thinking it might be the same person who shot Franny."

"I don't know anything about that," he said, his blue eyes glassy. "I always assumed it was the Twilight Bandit who took her out. Thanks to your detective work, you proved that was Donny, right? Good work on that, Detective. Too bad you had to give up one of your own."

"Yeah, well, Donny was a sweet old guy, but I can't imagine having to work with him back in the day." I lowered my gun. The distance between us was enough so that he couldn't jump me, and I needed to gain his trust. "You worked with him on the force, right? Was he always that goofy?"

Brown squinted at me, as if reassessing. He lowered his hands, relaxing a bit. "Yeah. Even worse. He was a know-it-all. Acted like he was God's gift to law enforcement."

"That must have been annoying. And I can't imagine how many times you had to cover for him."

"Constantly. He was a pain in the ass."

"And then there's Cribben, sucking up all the glory while you do all the work. Did you spend your entire career under him?"

"It was my curse," he said.

"He's such a stuffed shirt. Is he as brainless as he seems?"

"Not too bright. But a greedy bastard."

"Doesn't surprise me," I said, nodding. "I guess he tried to take more than his share of the Twilight money . . ."

The muscles in Brown's jaw tightened. "I don't know what you're talking about."

I'd pushed too far, too fast. "Oh, I guess he didn't share the profits with you, then. Hmm. He's going to be charged as an accessory in the Twilight robberies." If I couldn't spill it now, what good would it do later? "He and Dolly Redmond devised this whole system using blue cookie tins. You know, the ones those Danish butter cookies come in? They would take the cash from bank robberies and disburse it to everyone involved in covering up the robberies. But you weren't a part of that network?"

"Damn." He shook his head, feigning disapproval. "I always knew Cribben was a backstabber, but I had no idea he was dirty, too."

I knew he was lying. There was a reason this had been the longest civil conversation between Brown and me; we were posing, both of us lying.

Brown had been an accomplice in the bank robberies. He was likely the cop killer we were looking for, too. But maybe he was too smart to be sweet-talked into confession. He seemed to think he was still clean, that he was going to get away with everything, including shooting Z.

No need to burst his bubble, but I couldn't let him get away, even if he was twice my weight and had years of experience on the job and in the military. At the very least, the conversation was keeping him away from that trunk, and the rifle. I had to keep him going until backup arrived. The sirens had died, and I was hoping Ellie hadn't forgotten me.

"So what can you tell me about the chief?" I asked. "Do you think he's in this corruption business for the money?"

"He's got the worst kind of problem," Brown said. "A woman."

I tilted my head. "You're kidding me, right?"

"That's his weakness—Dolly Redmond. Apparently she was his childhood girl until Redmond went off, made a fortune, and stole Dolly away. It's a stupid rivalry, but the chief is determined to win. And that means getting Dolly back. But Dolly goes where the money is. So Cribben had to figure out a way to jack up his salary."

"You know a lot about Cribben's personal life."

"We're friends."

"So was it a friendly call when he phoned you Wednesday afternoon? Or was it business when the chief told you to shake Donny down? Did he tell you the evidence pointed to Donny pulling Monday's bank heist? Or maybe he kept it simple and just told you to visit Donny and collect your share of the money."

Brown's eyes opened wide for a moment—I think he was amazed that we had figured so much out in so little time. He quickly turned away and squinted, calculating. Plotting. Fabricating new lies.

The sound of footsteps in the entryway had us both turning to look back. Cranston came traipsing toward us, pushing his SLPD baseball cap off his forehead as if he couldn't believe what he was seeing.

"I knew it was you," Cranston said, his gaze fixed on Brown. "You stepped in it deep this time."

"Hey, buddy," Brown called to him. "Looks like we just missed the shooter here."

Cranston's anger with Brown was obvious, but I wasn't sure how it all fit in. Was Cranston part of the ring, angry that Brown had screwed up and exposed himself? Or was he one of the good guys, ready to shut Brown down?

"Don't try to smooth this one over, Brown. You freakin' traitor. I should have known all along. I should have known you had no decency inside. It's so easy for you to turn on someone. Pull the trigger on a fellow cop. Kill Donny with your bare hands."

"Whoa, there." Brown's face remained stoic. "Those are pretty strong accusations."

"But there's proof." Cranston's voice was low, steeped in fury as he cornered Brown against the car. "The FBI nailed you! They found Donny's blood on your uniform."

"What are you talking about?" There was a flicker of something in Brown's steely eyes—a surly edge.

"The FBI searched the lockers at the precinct this morning," Cranston said. "They found your bloody uniform pants all balled up in the bottom of your locker. They know, Brown. They know you killed Donny."

34

waited for Brown to react to the news, but he remained stoic, his expression stiff as a mask as his former friend delivered the damning news.

So the locker searches had revealed new evidence incriminating Brown. This was news to me, and with the amount of time it took to process evidence, I could tell Cranston was exaggerating. Still, I felt confident forensic tests would prove that Brown had been at the scene of Donny's murder.

"You killed Donny," Cranston said, his voice cracking with emotion. For all of his obnoxiousness, the man had a soft spot for his friend. "You and that juvenile delinquent that Dr. Mack coddles like a baby."

I looked from Cranston to Brown, but Brown didn't seem to react when Jason MacKenzie was mentioned. Still. Where there's smoke . . .

"I didn't want to believe it," Cranston said. "I gave you the benefit of the doubt, but now I know. You killed our friend, man."

"Don't go saying things you don't know. Besides, Donny was a pain in the ass, and he was on his way out anyway," Brown said. "Why does it matter who killed him?"

"He was our friend," Cranston said. "He was a person. Not some stinkbug you stomp out."

"And you think I killed him?" Brown said. "All because his blood's on my pants? Did you see that crime scene? It was a shit show. Maybe I leaned too close when I was checking his vitals."

I frowned. "Part of the problem was that you and Rivers neglected to check his respiration and heart rate."

"A mistake, but I'm trying to tell you, there's an explanation for everything," Brown insisted. "You can take me in for questioning, but I'm sailing away from all this. Free as a bird."

For the moment, I thought it was best to let Brown live with that illusion, thinking he was off the hook. It would be easier to cuff and arrest him before revealing the comprehensive evidence against him.

But Cranston wasn't backing down. "You think you're getting off with a few questions? A cop killer like you, you're lucky I'm not beating you senseless. You're lucky I have self-control."

I blinked as Cranston came forward, squaring off with Brown, who backed against his car. "Easy, man," Brown said, "Calm down."

"I'm perfectly calm," Cranston said, stepping toward Brown. "Copacetic. That makes it easier to remember all the things you did that didn't make sense. The lies you told me."

Brown shook his head, dismissing his friend. "You got nothing."

"I got the night Franny was killed, when you say you found that revolver in the bushes. But when I looked over at you, you were wiping it down. Why was that?"

"I lifted it with a rag. I didn't want to get my prints on it."

"But your prints were already there, weren't they?" Cranston was shoving Brown in the chest. "You were the shooter, over here at the freakin' playground. And afterwards, you ditched the gun to make it look like the Twilight Bandit shot her. Only you ditched it in a stupid place that made no sense. Ya freakin' moron."

"The police report says we both found that gun in the bushes," Brown insisted.

"You found it, because you planted it there. And I'm going to go in and make sure that report gets amended. I've had it with you, Brown. Your lies and your orders and your bad moods. You killed two cops, and I'm not going to let that go."

"You don't know what you're saying, man." Brown kept inching back, toward the rear of the car. "You're all riled up. You need a couple of beers and this will all blow over."

"Stop pretending it doesn't matter!" Cranston said, shoving Brown with each word. "Rivers knows, too. He saw you come back from meal with that bloodstain on your pants. The meal you caught with that tattooed freak."

"His name is Jason," Brown growled.

"Jason MacKenzie," I said, "and we have him on video attacking my sister and damaging my car." I moved toward Brown's car but kept a safe distance from the two men. "Because you sent him to deliver a threat, Brown. You wanted the investigation on Twilight stopped."

"I don't know what the hell you're talking about," Brown complained.

"And when Cribben told you to shake the cash from the robbery out of Donny, you brought Jason along to add some muscle to the threat. He met you during your meal break, and you cruised over to Donny's for a surprise visit."

"You can't prove that—"

"We have a witness who saw the two of you pull in," I said.

"That's impossible." Brown straightened. "Nobody could identify us."

"Because the two of you were wearing ski masks?" I said. "Trying to hide your identity. But the witness noticed your uniform. A Sunrise Lake cop. That narrows down the range of Donny's visitors that night."

"You scum," Cranston muttered, calmer now.

But Brown's face glowed red, his eyes bright with frenzy as he separated from Cranston, lifted his hand, and squeezed the key fob. With a chirp, the trunk popped open.

My heart seemed to fall as I realized Brown was making a move. I was already racing toward the rear of the car, shouting to Cranston. "He's got a rifle!"

In the scramble that followed, Cranston tried to grab Brown, but Brown shoved him off and moved toward the trunk. I got to the tail of the vehicle as Brown was already leaning inside. I reached up to get a grip on the trunk and slammed it shut with a desperate grunt. "Ung!"

It banged against Brown's shoulders and bounced back up.

He bellowed a curse, stunned and hunched over, but only temporarily.

As I was grabbing the trunk to slam down a second time, Brown protected his head with one arm while he reached with the other. The trunk popped up, and Brown emerged from the dark space, swinging his rifle.

I flew back, stumbling to the pavement, but Cranston caught the impact of the butt of the rifle against his head. He groaned and staggered back out of my line of vision.

Because I couldn't take my eyes off that rifle. Yes, Cranston and I wore Kevlar vests, but one rifle shot to the head or femoral artery in the leg would silence us forever.

Don't let him get the chance to shoot, I thought, my heart racing. *Get the rifle away.*

But Brown was already pivoting toward Cranston, butt of the rifle tucked under his arm to take aim.

"No!" Adrenaline surged through me like quicksilver as I leaped onto Brown's back, jumping high enough so I could reach over his shoulders, grab the steel nose of the rifle, and yank it toward the air. The element of surprise was on my side. Gritting my teeth, I fumbled with my right hand to wrest the gun from Brown's grip. He held on, but I managed to maneuver it across his chest and pull so that it was wedged against his throat.

Brown reared back against the car, trying to knock me off, but the rear of the car came up only to his hips, placing the brunt of the blows on the backs of his thighs. I tugged hard on the rifle, trying to mash it against his throat, but he had a strong grip, too, rendering me ineffective. With a guttural growl, he heaved his large body back and forth, trying to throw me off. It was getting hard for me to hold on.

"Let go of the rifle, Brown. Let go. Now!"

There is something very convincing about looking up the barrel of a gun pointed in your face. Since my head was inches from Brown's, I was getting the same view at the gleaming nose of Cranston's gun.

Brown stopped moving, obviously considering. When he lowered his hands from the rifle, I hoisted it off to the side, where it clattered onto the pavement.

Adrenaline was still buzzing in my veins as I dropped from Brown's back, stepped away from him, and went to retrieve the rifle.

"That rifle belonged to my old man," Brown said.

"Shame on you for abusing something your father passed on to you." I considered unloading the rifle but wanted to leave it intact for forensic evidence. I handed it to Cranston, who kept his handgun trained on Brown.

"It's over," Cranston pronounced. "You're done. Cuff him, Mori."

I pulled Brown's arms around to the base of his spine and snapped handcuffs around his wrists. A pat-down revealed a pack of bullets in one of the deep pockets of Brown's camo jacket. He'd been prepared.

"Come on, Cranston," Brown said. "We've had a misunderstanding here. Help me get this sweet tart out of the way, and you and I can go find the real bad guys."

"You never give up, do you?" Cranston said, lifting the rifle to his face. "I can smell the gunpowder. This one's been fired recently."

"He shot Z," I said.

"You're a real piece of work, Brown." Cranston's upper lip curled in disgust. "And just for the record, I'm no buddy of yours. I may be a crusty old bastard, but I'm no dirty cop. And there's nothing I hate more than a cop killer."

Catching our breath, Cranston and I stood side by side and took an odd moment together. As my training officer, Cranston had proven himself to be an obnoxious, sexist jerk. None of that had changed. But today he'd proven himself to be a decent cop.

Just then I heard a scuff on the pavement behind me. Omak and Derringer came up the parking lot entryway, guns drawn.

"The threat is contained," I told them.

"Yeah, and where were you guys when we needed you?" Cranston complained, rubbing the side of his head. "I think I got a concussion brewing here."

"We made the dispatch of Detective Frazier to the hospital our first priority, but you seemed to be holding your own," Omak said. "Don't forget to Mirandize him. Everything by the book."

"Of course," I said, my nerves singing, still hopped up on adrenaline. "And Cranston? Thanks."

Cranston squinted at me and nodded. "You got a good way of handling people, Mori."

It was the first and probably the only compliment I was going to get from Cranston, but I was grateful. And he wasn't the only one who had heard Brown's confession.

"Ellie, you still there?" I called into my radio.

"Roger that," she replied. "I recorded everything."

35

That evening at the precinct, I gingerly hugged Z, who was badly bruised from the impact of the bullet still embedded in the Kevlar lining of his vest. He had been treated and released from the hospital, and he should have gone home, but he couldn't stand to miss the wrap-up of the case that had come to haunt him.

"I'm so glad you're okay," I said.

"Me, too," Z said, tearing up a little. "Thanks for watching my back, partner."

"Aw . . ." My eyes started to mist over, too. "Is that the first time you've ever called me partner? I think it is."

"It's a figure of speech. Cop lingo. You don't have to go getting all sentimental."

I patted his shoulder. "You can count on me to have your back."

After we'd brought Ward Brown in, Omak had called me into his office with Derringer to discuss how the case would proceed. The homicide charges against Brown were intertwined with the larger corruption case involving Chief Cribben, and the FBI was going to take the lead in the prosecution. I hoped that meant Derringer would be able to stay on here for a while to fine-tune the case.

"We've all been impressed by your interrogation skills, Mori," Omak had said, "but I think you can understand why the prosecutors don't want any of our precinct cops interrogating their former colleagues or the chief."

While I regretted stepping aside, I got it. I wouldn't be questioning any of the suspects in the case. It was inappropriate for anyone in the Sunrise Lake Police Department to be involved in that capacity, though Esme Garcia and I would be working behind the scenes, filling in details and helping the FBI agents organize the case.

Garcia and I had been permitted to accompany Derringer and two other FBI agents serving the arrest warrant at Cribben's house this evening. On the way over, Garcia had explained to me how she had managed to track Cribben's infusion of cash that dated four years back.

"When the neighbors complained of the luxury cars that began to appear on the street, I tracked the vehicles to the dealership that sold them, Fast Treasures," Garcia explained. "Their accountant was helpful. She looked up the records. Turns out Cribben paid hefty down payments in cash on both cars but took out loans for both of them. The down payments align with the times when he would have cash from the robberies."

"That's some tidy financial investigation," I said.

"The marina where Cribben purchased his boat gave a similar account. A cash down payment four years ago, and then a loan." Garcia pointed a finger in the air. "And get this. A little more than two years ago, Cribben put the boat and both cars up for sale. By then the robberies had tapered off, and I figure he started to get short on cash. We know his salary is close to a hundred grand, but it would be hard to sustain luxury cars and a boat on that, not to mention if he has a mortgage payment."

"I'm impressed by the fairly complete financial picture you've been able to get without having access to Cribben's bank accounts," I said.

"Garcia has uncovered enough to charge the chief," Derringer said.

"And we'll learn more when we can look at his personal accounts," Garcia said. "After we bring him in."

It had been satisfying to interrupt Cribben's chicken piccata dinner with Dolly Redmond that evening. The chief kept insisting that someone had made a huge mistake, even after he found his reading glasses and studied the warrant with his name on it.

"Someone needs to explain to me exactly what this means, that I'm an accessory to the Twilight robberies?" He blew air into his cheeks and shook his head, resembling a puffer fish. "How can that be, when we've determined that Donny Gallagher pulled those heists?"

I knew that some of the phone records implicated Cribben in Donny Gallagher's murder, but for now the prosecutor had decided to charge him with only accessory to robbery and possession of stolen property.

"This is a mistake," Cribben insisted, slapping his linen napkin onto the dining room table.

"Buzz . . ." Dolly put her hand on his arm. "Take it easy. Just go along with the officers and I'll call a lawyer and have you out in a few hours."

"That's not going to work, ma'am," Derringer said. "Dolores Redmond, correct? We also have a warrant for your arrest. The charge is possession of stolen property."

"What?" Dolly gasped. "Oh my soul. That can't be right."

I couldn't deny feeling a sense of satisfaction as I moved around the suspects to search the house. Back at the precinct there had been talk of arresting Dolly's aunt Peg, too, but the district attorney had interviewed her and thought it best to simply confiscate the cookie tins as stolen property and get her sworn testimony that the canisters belonged to Dolly.

From the kitchen, I heard Derringer try to explain that the charges were correct and that he would need to handcuff Cribben and Mrs. Redmond. "Procedure," Derringer said. Checking cupboards and drawers in the kitchen, Agent Darren Kapowski and I were focused on our search. He reached up to look behind bowls and pitchers in upper cupboards as I opened the double doors of the pantry.

"Jackpot," I said, spotting the blue cookie tins, neatly stacked on a shelf. Garcia and Kapowski joined me in the pantry and I pointed. "Six of them."

Gently, Agent Kapowski opened the top tin and whistled at the stacks of cash bundles inside. Three bins contained cash, two were empty, one had butter cookies inside. We confiscated all of them.

As we carried the tins out of the kitchen, Chief Cribben recognized me suddenly and paused his monologue of how he was innocent and would be released soon.

"What are you doing, Mori? Those are my possessions."

"We're executing a search warrant," Derringer said.

"It's all evidence now," I said. "We'll take good care of it, make sure it's all inventoried."

"I don't trust anything you do," Cribben said. "You were supposed to keep me updated on the case. You were supposed to arrest Blackstone. And you were warned to stay out of the Twilight case."

"I was warned by anonymous threats," I said, maintaining composure. "Not direct orders."

Unrelenting, the chief folded his arms. "Nothing worse than a cop who can't follow orders."

"Mori is a detective," Derringer said patiently, "and Sunrise Lake is fortunate to have a detective dedicated to her job. Someone determined to follow the trail of a crime, despite major obstacles like corrupt cops and administrators."

The chief growled and turned away from Derringer, who allowed himself a rare smile. "I'm not saying anything else until I get a lawyer," Cribben said. Our cue to stop questioning him. And at least he stopped talking.

The chief remained quiet as we filed out of the small but lavish home with double doors, shiny marble floors, and a windowed alcove with a baby grand piano. Collecting the blue tins from his pantry and carrying them out over the marble and past his rocket-shaped expensive cars, I imagined myself returning some balance to the scales of justice.

*　*　*

Back at the precinct, Omak expressed surprise that we had found Dolly Redmond at Cribben's place, as well as those containers of cash. "You'd think they would work harder to keep things hidden," he said.

"Not Cribben," Garcia said. "One thing I've learned from investigating, he's not a cautious person. But that fits the profile of some people in high places. They think they'll never be caught. They think they're above the law."

I nodded. It seemed an apt description of Cribben.

"I regret that this investigation dealt Mayor Redmond a personal blow," Omak said. "He brought me on to find corruption in the department, and from my interactions with him, I don't think Ron had a clue that the foul play involved his own wife."

"That's got to be tough," Derringer said, "ordering an investigation that ends up putting your wife behind bars."

"The mayor and the police chief had a rivalry dating back to high school days," I said, explaining how Dolly's affections seemed to be one of the many things the two men had been competing for. "I guess Cribben won Dolly, but at what cost."

Omak reported that Taz Wilson, an FBI interrogator, had spent hours interviewing Brown with little success. "And we've run into a problem with Jason MacKenzie. The cops we sent out to question him weren't able to find him at home. They broke in and searched the house. Some items with bloodstains were brought to the lab for analysis. But MacKenzie never turned up. Not knowing the case, they didn't know where else to look."

Derringer and I exchanged a look of concern. "This guy might have been a murder accomplice. We need to get him off the streets, now."

Derringer started a search on his laptop. "Do we know where to find him? Did he have a job? Some friends in the area?"

"He's home from college for the holidays," I said. "I don't know much more about him." I found Dr. MacKenzie's number on my cell phone and handed it to Derringer. "Call his mother, Daphne MacKenzie. She'll take it more seriously if it's from you."

"Isn't she the one on our suspect list for—"

"We need her help right now. And I think she'll be motivated to help, for the sake of her son."

Derringer left a message, but she called back within a minute, and when Derringer told her it was an emergency involving her son, she agreed to cancel her next session and meet us in her office. "It's not far," I told Derringer, "and this merits a face-to-face."

Walking into Dr. Mack's office, I realized I was calm this time, in control and focused, while the doctor seemed flushed and scattered. This time I had the upper hand in the meeting; I held the power. It made me more confident, but sad in a new way.

She didn't know Brown had been arrested. He wouldn't have been allowed to call anyone but a lawyer, and although the press was reporting the shooting of a cop outside Pacific Lake Bank, the arrests would not be announced to the media until our major players were all in custody. Jason was the last of the trio to be collected.

Did she know Z had been shot? Had she been involved in that plot? She didn't tip her hand either way.

"I've been worried about Jason these last few days," she said, leading the way into her office in ridiculously high heels. She sat at her desk and raked the hair off her forehead, revealing weariness in her eyes. "Is everything okay?"

"Jason is a suspect in a homicide. We have a warrant for his arrest." I wasn't going to mince words. "Some of our officers went to your home looking for him today, but he wasn't there. We need your help finding him."

"Homicide? Who was killed?" she exclaimed, pressing her palms to her cheeks. "I knew something was wrong. He's been coming in late, unable to sleep, and he didn't come home at all last night . . . anyway, who do you think my son killed? Was it some accident?"

"Donny Gallagher," Derringer said carefully. "We think Jason was with Ward Brown Wednesday night. Gallagher was found beaten at home, and later died at the hospital."

She began to cry. "It can't be." She grabbed two tissues and pressed them to her eyes. "And Ward, too? This is my worst nightmare."

"We need your help finding Jason, before the situation gets worse," I said. "Does he have friends he's staying with? Or do you think he went back to school?"

"No. He's a loner, and he didn't like college. He's definitely not back in Bend."

"Who does he spend time with?" I asked. "Who can we call?"

She drew in a breath as she looked at me, and then sobbed. "Ward. He's been spending time with Ward, and I thought it was a good thing. A mature male role model." She shook her head.

"He's not with Ward Brown now," Derringer said.

"He texted that he was at Ward's last night, in Portland."

"Doesn't Ward live in West Green?" Derringer asked. He had arranged for officers to search Brown's apartment earlier today.

She nodded. "He does, but Jason likes Ward's boat. It's at the marina on the Willamette River. Jason might be there now. If he's not home."

"Why don't you text him," I suggested. "Do you have a way to track his location on your phone?"

"I do. He doesn't know about it, but I do." She opened a drawer and removed her cell phone.

I took a deep breath, trying to be patient as Dr. Mack texted her son, then tapped the locator icon. "He's at the marina, just as I thought." She sighed. "What's going to happen to him?"

"Get your bag and coat," I said. "We are going to go pick him up right now."

36

While Derringer drove, I explained to Dr. Mack that Ward Brown was a primary suspect in the murders of Franny Landon and Donny Gallagher, as well as the shooting of Zion Frazier.

She burst into tears again when I told her that the bullet had hit Z's body armor and he was recovering from the blunt-force trauma. Almost thinking out loud, I mentioned that he would have been killed if he'd been hit in the head. I also wondered why Brown had stopped at one shot. Had his rifle jammed? From my encounter with Brown, it seemed clear that he thought he'd killed Z with one shot.

"And you gave him the information he needed to take that shot. You knew Z and I would be outside the bank, and you told Brown. You set us up."

"No, I didn't know! I never expected that! Yes, I told him. He kept asking about Z. He said he needed to resolve what had happened the night Franny died. Ward said there was a lot he couldn't remember, and we thought that the sight of Z on the premises might jolt Ward's memory, too."

"You didn't realize he was a bully?"

"I knew that Ward had issues, but I had no idea he would act in a violent way," MacKenzie said.

I had trouble believing her. "How could you not be aware of the anger simmering beneath the surface? His animosity toward . . . well, just about everyone."

"That surliness . . . it's hard to explain, but honestly, the rugged cowboy thing is part of the attraction for me."

"But you're a mental health expert," Derringer said. "You didn't realize that he takes the macho act to the extreme?"

"I guess I was blind to some things."

I stared ahead at the road, not sure whether I believed her or not. It really didn't matter. It wasn't up to me to determine if Dr. MacKenzie was an accessory in the attack on Z, and the medical board would determine if she had violated ethics by sharing patient information. For now, we needed her help apprehending her son.

Daylight waned as we neared the riverfront marina. The western sky was a wash of pale gray, while the eastern horizon was dark as witch's brew.

"You'll need your flashlight," I told Derringer.

He opened his arms, miffed. A guy in a tailored suit doesn't have a flashlight on his belt. "Then use the flashlight on your phone. The waterfront is dangerous at night. One wrong step, and you're in the river." Life on the lake had taught me a few things. The vista of water that sparkled in the day became a black hole that played with your depth perception at night. Even if you could swim, the impact of the dock or rocks or a boat could be deadly.

The entry to the marina was a well-lit, paved surface that quickly gave way to a network of dark, wooden walkways that stretched over the waterfront. Dr. Mack led the way, walking with authority at first, and then struggling when her high heels wobbled on the uneven, scarred wood.

"I forgot my boat shoes," she said, slowing her pace.

I extended an arm and walked alongside her, my flashlight illuminating the way.

She led us nearly to the end of a dock, then stopped and pointed at a boat. The twenty-one-foot cabin cruiser, or so

MacKenzie had described it, was like many craft at the marina. It had an open back deck with bench seating along the sides and a closed, windowed cabin at the front to house the steering wheel.

"See the light inside?" she asked, and I noticed the dim glow inside the cabin. "He's in there."

The doc removed her shoes, dropped them onto the dock, and climbed onto the back deck, making the boat bob slightly. Derringer and I left our shoes on but stepped onto the boat, careful to mind the gap. We stood back as Dr. Mack knocked on the glass window, called to her son, and opened the door.

"Jason, it's Mom. I've been worried about you." She positioned her face in the open doorway and peered in. "What's going on?"

"Nothing." The answer was low and monotone. "I'm just tired."

She turned to us. "He's sleeping. Jase, you need to come out here. I have someone who wants to talk to you."

Jason objected, but Dr. Mack persisted, and after some back and forth the door opened wide and a tall, thin man in jeans and a gray hoodie stepped out on to the deck. He moved gracefully, but his face looked gaunt and pale, in stark contrast to his black soul patch and mustache. The tattoo on his neck was muted by shadow. The swashbuckling air of a pirate was gone, and in its wake Jason MacKenzie was shaky and overwrought.

His anxiety was amplified when he caught a look at our SLPD uniforms.

He breathed out a curse and turned back toward the cabin door, but Derringer and I quickly crossed the deck and grabbed him by either arm.

"Jason MacKenzie, you're under arrest for the reckless homicide of Donald Gallagher," Derringer said.

"Mom? You brought them here?" In the dim light Jason cast a desperate look at his mother, then let his head drop to his chest in utter defeat. "I'm screwed."

"I'm so sorry, honey. I'm sorry that I ever introduced you to Ward . . . that I ever got involved with him."

Derringer read Jason his rights as I handcuffed his hands behind him and patted him down. No weapons. Only a wallet and cell phone, which I confiscated.

Dr. Mack was crying again, and she came over to Jason and rubbed his upper arm in a soothing way. I looked at Derringer for a cue, but neither of us had the heart to stop her.

"I totally screwed up," she said. "I had no idea where Ward was leading you."

"I did what I did," Jason said. "I feel sick about the old guy, but in the beginning it was fun. Following you around," he said to me. "Smashing up those headlights. It felt good. Like, I could've been on *Jackass*, but I was the dude that got away with it."

"But you know better," Dr. Mack said.

"So does Ward, but he breaks rules, all the time."

Lifting my flashlight slightly, I noticed that Jason's eyes were swollen and red and his hands were shaking. He was a mess.

"I knew it was wrong, okay? But I was making some money, and I'd screwed up with school, so I thought maybe I could do better doing odd jobs for Ward here and there. But then we went to see the old guy, and . . ." His voice cracked as he fought tears.

"Don't say it," Dr. Mack said softly.

"I didn't mean to kill him," Jason sobbed. "I didn't even want to hurt him at first, but Ward said he was a cheat and a backstabber, that he deserved a beating. He told me to focus all my anger, take it all out when I punched the guy. And I did. And at first it felt good. I pretended I was punching a bag at the gym. You always tell me to let things out, to let go. So I did. I got in the zone and let it rip."

"Honey, you can't let your anger out on another human being."

"Don't you think I know that now? But Ward kept telling me the old guy was nothing. Worse than useless. He said he was a cheat and he deserved to die. So I went with that, and I thought I was going to be okay with that. Until later." He tried to wipe his cheek against one shoulder. "It didn't take long. That night, I got sick. Started throwing up, and I couldn't stop thinking of the old man. Couldn't stop seeing his face, all panicked and scared. Like a little kid. I asked Ward if the old guy was okay, and he said yeah. No problem. But I felt like shit. That's not who I am."

"I know it's not," his mother said. "I know."

"Then Friday morning it was on the news. They said the old guy, Gallagher, that he had died from the assault. Ward and I had killed him." He shook his head. "I never wanted to kill anyone. And it's wrecking me now. I don't know how to go on."

"You will go on." Dr. Mack took her son by the shoulders and looked into his eyes. "You are going to pay for your crime. And while you're in jail, you're going to get therapy and start working on yourself as a person. Start building your self-esteem and discover ways to make amends for your crime and contribute to the people around you."

"I can't," he said. "I can't get over this."

"You can heal, Jason. You can, and you will."

We waited as they hugged, then helped Jason off the boat and began to walk them back to the patrol car.

We had our confession, and I felt sure that Jason MacKenzie would be more than willing to testify against Ward Brown. Slowly but surely, all the investigations were wrapping up.

* * *

After twenty-four hours in jail, Chief Buzz Cribben was eager to be interviewed Monday morning. As I watched the interview on videotape from a room down the hall, Cribben confirmed many of the things we suspected.

"So help me out here for my report," Derringer said. "Chief Cribben wasn't the mastermind, but he was allowing the bank robberies to happen, right?"

"That's right," I said. "The kingpin of the operation was Ward Brown, who has a talent for getting others to do his dirty work. Brown knew about the chief's affair with the mayor's wife, and he used it to force the mayor to look the other way while the Twilight Bandit did his hits. It probably didn't seem like a big deal in the beginning, and maybe it seemed worth the risk when some of the cash landed in Cribben's pocket."

"But the stakes went up when Officer Landon was killed," Derringer said.

"It posed a huge problem," I said. "Brown killed Franny to stop the Twilight investigation. The chief claims that he didn't know that Brown planned the murder, but it backfired when Donny freaked out and shut down operations. No more bank robberies."

"And no more cash flow for Brown and Cribben," Derringer said.

"After that, Cribben destroyed some of Franny's paperwork, and Brown leaned on Cranston to give up on the investigation." Omak rubbed his knuckles against his chin, his eyes shadowed with regret. "It's still not clear who was involved in that cover-up. Cranston botched the report, but was he trying to protect Donny? I've confiscated his gun and badge until we've investigated his role. Sergeant Gil Stanford was the supervising officer at that time. Also under investigation, but I don't think there was intent on his part. I suspect Stanford will be slapped with department charges—failure to supervise, something like that. Cranston might also get a letter of admonition for failure to follow police procedure. May lose some vacation time."

"If you had told me to pick the source of corruption in our department, I would have chosen Cranston, all day, every day," I said.

"He's obnoxious and he's let a lot of details slip in his work lately," Omak agreed.

"But in the end, he helped me apprehend Brown," I said. "And I don't think he was involved in the bank heist at all. He was just trying to be a good friend to Donny."

As we were finishing up, Garcia came in and handed Omak a sheaf of papers. "My report, the last of it."

Omak nodded. "Good job, Garcia. I'm grateful for the work you did on this case. It's not easy going undercover in your own workplace."

"It had to be done," she said. "I couldn't stand knowing that crooks were operating under the guise of cops."

"So are you going to reveal the undercover operation to the other cops in the precinct?" I asked.

"That's the problem," Garcia said, looking casual with her hands in her pockets. "Once this case goes to trial, and there will probably be a few separate trials, I'll need to testify and my identity will come out. There's no putting the genie back into the bottle."

"So we're hoping to get her hired in our forensic investigation division," Derringer said. "Garcia has proven her skills in forensic accounting."

"I would hate to see you go," I told her, "but is that a goal for you?"

"You kidding me? I've always wanted to be a G-man," she teased.

*　*　*

Out in the squad room I sat at my desk and looked across at all my colleagues' desks. A few cops and detectives were huddled that Thursday afternoon, talking about a rash of bicycle burglaries that seemed like a game compared to the arrests we'd made earlier in the week. The news of corruption charges at the highest levels had shot through the department like fireworks, but the noise was finally beginning to fizzle. Z stood at the window, drinking a cup of tea. He pointed outside to two squad cars in front of the precinct.

"Look at that. Your buddy Ward Brown is back for a visit from the county lockup." Z shook his head and took a sip of tea. "It's been a really weird week."

As Z spoke, Milewski escorted a handcuffed Ward Brown through the precinct and into an interrogation room. With his drooping mouth and rumpled hair, Brown had lost his veneer of cowboy charm. Being under arrest was not a good look for him.

"I guess he won't be sailing off into the sunset after all," I said, watching him walk past.

"Do you think he'll finally come clean with the FBI interrogator?" Z asked.

"I don't know. With two homicides, one assault, and multiple bank-robbery accessory charges he's looking at a long sentence, even if he cooperates."

"The worst part is the other people he brought down. He might have screwed Cranston, and Jason MacKenzie was just a kid. It's just so wrong. And you know, Dr. Mack really was a decent therapist. It's a shame she wasted her talents getting involved with Brown."

"Maybe she'll find her way to helping people again."

Z gave a snort. "Not me. I'm cured."

I smiled. I knew Z was planning a few sessions with a private therapist, and that was a good thing. I still considered psychology a noble profession, but today I was elated to be a police detective. I liked being on the right side of the law, and I loved being a good cop.

37

A few days later on a Saturday morning, I woke up to pristine white falling snow, including several inches already accumulated on the ground. The thick boughs of the Douglas firs were draped in white and there was a peaceful hush, as if every living thing were in awe of the descending white flakes. Snowfall of this magnitude was rare in Sunrise Lake, and it brought back childhood memories of making snowmen with my sisters and brother. I spent the morning hanging with Natalie at home, cradling a coffee mug in my living room, and watching fat snowflakes soundlessly hit the ground.

"This is the Sunrise Lake we grew up in," Natalie said. "Peaceful and perfect."

I smiled, knowing that no place was perfect.

"Sometimes it's actually too peaceful around here," Nat said. "When the big story of the day is a snowstorm? Really?"

I tucked my feet up on the couch and sighed. "There's no such thing as too peaceful."

"You know what I mean." Earlier that morning Natalie had gotten a call from the news division asking her if she wanted to come in on her day off to cover the weather and traffic situation—the lead story for a snow day. She had declined the offer, wanting to have the day off for the holiday party at my parents' house.

"Sometimes I wish for a little shake-up around here," Natalie said.

"Oh, I think we've uncovered enough of the ugly underbelly of this town," I said. "A cop gunning down his colleagues. The police chief sleeping with the mayor's wife and taking stolen cash to keep quiet about a serial bandit who strikes banks after dark. A young thug beating a debilitated man to death. Not to mention the Lost Girls' bodies found in the woods. Really, Nat? Haven't I churned up enough exciting crimes for you to report on?"

She winced and tossed a pillow at me. "That's not what I meant."

I deflected the pillow with my foot, saving my warm coffee from a spill. "And need I remind you that one panel of the window behind me was just replaced because some stalker of mine smashed it with a brick? I think that's plenty of action."

"Yeah," Natalie said. "Way to lure the criminals to our house, Laura."

We both laughed.

"Did I tell you that my Twilight Bandit coverage last week was one of the most watched pieces on the website. Ever! It broke records for the station."

"Congratulations!"

"People seem to be intrigued by someone with the nerve to keep walking into banks and demanding money. I think people can't help feeling a little sorry for Donny Gallagher, in failing health and manipulated by his friends. And then there's the love triangle with Dolly Redmond. I think the crimes sucked readers in, and the backstabbing wife and friend cinched the deal."

Just then my phone rang, and I plucked it from the sofa cushions where it liked to sink away. "It's Alex." My brother was home for a brief holiday break from med school. I answered the call: "Hey, bro, what's up?"

"Mom has us chopping melons and making hundreds of little pinwheel thingies, and Dad said we need to clear the snow off the dock so the guests can go out back. When are you getting here?"

"Much later, if that means I can avoid doing the catering and snow removal."

"Get it in gear and get over here." Alex and I had bossed each other around all our lives, and we secretly loved it.

"I'll be over as soon as I grab breakfast and a shower," I promised.

"Breakfast? It's almost noon."

"I love you too," I said. "See ya soon."

* * *

By five PM the annual Mori Christmas party was in full swing. My father, Koji, played the piano while crowds of partygoers sang along and munched on homemade hors d'oeuvres. My parents' Sunrise Lake home was decked out with twinkling white lights, which were mirrored by the still waters of the lake beyond our back deck. I'd helped decorate, hanging blue and silver ornaments on the tree, stringing a lit garland along the banister, and placing candles in every window. My grandmother used to tell me that a candle in the window was a sign of welcome and aid to weary travelers, which explained my mother's penchant for those electric candles at Christmastime.

I'd also made sure there was lots of mistletoe. My brother Alex and I had actually gone on a special trip to the local nursery to buy it fresh.

"A mistletoe run." Alex had tapped his fingertips on his knees as I backed out of the driveway. "So Hannah was right. You are crazy in love."

"Oh, stop with the hyperbole. I'm seeing someone, okay. And yes, I'm crazy about him. Kind of. The thing is, he's not from around here. He lives in Seattle."

"And he's not Japanese."

"Yeah, well, that, too, but Mom and Dad will just have to get over that."

Alex grinned. "Our little *gyoza*, all grown up."

Once my friends arrived, I settled happily on the sofa between Natalie and Neen, my college roommate who was in town from

Sweden to visit for the holidays. My other best friend Becca was off in France, doing a whole immersion thing and bravely spending the holidays there on her own. Derringer and Z snagged the upholstered chairs, talking sports as if they'd been friends for years. We chatted for a while, and then Z and Derringer made off for the bar to grab cocktails for all of us.

"He's really cute, Laura," Natalie yelled over the din of the crowd.

Neen nodded. "How many dates have you been on?"

I held up two fingers. "We went snowshoeing at Mount Hood last weekend," I told them. "I only fell a couple of times."

"I wouldn't mind falling either, if he was the one to catch me," Natalie said.

I swatted her. "He's also a fine detective," I told them.

Neen tapped her chin, her face in a deadpan expression. "Quite fine, I'm sure. I'm glad you appreciate him for his professional skills."

I saw Ellie across the room and excused myself to chat with her for a few minutes. We hadn't had much time to talk after Brown's arrest, and I was glad she'd accepted my invitation to come to our family holiday party.

"Your dad is a delight," Ellie said, giving me a quick hug. "I have to get to the restaurant next time I'm in Portland. He promised me a kitchen tour." As always, we started talking shop right away. "I really hope Omak gets the promotion to chief. He deserves it."

I agreed. "Cribben's arrest is really shaking up the department."

"True," she admitted, "but Cribben wasn't a strong leader, so I think most of us are a little relieved."

Ellie nudged my shoulder with hers. "I can't believe Cranston is taking so much credit for Brown's take-down. He made himself out to be the hero, but depending on the investigation, he might be booted from the job. I'd be pissed if I was you."

I shrugged. The people who had heard the taped recording of my confrontation with Brown—Ellie, Z, Omak, and Derringer—knew the truth. "Cranston made some big mistakes, but he did have my back when it mattered."

"You are way too nice," Ellie said.

My sister Hannah sidled up beside me and, looking mysterious, handed me a fortune cookie.

"Ellie, have you met my sister?" After making introductions between the two, I turned to Hannah and held up the cookie.

"Tell me there's the key fob to a new car in here," I joked. My poor car had taken a beating in the past few weeks.

She shook her head and laughed. "You wish. Open it!"

I cracked open the fortune cookie, and inside was a slip of paper with a note saying that Hannah had been accepted to Columbia. "What?" I let out a whoop of joy, then covered my mouth as I realized I was making a scene. "Really?"

Hannah nodded, her eyes brimming with tears.

"I'm so proud of you!" I threw my arms around my sister and hugged her. I knew this school was Hannah's dream, even if it was across the country in New York City. I would miss her next year, but for now, I had to share her joy.

"That is great news," I said, noticing now the high color in her cheeks and the gleam in her eyes. "And you worked hard for it. You deserve it."

"What's all this yelling about?" My mother joined us, her eyebrows knitted together in concern.

I showed her the fortune, and Mom's lips curled into a huge smile. "Oh, I'm so happy! Let's tell Koji right away." We corralled the siblings beside the piano and assembled near my father. Alex and Koko hugged Hannah. Years ago, I might've felt a twinge of jealousy that Hannah was receiving such praise. But tonight I understood that my whole family had high expectations of each other so that each person could find fulfillment. I was no longer the family member who fell short. Tonight, I was proud of the work I'd done, solving the Twilight Bandit case as well as two homicides. Our investigation had removed some dangerous men from society. I could afford to be truly happy for myself, my sister, and the rest of my family, too.

"Hey, you." Derringer came up beside me and put his arm around me. "I've been looking for you." He handed me a martini with extra olives—just the way I liked it. "What's all the hoopla about?"

"My sister Hannah got into her first choice for college—Columbia."

He smiled. "So, are all your siblings as smart as you are?"

I rolled my eyes. "They're a little more impressive in that department, I'm afraid."

"Apparently they haven't seen you in action, cracking tough guys. Squeezing confessions out of suspects."

I laughed. "Well, that can be our little secret."

He turned me around and walked me outside to a quiet area on the deck. Above us, twinkling lights mimicked stars. Their lights glowed on through the dusting of snow. Beyond the deck, the cold lake mirrored our home's warm ambience, and other houses twinkled on the opposite shore. Derringer held a sprig of mistletoe over our heads.

"I know what you're up to, mister," I said.

"See, you're very intuitive, Detective Mori." Derringer leaned down for a gentle kiss. I felt my body pulled toward his, as if he were a magnet. He brought his hands up to cup my face and kissed me again. It was so nice, we kept at it for a breathless spell.

Afterward, Derringer pressed his forehead to mine, then looked me in the eyes. "Laura. I'm leaving for Seattle next week."

"I know."

"Funny, my first few days here, I couldn't wait to wrap things up here and get back to Seattle. Now I'm sorry to leave."

"I'm sorry too. I don't want you to go," I said, trying not to be too dramatic. If I started talking about the depth of my feelings, I was going to be gushing like a creek after a storm.

"When you're not too busy fighting crime down here, will you hop up to see me?" He pushed a strand of hair out of my eyes. A natural gesture, as if he'd known me forever. I liked that feeling.

"I've always liked Seattle," I said. "And I've got some vacation time to burn."

"So come on up. Maybe after Christmas?"

The thought of spending time outside of work with Derringer was exciting and scary and romantic, but I just said, "Sure!" like a junior high cheerleader, and that made him smile.

"I'll be back to work with the prosecutors when we get closer to a court date," he promised. "Maybe I can come by your place and you can make me a martini?"

"I'd like that. A lot. And there is this invention called a cell phone. We can talk. Video chat." I grabbed hold of his shirt and pulled him closer. "I'm not letting you go without a fight."

"No fight required." His eyes crinkled in a deep smile. "You got me, Mori."